Out
of the
Bower

~ A DURBIN FAMILY NOVEL ~

A. E. Walnofer

Visit the author's website at
www.aewalnofer.com

Cover design by Jenny Q of Historical Editorial

ISBN: 9798587033276

DEDICATION

This story was written for anyone, anywhere
who is affected by the grievous sin of another.
Their sin neither taints nor defines you.

Any sexual incidents in this story are described in
limited and non-gratuitous detail.

CONTENTS

Out of the Bower

SACRED BLATHER

Just outside St. Paul's, the Actors' Church, Covent Garden, London
September, 1817

IT SEEMED THE two harlots had drawn nearer.

Perhaps they want to hear me better, Barclay thought, pleased though his heart pounded a bit faster.

The women — they were just girls, really — now leaned upon the churchyard fence, only a few yards away. The young street preacher had never before seen a pair of what his elder brother, Clayton, referred to as 'doxies'.

Yet here they are — I am sure of it for what else could they be?

Their faces, garishly painted with pinks and reds, were the brightest spots of colour in Covent Garden outside of the flower market. Yet, they looked far more docile than he had expected.

Father, which verse would cut them to the heart? Barclay flipped through the pages of his Bible before settling on one, then steadied his voice.

"The Lord has said, 'If any man thirst, let him come unto Me and drink!'" His voice called out across the cobblestoned street, sounding bolder than he felt. "But good people, I assure you, it is not only men He invites. Come, children! Come, women!"

Here he swung his arm toward the harlots. Moments earlier, a few dirty urchins had lingered nearby, but they had now vanished.

"Come unto Him, all ye that la – labour –"

Barclay's voice caught on this word as he considered how the two painted creatures hearing him likely laboured.

" – and are heavy laden, and He will give you rest!"

Pedestrians hurried past with baskets of foodstuffs from the market. Some sneered at Barclay but most ignored him completely. Just these two young women paid him any steady attention, though they did not approach him as he spoke on. And he, certainly, dared not acknowledge them directly.

Lord, may Your words prick their consciences and bring salvation to them this day, Barclay prayed.

A boorish-looking man now sauntered past, stopping a moment to look the prostitutes over. The taller girl shifted on her feet, leaning further back against the fence, clearly aware that the fellow was assessing her. She pushed her long, curled locks over her shoulder to dangle down her back. Her sleeve slipped down, revealing a smooth, white shoulder.

To his deep chagrin, Barclay felt something stirring within him at this display.

Was it a mistake to come here, Father? he asked. It was only because his younger brother, Jasper, had not ventured into London with him that day that Barclay had dared go to Covent Garden. He suspected their mother would have disapproved heartily, and now Barclay was beginning to understand why.

But Lord, aren't these the ones who most need to hear Your message?

In spite of this conviction, Barclay knew that peek of silky flesh would likely haunt his daydreams for weeks.

...make not provision for the flesh, to fulfil the lusts thereof, he chided himself.

With a final sweeping glance around the street, he shut the Bible and pushed it into his leather satchel. As he did so, he heard a nasally voice at his elbow.

"This is not your parish."

Barclay looked up to see a middle-aged man bedecked somberly in all black. Though he was a good two inches shorter, the man somehow managed to look down his nose at Barclay.

Believing that direct honesty was best, Barclay replied, "That is true, sir."

"Of course, it is. Moreover, you have not been granted permission to stand here and blather on as you have done these past few moments."

'Blather'? Barclay's cheeks began to burn. *Did this fellow, a clergyman by the look of his garb, not recognize the Holy Writ I quoted?*

"But sir, just as our Lord and His disciples declared the gospel to the downtrodden, so do I seek to share it with these peop—" Barclay's voice broke off as he swept his hand toward the indifferent pedestrians hurrying down the street. Now even the two painted girls were gone.

Smirking, the man sniped, "Get thee gone, stripling. I doubt you could afford the fine levied for preaching in another's parish."

Bristling, but determined to say nothing that might grieve him during later reflection, Barclay squared his shoulders, lifted his satchel and turned to go.

At least those girls heard a bit of 'sacred blather', he consoled himself, regretting no one was there to share his joke. He wondered though if they had disappeared with the leering man to partake in lewd and mysterious acts.

And no one else listened at all today.

Deflated at what felt like a waste of his morning, Barclay adjusted his hat as he continued down the street. Head down, he ducked into an alley, a shortcut to where he had stabled Caleb. He was several steps in when he heard a faint giggle. The hair on the back of his neck rose but he continued forward into the shadows. Out of the corner of his eye, he saw just feet away, the very same two girls who had been listening to him so intently. One leaned against the brick wall and the other, the taller one, sat on a discarded barrel, her skirt lifted to reveal her ankles.

The stable is just at the end here. It would be silly to go all the way around. Barclay's reasoning was sound, but his heart pounded noisily in his ears.

With his attention trained on the cobblestones ahead, he could feel the girls' eyes boring into him as he hastily made his way forward. Just as he passed, the girl on the barrel purred, "If any man thirsts, let 'im come 'n drink."

Leaning forward, she sighed suggestively and the pale bulk of her bosom spilled out of the top of her bodice.

Biting back a gasp, Barclay somehow kept his gaze steadfastly forward and tipped his hat in the women's direction, using the brim to block the alluring spectacle.

"Good d-day, ladies," he stuttered.

Lilting, raucous laughter filled the narrow passageway, and he quickened his pace.

Seconds later, Barclay emerged into the sunlight with his head held high, shaken but feeling victorious.

A BAWD'S EXHORTATIONS

Titania's Bower, near Leicester Square
Late October, 1817

"IF ONLY YOU would *eat* more, Celia," Dovey said, circling the prostitute like the vulture she was. "Get a little softness on those bones and you'd be the prettiest of all my girls – well, the prettiest except for Molly, of course, but I readily forgive you for *that* shortcoming!"

The bawd's laughter filled the plushly decorated bedroom as Celia tried not to squirm upon the velvet chair. Staring at her hands in her lap, she murmured something indistinguishable. She knew the desired response was at least to smile at Dovey's cajolery – that might even bring the woman's exhortations to an end sooner – but she hated giving Dovey what she wanted.

"I have several lovely dresses that would become you very well," Dovey continued, motioning a long arm toward the three wardrobes across her room, "if only you had more to put *into* them! You know I'm always wanting to improve our lot here, and *you* can play a part in that. If more wealthy gentlemen prefer Titania's Bower, they will frequent it over other establishments."

Yes, yes, Celia thought impatiently. *And what would the prize for that be? Ugh!*

"Those dresses are just waiting for you to don them and stroll around the park as you're wont to do." Dovey turned to face Celia again, peering intently at the girl. Her voice slowed as she added, "Wearing one of them, you just might be mistook for a proper lady."

Celia's breath caught in her throat.

How does she know what I pretend? I've never said a word of that to anybody!

As Dovey waited for a reply, Celia stumbled around in her mind for anything that would divert the madam from peering into her soul. Thus mortified, Celia was thankful when the procuress sallied forth onto a different course of admonition.

"And why do you so rarely smile, dear girl? There is much to be pleased with! Roads and bridges are being built all around us, sure to bring in more custom, and any day now, Princess Charlotte will be delivered of the royal baby. It is a marvelous time to be alive in London, the greatest city in the world!"

A marvelous time? Greatest city?

The thought of the many filthy, starving wretches Celia often saw sitting by the side of the road, just a few streets away from the Bower's door flashed into her mind, but she forced a little smile, hoping it would be enough to satisfy Dovey and end her sermonizing.

The bawd took two steps toward the window and gazed out on the street below. She breathed in deeply, and with hopeful longing in her voice said, "I have wonderful plans for the Bower, Celia."

And it is my dearest hope that I shan't be here to see them, Celia responded silently.

"You may finish your chores now. And if you're quick enough, you may go for a walk in the park afterward — but be home for an early supper."

Celia knew there was no chance of her washing all the soiled napery piled up in the laundry room before suppertime, so Dovey's offer of a walk was calculating and ridiculous.

As is everything else about her, Celia thought as she rose with a barely perceptible nod, and made her way out of Dovey's chamber.

INTO THE BOWER

WITH THE GIRL gone, Dovey leaned back against the wall, drumming her fingers on its wainscoting.

Ugh, Celia! When I grant Doris an afternoon off work, she regards me as her patroness. And last week, I gave Molly just enough money for a new hat – a tawdry one at that! – and she made herself my pet. But Celia! To her I might grant allowance to walk from the Bower to the sea itself and all I'd get in return is a sullen look and a mumbled answer.

Celia's morosity was a particular stitch in Dovey's side as it spoiled the girl's perfect porcelain skin and large green eyes. Both were strikingly enhanced by the dark ringlets that hung naturally about her face.

If I could simply inspire the girl to improve and parade herself, then much profit would abound!

However, Dovey's irritation was diminished by what she had just realized about Celia – the girl's guilty response had given her away.

She longs to be thought a fine lady as she strolls through the park! I shall use that to my advantage somehow.

Within the bawd's bedroom were three large oaken wardrobes, situated in such a manner to leave just enough room for a bed, a small desk and the velvet chair Celia had been sitting upon. Opening the doors of the middle wardrobe, Dovey rifled through the crushed stacks of paper-wrapped dresses which were stuffed into its confines. A sprig of dried rosemary – meant to combat the fustiness – dropped out onto the floor as her eyes fell on a fold of sprigged muslin, speckled with little blue flowers.

Ah, the perfect one! she thought, tugging the entire gown out of its place and tossing the paper aside. Pinching the shoulders, she let the length of the skirt fall. *Yes, lovely. But what is this?*

Looking at the back, she found that a portion of the skirt hung in tattered ribbons.

Who would dare do such a thing? she fumed.

Her mind immediately went to Molly. They had quarreled just the day before about a pair of shoes Molly was determined to have at Dovey's expense.

But no, surely even Molly wouldn't dare come into my bedroom unbidden.

Pulling several other garments from the wardrobe, Dovey was dismayed to see that another two gowns were spoiled, though not as extensively. Behind them all, a hole about the size of a plum had been gnawed through the wood backing of the furniture. Little scraps of paper littered the area and jagged strips of fabric had been pulled through as if something had tried to drag them away.

A rat! Dovey shuddered. *But what is it after? There are no crumbs of food here!*

"Damn vile creature," she muttered under her breath before shoving all the things back into place. As she did so, her eyes fell on another gown, finer than the sprigged muslin. It was of thick, lavender silk, its colour changing in her hands by how she held it in the light.

Hmm...subtle enough to suit Celia's taste, yet fine enough to honor the Bower.

Shaking it out to its full length, she saw it was undamaged and quickly assessed how it ought to be altered to fit Celia properly.

Yes, she would feel herself a fine lady in such a gown...stupid girl. With needle and thread in hand, Dovey pushed the chair toward the sunlit window and sat down to begin some minor alterations.

As she did so, the questions that forever niggled at the back of her mind spoke loudly to her.

How can I improve the Bower? What can I offer that men truly want?

Over the years, she had observed there were countless answers to this last question since what lit the fires of desire in one man's belly, merely aggravated the indigestion of another. But she also kept to mind what sort of fellows she wanted to attract to the Bower. Never had she painted the faces of any of her girls and sent them out into the streets to attract custom. The fellows drawn to that garish falsity were usually rough, coarse, and rarely had two coins to rub together.

Keep those wastrels at bay, she thought, pinning a tuck in the bodice.

It's the jangling pockets I want here.

To tempt the monied fellows, Dovey kept a wide variety of girls at Titania's Bower. For economic reasons, as well as keeping the girls from idleness, Dovey required that in addition to their evening entertaining, every girl perform chores about the place.

Doris – who swept and mopped floors – was a delightful chameleon, able to adapt herself to whatever she sensed a fellow wanted. However, his cravings had to get past her face as she was not very pretty – her nose too sharp, her teeth protruding.

Molly was undoubtedly the most beautiful girl at the Bower. With her wavy golden hair and large blue eyes, she was cosseted by Dovey accordingly. Her mere presence in the Mingling Room drew in more men than could possibly be served by her, which resulted in overflow custom for the other girls. Reveling in her own loveliness, Molly shirked most of the dusting and polishing of furniture that she was meant to do. This bred resentment amongst the other girls, but it seemed that Molly found all the female companionship she needed in the depths of her mirror. What Dovey found most trying about the girl were the fits of giggles to which she was prone – reportedly even whilst in the throes.

When Lyla was at the Bower, she had washed the windows. With her thick rump and sultry voice, she had been a prize, but Mr. Shaw had thought so too, and convinced her to run off with him. Though sorry to see her go, Dovey knew the romantic storyline of her departure appealed to the other doxies, and she encouraged the opinion that if *they* kept working, they also might earn a rich man's favor and a permanent place in his keeping outside of the Bower.

There were more girls – Nancy, Alice and Lorelei – within the Bower's walls, none terribly impressive, but they kept all the food served, the dishes washed, and the men found them more than tolerable. Mostly, Dovey regarded them as good girls who played their parts while causing very little trouble.

And then there was Celia, the laundress – someone who *had* run off in her first month of employment, only to return one dark night after a three-day absence, wet to the skin and faint with hunger. Tall, dark-haired and brooding, she carried herself with the air of a young widow – reclusive and wholly distracted. She didn't entertain customers as often as the other girls as there weren't many men drawn to her chilly presence in the Mingling Room, but she had earned the devotion of a few well-paying fellows.

She has the look of a 'good' girl – wholesome and clean – just as any girl of the Bower ought to be. And she gets the linens cleaner and brighter than anyone else ever has, Dovey thought as she stitched a seam in the bodice. *Thus, I house and feed her and hope for a change in her deportment.*

From the outside, Titania's Bower appeared to be nothing more than a coffee house tucked away in an inconsequential court off of St Martins Lane. Between the hours of four in the afternoon and two in the morning, anyone within ten yards of the front door was enveloped in the rich redolence of the freshly-brewed beverage. Thus disguised, Dovey's brothel was close enough to Covent Garden for the convenience of wayward gentlemen, but far enough away from it as to retain a sense of respectability among the naïve and ill-informed.

Though she had never seen it, a client had once told Dovey of a booklet – *Mr. Peter's Guide to the Nocturnal Metropolis* – which detailed various establishments much like her own, advising its readers on their particular worthiness. Apparently, Titania's Bower had earned a couple of sentences within its paper-bound breadth, which extolled the coffee house's ability to slake one's yearning for *café* before offering satisfactions of another nature. Though the man reported that the book often named and praised prostitutes specifically, none of the Bower's girls had achieved this particular distinction, which vexed Dovey to no end. Her hands itched to get ahold of the volume to see exactly what it *did* say about her brothel, but the fellow wouldn't let her touch it, claiming that its contents were of too strong a nature for the eyes of a woman.

Ha! I am a bawd, *you fool!* She had nearly shouted. *I have made arrangements just this week that would make you blush and duck your head!*

But she had held her tongue. To openly scorn a man – no matter how ridiculous he was – would be to lose his custom, and *that* Dovey was not willing to risk. Instead, she smiled at even the stupidest men, catered to their desires, took their money and then retreated to her private bedroom to sit upon her velvet chair where she plotted how to get *more* money whilst sipping Madeira from a crystal goblet.

Dovey knotted and snipped her thread, then let out the skirt's hem to where she envisioned Celia's ankles would be.

If I had a houseful of pretty Dorises, there would be no need for such a handbook as Mr. Peter's Guide as all other *houses of pleasure would be abandoned! But I have only* one *Doris, and a plain one at that...*

There was a sudden knock upon the front door. Had anyone still been in the room with her, they would have seen that this sound transformed Dovey's demeanor entirely, from conniving to convivial, from greedy to accommodating. She glanced at the clock on the mantel as she laid the lavender dress aside.

Early today, aren't they? She laughed to herself.

Then, settling her face into its 'welcome, you naughty gentlemen' look, she headed down the stairs to the vestibule.

When she opened the door, there was not the group of raucous men bent on obtaining pleasure that she expected standing on the doorstep, but a young woman – a pretty one – who held a folded sheet of newspaper in her hand.

Dovey's expression changed to one of haughty suspicion as she stared down her full height at the girl.

"May I help you?" she asked, though nothing in her tone implied she intended to offer a service of any kind.

If you've come to draw your man out of my grasp, you shall go home empty-handed.

"Ah, yes. I've come about the work in the kitchen. This is…" Here the girl glanced at the paper in her hand. "…Titania's Bower, is it not?"

Kitchen work? Hmm, Sally did say something about placing a notice, but a girl this young and pretty wants to moil away in the kitchen?

"That's right. This is The Bower."

Dovey began the quick but thorough assessment she made of all people upon first acquaintance. The girl had chestnut coloured hair, wide hazel eyes and a quick smile. She spoke assertively like a lady's maid – the words clearly formed and not lingering in her mouth.

Noting the small satchel next to the girl's feet on the stoop and the pelisse she wore in spite of the warmth of the day, Dovey thought, *Well, refined or not, she looks as if she has nowhere else to go.*

A plan began to form in her mind. Smiling, she threw the door open wide.

"Please come in. It's Sally you'll be wanting to talk to. What name can I give her?"

"Honora." The girl said, sticking her hand out. "Honora Goodwin."

Dovey took it in her own. The girl's shake was firm, certain.

This one may be hard to break, she assessed, but the promise of a challenge stirred something deep within her.

"Very well, Miss Goodwin. I am Mrs. Dovey. I shall inform Sally you are here to speak with her. You may wait here. Oh!" Dovey suddenly narrowed her eyes and tilted her head as if to examine the girl's face very closely. She dropped her voice to a whisper. "Whilst I'm gone, you may want to use your handkerchief. There's a..."

She didn't finish her sentence, but dabbed cautiously at her own nose as if by example. In truth, Honora's nostrils held no offensive particulates. But the resultant sight of the discombobulated girl swiping vigorously at her nose swelled Dovey with satisfaction. Thus gratified, Dovey strode down the hall, her shoes clicking as she passed the main dining room, and turned to enter the kitchen.

Sally was hunched over the stovetop, but her back straightened at Dovey's entrance.

"Ahem," Dovey cleared her throat.

The usual slow turn of Sally's head brought her plain face around for Dovey's observation, though their eyes didn't meet. Sally rarely looked Dovey in the eye.

"Sally," Dovey said. "There is a young woman at the door who is interested in working here in the kitchen with you."

The older woman's head bobbed faintly in acknowledgment.

"Ask her a few questions, then hire her, even if she doesn't seem suitable for your purposes. If, after a week, when she's serving the gentlemen, you're not pleased with her, you may search for a replacement. Say nothing of this to her. Show her upstairs to situate herself and her things in one of the bedrooms. Then start her to work right away."

"Yes, ma'am," Sally said quietly. It was a convenient, yet uninteresting response.

The fight's all but gone out of her, Dovey thought, annoyed at the woman's lackluster. The appearance of both fear and anger in another's eyes always drummed up something within Dovey's heart, but dullards bored her.

The madam spun on her heel to return to the vestibule, hoping that Honora would still be wiping at her nose.

DAYDREAMS AND POSSERS

AS THE LAUNDRY ROOM was adjacent to the kitchen, Celia could hear the low rumble of Dovey talking to Sally through the door. Yet, she paid it no mind, very much wanting to remain alone with the piles of soiled napery about her.

If Dovey recalls I'm back here, she might bring me a whole rasher of bacon and force me to eat it whilst she watches.

Celia added a chunk of lye soap to the hot water in the tub and used a long wooden posser to stir the steamy, acrid soup. When the soap had dissolved, she dropped tablecloths in, the less soiled first, and continued her stirring.

I couldn't possibly finish all this in time for a walk before supper, she thought, looking discontentedly at the mound of wadded up linens on the floor next to the door. *And I have yet to get any of the girls' monthly cloths. Who's due for that?*

She thought through which prostitutes were likely bleeding just then.

Alice, definitely. Lorelei, if not today then soon.

She always waited until the end of her laundering to fetch the fetid rags, determined to not be closed up for long in the laundry room with them as they fouled the air. She herself had not menstruated once since entering the Bower six months earlier. Though she did not understand this was due to how little food she ingested, she was thankful for the cessation.

Once she settled into the rhythm of stirring the sloshing vat, Celia's mind drifted outside the confines of the Bower's laundry room.

In her mind's eye, the trees of Hyde Park loomed above her. She stared up into their lofty tops, listening for the gentle hoot of the wood pigeons and the joyful chatter of the sparrows. Lime trees lined the walkways, their abundant foliage fluttering delicately in the breeze. She ran her thought-born hands over the twisted trunks of sweet chestnuts and admired the oak trees' lovely leaves, all bordered with curves and notches, much like puzzle pieces.

Once Celia had brought an especially frilly one back to the Bower and stuck it under her pillow. She often touched it as she drifted off to sleep, to remind herself that there existed things other than soiled laundry, rutting men and the oppressively looming Dovey.

Ugh, Dovey!

Celia's mind jarred back to the recent chiding of the bawd.

Wear fancy dresses that I might be mistaken for a fine lady? How does she know what I play at when I'm out for a walk? She shook her head as she plunged the dolly-peg deeper into the water, swirling the third of six tablecloths about. *But it ain't a* fine *lady I want to be — not exactly. I just want to be someone else. Anyone else.*

Anyone but me.

When Celia went out walking, she rushed down the pavement away from the Bower, and got as far away as she could, as quickly as she could. Shirking attention, she strove to blend in with the other Londoners milling about.

There were other doxies who ambled about town, certainly. Celia recognized some every time she went out, but unlike her, they sauntered, the fringe of their shawls sometimes dragging on the pavement behind them. Some had made up their faces brightly, emphasizing their lips and cheeks. They looked about languorously, tilting their heads at passersby, pursing their scarlet lips as if they were just waiting for something or someone. Celia knew that to simply be out walking without a chaperone – or at least a companion – made her morality suspicious to passersby.

That I look at no one and rush past all may gain me some respect in leery minds, she reasoned.

It was the industrious young women who were always hastening on whom Celia tried to emulate: maids sent out on errands, nannies pulling perambulators behind them, girls dressed to help shopkeepers sell their goods. Some of them carried small canvas bags which were full and lumpy in the mornings, but empty in the evenings. Presumably they contained their dinners. Celia filched an old flour sack from the Bower's kitchen that she might have one of her own to carry about. If she was on a morning walk, she stuffed this makeshift reticule with a dry roll and apple from breakfast, sometimes a bit of ham. Once at the park, she would sit beneath a tree, prop her parasol up as a blind and eat whatever she had brought. So much exercise kept her hungry, though she had difficulty ingesting much of anything back at the Bower under the attentive eye of Dovey.

The navy-blue parasol she took with her even on dreary days had the barest stretch of lace, flat and scratchy, around its perimeter. Though of the cheapest sort, it allowed her to adequately hide from the sun – and people – beneath its span. She wielded it expertly to shield herself from men whose eyes she caught as they moved past her.

Why must they always be gawking? What was Dovey getting at going on about how pretty I'd be if I just fattened up? Why would I want to be looked at more?

Lifting a tablecloth, heavy with water, from the vat, Celia fed it into the wringer. Once she had cranked it through, she turned back to the remaining piles of laundry.

There were no men's garments awaiting her attention. When her grandmother had taught her to launder, it had been mostly men's shirts and drawers. Living just south of Cheapside, they were surrounded by hard-working men who came home covered in dust and mud after spending their days building the many roads and bridges that were snaking through London to unite the city. There was plenty of laundering work for two females willing to scrub and flog it. Their lodging rooms allowed for this work, providing an unusual amount of space for the vats and racks. It even had its own little back garden which on every sunny morning or afternoon had several rows of shirts, trousers and drawers strung from lines, drying. Nana always had a watchful eye, looking out the window to make sure no one snuck over the little fence to nab a garment.

As for Celia and herself, Nana always wanted them to look clean anytime they left the confines of their home – said it was good for business.

"We mayn't have much, but even poor folk can look and smell nice," she'd say.

And Bill was always tidy when he struck out in the morning, though he never was when he returned! Celia recalled, smiling at the memory of her younger brother sitting down to supper after running messages all around

London. His dark hair was always tousled, his collar creased and askew.

"Which of your lovelies did you see today in your venturing, lad?" Nan would ask.

And Bill might answer, "Well, a bay mare called Meadow was clipping down Fleet Street. She had the merriest tail flicking back and forth." Or, "A *perfectly* matched pair of white geldings was waiting for a lady and her maid at Bedford Square. I didn't hear their names, though."

With a ubiquitous ache in her heart at the thought of Nan, Bill and his reliable prattling of the horses he saw each day, Celia pushed another tablecloth into the steaming vat and willfully turned her mind back to the towering lime trees of Hyde Park, swaying in the breeze.

A FOOL TO NONE

WHY, THIS IS nearly lovely, Honora thought, looking around the bedroom to which the woman called Sally had led her.

Not at all the grimy garret I would have expected to be housed in.

The room was small, but sound. There were no brownish stains from a leaky roof on the ceiling boards nor any holes in the walls. There were even two small windows, both open, letting in the afternoon breeze.

How indignant Lady Eliza would be that I have a job and a room on my very first day out of her clutches! Honora glanced again at the narrow breadth of the room. *Well, she might* laugh *at these quarters, but I never expected anything quite this nice for myself. If I had gone on to be a governess as they all planned for me, I'd likely have a similar room to this in some household – though probably to myself.*

Honora eyed the evidence of the room's other inhabitants – the folded clothes on the open shelves above the beds, the comb and pins littering the ewer table. Several long blonde hairs were caught in the comb's teeth.

But I'd much rather share a cozy room with a couple of other girls and work in a nice kitchen, than act as governess to children quite possibly as atrocious as Eliza herself!

She breathed in deeply. *And the glorious scent of that coffee drifts all the way up the stairs!*

For the first time, Honora was certain that she had made the right decision in leaving Stagsdown House early that morning. Though she had lived there all her life, it had become unbearable after Lord

Beeman's death as he was the only effective buffer to Eliza's antipathy to Honora.

Honora continued to survey the room with a sense of triumph in her gaze. There were two beds in the small space, one wide and one narrow.

Where shall I sleep? Certainly, as the new girl here I won't be allowed the luxury of a solitary bed. So I predict that means I'll share the larger one with another girl.

The shelf above the larger bed was long and the belongings it held were spread out upon it. Pulling her own few articles of clothing out of the satchel, she folded them neatly and placed them on the shelf's far end. A pile of flimsily bound books was spilling over into the limited space. She read the cover title with surprised satisfaction as she straightened the stack.

Someone living in this *little room subscribes to 'La Belle Assemblée'?*

She had leafed through many of this periodical's issues once Eliza had cast them aside. The ones at Stagsdown House had had the hand-painted fashion plates, but these on the shelf looked to be the less expensive, uncoloured ones.

Well, it seems I'll have something to discuss with at least one of the girls who lives here.

Stepping back, she surveyed the placement of her belongings with gratification at its neatness and convenience.

But where to put my coins?

Until twenty minutes earlier, she had rightfully regarded the little bit of money she carried as the difference between eating and not eating for the foreseeable future. Now that she was employed, she was assured of three meals a day, and the provisions in the kitchen had looked fresh and tasty. The previous evening, she had stuffed the two coins into a tiny pouch and tucked it into her pelisse's inner pocket. Now, she clutched the little bag in her hand, eyeing the stack of clothes she had just placed on the shelf.

I could put them underneath all of the clothes, but if someone went through it, they'd find them straightaway.

Honora's internal debate was cut short when the door to the room opened. An unusually beautiful girl with blonde hair, about Honora's age, stepped into the room, then stopped abruptly.

"Who're you?" the girl asked, her obtuse manners sullying her lovely features.

Honora clutched the little pouch, hiding it in her hand and responded, "I'm Honora. I'll be working in the kitchen with Sally. And you are?"

"Dovey put a *cook* up 'ere with us?" The girl giggled as if this were the most ridiculous decision imaginable. The amusement passed and she shook her head as she pointed at the left part of the bed, "Well, this is *my* side of the bed as the mattress 'as fewer lumps over 'ere."

Glancing at the shelf above the bed, the girl went on, "'Ave you been lookin' at my 'Bell's Semblies'? It looks as if you mussed 'em about."

She reached up and clapped her hand possessively over the pile, suspicion marring her face further.

"No," Honora said, suddenly flustered. "I merely straightened the stack."

"Well, don't touch 'em. That's *my* shelf, so you'll 'afta find somewhere else to stash yer truck."

Reaching over to where Honora had neatly laid her few folded articles of clothing, she pulled them all down, tossing them onto the bed.

Honora's face burned hot and she swallowed hard before asking, "Where ought I to put my things, if not there?"

"Dunno," the girl responded, digging through a small drawer in the ewer table. Pulling out a velvet hair ribbon, she went to the small looking-glass on the wall, tied it in her hair, adjusted a few locks, smiled at her reflection and then was suddenly gone out of the door.

That was poorly done of her. And poorly done of me that I didn't defend myself, Honora thought. Her late father's words rang in her mind, 'Be a respecter of all, but a fool to none.'

Surely it is intended that everyone in the room have a place to put their things.

Though her hands shook and she listened for footsteps approaching the door, Honora refolded her clothing and returned it to the same spot on the shelf. But she knew she could not put the coins under it all as the whole lot might be tumbled down again when the girl returned. Instead, she stuffed them back into the inner pocket of the pelisse she'd been granted by Lady Beeman many years ago, a remnant from the days when fine, cast-off clothing was given to her. Hanging it on a peg on the wall next to what had been declared *her* side of the bed, she left the room to return to the kitchen.

If I'm to share a room with that girl, I cannot allow her to bully me. Living with Eliza all my life, you'd think I'd have perfected the art of standing up for myself by now!

"Be still," Honora whispered to her quaking hands as she descended the staircase.

The door swung open at her push and she found herself standing face to face again with the woman called Mrs. Dovey. Quiet, Sally stood behind, scrubbing vegetables with a brush.

"Ah, there you are!" Dovey said, with something approaching jolliness. "All settled in upstairs, are you? Well, you are to start in your work right away." She pushed a broad, shallow basket across the table toward Honora.

"Silly Sally didn't get enough celery root when she went shopping this morning. You're to go and purchase more at the grocer's. Tell her to put it on the account of *Titania's Bower*, then come straight back and do whatever Sally tells you to prepare this evening's supper."

Honora surveyed the pile by the sink. *So much celery root already! Coffee houses serve such things? I thought it would be all little cakes and pastries.*

"Well, don't just stand there!" Dovey laughed but there was an edge to her voice as she pushed the basket into Honora's arms and waved her out of the door.

"Left here, take the next two rights, then it'll be on the left, halfway down the street. Remember, it's the account for *Titania's Bower*," Dovey reiterated, then shut the door, leaving Honora at the foot of a narrow staircase that led up to the dusty courtyard above.

It was an odd sensation to be shut out of her new home, and Honora realized how little she liked the tall, brusque woman.

I shall have to watch my tongue whilst addressing her, I suppose, she chided herself.

Honora knew that at times her arch manner of speaking bordered on impertinence. Her father had shushed her on more than one occasion whilst Lord Beeman and his ilk were present. Even Polly, the cook at Stagsdown House who seemed to esteem everything about Honora, had cast her pointed looks from time to time when Honora was mid-prattle. And yet, in most situations, Honora knew herself to be clever and correct.

Surely there ought to be allowance for a hint of cocksureness when both of those attributes abound! Yet, Mrs. Dovey may not see it that way, and she is my employer now.

Still, even this realization could not sink the elation she felt at having found a job in such a short time – and a well-paying one at that – as she paced down the pavement. Swinging the basket on her arm, she wished that nasty Lady Eliza could see her at that very moment.

A BAWD'S MULLINGS

DOVEY WATCHED THROUGH the kitchen window as the new girl's feet disappeared up the stairs.

Those are fine shoes, she thought, wondering at Honora's history. *Somehow, somewhere, she comes from a monied household.*

She wouldn't ask the girl about it, though. Dovey was parsimonious in her questioning of young women who arrived on the doorstep of the Bower. She asked just enough to ascertain how badly they needed a place to live.

This girl asked no questions beyond if the cook's job was still available. She is either completely desperate or utterly naïve.

Either was fine with Dovey as they would both lend to her domination of the girl.

She lacks the coldly prim look of so many snobbish women, yet it may prove difficult to get her used to what she must do as one of my girls. Though she is lively, she is yet 'proper' as her sort like to call themselves.

Dovey hoped she had just secured Honora's place at the Bower by sending her on this errand.

When the grocer's wife hears 'on the account for Titania's Bower', she'll flit around, telling all the other prudish shopkeepers that this new girl is one of mine. Soon, there will be no other place for this Honora anywhere in this part of town, though she's yet to lift her skirts for anyone.

Dovey turned away from the window, pleased with her easy day's work.

Sally had paused in her task.

"What?" Dovey grunted.

"Nothin'", Sally murmured, dropping her eyes to the pile of potato peelings before her.

"Do you think she can truly cook?"

"Said she learned to bake when she was a wee thing. Looked right proud of 'erself when she said it, too."

"Hmm." Dovey thought a moment. *I ought to keep her happy in her first days here, certainly until her tainting.*

Turning toward the swinging door, Dovey said over her shoulder, "When she returns, tell her to bake a cake for tonight, whatever sort she likes."

Sally grunted her assent.

Once in the vestibule, Dovey donned her pelisse and hollered up the stairs, "Molly! I'm going out!"

Everyone hearing this, knew it meant that in Dovey's absence, Molly ought to answer the front door should anyone knock upon it. As the Bower's most beautiful girl, it was natural that she ought to be its primary representative.

Dovey listened for three knocks upon an upstairs wall which signified Molly had heard the commandment, then headed out the front door to hire a hackney coach. The weight of her bulging coin purse filled her with a heady satisfaction as she climbed into the conveyance. That, and the thought that she had likely just ensnared another doe for her brothel.

"Corrington and Boyce," she told the driver though he had already started off toward the Strand as he often transported her on her excursions.

About once a week, Dovey journeyed to various banking institutions on Fleet Street or the Strand to change the coins she had collected into banknotes. Although coinage was the preferred currency for some, Dovey had more faith in its paper counterpart. Notes which said "Bank of England" across their tops in a flourishing script appealed to her hearty sense of patriotism. Also, she felt she could hide the paper leaves more easily than she could heavy coins. As a wealthy madam who did not want to employ a burly guard to fortify the Bower – she hated men near her to think themselves more powerful than her – she pleased herself by stuffing rolls of notes into the toe of a silken stocking, reasoning that anyone rifling through her wardrobes would be listening for clinking instead of rustling in their search.

Always attentive to talk of money, Dovey had heard patrons decry the possession of banknotes to one another with, "Why get paper when coins that will neither burn nor wash away can fill your purse?"

Comforting herself with the knowledge that the Bower's walls were built of stone and situated far from the flow of the Thames, Dovey did not cease in her banknote collection.

Early on, her jaunts to banks served another purpose as these institutions were full of men, the precise animal whose interest she needed for success in her business. When she had first entered one of the buildings, a woman without a man at her side, all eyes had turned to her, some curious, others derisive. When soon after she had produced a weighty purse while declaring her intentions to obtain banknotes, the entire bank went abuzz. Though the rumours men spread about women are often baseless, the bankers' suppositions proved true: The bawdy house this woman ran must deliver satisfaction as evidenced by the mint's worth she had in her possession.

The amorous and inquisitive had soon made their way to the doorstep of the Bower where Dovey jollily assured them with a wink that they could get a superior cup of coffee for their coin and other pleasures afterward, should they desire them.

The hackney coach pulled to a stop before a three-story building which had six pilasters, lending it an air of especial solidity. Up the steps and through the large, oaken doors she went, wondering, *Which idiot will I encounter today?*

The answer sat at a walnut-wood desk to the far right of the room in the form of a man she had dubbed 'Mr. Pilven' at his first visit to the Bower during the previous week.

His station was the only one without a customer standing beside it, so Dovey approached him.

Ah yes, she thought, hoping to see him blanch at first sight of her. *I would recognize that curly head of hair anywhere. He was entertained by Doris, I believe.*

As he glanced up, Dovey saw a quick change behind his eyes. They said at first, 'How can I help this next patron?' then immediately began to beg, 'Dear God, don't let this madam unmask me!'

You needn't worry yourself, Pilven. Your shameful lusts are safe with me, for the by and by.

"How may I be of service?" he asked, his voice polite yet steely.

In a civil, disinterested tone, Dovey responded, "I should like to change some coin for paper, sir."

"Ah, yes," he said. Seemingly assured that she was not bent on exposing him, he relaxed into congeniality. "I should be delighted to help you with that, ma'am."

After she counted out before him a pile of coins — *Yes, perhaps your fingerprints are yet on a few of these, sir,* she thought — he reached into his desk for a fresh note and filled it out. When finished, 'Pilven' stood and went to the chief cashier on duty behind a high counter, to exchange the coins for a signature upon the note. Returning, he gave the paper to Dovey along with a courtly nod. As was her habit, she folded it in two and pushed it into the buxom bodice of her gown. The gesture was deftly done, without embellishment, but it raised a blush of colour upon the clerk's cheek, much to Dovey's satisfaction. She liked to remind the men around her exactly how her money was acquired.

In this manner, her trips to the banks served as free advertisement for the services she offered. Additionally, they allowed her to keep an eye on various men who had wandered into her brothel at one time or another. Information about a patron, she learned, was invaluable. Due to the delights reportedly found at the Bower, word of it had spread beyond the banking sector to other branches of the business world, ensuring Dovey's continued achievement. By lingering attentively in the Mingling Room, Dovey became shrewdly aware of which fellows knew the most about the others. She privately plied these preferred few with drink and favors from any girl they relished in exchange for gossip about various families and workplaces. She never needed to write anything down as her mind was a bear trap for anything that could be used to her advantage.

And now, Mr. Pilven, she thought, exiting the bank to climb back into the hackney coach. *I know exactly where you work.*

CALLING-OUT

Crawton Green, London

"IT WAS MUCH BETTER when we brought the apples," Jasper said, looking out from Crawton Green where he stood with his brother.

Barclay noted these words were stated in the slightly whingy voice Jasper used when he was growing weary. The sentiment was understandable. Attempting to engage a crowd which walked indifferently past them was exhausting.

"Yes, you're right," Barclay replied, then looked down at the stack of small religious pamphlets in his hand. When the brothers handed out apples along with the tracts, people took them, thanked them even. Whether the recipients ever read the tracts – or even possessed the ability to read them – remained unknown, but there was at least a sense of satisfaction at the end of a Calling-Out day when Barclay returned home empty-handed.

Emboldened perhaps by Barclay's affirmation, Jasper spoke on, "And I don't know why you insist we ride in on this rickety cart instead of astride our perfectly good horses. I feel like a play-actor."

Barclay motioned to the people on the street and answered in an affectedly patient voice, "Look around you, Jasper. These before us have no finery. Many even lack necessities. Arriving on a simple cart helps our message to seem more attainable."

And, he added silently, recalling his encounter the previous month in Covent Garden, we are less likely to draw the attention of crotchety clergymen who pay mind to whose parish is whose.

"Well, if declaring the gospel is our sole objective, we oughtn't to ever bring apples, either," Jasper persisted.

Barclay sighed and took a sip of water. The reasonableness of Jasper's observation struck at his heart in a way that his younger brother could not know – likely would not pursue had he known the power of it. When Jasper complained, it was not usually done without some merit. He was not snide. Barclay would not have brought him along to London with him if he were.

And in this instance, he's absolutely right, Barclay lamented silently, gazing out at the masses milling past. Dear Lord, did You encounter such indifference from those You sought to help? Yes, I know You did, and much worse than mere indifference – they crucified You.

The sun beat down on the brothers as they sat upon the green, their backs resting against one of the reviled cart's wheels. The silence between them was drowned out by the steady hum and patter of the many other people going past.

"Well, best get on with it so we're home for supper," Barclay said. He handed the bottle to Jasper and stood to his feet.

Trying to shake off the frustration and nagging doubts he felt, he began to flip through his well-worn Bible.

Which passage, Lord? Which words will draw these people, any of them, to You?

Settling on a dog-eared page, his eyes fell on several words that were underlined neatly.

Heartened by the verve of the black words upon the white paper, Barclay cleared his throat to speak in his clear, strong 'calling-out' voice, and looked up at the people walking past. Some glanced at him, their eyes hinting at mockery waiting to be unleashed from the tips of their tongues. Most ignored him altogether however, having seen him here so many times before. But as he surveyed the crowd on this morning, his eyes met those of an unfamiliar girl as she made her way past the green. Pretty though she was, it was not the shape of her features that arrested the scripture on his lips.

Her eyes looked back at him in a playfully confident manner, and her mouth was slightly pursed as if she knew something and was trying not to smile about it. On her arm was a large basket which she carried past, steady to her purpose. He tipped his hat reflexively, to which she nodded slightly, the faint smile growing on her lips. Then she was beyond him and her direct gaze no longer held his own.

"Well, come on then!" Jasper urged with a chuckle. "No need to be waylaid by a pretty face."

Embarrassed that his brother – and possibly the girl herself – had so clearly seen the reason behind his distraction, Barclay forged ahead, reading the chosen verses loudly that they rang across the green and street.

"Take my yoke upon you, and learn of me; for I am meek and lowly in heart: and ye shall find rest unto your souls. For my yoke is easy, and my burden is light."

As he recited familiar verse after familiar verse, Barclay's mind again strayed back to his one foray into the heart of Covent Garden. That day, Jasper had stayed behind at Singer Hall, recuperating from a fever. Barclay, who had long wanted to try his hand at calling-out in needier, more dissolute parts of town, had gone there, never saying a word of it to anyone at home.

There, he had encountered the two painted doxies and walked within feet of a disclosed bosom. The memory visited him regularly, both thrilling and mortifying him, as it did now, so he kept on reading.

Finally, after a sixth verse, he looked around at the unresponsive crowds, milling past.

But wait. Who's this? Barclay's breath caught as two young men on horseback rode nearer, their faces turned to Barclay in amused astonishment. Their black, silk top hats and velvet, tailed coats declared them to be gentlemen.

"I do believe we've sighted Clayton Durbin's younger brothers!" one man told the other in an affectedly disapproving voice. "The Seville Orange hair on both confirms it."

Though the vivid colour of his hair no longer perturbed Barclay as much as it had when he was a child, he prickled.

"Ah, yes!" The second man said, regarding the Durbins just as boldly and with as much disapprobation. "And what are they doing – sermonizing? Good god! Clayton's been bred amongst radicals!"

Laughing, the gentlemen heeled their horses' flanks, trotting down the cobblestoned street.

"Sodders," Jasper muttered.

"Jasper!" Barclay exclaimed, suppressing his urge to laugh. "We're here to uplift people of all classes, not insult them."

His little brother shrugged as Barclay's own thoughts continued.

Why are the monied some of the nastiest people of all? How glad I am that the girl with the basket was not passing just then to hear them.

His frustration returning in full force, Barclay slapped the book shut.

"Our work here today is done," he announced as cheerfully as he could.

Jasper made no complaint at this pronouncement and soon the brothers were atop the cart and navigating the congested streets. Feeling the rough jostle and sway of the cart under him, Barclay had to agree silently with Jasper once again.

I do feel like a play-actor atop this silly conveyance.

A SOURING OF SENTIMENT

STILL SIMPERING OVER the way the street preacher had looked at her, Honora soon located the grocer's. Entering the storefront, she found herself alone with a pleasant-looking woman who was sweeping up the papery husks of onions from the floor.

"Might I help you?" the woman asked, putting her broom aside.

"Yes, please. I need several bulbs of celery root." Honora settled the basket on the table.

"Ah! It's good you come when you did, as I've not much o' that left!" The woman laughed, then lifted several nobbily vegetables from a box to nestle them into the wicker confines.

"Won't have to scrub those much!" Honora said amiably. "Thank you for offering such clean vegetables."

"I find it keeps the customers comin' back if I do a bit of the work for 'em. And I'm here all day, so's might as well keep meself busy with a scrub brush." The woman smiled, placing the last bulb. "There. That's all I got. Will that do?"

Honora nodded.

"That'll be five pence." She stuck out her hand.

"Oh, Mrs. Dovey says it's to go on the account for Titania's Bower. Is that alright?"

Though Honora made the request cheerfully, she noted an immediate sour turn of the woman's expression.

Ugh. The bill must be quite high already, Honora deduced cringingly as the woman silently pushed her basket at her, then waved her away toward the door.

"Thank you," Honora murmured, but heard no response. The spoiling of the pleasant moment was like a foul odor in the air.

No wonder Mrs. Dovey sends others to do her shopping. She doesn't want to face her creditors herself.

Holding her head up high, she grasped the basket's handle and headed out of the door.

CELIA SMILES

ENTERING THE DINING ROOM with a ubiquitous mantle of dread over her shoulders, Celia immediately sensed a change there. The scent of apples, and something even more piquant – cinnamon – filled her nostrils. She felt as if a cord in the top of her head had yanked her upright and she came into the room taller, and alert.

Her eyes were immediately drawn to the front table. Besides the usual plates of chicken and boiled vegetables, were plated wedges of cake. Behind them stood a girl Celia had never before seen. Her wavy hair was reddish brown, and her modest clothes were neat and well-fitting. She stood almost proudly, erect while she surveyed the other girls approaching the tables to walk away with their supper.

So that is the new girl the others spoke of this afternoon.

Celia stepped up to the serving tables, but tonight she did not make a pretense of selecting a plate of chicken and celery root, of which she would eat no more than three bites. Instead, enlivened by the scent in the air and her curiosity at this strange new girl, she went straight to the cake.

Though she intended to lift her own piece from the table, the girl anticipated her approach and selected one for her. Holding it out with a confident smile, the girl's eyes locked with Celia's for a moment and Celia nodded slightly to her, then scurried off to the table against the wall where she always sat when she was pretending to eat.

The cake's sweet, heavy scent filled her nostrils, even seeming to warm her lungs. With her fork, she lifted a small bite, then tasted it, closing her eyes as the slight burn of cinnamon tingled her tongue.

Saliva filled her mouth as she felt the creamy topping smearing across the tines. It had a tinge of sourness that balanced out the bright, sweet apple flavor. After her second bite, Celia looked again at the girl who had served it to her.

Is this the sort of thing she will be serving every night? she wondered. *She must have baked this, as Sally wouldn't take the time to make or decorate anything so fine for us girls.*

Celia put another forkful of cake into her mouth and let it turn to delightfully rich mush.

Look at how she stands beside her cake, looking out at anyone who's got a bit of it on their plate, as if she's just waiting to see if we like it. No, looking to be certain we know we ought *to like it. But who could not? It's perfectly lovely.*

She caught the new girl's eye and faintly smiled. The girl returned the expression with a little nod.

The cake reminded Celia of something Nana had baked for Old Michelmas Day when she was very small. It had been laced with apples and cinnamon, its sweetness lingering upon the tongue. But this girl's cake was much more refined, not dark and heavy, with a lightness to its crumb and a creamy sauce over the top. Celia imagined it was something the finer gentlemen who visited Titania's Bower would eat when they took tea with their wives.

When Dovey said she had plans to make the Bower a finer place, I'd no idea it would start tonight or like this.

Wanting a second piece, Celia saw there were several wedges left, but Dovey sat just a few feet from them. After the bawd's exhortation earlier that day to eat more, Celia couldn't bring herself to get another helping of something so thickening right before the woman's eyes.

At that moment, Doris approached the table and chirpily asked the baker to put a second serving of cake on her outstretched plate.

"The finest thing I ever tasted!" she declared, then marveled animatedly as the gooey piece was transferred over to her.

Well, at least it's getting a bit of praise from Doris, Celia thought. *Though Doris's praise is as abundant as flies in summer, so you wonder at its worth.*

Of all the girls at the Bower, Doris was the one Celia pitied the most, though this wasn't due to her unfortunate facial features. Doris's eagerness to please anyone on any level seemed moored in a need to be wanted, appreciated – even simply noticed. There was no light in Doris's face unless someone was speaking to her, no spring in her step unless someone's eye was upon her. It was as if she thought she did not exist unless another being was presently acknowledging that she did.

On a couple of occasions, Celia had been especially kind to Doris, but Doris's resultant devotion had made Celia itch with irritation. Thus, she had settled into doling out a few civil words when situations required her to speak with Doris, but a general cold, disinterest prevailed.

The baker looked pleased at Doris's effusion, so Celia silently blessed the annoying prostitute while licking her fork clean. She cleared her dishes before heading upstairs as it was her custom to withdraw from the others that she might dread the arrival of the gentlemen in solitude.

Ugh, the filthy rutters will be here soon.

As soon as she entered the bedroom she shared with Molly, she knew something was different. Looking around, she saw things that belonged to someone else, someone new, on the shelf above Molly's bed.

Did Dovey put that cake girl up here with us? She's to house her prized baker with her tainted dollies? Well, I guess I best help the new girl out then.

With nimble fingers, Celia carefully picked through the newly arrived belongings on the shelf above the bed, recalling how each item was placed before lifting it to peek under. She patted everything, feeling for lumps. In the pocket of a linen apron, she found a wick trimmer. Though its tiny blades appeared newly sharpened, the instrument was too utilitarian in design to excite any envy in Celia's heart. She dropped it back into place, and returned the apron to its shelf. It was only a moment before she found what she was really looking for in a fine coat hung up on the wall: two gold coins in a pouch in an inner pocket. Celia lifted them out, her heart thumping madly in her chest, and proceeded to transfer them to her own secret, hiding place.

Then, instead of resting upon the bed as was her usual habit before the evening's obligations, she exited the room, determined to be found anywhere but there.

***

An hour and a half later, Celia stared at Mr. Howrood's cravat. It was strewn across the top of the settee. She always chose something to stare at during a forced dalliance.

Untied, cravats are such silly looking things — long and thin, like cloth serpents.

The hum in her brain from the wine she had gulped down in the Mingling Room had started to wear off. Dovey only allowed Celia one large glass of the cheapest stuff each night as she awaited the approach of any man present. Gin would have been less expensive and more effective, but Dovey said it would take a toll on her girls' looks.

Since the wine's dulling only lasted so long, Celia often had to resort to studying garments in close detail to carry her through the final moments with a man.

Fly to the devil and be done with it! she thought, noting the change in Howrood's breathing as she stared harder at the cravat.

Dark blue with a herringbone of black running through it. A smart but subtle pattern.

Often, the men left articles of clothing on the floor or flung over the furniture, forgotten cast-offs in their excitement of the moment. There were boots, waistcoats, shirts, drawers, all of which Celia had inspected in earnest as she waited.

It was a strange practice, transporting her back to the time when she did not yet know what men were capable of. Since she was young, she had handled men's garments, laundering them alongside her grandmother. The two of them would compare the rough skin on their hands, coarsened by hot water, lye and the calluses born of handling of the posser, a sense of pride welling up within them over their similarity and hard-work.

Since she could remember, Celia had turned shirts and trousers inside out, rubbing the yellow spots with a cake of soap that made her eyes burn, displeased when the stains proved too much for her efforts.

"'S'alright, darlin'," Nana had said. "You done your best. That's all these brutes'll be expectin'."

Nana had taught Celia many other things as well, like how to read. One newspaper story Celia recalled was of Snow White. When she sounded out the part where the lost princess bit a poisoned apple, Celia thought nothing could be worse than such a fate. Now she knew how wrong this assumption had been.

Nana grew gravely ill when Celia was thirteen, requiring Celia to tend to her *and* continue the laundering of what seemed like half the neighborhood. Nana's descent into the grave was slow, but steady. Celia watched as the fifty-four-year-old woman harrowingly became a hideous and deflated version of herself. It took two years, during which time Celia transformed from a gangly, awkward girl into a beautiful young woman, in spite of the horror of watching her sole caretaker die. Her mother had died birthing Bill and their father had sailed away to the East Indies years earlier without a word since.

One of the final things Nana had said to Celia was, "Protect your virtue, my lovely. As a poor girl, it's all you've got in this world of men."

Too ashamed at her own ignorance, Celia did not ask Nana what her 'virtue' was, nor how to protect it.

Perhaps Bill will know, she had thought, though she never pressed the point with him.

Now, as she lay on her back – the weight of a naked man bearing down upon her – Celia reminded herself that not all men were rutting, obscene creatures – though since her tainting, she supposed the ones who weren't couldn't bear to look at her. As she continued to study the black lines running through the blue cravat, she was certain that all virtue – had she ever had any – had all but disappeared and no amount of scrubbing with lye soap could restore it.

A GENTLE INQUIRY

Singer Hall

THAT EVENING, when Barclay sat down to supper, he was not expecting to be ambuscaded, though he realized that he should have been prepared for it. Silver candelabras at either end of the table illuminated the food as well as the faces of his mother, Clayton and Jasper. Martha, the ever-present servant, stood three feet away, her face floating like a specter in the near dark beyond.

The three brothers were avidly feeding themselves when Mrs. Durbin broached the troublesome topic in her smooth, gentle voice.

"Barclay, have you thought more on your Uncle Allard's offer?"

Looking up from his plate of roast beef and peas, Barclay saw that both she and Clayton were peering hard at him, though Jasper remained bent over his food, shoveling it in. Even Martha looked as if her ears were perked, her hand steady on the soup tureen's lid.

Yes, even Martha has a horse in this race. Though hers may be of a different colour. Stifling the sigh that brewed in his chest, Barclay thought, *Well, may as well have it out and be done with it.*

"I'm thinking not to take it, Mamma, as I doubt it would afford me the opportunities I prize most highly."

Mrs. Durbin had already taken a breath to answer, though she dropped her gaze to her plate. "But Barclay, if you *were* to become the curate at Southby, think of the influence you would have!"

Martha loomed at the table's end, looking even more alert than usual, if that was possible. Even when required to stand in one place, the woman's eyes flitted about, blazing with the realization of potential activity.

Barclay resisted the urge to glance at her as he waited for his mother to continue.

"It would be a first step in securing your future." Here her voice dropped as if what she said next should only be spoken of in hushed tones, "Upon your uncle's passing..."

"Mamma, there is no assurance that Barclay would ascend to the living in my uncle's stead," Clayton spoke for the first time.

"Surety, no, but it *would* be likely."

If things were truly the way his mother described them, then her scheme might be a sound one, but Barclay had attended the church at Southby on many occasions while visiting his uncle. In conversing with its congregants, he had determined that although they were amiable and generous in their own bloated way, they were also stuck in the throes of societal surfeit. He had explained this to his mother before, but she had ingested it all with a look of hurt, reminding him that her greatest wish was to see her children suitably settled.

Since Barclay had shown especial interest in spiritual matters even as a young boy, his uncle who was a rector, always singled him out during his regular visits to Singer Hall. Now that Barclay had recently graduated from Cambridge, and had continued to maintain an unblemished reputation – a rarity amongst young gentlemen – Uncle Allard's attentions to him had become more frequent.

And now that I am ordained, I cannot trespass on Clayton's hospitality here at Singer Hall indefinitely. We're getting on well now, but that oughtn't be tested too long.

Looking from his eldest brother to his youngest, Barclay's eyes fondly settled on Jasper who was watching hungrily as Martha forked another slice of beef onto his plate.

Yet, if I was to leave here for Southby, I would be separated from Jasper. He felt a frisson of regret. *Surely another year or so before my future is settled will not hurt anyone.*

Martha was now at the other end of the table – the woman was never in one place for long – lifting the lid of the parsnips and carrots to peek inside the bowl.

Yes Martha, feign interest in the number of peas left as you listen intently.

As a woman of terrific energy, her wiry form was never still. In her youth, this restlessness had earned her dismissal from a position at another great house. The master claimed the vigor she emanated jangled his nerves. Therefore, at the age of one and twenty, she had gained a place at Singer Hall and remained there for nearly fifteen years thus far.

Hers was a peculiar sort of domestic servitude within Singer Hall. Her appointment there had originally been as a parlor maid, but her diligence and reliability had resulted in the family's utter dependence upon her. She did the work of two maids at once and knew the tasks of every servant on the grounds. Therefore, her role could not be confined to any particular title. She was simply "Martha".

Barclay's true bonding with Martha occurred in his sixteenth year. Prompted by a pervasive dissatisfaction within himself, Barclay had attended an evangelical meeting in town one summer evening. At its end, he went forward to confess his sins and receive forgiveness. A number of other gentlefolk from the great houses nearby had been in attendance, but he alone had had tears streaming down his face, his head bent in contrition. After the minister had assured him that he was now a member of the family of God, he had turned to see that Martha was there, gazing in wonder at him as all the others filed out of the chapel. He felt his wet eyes shining as he beamed, announcing, "Martha, I am born anew."

It was as if the Lord Himself had revealed to Barclay that in spite of the differences of their ages, and their social standing, he and Martha were now brother and sister in Christ.

After the meeting's conclusion, the new spiritual siblings had walked back to Singer Hall together, she slowing her usual pace as he led his horse by the reins beside her. They passed chaffinch-filled hedgerows as the golden sun lowered itself heavily to the horizon while they affirmed to one another the goodness of God and His forgiveness. The warmth of the waning sunlight, the calls of the birds, the joy of the deep commonality the two now shared was nearly intoxicating as they made their way back to their stately home.

Thus, began the unusual nature of the relationship between the middle-aged maid and the teenaged boy, him often going to her when he needed advice. Just six months earlier when he had returned home from university, he had approached her in the parlor where she was dusting and burst forth with, "Martha, I cannot bear that I have such an easy life when others know not what they will eat for supper this very night. But what can I do of it? Clayton wouldn't want Singer Hall crawling with alms-takers. And even if he did allow for it, would simply doling out food, day after day truly halt their suffering?"

Martha had listened as her wrist flicked the feather duster expertly over the tables and chairs at each of his words, then thought for but a moment.

"Master Barclay," she said. "Why don't you go to those poor, find 'em wherever they are and tell 'em where they'll find food – the sort that don't dry up or molder – food for their souls."

His relief had been immediate and mixed with excitement at her suggestion.

"Yes," he'd said. "They have minds as well as I do. And what they do with the message of Truth once told would be their own decision."

Before the week was over, Barclay had climbed atop his horse and trotted off to London in search of endangered souls to reach and captivate. Thus, he had begun his regular practice of calling-out in town.

"I should very much like you to seriously consider taking your uncle's offer sooner than later," Mrs. Durbin said, bringing Barclay's mind back to the dining room.

Barclay simply replied, "Though there would certainly be benefits, Mamma – that I won't deny – I fear they would not outweigh the disadvantages. Those people know the Lord and I strive to spend my days drawing to Him those who *don't*. Let another go to Southby as I prefer to labor in Covent Garden."

"*Covent Garden?*" Mrs. Durbin asked, putting down the roll she had been buttering, her brow furrowed with worry and disdain. "Have you been calling-out *there?*"

Oh Lord! Why did I say that? Now they all know, even Jasper!

This time, he couldn't help but glance at Martha. She, too, had paused at his words, the soup ladle aloft in her grasp, dripping into the tureen.

Unwilling to lie, Barclay wiped his face, and replied, "Just once."

"I marvel you go *there*, son. It's not a *heavenly* place."

"Which is precisely *why* I went there, Mamma – to reach those in the gravest of straits."

"But there are certain…*temptations* there that you mightn't be immune to, brother," Clayton said, his eyes sparkling at the turn of conversation.

Here, Mrs. Durbin's eyes flitted uneasily toward Clayton before settling again on Barclay.

"Yes, son," she said rather quietly while focusing on her plate. "It wouldn't do at all for you to fall into the fire whilst trying to pluck others from the flames."

Barclay replied, "Mamma, the poverty and depravity I see each time I call-out portrays before me so clearly the consequence of sin, that I have never once considered falling in with those who practice it."

These are the words he spoke, solemnly and sincerely, but simultaneously, the memory of the painted doxy on the barrel slipped into his mind again – the pale shoulder, the purring voice.

Yet there was a thrill in his heart every time he recollected the victory of his spirit's will. He felt it now, suppressing a smile as he cut through the slice of beef on his plate.

Oh Lord, if only I could tell them all how I kept my eyes averted from what that woman bared before me – how strong I proved myself to be!

Jasper spoke then, spoiling Barclay's recollection of triumph.

"We don't need to go to Covent Garden for Barclay's head to be turned. Just this afternoon, he opened his Bible to preach when a pretty girl walked past. He stood there with his mouth gaping, dumb as a doorpost!"

"Jasper, I hardly think that an accurate description, and exaggeration does not become you."

"Oh, ho! I, for one, am pleased to hear that there is the heart of a man thrumming away underneath that waistcoat of yours, as sometimes I wonder!" Clayton teased.

Ignoring Clayton's gibe – as he had become an expert at – Barclay thought back on what had truly happened earlier that day. With renewed appreciation, he recalled the brightness of the girl's eyes as she turned them confidently in his direction, the hint of a smile at her mouth's corners when she saw him looking back at her. He had tipped his hat at her, just as he had at the doxies a month earlier, but this lovely young woman had simply nodded, then squared her shoulders and walked on.

What was it about her? Barclay wondered. *She was comely, yes, but there was something about the way she moved, as if she knew exactly where she wanted to be and was on her way there just then.*

"Well," Mrs. Durbin finally said. "I would much prefer that you stay away from Covent Garden. There are certainly many other parts of town where people might benefit just as much from your calling-out. And I do hope you will ponder all the benefits of taking the curacy at Southby."

"Hmm, I will keep them to mind, Mamma."

Barclay reached for the water carafe to mask the perturbation he felt.

"Don't think on it too long, Brother," Clayton put in. "I've had a letter from Uncle Allard myself just this week. He is growing restless, wanting to fill the vacancy."

With a faint nod to his brother, Barclay hid his frustration, thinking, *But surely you all know I will not commit to anything that violates my sense of what the Lord is calling me to do.*

INNOCENCE AIN'T A BAD THING

Titania's Bower

WHILE RETYING HIS cravat, Mr. Howrood said nothing and Celia stole out of the salon into the hallway. She made her way up the stairs to her bedroom door.

Will she be here? she wondered uneasily.

Upon entrance, Celia immediately heard a deep, even breathing from the far side of the room.

Oh, she's asleep already, she thought, staring through the near dark at the lump of a blanketed body.

After stripping down to her shift and neatly putting her dress away, Celia settled herself in the smaller bed and wondered at her ambivalence.

Did I want *to speak with her? What would I say? 'I liked your apple cake.' I'd sound like a child!*

There were footsteps in the hallway and the door creaked open. Celia feigned sleep as Molly stepped into the room.

The gambit was no deterrent and Molly spoke as she stepped out of her dress. "Celia?"

Ugh! Can't you see I'm trying to sleep?

"Celia, I've got the piss-fire startin' again," Molly whispered, climbing into the larger bed alongside the new girl's immobile frame.

Though annoyed at the disruption, Celia was sorry for Molly. She herself had suffered similarly only the month before.

"Mmm," she groaned sympathetically.

"Every wee feels like I'm birthin' a Guy Fawkes bonfire," Molly whispered. "And last time I had it, Dovey weren't please to give me brandy though the doctor said to."

"Maybe she'll give you a few days out of the Mingling Room," Celia murmured groggily. "Until your water runs yellow again."

"But if I'm away from the gent'men, Mr. Jewel and Mr. Lodestar might forget 'bout me," Molly said.

At this answer, Celia's pity waned.

"Shh. You'll wake the new girl," she said quietly, though there was no break in the steady breathing coming from the other bed.

"Wake *Honora*?" Molly scoffed. "Who cares?"

Suddenly, from somewhere else in the Bower, the sound of a woman moaning loudly began to emanate through the walls.

Sounds as if Doris is almost done for the evening, Celia thought.

As the moans swelled into primal cries, loud and long, Honora awoke and sat upright.

"Dear god!" she cried, throwing off the covers and jumping up to stand on the floor.

In the moonlight, Celia discerned the quivering of Honora's silhouette at the door now, her hand on the knob.

"Who is that? How can we help her?" Honora whispered urgently.

"'*Elp* her?" Molly snorted derisively. "Doris don't need 'elp!"

As if proving a point, the screaming suddenly stopped.

"But...but who's hurting her?"

At this, Molly began to giggle uncontrollably, then turned to Celia.

"Who is '*urtin*' 'er, Celia?" she finally wheezed, then melted into another fit.

"Shut up, Molly," Celia said, sitting up in her bed to reach for a candle on the shelf above her. Once lit, the faint light revealed Honora, her brow a map of fearful creases.

"Go back to bed," Celia said gently, "Doris is fine. There ain't murderers roaming the halls."

Molly laughed again but it sounded bitter now.

"Well, I'll go and make sure," she said, crossly. "We cain't be too careful, can we?"

Climbing out of the bed, she pushed past Honora and exited the room.

Celia rolled her eyes as Molly slammed the door shut, then noted how Honora's lower lip trembled in the candlelight.

"Don't cry," she said, reaching out to touch the sleeve of Honora's nightdress.

Crying changes nothing, she thought, remembering weeping over her grandmother's dead body.

"You heard the screaming as well as I," Honora said, but she slowly lowered herself onto the larger bed.

Celia shifted uncomfortably. *She really doesn't know where she is, does she? I don't fancy telling her. Innocence ain't a bad thing. And Doris does sound like she's getting her head bashed in when she's pretending to be in the throes.*

Celia finally responded, "Doris sometimes has nightmares."

"Oh, how perfectly awful!" Honora replied, taking a big breath. "Does she have them often?"

"Yes, so don't be frightened when you hear her again." Celia hoped they were done speaking of it as she liked this girl and hated lying to her. On she rushed with, "Oh, I must tell you that the cake you made tonight was delicious."

"Cake?" The distracted look in Honora's eyes stilled and her breathing began to slow. "Oh yes, the apple cake."

"How did you learn to make that?"

"Polly taught me."

"Polly?"

"The cook at Stagsdown House. When I was a tiny thing, Polly had me measuring flour and stirring batters. That cake was one of the first sorts I baked entirely on my own."

"It reminded me of something my Nan made once. I nearly had a second piece."

"Thank you. And thank you for standing up for me to Molly." Honora picked at the bedclothes. "I don't think she likes me much, though I don't know why."

"Don't let Molly trouble you. She's not truly nice to anyone…unless they've got something she wants. Then she's friendly enough, so watch out for that."

"Does she actually read those?" Honora pointed at the stack of the 'La Belle Assemblée' upon the shelf.

"What, Molly *read*?" Celia scoffed. "Good lord, no! Mr. Boxem brings those to her once his wife is done with them. Molly just stares at the drawings of the bonnets and gowns on the fashion pages. Oh! While she's gone, I've something to show you."

Honora's troubled eyes settled on Celia.

"This afternoon when I saw you'd moved in, I hid something of yours so it wouldn't get filched by anyone who might sneak in to poke around." She climbed out of the bed and crouched on the floor, beckoning Honora to join her. "Here."

Celia cast the candle's light upon the wall under the chair rail which spanned each wall of the small bedroom. The two girls' heads nearly knocked together as they peered at what Celia had wedged into a crack underneath the board.

Honora gasped. Two gold coins glinted in the candlelight, inches away from the few coins of Celia's own that she had hidden similarly each rare time she got one.

"It gave me no pleasure rifling through your things, but I knew others would do so before long and I ought to hide for you."

At her confession, it was difficult for Celia to interpret the look on Honora's face. It wasn't one of anger nor displeasure.

Sadness, perhaps. Celia had seen plenty of that on the faces around her in her short seventeen years.

"Well, thank you then," Honora said, flatly. Little flecks of tears still sparkling on her lower lashes.

"There's a little room for more should you get it," Celia said, pointing at a furtherance of the crack. "Just don't stow it when Molly's around. She hasn't found mine yet, but if she sees you crouching down here, she's sure to look closer."

Celia glanced at the stash again, comparing Honora's money to her own little pittance nearby.

Two gold coins! Why'd she come to work here if she's got that much money, and how'd she get that lot in the first place?

48

Though she was vastly curious, Celia saw that Honora was too tired and overwhelmed just then to give a history of herself.

"Why don't you try to sleep?" she encouraged. "It's late and I think all will be quiet now."

The girl nodded dumbly, then lay down upon her bed.

Celia settled herself onto her own mattress and blew out the candle, thankful for the dark enveloping her. Thoughts filled her mind of how having two gold coins herself just six months earlier might have kept her out of the Bower.

Upon her grandmother's death, Celia and her brother had in their possession just twelve shillings and a few pence.

In Nana's last weeks, Celia and Bill could not bear to deprive her of a few bare comforts. When she stopped eating, weakly brewed cups of tea were the only thing she craved except for oranges. When the fruit sellers had boxes of the golden orbs, Celia would buy one each day, and take it home to cut it into wedges. With the little strength she had, Nana would weakly nibble at the pulp until she fell into one of her deep sleeps. Then, Celia would pry the pungent peels out of her hands and wash her sticky fingers with a damp rag.

While Nana lay dying upon the cushioned pallet under the sitting room's one window, Celia had taken on the arduous task of laundering every order on her own. Bill went out during the day to earn a few coins running errands and carrying messages across town.

It was one week after Nana's passing that Celia had shown Bill the limited remains of their savings.

"That's it?" Bill had asked as Celia spilled the measly contents of their purse into her hand. Though the dull coins filled her palm, they both knew how quickly they would disappear once the rent was paid and a little food was bought.

Dropping the few coins back into the bag, she had tucked it into the top of her stays and said, "Now that you've seen what little we have, come walk with me. I must speak with you."

"I been running all over London-Town since morning," he had responded, settling himself further into the wooden chair. "I'm tired."

"As am I," she had said simply, extending her hand to him. "Come."

With an exasperated sigh, her younger brother had plucked the last roll from a crumb-filled plate on the table and stood, ignoring the hand she offered him.

The dark-haired siblings exited the apartment and descended the dark staircase to the street below. Falling into quick step beside one another, they had been silent at first. When the water of the Thames came into view at the end of Queen Street, Celia had finally spoken.

"We've got to earn more money."

"You got me off my chair to tell me that? I ain't blind nor stupid, Celie," Bill said, stuffing the last bite of the roll into his mouth before brushing his hands off on his worn-out trouser legs. Celia saw they were two inches too short – his legs were growing longer at an astonishing rate though he was still rail-thin – and the sole of his right shoe flapped on the pavement with each step.

"I neither thought nor said you were, Bill. But we've got to do something about it. I've a plan, but don't think you'll like it."

"Nor do I like being as poor as we are, so tell me."

They had reached the end of the street and were peering down the banks at the slow-moving Thames. The days were lengthening at this time of year and the sun was hovering at the horizon, glinting off the water.

"Two bedrooms and a sitting room is far more than we need. We've got to find a single room somewhere. Meanwhile, I'll give up laundering and try to find work as a maid in an inn or a grand house." She turned to look at him. "If I work for a great family – or at least a place where great families sometimes stay – they'll get me known to others like them, and maybe one of them'll have a clerk's job for you. You read and write well enough, and running messages around London ain't the type of thing you ought to be doing at fourteen unless you want to do it the rest of your life."

To her surprise, Bill had grunted what sounded like an affirmation.

Staring out over the gray waters rolling past, he said, "Working as a clerk all day can't be so bad if there's a plate of hot roast and 'tatoes on the table at the end of it."

As relief flooded Celia's heart, they had turned and started back up the hill.

"Where will you look for work, Celie?"

She placed her hand on his shoulder and was pleased when he didn't shrug it off.

"Well Bill, you're not the only terrific walker in the family. Tomorrow, I'll go deep into the finer parts of town and knock on doors."

And the very next day, I washed my face, put on my better dress and climbed the steps to the Bower's front door...

Recalling the feel of his rough shirt under the palm of her hand, the warmth of his bony shoulder underneath it, Celia now reached under her pillow, tears stinging her eyes.

Through the darkness, three faint words drifted to her, pulling her out of her memories and back to the present.

"Thank you, Celia," Honora said, drowsily.

"Mm-hm," she murmured, tracing the edges of the oak leaf over and over with her finger tip

THE FIRST SIGNS

HONORA WOKE WITH a start, the strengthening sunlight filtering through the windows was an alleviation after the scare of the night before. Still, awakening in the dark whilst a woman screamed just rooms away had knocked the joy out of her gaining employment so quickly.

Am I late? She worried. Yet beside her, Molly slept deeply, a light snore escaping her slack lips. In the other bed, Celia's body was still, her dark head resting heavily upon her pillow. Carefully, Honora climbed out of the bed and donned her dress and apron.

Ought I to wake them? She wondered. *Surely their day's work starts soon though perhaps not as early as mine. I do wonder what they do here. Sally and I were the only ones in the kitchen last night.*

Had Celia been in the bedroom when Honora retired the night before, she might have asked, but the room had been empty. Exhausted, Honora had gone to bed, waking only slightly when Celia had come in later, then fully when the nightmarish screaming had sounded.

Deciding to let the other girls sleep on, Honora let herself out into the hallway. It appeared as mundane as it had the day before.

There are no bloodstains upon the floor boards, she noted. *Nor any clumps of torn-out hair scattered across the rug. So, it truly was* just *a nightmare she was having?*

The memory of the cries, part howling, part shrieking, sent a thrill down Honora's spine.

Celia was kind, but that Molly mocked me to my face.

It wasn't the words Celia had spoken that had eased Honora's fears. It was the calm she had displayed, as well as the willingness of Molly to go out of the room just moments after the screaming had ceased. Clearly, they both were accustomed to such horrific sounds, and had no fear of what they might indicate.

I must rally and focus on the good, Honora urged herself. *I can earn my keep here by cooking in a well-equipped kitchen instead of schooling some naughty children hand-picked by Eliza. Now, downstairs to begin my day's work.*

She hurried down the flight of steps and pushed into the kitchen. Sally was already there, stoking the fire in the oven.

"G' mornin'," the older woman said, surprising Honora. It held no tone of frustration at Honora's hour of arrival.

"Good morning," she replied.

"Mrs. Dovey says yer to do the shoppin' this mornin'. She's left a list on the table fer ya. And yer to bake another cake when ya return, whatever sort ya like."

Pleased at this news, Honora made her way to the list which was next to the big basket on the table. She noted with relief that there were five coins beside it.

Perhaps the grocer will not recoil from me once I hand these over. But can they be enough? She was sour as rhubarb about extending the credit.

Ah well. Here I go to discover it!

Pocketing the coins, she lifted the basket and made her way out of the door.

***

The street was narrow and cobblestoned with a roughly paved walkway running parallel alongside it. It was the middle of the morning bustle and many people brushed past or bumped into Honora as she walked along. She followed the street to a square where the buildings were further apart and the street split to accommodate a grassy median where a couple of goats were tethered.

Alas, no cart with young preachers today, she regretted, recalling the two fellows who had stood on the greensward the day before. The elder had been about to address the crowds when she had passed, catching his eye, causing an elongated pause in his declaration.

Had Eliza seen that, she would have accused me of flustering him on purpose. It did make me laugh — his eyes locking with mine as his mouth hung open, ready to speak, then silent — I must confess!

The thought of it now cheered her immensely.

Another stretch of roadway brought her to the grocer's and with a small measure of anxiety, she went in the door which rang its pleasant bell. Two other customers were there, perusing the goods on offer.

"Good morning," Honora said quietly as she ventured further into the shop, the coins in her palm, ready to be handed over immediately. At her approach, the woman behind the counter looked up, the amiable expression upon her face taking a quick turn to consternation. She glanced at the other customers and beckoned Honora towards herself, shaking her head all the while.

Grabbing Honora's arm, she pulled her through a doorway into the back of the shop and hissed, "Don't come in the front."

Shocked, Honora stuttered, "Par...pardon me? But here is payment. I hope it's enough for now."

"I know you lot've got to eat," the woman said as she took the coins and list from Honora's hand. Squinting at the paper, she hurriedly piled carrots, apples and sprigs of parsley into the basket. "I don't begrudge you that. But I *insist* you come in and out through *there!*"

She pointed at a door at the back of the room.

"You stay back here till I come and get you yer truck. I see you brought a wee bit of money, but tell that Dovey woman her tab's gettin' high and if she wants more goods for you and yer sort, she's got to pay it all. Now off you go!"

The woman stood between Honora and the storefront, shooing her toward the backdoor.

"If I see you up front again, there'll be nothing more from my shop for you lot at the *Titania's Bower.*" She whispered this as if doing so filled her mouth with bile.

Too stunned to protest at such treatment, Honora stepped out the backdoor and found herself in a narrow alleyway, the door swinging shut behind her.

Why would she hate Mrs. Dovey so? Honora marveled as she began to make her way toward the street. With as much dignity as she could gather, she folded the edges of the cloth over the groceries, tucked the basket firmly into the crook of her arm and stepped around little piles of filth that littered the alley on her way back to the Bower. Sunlight warmed her bare head as she stepped into the square with the green.

"Good morning to you!" a voice called brightly. "Would you like an apple?"

Looking up, Honora was surprised to see the young man who had gazed upon her with such interest in his eyes just the day before. But today, instead of a leather-bound volume in his hands, he held a greenish fruit, extending it toward her.

So they have arrived after all.

Three more steps brought her directly in front of him and she smiled, reaching for the gift.

"I thank you," she said, wrapping her fingers around the smooth, cool weight of it.

"Taste and see that the Lord is good," the man continued, dipping his head toward what he had handed her.

This comment drew a faint scoff out of the person standing beside him.

Ah, yes. He *was here yesterday as well,* Honora recalled, glancing at the slighter fellow. Seeing him up-close now, she saw he was a mere, tall boy.

The two were obviously brothers with their warm blue eyes and their reddish hair bright against the dark brims of their hats.

Unsure if they meant for her to eat the apple right then, she clutched it to her belly, thankful for the kindness it signified but unwilling to be observed by two strangers at its ingestion.

Honora and the elder fellow beheld one another dumbly for a moment.

Glancing at her basket, the younger boy dryly announced, "She's already got a whole peck of apples, Barclay. Whyn't you share the message with her, as that *is* why we're here, is it not?"

He laid a tract on the produce in Honora's basket, then stepped back as if watching a play upon a stage.

"Oh yes, of course," the elder said, clearing his throat. "I am Barclay Durbin, and this is my brother, Jasper."

Jasper tilted his head at Honora, smirking all the while.

"We're here today," Barclay went on, motioning toward the pamphlet, "to call-out to the people of London."

"Call-out?" Honora asked, her head full of memories of the prior morning – her first day in London – when she had walked past hawkers of all sorts on the busy streets. Countless girls had cried out about the flowers and ribbons they were selling. One man had hollered many times "Fish! Eels!" though the pungent smell of his cart negated any need for such declarations. She wondered for a moment if the street preachers before her expected her to pay for the apple and pamphlet, feeling a thrill of horror as she had not a ha'penny upon her person.

"Yes, we call-out as those who are in the wilderness to make straight the way of the Lord," Barclay said. He dipped his head again to the apple she held. "And we find that people are readier to listen when we sweeten the message with the gift of such fruit from our orchard."

Ah, a gift! Thank goodness! With her mind now at ease, Honora asked, "And how are you 'making straight the way of the Lord'?"

Clearing his throat, Barclay delivered an answer that seemed practiced, yet somehow sincere.

"By alerting the multitudes of God's love for them and His ever-ready aid for them."

"Hmm. In what forms might this love and aid present itself?"

Had he been another religious zealot, she mightn't have asked, but she longed to continue her observation of the admirable fellow before her.

"Oh, many!" Barclay replied.

A few feet away, Jasper extended an apple and pamphlet to an elderly woman who was tottering past. While he helped her tuck them both into the small basket she carried, Barclay leaned in slightly toward Honora and quietly said, "It is my hope in the future to establish a school of sorts where impoverished young men can learn reading, writing and ciphering that they can find employment and elevate themselves from destitution."

"Hmm. That *is* a worthy venture." Honora's appreciation of him expanded further, and she asked, "And what of the girls?"

"Girls?"

"Yes. For every boy in poverty there is certainly a girl stuck in the mire beside him. Would the Barclaian School of God's Love and Aid have a wing for girls that they might learn a trade and elevate themselves?"

With a guileless expression, he responded, "I hadn't thought that far in advance. One step at a time, I suppose."

Honora warmed at his humility, so unlike the many men who had come to Stagsdown House to court Eliza. Barclay spoke neither with conceit nor affected gallantry.

A young gentleman — for a gentleman he surely is! — whose mind isn't solely fixed on horse races and hunting foxes? Remarkable!

Honora felt she could breathe while faced with him, and breathe deeply.

His eyes were wide and earnest as he spoke on. She heard the soothing timbre of his voice and watched his lips and even teeth form his words. The soft look in his eyes reminded Honora of other young men who had looked at her with fondness. It made her feel playful and she wanted to extend the conversation.

Oh, what would Lady Eliza say of me? she asked herself.

But now, Barclay's mouth had stopped moving and Honora realized he was awaiting a response from her. Jasper, beside him, was also attentive to her, and looking sly.

"Would you like to hear more of the gospel?" Barclay asked, apparently for the second time.

Embarrassed, Honora nodded her head, but lifted higher her produce-filled basket and replied, "I *would*, but unfortunately, I must be on my way now as I'm expected back."

"Oh," Barclay's face fell, then lit again. "Very well then. I shall see you again when you have more time, perhaps. Jasper and I call-out here once or twice a week. In the meantime, please read the tract and write down any questions you might have."

He grew suddenly serious. "You…you can read and write, I suppose?"

This question from anyone else might have lit her ire, but from this gentle, warm fellow, it struck her as highly amusing. She couldn't help but throw back her head and laugh.

"Yes. Yes, I can," she said. Then, "And I thank you for the apple."

With one final glance at Jasper and a slightly longer look at Barclay, Honora bobbed her head and began her walk back to the Bower, still giggling and with a much lighter heart than a few minutes earlier.

STRANGE FIRES

WITH HIS FACE AFLAME, Barclay heard Jasper's low chuckle as they watched the girl walk away.

"'You *can* read and write, I suppose'," Jasper said in an affectedly lowered voice, then patted Barclay on the back. "Well, brother, that's certainly one way to impress a woman."

Barclay bit his lip and said nothing.

Why did *I ask her that? Just hearing her speak — the words she used — she is undeniably literate.*

This was not the first time that Barclay had felt foolish whilst standing on Crawton Green calling-out. Once in his early days, he had been loudly imploring the passersby to repent of their sins and turn to a loving god in humility. A woman walking past had stumbled and sloshed him with a bucket of sour milk. Though she apologized as if it was an accident, the smirk on her face implied otherwise. The cold, wet shock of the wave splashing over his head had brought about an immediate change in Barclay. He was still committed to calling-out, but his manner in doing so was transformed in a saturated instant.

If I am asking them *to be humble before God,* he had reasoned as the milk dripped off his hat and shoulders, and the laughter of those nearby rang in his ears, *then it is only right that* I *should stand humbled before them. I am a fool, yes, but I am the Lord's fool, so it isn't all for naught. At least, I hope not.*

From then on, he never raised his voice in tones that could be regarded as angry and accusing. Rather, his loudest cries were reserved for when he spoke of his Lord's infinite love and mercy.

However, this was the first time he had felt embarrassed on the green in regards to a young woman who had caught his attention. Feeling foolish before her was a very different sensation than the humiliations to which he had formerly inured himself. He often read in his Bible of the prophets of old and what they had endured, some of them to the point of death.

But today, what verse will solace me in this shame? He wondered. *Neither Isaiah, nor Jeremiah spoke of their tender feelings for women and how they navigated such waters.*

Years earlier at his conversion, his heart had burned within him, longing to be completely devoted to the service of his newfound Lord. Thinking through the practicalities of this, he foresaw simplicity for this pursuit if he were to remain unmarried. He was, after all, the second son of a gentleman's family, and his inheritance would be paltry compared to that of Clayton.

As a single man, I would never have to choose between the comfort of my wife and children and ministerial opportunities, he had rationalized.

But there was another fire – a strange one – that had begun to burn within him. Irreligious and embarrassing in nature, it would smolder, then suddenly blaze, overtaking his mind and body. Inexplicably, he would find himself thinking things he oughtn't think, longing for things that were not his for the taking, and all with such undeniable and fervent physical manifestations. He was at a loss to reconcile this relentless distraction with the call he was certain God had placed upon his life.

With shame and vigor, he begged God to 'heal' him of his yearnings. He found himself withdrawing from society, particularly young women as their presence tended to undo any progress he felt the Lord had recently made within him. As time went on, he became more and more miserable and the loneliness that accompanied this was like the darkness of a silent, starless night. He considered speaking with Martha about it, but humiliation kept him dumb. One day, at the peak of his frustration, he was forlornly flipping through the pages of the Bible when he came across a group of verses. Reading them, his faith – not only in his god, but even in himself – was salvaged.

'It is good for a man not to touch a woman.'

Yes, yes, I know! he had thought miserably before reading on.

'Nevertheless, to avoid fornication, let every man have his own wife, and let every woman have her own husband...I say therefore to the unmarried and widows, it is

good for them if they abide even as I. But if they cannot contain, let them marry: for it is better to marry than to burn.'

The final few words emblazoned themselves across his mind, heartening his soul. To see that the recommendation for marriage was in the very word of God itself, evaporated his shame as a deep peace flooded his soul. Suddenly, he understood that though some were meant for singleness, he was not of that number and his confidence grew that God, Who had fashioned him this way, *wanted* him to have a wife. To feel shame over it would be to discredit God Himself. Even his mother, who knew nothing of his struggle, commented on a change in his demeanor in the days afterward.

Believing that his intended spouse was somewhere out in the wide world, and that the Lord would bring them together in His perfect timing, put Barclay's heart at ease.

So upending had been this crisis, and so relieving its resolution, that Barclay had watched Jasper age with astute concern. He hoped to aid him in overcoming any similar upheaval with less heartache and confusion. There were little signs here and there that indicated Jasper was moving into this stage in life, but Barclay suspected that the boy had a clearer understanding of many things that he himself had found puzzling. Therefore, in spite of the irreverence that often poured forth from Jasper's mouth, Barclay gave allowance for the boy's pert observations that bordered on appreciation.

Such was his feeling in this moment on the green, watching the girl with the basket disappear into the crowd.

Jasper is right, he thought, forming a smirk of his own. *If I am to impress a member of the gentler sex, I'll have to do much better than that!*

Turning to his brother with a gleam in his eye, he said sheepishly, "I didn't think to ask her name!"

Jasper's eyebrows rose in interest. "So you do have designs on her?"

With a good-natured shove, Barclay replied, "Don't use so obtuse a term. She has a certain air about her, something beyond mere prettiness. Don't you think?"

Jasper shrugged, "I don't know, but I'd venture to say she thinks well of you, as well."

Barclay couldn't refrain from smiling. "Why say you so?"

Again, Jasper shrugged. "You looked a right fool, stammering and stumbling while speaking to her, and she *did* laugh, but not scornfully so. She seemed pleased, rather."

"Hmph," Barclay responded, eyeing his younger brother. *That's as close to encouragement as I'm likely to get out of him, yet there's truth in it. She did laugh happily as she walked away.*

"Well I thank you for such affirmation, brother. Here." He slung the sack of apples over Jasper's shoulder and took the tracts from the boy's hands. "You hand out the apples now. It's early yet, and we've much good to do before we return home."

With revived spirits, Barclay turned his attention back to the crowds.

"Come!" he called out to them. "Hear of the Lord's great love for us all!"

A GOWN FOR HONORA

THOUGH IT WAS NOW late morning, Dovey was still wrapped in her green silk dressing gown, posted at one of her bedroom windows, watching for Honora. The door was locked as she counted out the wad of paper bank notes she kept rolled up in her drawer. She reveled in this weekly ritual of seeing how her hoard had grown.

While smoothing the notes out into denominational piles upon the desk, she waited to see which of the countless emotions Honora would exhibit upon her return. Discerning such would inform her how to proceed in ensnaring the girl.

When she had chosen this building fifteen years prior, it had been because its location afforded a shroud of propriety for the brothel she wanted to establish. The men who frequented it, if questioned by their wives or mothers, could say honestly that they had not been to the more dissolute parts of town the night before. The fact that Titania's Bower served robust coffees and complementing comestibles furthered the ruse. Even the name had a ring of elegance. Any naïf hearing it might smile, thinking of Shakespeare, and query, "It sounds lovely, but are they scant with the cinnamon in their sagoo custards[ii]?"

Likewise, when she chose her own bedroom in the building, she had considered many things. Although some madams would want a room on the lower story to better control the comings and goings of their patrons and their girls, Dovey had chosen a bedroom on the second story. It had two windows, one facing the courtyard from the front and the other giving her eyes further up the nearby street, to the west. This afforded her a view of people who didn't know they were being watched, which of course is when they committed their most telling behaviours. At a gentleman's approach, she could see if he was drunk, nervous, saddened, angry, being pursued, or feeling celebratory. Likewise, on the occasions when her girls went out, she could watch to see how comfortable they looked as they ventured into the outside world – how eager they were to be out of her clutches. These observations helped her to scheme how to handle them all, men and women alike. And now, her focus was set on Honora who would be returning having likely encountered some prejudicial treatment from the grocer's wife. Dovey was anxious to see how she would bear such disapprobation.

Ah. There she is at last, thought Dovey as the girl came into view. She was clutching the basket and something in her hand.

What is that, a pamphlet of some sort?

Her head was not hanging in shame, nor did her back look rigid with indignation. In fact, there was a spring in her step and as she turned her head, Dovey saw a faint smile on her face, as if she was amused by some quiet thought. Then, she was under the window, leaving only the top of her head to be seen.

Hmph. She doesn't seem bothered at all. Perhaps the shopkeepers have not yet realized she's one of my girls? Ah well, I'll have her chained to the Bower soon enough.

Dovey's disappointment dissipated as she tallied up the four piles of banknotes.

Two hundred and twenty-five pounds! She smiled down at the stacks of creased paper. Elated, she rolled them all together into one fat cylinder. Stuffing the money back into the sock, she dropped it into the middle wardrobe's drawer with a satisfying thud. After piling a few loose shoes over the top of it, she shut the drawer and began to sort through a stack of gowns as her next plan required one for Honora.

Pity I don't have time to alter it nicely. A few pins'll have to do, and Molly can help her with that.

***

A few hours later, Dovey stepped into the kitchen, a blue dress draped over her arm.

"Ah, that is beautiful!" she said, stepping over to where Honora stood.

The girl looked up from the cake she was decorating, a look of gentle pride in her eyes.

"Thank you, Mrs. Dovey."

Truthfully, it was a lovely sight with its three even layers over which a thick glaze was being poured.

Dovey studied her closely as Honora continued to expertly drizzle the sugary syrup.

"I've asked you to bake that because a special group of people is meeting here tonight." Dovey smiled at Honora as if she had an exciting treat in store for her. "And, it would only be fitting if you were to wear a lovely dress whilst you presented such an offering, so here you are."

Stepping back, Dovey held the dress up to her own chest and let its heavy skirt drop to its full length. Humming lightly, she swayed back and forth, then spun around with a little giggle that belied her age and size. "Isn't it beautiful?"

"Oh." Honora had halted in her task. "Yes, but…I don't know that it would fit me."

"Nonsense!" Grabbing Honora's wrist, Dovey shook the spatula out of it, then pulled her toward herself. With one hand, she held the garment to Honora's front and with the other, she patted it into place upon the girl's body.

A flat belly and nice, firm breasts, she thought, ignoring the alarmed look on the girl's face. *Yes, some eager rutter will pour gold into my hand to deflower this girl.*

"A few pins in the right places will work wonders! I'll go and put it up in your room, out of your way," she said, petting the blue skirt, now draped again over her arm. "Now Honora, the gent– the party – will arrive around seven o'clock. Before they get here, you are to prepare yourself in order to present the cake. Molly can help you. Be downstairs before the bell rings thrice. In the meantime, it looks as if you have finished your duties here. You may have the afternoon off!"

Sally looked up from the onions she was dicing, irritation souring her drab face.

"Call down Doris or Nancy to help you," Dovey murmured to her, then left the kitchen with a swish of her skirts, feeling victorious

A RELUCTANT PREENING

CELIA ENTERED THE kitchen, parasol in hand, and stopped to watch Honora carefully place a fan of thinly sliced candied lemon peel on the shiny glazed top of a three-tiered cake.

"It's lovely," Celia said quietly, surprising herself.

Sally looked up from the chop block and gazed for a moment at Celia.

Yes, I do *speak, Sally,* Celia thought. *No need to stare.*

Honora let out a shaky breath and laughed.

"Thank you. It'll do, I suppose," she said, surveying her work, then eyed the parasol Celia carried. "Where are you off to?"

"Hyde Park," Celia said softly.

"Ah, lovely! Might I join you?" Honora asked, her eyebrows lifted, her eyes smiling. "I believe I'm done here for now."

"Oh…um, yes. Of course." Celia stammered.

"Wonderful!" Honora said, untying her apron. "A turn in the fresh air will do me good."

Sally was gawping again, this time with her mouth agape.

I don't always have to go alone, you old bat! Go back to your onion.

The girls exited the kitchen and climbed the outdoor stairs to the street above. Upon reaching the pavement, Honora asked with subtle excitement in her voice, "Which way from here?"

Celia gestured to the right, her stomach fluttering. *What am I to say to this girl who smiles so freely and bakes beautiful cakes as if it were easy? Perhaps I'll cut the walk short today.*

"How often do you walk out like this?" Honora asked.

As always, Celia strode quickly, anxious to put space between herself and the Bower. "Every Friday, for certain, and whenever else Dovey lets me."

Honora guffawed. "Whenever Mrs. Dovey *lets* you? Is she so mean as to restrict you from walks in the park?"

Ah, criminy. Why did I say that?

"She's a bit bossy is all."

"Yes, I gathered that! Sometimes I think she likes me and other times, I don't. Oh! I wanted to ask you, what does Molly do at the Bower?"

Suddenly, it felt as if something was gripping Celia's heart.

"I know *you* launder, and I cook," Honora continued, almost tripping on the uneven stones. "Can we slow down a bit? But how does Molly earn her keep?"

"She dusts and polishes."

It's true, Celia excused herself for the deception, thinking of the one time she'd seen Molly burnish the bannister with a rag. Not for the first time, envy gnawed away at Celia's heart as she regarded the girl walking along beside her. But the resentment was immediately overcome by a twinge of guilt as Celia realized again that she genuinely liked this girl. Honora was kind, friendly and amusing.

She truly doesn't know what the Bower is, does she? Well, I won't be the one to tell her.

That Honora was ignorant in some matters in spite of her obvious overall intelligence did not surprise Celia.

I knew nothing of bawdy-houses before I found myself trapped in one, and I grew up rougher than this girl. She's been primly tucked away somewhere for most of her years.

"Where were you – before?" Celia asked. She was truly curious, but also anxious to steer the conversation away from roles at the Bower. Suddenly something caught her eye and she grabbed Honora's arm to yank her toward herself.

"Sorry!" she exclaimed. "Mind where you step."

She motioned to a two-inch deep hole in the pavement, left there by a missing block of stone.

"I've stepped in that before," Celia said, smoothing out Honora's sleeve, rumpled by her frantic grasping.

"Oh, thank you!" Honora said, glancing over her shoulder to eye the pothole. "Making my way around the kitchen would be a bit harder with a turned ankle. But you asked where I was until yesterday…now *that* is a long, tragic tale."

She said this lightly, as if she was about to describe a pair of new gloves. "The truncated account is that my father was a steward to a wealthy Lord. Their intention was to train me up as a governess that I would have a trade to ply once I was grown."

"That's why you talk so proper-like," Celia laughed. "I never heard but half the words you say. I just pretend to understand you!"

"*That*, I do not believe!" Honora laughed also. "You speak well enough yourself!"

Celia felt a warmth spread through her chest, surprised and pleased that this fine girl found them on more equal footing than she herself thought possible.

They were still yet far from the park. Celia usually kept her head down until her feet felt the crunch of the park's gravel path underneath them, but conversing with Honora, she found herself looking up more.

The butcher has a blue awning over his doorway now. And oh! I can see the roof of the cathedral from here. It's not so very far off after all.

"What is a 'gova'…a 'govress', and why are you not one now if they meant you to be?" Celia prodded.

"A *governess* is a teacher of girls who lives with the girls' family," Honora explained. "Well, in the past few years, both my father and his employer passed away and I was left under the *care and guidance* of the good gentleman's mean-minded daughter, *Lady Eliza*. This was especially difficult because we are nearly the same age and – I hate to sound unkind but – she possesses none of the good sense that her father had but has all of the resentment that an insecure being is wont to feel. Living with her, I was made to feel that I was forever ruining her prospects."

"What can you mean?" Celia furrowed her brow. They were on a wider street now, more traffic rushed past, and innumerous pedestrians pushed by on the walkway. The buildings had opened up as well, their fronts no longer shooting straight to the sky from the girls' elbows. The resultant space allowed the sun to shine directly onto them and Celia felt sweat forming under her arms.

Honora lifted the parasol in Celia's hand and opened it, ducking under to walk alongside its owner in the shade.

"Oh, well certainly it was *my* fault that any young man who came to see her soon realized she was not the goddess Diana! It had nothing to do with the fact that she was stupid and dull. No! It was because I was – as she called me – a *coquette*."

"What's that?"

"A *flirt* – a woman *without discretion*. Which is ridiculous as I never spoke to any of her guests unless they addressed me first. What did she mean for me to do – stare at them dumbly when they asked me a question and then pantomime an answer?"

Honora threw back her head and laughed, causing a couple walking past to look at her, and Celia to flinch.

"Once she accused me of lurking in the garden where she was walking with a possible suitor with the aim of luring him away!"

Into Celia's mind flashed a picture of Honora posing provocatively alongside an oak tree, just waiting for the unsuspecting couple to stroll past, and she joined Honora in her laughter.

"She's terrible plain then, is she?" Celia asked.

Honora considered this for a moment, then said, "No, she is fair enough when she isn't sour-faced, though that is a rare occurrence. Most often, she wears the expression of someone who has been cheated out of something." At this, she pulled a face of irritable disdain, turning it to Celia's full view.

Celia giggled. "A gentleman's daughter felt cheated? Good lord, she must have her own bedroom and never washed a garment in her life!" She adjusted her shawl, feeling the roughness of her hands catching on its fibers.

Honora tucked her hand into the crook of Celia's arm.

"Oh, yes! And don't forget her *twelve* parasols – she had me recount them every April! So you can see why I am now so delighted to be at Titania's Bower baking cakes miles from Eliza and her queer accusations."

At the mention of the Bower, Celia glanced at a man walking past though he didn't seem to overhear it. He did, however, return the look, a glint of appreciation and interest in his eyes.

Celia's gaze fell to the ground. She'd had enough looks like that to last her a lifetime. She considered Honora's last words *'...I am so delighted to be at Titania's Bower...'*

'Well you oughtn't be!' she considered saying, wondering if she should warn this girl. Yet, she held her tongue. *Surely Dovey doesn't mean to put her to work like the rest of us. Just look at her! Listen to her talk! She's nothin' like us.*

"How came you to London," Celia asked. Having never exited the city in her entire life, Celia imagined the countryside to be a very large park, but dotted with livestock instead of parasol-twirling ladies. She couldn't fathom that anyone would want to leave there, even if that place held a jealous girl who was liberal with her finger pointing.

"By coach," Honora replied succinctly. "For years I watched it pass Stagsdown House nearly every morning, just after sunrise. How many times in the past two years did I dream of claiming passage upon it to escape Lady Eliza's disdain? And last week I finally did! Though I must confess that when at last I climbed aboard, I found it over-stuffed with smelly humanity."

Celia smiled. Having never been inside a carriage of any sort, she had seen countless roll past upon the London streets and always regarded them as unpleasant, jam-packed conveyances.

Honora continued, "And you? How came you to the Bower?"

Unprepared, Celia paused to avoid stammering. Here was someone who would not be fooled for long by carefully crafted words. Though she knew the ruse would likely be exposed within a week, Celia couldn't bring herself to own her purpose at the Bower, not directly. The truth was too vile. With most of the other prostitutes, there was an unspoken understanding that what they did behind closed doors could be laughed about at times, but never spoken of in meaningful terms – never regarded as the humiliation that Celia knew it to be and suspected the others did as well.

"Not much to that tale," Celia finally said. "I needed work, and Dovey set me to it. My Nana taught me laundering before she passed."

It was true. Upon her arrival at the Bower, Dovey had given her a few small loads of napery and sheets, promising to feed and house her if she was a very good girl who did what was asked of her. Just on the heels of a very hungry winter and the death of Nana – Celia worked hard to prove herself worthy of her place and earnings at the Bower. She felt her and Bill's futures depended upon it.

"So you see, I was much like you, needing work, but I didn't come from a grand house before mooring at the Bower."

"Well, I lived in a *very small corner* of a grand house, as I was merely a steward's daughter. *And* after his passing, no one could locate the last will and testament that I'm certain my father wrote, so any provision he may have left for me is unverifiable." Honora laughed lightly. "So you see, I did not much benefit from the grandeur."

I've seen and touched your fine pelisse, Celia thought. *I tasted the cake you learned to bake so nice. I hear you talking proper. You benefited lots.*

"Oh, look!" Honora pointed delightedly up into the sky. "A kite!"

They were nearing Hyde Park now – only the busy Park Lane between them and it – and above its trees, a bright red, diamond shaped object dipped and crested upon the wind. A short tail dangled underneath it, whipping about wildly, and a long cord tethered it to something or someone unseen on the earth below.

A kite, Celia said to herself, storing the word away. She had seen these whimsical objects, bobbing above her in the sky a few times, but hadn't known what to call them.

"Where you seen one of them before?" Celia asked.

"Lord Beeman entertained Lady Eliza and myself with them on the Great Lawn at times when we were small. The day has to be just right, though – clear and windy. Have you never flown one?"

"No, I..."

Celia's gaze dropped from the sky above to Honora's face, but was arrested by someone just over her shoulder. At a distance of thirty feet, the sight of this dark-haired fellow was enough to take Celia's breath away, silencing her immediately.

Bill.

Dressed in the same coarse coat and hat she'd last seen him wearing, her brother sat upon a cart loaded heavily with barrels, staring up at the same sight in the sky that was still bewitching Honora.

Instinctively, Celia darted behind her new friend, but peered out carefully to behold the boy fully.

He looks well, she thought, her heart beating so hard that she felt faint. *His cheeks ain't hollowed out, so he's eating just fine. Lor'! Look at the length of his legs!*

This was only the second time she had seen him in six months. The first had been on a gray, drippy day.

"You might as well go out walking!" Dovey had said to Celia as she peered out of the window at the gray drizzle. Celia had perceived the invitation as malevolence, but she had waited for the bawd to swish out of the dining room, then went out the door.

Not far from the Bower, she had seen him, sitting on that same cart where Coventry Street met Hay Market.

He's working for a drayman! She had realized, pride swelling her racing heart as she had ducked behind a wall to stare at him.

But he had looked terrible then – his face gaunt, his dark hair shaggy as he hunched forward, staring gloomily ahead – haggard far beyond his sixteen years – waiting for the drayman to pull out onto the road for a right turn.

She stayed where she was, quivering with something other than the cold drear, waiting for the quick clip clop of the horse's feet to start and then fade as the cart made its way to other parts of town.

After that occurrence, she went on every one of her walks, finding herself caught between two intensities – desperate to see him alive and well once again, yet terrorized that he might spy her in return.

"What is it?" Honora said suddenly, glancing at Celia, then over in the direction of the drayman's cart.

Celia's head bobbed to stay behind Honora's shoulder, though her eyes didn't waver from the young man's face. He was glancing around now as the unfamiliar driver beside him readied to pull out into traffic. Then, with a *Haw!* and a slap of the reins, he was gone.

Celia nearly grabbed onto Honora's shoulder to steady herself, but took a deep breath instead, praying for the stilling of her heart.

Honora said, knowingly, "Oh, *I* see."

"Hmm?" Celia murmured, watching as the cart disappeared from sight.

With a faint smile, Honora teased, "Ah, what a shame the fellow's gone and there's only a kite above to gaze upon. Oh! That's disappeared now, as well!"

Saddened yet satisfied that the boy was truly out of sight, Celia readied herself to resume normal conversation. Glancing up at the sky, she saw that the kite had in fact disappeared.

"Maybe they'll have it up again before we hafta go back," Celia said, forcing herself to look hopeful, wondering if her comment made much sense as her heart and mind continued to race.

His clothes looked clean. Still wearing those patched trousers. How many times did I wash them trousers?

Tucking her hand around Celia's upper arm, Honora pulled her forward and said, "He was rather handsome. A bit old for you though, wasn't he?"

She musta thought I was looking at the man driving the cart and not the boy beside him.

Relieved at the unsolicited alibi this presented, Celia forced something that almost sounded like a giggle.

"Yes," she said, and allowed her new friend to pull her toward the park's entrance. "I suppose he was."

***

They were late. Celia was supposed to return from her walks in time to eat supper and prepare herself for what the evening held. Talking with Honora and then having sighted Bill, Celia was flustered and distracted. Attempting a poorly-planned short-cut back to the Bower had only compounded the problem. She expected that the instant they came through the front door, Dovey would strike her – on the back of her head of course where her hair would cover any bruises. But when they arrived, the bawd was not looming in the vestibule, waiting for them. The other girls, however, were clearing their dishes from supper.

"I hope you weren't terrible hungry this evening," Celia said apologetically as they hurried up the stairs. "It looks as if we'll have to wait until later to scrounge up something to eat."

"If you *must* know, I licked the glaze bowl clean – that lemon is one of my favorites!" Honora replied as they burst through the door to their bedroom. "So I couldn't have eaten much just now."

Thirsty after their rush, Celia went straight to the pitcher of water on the ewer stand and poured herself a large cup. She saw in the mirror that Honora was looking at a blue dress, its skirt smoothed and splayed out upon the bed.

"What's that?" Celia asked after a large gulp of water.

"Oh," Honora laughed with a wave of her hand. "Something I've been told I must wear tonight whilst serving cake."

What?

Celia sputtered, then began to cough violently.

"Are you alright?" Honora laughed, patting Celia's back.

With her eyes watering, Celia wheezed, "Dovey brought that to you to wear?"

"Yes." Honora turned back to the frock, lifting one of its long sleeves from the bed to examine the lace at the cuff, saying airily, "Apparently, my own clothes aren't fine enough for patrons to see me in."

A cold thrill ran down Celia's spine.

No! She can't mean to turn Honora into one of us. Honora's too smart – too fine!

"What's the matter?" Honora was looking at Celia expectantly.

Ought I warn her?

Celia sipped her water, her thoughts dashing about.

No, it's early yet.

"Celia?"

I was here nearly two weeks before my tainting. And this is just Honora's second day.

"Hmm? Sorry, I was thinking how you ought to dress your hair."

Honora sighed. "Truth be told, I'm hopeless at the arrangement of hair. That's why I always pin it up in precisely the same way. You'd think that someone who can decorate a fancy cake could beautify their own person, but I defy that supposition! Will you help me?"

Help you? I can't make you pretty for the picking in the Mingling Room.

"*Your* hair looks nice," Honora went on.

But need I pretty her up?

A plan was birthed in that moment.

"Uh…thank you. Yes, I'll help you," Celia replied slowly. "Though I don't claim to do hair well myself."

"Ah, bless you," Honora said with a smile as she slipped out of her dress.

Celia watched her friend in the mirror, the cup still at her lips.

Surely, she is untouched, she thought, her eyes resting on Honora's long pale arms as they lifted the blue gown from the bed. *She doesn't cringe and cower whilst undressed.*

Honora was struggling to get the plenteous cloth over her head, and Celia stepped over to help. Together, they got Honora's head through the bottom of the skirt and lowered the bodice to rest on her hips.

"How is this to stay up?" Honora giggled, leaning forward to show the gaping of the neckline. Above the simple stays she wore, the tops of her round breasts were unmarked. Celia felt as if her own chest had blots and smudges all over it, even had dreamed of large handprints marring its breadth on more than one occasion.

76

"I'll pin it for you," she said, retrieving a pin cushion from the ewer table's drawer. Pulling and folding, she covered as much of Honora's flesh as she could, securing it all into place. There were many tucks she could have pinned to accentuate Honora's waist and hipline, but these she left billowing.

"And the hem," she said, kneeling by Honora's feet. Lifting the skirt, she revealed Honora's legs. Her calves were firm and muscular, her feet broad across the ball.

Good for kicking a man should he get any ideas, Celia thought as she began to pin the skirt to a length that fell just below the ankle. *There – long enough to cover her, short enough she can lift it and run.*

In a few moments, she had finished and stood, circling the girl, pleased to see how shapeless she appeared. *What else might I do?*

"Now for your hair," she murmured then motioned that Honora ought to sit on the small bed, so she could crouch before her, scrutinizing.

Her face is rather square. Fullness at the sides would make it look more so.

With her bone comb, Celia parted Honora's hair right down the center of her scalp. Pulling the locks down straight on either side, she twisted them separately to form two large flaps. With hairpins, she secured one above each ear. The style itself was handsome enough, but it did not suit Honora. Her head looked like a big, flouncy block above the pinned neckline of the blue dress, much to Celia's satisfaction.

There! Now she'll not turn any gentleman's head while doling out cake.

"Done!" she said, then lied. "It's the latest fashion and looks well on you!"

How can I keep her from looking in the mirror? She may try to fix it if she does.

As if on cue, the calling bell sounded.

"Oh!" Honora said, standing up from the bed and turning toward the door. "Mrs. Dovey told me to be downstairs *before* the bell rang! Thank you for your…"

Her gratitude was halted as she glanced in the little looking-glass, her hand upon the doorknob.

"Uh, thank you…for your help," she said, patting awkwardly at the voluminous puff of her stylized hair.

There was concern in her eyes, but Celia said brightly, "You're welcome. It turned out better than I thought it would. You ought to go down now. They'll be wanting that lovely lemon cake."

Honora regarded herself one last time in the mirror, but said nothing. Celia could see the dissatisfaction in her eyes and was glad at the limited view the small looking-glass allowed.

The hair appears ill on her, certainly, but the fit of the dress is worse, she thought. *She looks like a bit of laundry drying on the line in the alleyway.*

The bell sounded a second time at which Honora squared her shoulders, saying simply, "Yes, it won't do at all to be tardy."

Then, she was out of the door, leaving Celia alone to hope for her ignorant friend's well-being.

A PECULIAR EVENING

CARRYING THE CAKE, Honora headed toward the room to which Dovey had bade her come. Passing a mirror, this one larger than the one in her bedroom, she glanced into it and confirmed her thoughts.

Ugh! I do *look a fright!* she thought. *Oh well. Celia is not a fine hairdresser, but she meant well, and no pair of shears was involved!*

She was thinking of the time she had foolishly bemoaned to Eliza how ill-equipped she felt to style her own hair. A large party of guests was coming to visit and all of Stagsdown House was abustle. Eliza had said she knew of a style that would suit Honora marvelously. This was in the time before their fathers had passed, when Honora still hoped to make Eliza her friend. And so, she had consented – though the daughter of a servant can hardly decline the request of a master's child. Happily, Eliza had situated Honora at her own vanity table, but with her back to the mirror as she stated the final result ought to be a surprise. Trying to hide her nervousness, Honora let down her waist-length hair. After much rough and painful combing – throughout which Honora stayed mum – she heard a snipping sound at her left ear. In horror, she saw and felt a freed lock of hair fall from her shoulder to the floor.

"NO!" she had cried, jumping up from the padded velvet seat. Spinning around to face the large mirror, she saw Eliza who stood with a pair of shears – previously unseen – in her hand. Staring past her, Honora's reflection showed the butchery of an unskilled hairdresser upon a trusting subject.

"You said nothing of *cutting!*"

"You needn't look so horrified," Eliza had said. "I'm not yet finished. Sit down!"

But Honora wouldn't.

"Well clean up this mess then!" Eliza had said crossly, dropping the shears on the seat and waving her hand at the clump of hair on the carpet.

Determining to never again trust Eliza, Honora had tucked her shorn lock into her pocket and retreated to the kitchen. There, Polly placated her by setting her to make macarons – over which the Stagsdown House guests had been ecstatic later that evening.

Now in the Bower with a lemon cake balanced on the plate in her hands, Honora turned away from the mirror and sighed, reminding herself, *I've felt unsightly before and lived another day. And, at least the* cake *looks good.*

If she had to choose, Honora would prefer her baked goods appear more attractive than her own person, and this one was a delight to behold. Its layers were high and level, the glaze smooth, the curls of candied peel a bright flash of yellow on the top.

Once at the parlor door, Honora heard Dovey announce to the dinner party, "I do believe we have some cake to complement your coffee! I'll just go see where it's at."

Oh dear, it sounds as if I'm late, Honora thought as the door opened.

"Ah, here it is!" Dovey called out, swinging the door wide that Honora might enter. As she did, she looked directly at Honora and her lip curled in disgust.

"Who did your hair?" Dovey whispered sharply as Honora passed her.

"Celia," Honora replied, her eyes set on the platter.

"God, what was she thinking? Well, there's nothing to be done about it now. When you've finished doling out the cake, you're to sit with Mr. Shiverly. He's the little, withered one in the corner. His eyes are poorly, so he mightn't be frightened at the sight of you. Smile a lot and speak loud enough for him to hear you."

Her ears burning with indignation, Honora surveyed the parlor. There was a table nicely laid out with clean plates, forks and napkins, but the people – the long-awaited dinner party – was a strange surprise. It consisted of about ten men of varying ages and sizes, who sat or milled about the room, essentially ignoring one another. Serving them were some of the women of the Bower who Honora had previously seen in the dining room or in the hallways.

Two girls – *Nancy and Alice?* Honora tried to recall – were at the table, one pouring coffee into cups, the other offering cream and sugar to the men who stood nearby. The little plain girl, Doris, who had been enraptured by Honora's apple cake the night before, flitted about the room offering napkins to the guests. There was something about the girl's manner that made Honora uneasy. It was far too familiar. She simpered coyly as she brushed past the men, her skirts catching on some of their trouser legs. A brash blond fellow reached out and squeezed her arm. Doris responded with a laugh and a lingering smile. Yet Dovey stood beside the door, overseeing everything with a look of contentment. But as her eyes fell again on Honora, she frowned.

Pushing her discomfort aside, Honora put the cake down on the table and began to cut into it with a fine silver server. Soon, she had several slices of cake plated and she took a turn around the room, offering them to everyone there, just as Dovey had instructed her earlier. She was disappointed that only three men accepted a piece.

One of the men was Mr. Shiverly.

"Oh! Cake, I see," he said, leaning forward and squinting at what she held out to him. "That looks delicious."

There was a slight tremor to the hand he lifted to take the plate.

Honora glanced at all the guests, pacing around the room as if waiting for something. She was dismayed at the many slices of cake that remained untouched on the table.

They don't even want it!

"Mm. Lemon! Very nice, indeed." Mr. Shiverly proclaimed, patting the seat of a wooden chair next to him. "Do sit down, young lady, and give me your company. All you girls here are so agreeable. Yes, indeed."

Wanting to flee the room, but finding a seat in the corner to be the next best option, Honora complied.

"And what is your name, my dear?" he asked, a few crumbs on his upper lip.

"Honora, sir."

He forked another bit of cake into his mouth, then spoke sloppily around it. "And am I to understand that you baked this delightful creation?"

"Yes, Mr. Shiverly."

"'Shiverly'?" His fork stopped halfway to his lips and he laughed. "Is that what you lot call me? Hmph!"

"Oh! Perhaps I misheard it. What is your name, sir?"

"'Shiverly' will do just fine." He winked.

So that is truly not *his name?* Honora's bewilderment deepened.

"Such lovely cake! My dear housekeeper, Gladys, used to make a most toothsome fruitcake. One Christmas, I insisted she show me how to do it, so we stayed up all hours of the night, chopping citron and sultanas, mixing spices – just the two of us." His rheumy eyes shone as he stared off into yesteryear, then sighed. "Well, she's gone now – God rest her sweet soul – and Phyllis takes care of me, though things just aren't the same at home without Gladys. She was a very dear woman. Beautiful, too."

Mr. Shiverly rallied from his melancholic nostalgia, and pulled his chair a little closer to Honora's. "Do you know what the secret is for a superior fruitcake?"

She shook her head as she leaned back from his hot, lemony breath.

"You are a baker of cakes, yet you do not know?" He beamed, obviously delighting in her ignorance. "The secret is, you must wrap it in heavy paper, tie it with a thick twine, then store it in a dark closet for months, not once peeking at it. 'Bake and hide it in September, feast upon it come December,' Gladys always said."

"Hmm," Honora murmured as she watched Dovey move around the room, asking the men if they needed anything, and if they required more to drink. Suddenly, Honora noticed that there were fewer men in the parlor now. Also, Nancy and Doris were gone, having finished their duties, Honora supposed.

Perhaps I can leave, as I am done serving, as well.

"That fruitcake sounds very promising, Mr. Shiverly, and December is not far off. But in the meantime, might I get you another slice of *this* cake?"

"Oh no, my dear. My innards can only take in so much, but I thank you."

Dovey's back was turned.

"Well, I'll clear this for you then." She took the plate from him and stood, ignoring the disappointed look in his eye and quietly said, "I wish you a lovely evening."

A MADAM'S MACHINATION

DAMN! DOVEY RAGED.

The plan to stir her clientele's interest in the new girl had failed shamefully.

What could a man find more delightful than to have a pretty girl bring in a fine-looking cake, baked by herself and served with her own slender, smooth hands?

Dovey had supposed it would lend a sense of refined domesticity to the Bower, appealing to the proper sensibilities of the men present. The sort of customer Dovey wanted to attract was a top-hatted gentleman who rode around town in a barouche, sipped tea in his mother-in-law's parlor beside his hideously ugly wife, all the while longing to be back at Titania's Bower where he got what he really wanted by spending a bit of his prodigious money – a man who approved of propriety as long as it didn't interfere with the satisfying of his base desires.

The parlor was full of such men last night and that stupid girl ruined it all!

She shuddered at the memory.

"Gentlemen," she had announced, her voice full of naughty promise. Rising from the settee, she had sashayed toward the door. "I do believe we have some cake to complement your coffee!"

The fellows who were familiar with Dovey's dramatic flairs had turned to watch. When she had opened the door, they all saw Honora walk in – looking ridiculous.

None of them showed any interest in her at all. And why would they? That horrible hair — Celia's doing, apparently — and that fine blue dress pinned onto her as if it were a potato sack! Only Mr. Shiverly — half-blind and decrepit as he is — found her worth talking to, and then she left him after a mere moment! How much money can be wheedled out of bursting pockets if only a girl feigns a bit of interest? How dare she leave the parlor so soon?

Turning back from flirting with the man she called Mr. Highbrow, Dovey had seen Shiverly alone again, blowing his ever-leaking nose on the foul handkerchief that seemed forever stuck to his hand. Her eyes had darted around the room, quickly counting the number of gentlemen in the room and which girls were still there. Honora was gone and had taken no one with her.

Not that I expected her to charm a fellow out of the Mingling Room last night. The naïve look on the girl's face flashed into her mind.

Does she at all suspect what is to be required of her? The sooner she accepts the arrangement, the sooner she'll turn a profit.

Dovey stepped away from the window and paced the room. Her eye fell on a slice of leftover lemon cake that she had set aside for herself on her desk.

She can bake; she speaks like a lady. I had hoped to make the most of her maidenhood — some men pay a high price to be the very first! — but if she got away now, she might be able to wedge herself in somewhere as a lady's maid or a cook, a place where the people have never heard of Titania's Bower.

Something more must be done to secure her place here — something irreversible. And soon.

Dovey settled into her velvet chair, picked up the plate and began to slowly eat, savoring the tangy flavor as she plotted how to assure that Honora would not elude her grasp.

To pin a man down, I must convince him of my undeniable ability to please him. But to secure my hold over a girl, I must humble her.

Yes, shame is the key to controlling Honora.

***

Eager to set her plan into play, Dovey left her room with the dirty plate in her hand. Molly, who was lackadaisically drifting down the hall, did not look up at Dovey's approach.

This little slut is far too comfortable and pleased with herself.

"Here," Dovey said, pushing the dish into the girl's hands. "Take this and wash it."

Stifling a small sigh of protest, Molly took it and headed toward the kitchen.

Smiling as she walked behind her, Dovey wondered, *Will she dare to say anything when she sees I'm going to the kitchen myself?*

They pushed through the kitchen door together, but the bawd's mind no longer dwelt on the blonde, as Honora was there, standing at the table, stirring a large bowl.

Stopping just inside the doorway, Dovey waited silently. Sally looked up and nodded dumbly in her direction. When Honora saw the procuress, her glance wavered only slightly and she said pleasantly, "Good morning, Mrs. Dovey."

"Honora," Dovey dipped her head stiffly. She continued to watch as Honora resumed her task.

When finally convinced of Honora's discomfort at being closely observed, Dovey said, "I've had a piece of the cake you made yesterday."

She waved her hand toward Molly who stood at the basin, wiping a dripping cloth over the plate and fork.

"It was quite delightful. Today, I shall charge you with baking another for tonight's guests, of whatever sort you want. But tonight, *I* shall oversee the dressing of your hair and body." She paused, her eyes boring into the girl, informing her in no uncertain terms that her appearance the night before had been unacceptably shameful.

Sally and Molly had grown still in their tasks, certainly curious as to how Honora would handle this scolding.

In no small voice, Honora replied, "I should very much like your help, and thank you for it. As pretty as it was, I'm afraid that blue dress did not suit me though Celia did her best with the pins."

Caught off guard by the girl's unexpected candor, Dovey steadied herself and said, "Come to my room tonight just before supper, and I shall find you something more suitable."

Dovey turned on her heel to go, but Honora spoke again.

"Mrs. Dovey, I wanted to tell you, if I may…"

Rigidly, Dovey slowly turned back to face her. "Yes?"

"I don't like to tattle but, I think you ought to speak with Doris."

Dovey's brow furrowed. "And why is that?"

With the self-possession of a schoolmarm, Honora said, "Perhaps you did not see it, but she was behaving in a very…*familiar* manner with one of the men last night. I fear such behaviour might mar the good name of Titania's Bower around and about town."

Stunned, Dovey felt one of her eyebrows involuntarily lift and a smile tickle her lips. Unaware, Honora measured flour into her bowl, but Molly met Dovey's eye. The two exchanged a look of covert amusement.

"Hmm," Dovey finally replied, biting the inside of her cheek. "It's not often things escape my notice, so I thank you for alerting me."

Honora looked up and bobbed her head affirmingly.

Can she not see the mockery in my eyes? Dovey wondered. *She's stupider than I supposed!*

This realization delighted Dovey to no end.

"I shall speak with Doris directly," she said as she started out of the kitchen, biting back a chuckle and saying over her shoulder, "Bake the cake, and I shall see you in my room before supper."

Still smiling to herself, Dovey went upstairs to her bedroom.

That girl is as ignorant as a baby, yet brazen as the noon day sun! Does she dare educate me on the state of one of my girls?

Oh, how I shall delight in the consummation of her tainting!

It won't be difficult getting her into the room, but keeping her there? Yes, that's the problem. Perhaps I ought to let her wear whatever she wants. She won't need to look too alluring as I'll make it clear to Mr. Rottem what I want from him. He'd complete the task even if I dressed her in a tablecloth!

Yes, all will be well. She sighed, satisfied.

But now, for Celia…

Stepping over to one of the wardrobes, she pulled the doors wide. The inside was jammed full of so many garments that it was difficult to understand a particular item without removing it to lay it out on the bed.

Anyone who dared to ask Dovey whence she had acquired the vast collection and why she kept it all – especially peculiar since most of it could not fit her tall frame – she would have honestly replied, "This was my inheritance."

As the daughter of a theater's costumer, she was left with the trove that her father and mother had designed and stitched over several decades. Along with it, she was granted a sizable nest egg which likely would have been spent on drink and prostitution had her father managed to live much longer. Together, this cache of clothing and money constituted the means through which Dovey established herself. The money allowed her to let a building – in her dead father's name – and the clothing had inspired her as to how she might build her business.

Growing up, surrounded by beautiful actresses, Dovey had seen at an early age that one season, a woman might be regarded above all others, but within a twelve-month the same woman was suddenly snubbed whether due to scandal, political maneuvering or simply a loss of her beauty. Most women's popularity summited at the age of two-and-twenty. Plain women, like her mother, who had a skill and stayed out of the public's attention, managed to maintain their place in the theater world much longer. Their lives lacked the glamor and fame of the beauties', yet they suffered less in the long run.

Upon her father's death, Dovey knew she needed to invest whatever resources she had if she wanted to survive. Seeing the power that the female body – particularly nicely decorated ones – held over men, she decided to open a brothel. Dovey's many costumes would fit the desperate and ignorant young girls around her who seemed willing to trust her to tend to their needs. Thus, Titania's Bower was born.

The dresses were all basic patterns underneath their varied embellishments and with some removals or additions could easily be made over into something a young woman might don as day or night wear. Having acted as a seamstress under the tutelage of her parents since her fingers became dexterous enough to hold a needle, Dovey had worked late into the night, pulling apart and making over gowns for her girls. Now, years later, the Bower's success was well enough established that it did not hinge on such careful management of its wardrobe, but Dovey still accessed the cache of garments whenever it suited her intentions.

Having just that morning finished the required fixes on the gown she intended for Celia, she lifted it from its shelf. Admiring how the lavender-coloured silk shimmered in the afternoon sunlight, she congratulated herself. With a quick snap of the cloth, the gown unfurled and Dovey thought again that it was an elegant yet understated gown, suitable for Celia's complexion as well as her demeanor.

Yes, with that dark hair and somber face, she'll look as if she chose this for herself, Dovey affirmed, smoothing the wrinkles out of the skirt. *The bodice will gape a bit over her lacking bosom, but the rest will do quite nicely. With a parasol and gloves, she'll feel a right lady prancing around the park in this!*

Quickly selecting these accoutrements to complete the outfit, she went out of the door in search of Celia.

And she'll be out of my way tonight as I secure Honora's place here.

DONNING LAVENDER SILK

THE WET FRONT of Celia's work dress clung to her flat belly. She noted with relief that her skirts were not dripping onto the wooden floor as she walked toward her room. Once, Dovey had slapped her for leaving a trail of droplets in her wake.

All morning, she'd been laundering, and thinking.

If Dovey didn't want to turn Honora into one of us, why would she parade her through the Mingling Room last night? Even if she doesn't mean for Honora to be a whore, just living here with us might ruin her. This is her third day here. If she left now, she could find work somewhere else and carry on alright.

But then she'd be gone and I'd be alone here again.

Oh! What to do?

With her hand on the bedroom doorknob, she knew her first step was to count the money she'd saved. Entering the room, she was pleased to see that Molly was not there.

Have I enough now? she wondered, kneeling by the wall to peer under the chair rail.

The two gold coins she had retrieved from the inner pocket of Honora's coat winked at her suggestively.

Perhaps if I tell Honora what is at stake, she will be willing to pool our money and we can plot together on what to do. We must leave! But without enough money, things will end just as they did for me the last time. And that I couldn't bear.

Never since she had started storing her little contributions had Celia been able to pull them all out and count them together in her hand. She wouldn't dare. Even now, as she hurriedly attempted to tally up their number, she heard footsteps in the hall and bolted upright. Grabbing the comb from the ewer table, she posed to begin combing her hair should anyone enter.

This proved prudent as within seconds, Dovey herself had opened the door without a knock and stood, looming tall and triumphant in the doorway.

"Here you are!" she said as if finding Celia in her own bedroom was one of the more surprising and delightful things she could have imagined. "My dear Celia, I have something for you."

In she came and caringly spread out a gown on the larger bed. "Remember our little talk a few days past? Though you still have some plumping to do, I believe that this handsome dress may fit you well enough. I saw that you ate a large piece of cake the other evening, and I wanted to thank you for taking my word to heart. Therefore, I give you leave for the entire evening that you might wear this and pretend you are the finest lady in Hyde Park!"

In spite of her skin crawling at the bawd's saccharine speech, Celia smiled.

I needn't work tonight? Celia marveled. *What a boon!*

Dovey smiled benevolently, waiting for a response.

Celia's grin widened. And *I can walk about all afternoon looking for places for Honora and I to go!*

"You do like it don't you?" Dovey asked, reaching out to squeeze Celia's shoulder. "And I trust you will look quite fetching in it."

Resisting the urge to shake off the touch, Celia eyed the gown with the scrutiny of a possible employer. Soft, delicate lace ran the length of the neckline which was high enough to be considered proper. A dark purple sash encircled the waist to tie at the back.

In this, I might look quite respectable. People will listen to me and grant me answers to my questions.

"Thank you, Mrs. Dovey," Celia murmured.

"Shall I help you put it on?"

"No, I'll do well enough on my own, I thank you," Celia hurried to say. The thought of Dovey seeing one of the unclothed bodies she purported to own and use for the enrichment of herself infuriated Celia.

"Very well," Dovey said with a shrug as if she was humouring a petulant child. She made a show of placing a parasol and gloves alongside the dress. "Be sure to use these as I don't like any of my girls to be sunburnt."

Ignoring the edge of authority that had slipped into this last line, Celia stroked the gown's slippery material between her fingers until Dovey exited the room.

Once the door was shut, Celia began the struggle of dressing herself – the fastening of the dress proving more difficult than she had supposed. But she persisted and soon stood before her little mirror looking perhaps the smartest she ever had in her life. Smoothing her hair into a neat knot, she pinned it in place and gazed with pleasure upon her person.

With a rapidly thumping heart, Celia grabbed the matching parasol from the bed and headed out of the door, though she was uncertain as to where she was going.

I need a plan before I tell Honora everything, or she might feel as hopeless as do I.

CELIA SEARCHES

"DO YOU HAVE a letter of recommendation?" The woman standing in the doorway of the servants' entrance did not look into Celia's eyes. Instead, she was examining Celia's dress, a puzzled look on her weary face.

"Pardon me…I'm sorry, a what?" Celia stammered.

I ought to have brought Honora along. She would understand such things.

"A letter of recommendation from your present employer." The woman glanced up now, lifting her eyebrows. "It would tell my mistress how well you work. Or how poorly. Ask your employer for one. He'll know."

There was an indiscernible holler from somewhere behind her in the hidden mystery of the great house's depths. The woman glanced over her shoulder into the dimness and called, "One moment! I'm nearly done here!" Then she turned back to Celia to say matter-of-factly, "Once you have that letter, come back and we will consider you at that time."

The door was closing already though Celia had said nothing in response.

It was the fourth door that had been shut in her face since she had donned the purple dress and left the Bower. She ascended the short staircase to the street above and stood for a moment, feeling muddled and a little fearful.

A letter from my employer? Even if I was stupid enough to ask for one, what would Dovey write of me? 'Celia Woodlow is a paltry whore who never smiles, eats little and runs off when frighted.'

Celia stood on the hard walkway, grim and uneasy, asking herself, *Where to next?*

The first house she called on was one she always passed on her way to the park.

It is so very large! Surely, they have a lot of servants, she had thought. *But perhaps they're in need of a baker and a laundress. How lovely it would be to work in a home so close to Hyde Park,* she had thought, noting that the park's trees were likely visible from its windows on the third story. Such fancies seemed trivial and childish now as she noted the sun's ever-lowering position, a trace of horror prickling her spine.

All of the subsequent houses, she had chosen just as haphazardly as the first. Now depleted of her few ideas, Celia began to walk aimlessly.

How's it I had a whole afternoon to search all of London and have nothing *at the end of it?*

We've got to get out of the Bower. How long before Dovey plans Honora's tainting? I was there but two weeks before mine.

Celia's first fortnight under Dovey's employ had been a whirlwind of activity. Anxious to prove herself, Celia had asked for more and more tasks. This was why she began to serve in the dining room and clear dishes, in addition to washing the laundry. She'd been so proud, returning home each night to the small room that she and Bill had found to let. Scraps from the Bower's kitchen fed them. The siblings would sit on the ends of their beds and natter about their days, while nibbling the meaty bits off of stew bones and imagining butter on the heels of their bread. In the mornings, Celia would return to the Bower, determined to impress her employer further.

Dovey had been kind, encouraging. One night, she had pulled Celia aside to tell her how delighted she was with her, how glad she was to have taken a chance on hiring a girl who had never worked outside the home before. Someone else had noticed Celia, Dovey said – a regular patron, a young man whose good standing in society Dovey could vouch for.

She confided all of this in a maternal yet conspiratorial manner as if it was a delicious secret to be enjoyed by only Celia and herself. That night, Dovey introduced Celia to Hal and gave her leave to neglect some duties that she might sit awhile with him and chat.

He was just about Celia's height, and reasonably handsome, though his chin was a little weak.

Nothing a fine set of whiskers couldn't hide, Celia had told herself. *Yes, if I could return home to introduce Hal to Bill, I could feel right proud of that!*

Hal had seemed almost shy as he asked her to sit down with him, and he had listened with interest as she gave stumbling answers to his questions about herself. She feared she would prove to be the dull creature she thought herself, but his eyes had glowed with warmth when gazing upon her.

The next night, he returned and sought her out again, all under the watchful eye of Dovey. On the third evening of their acquaintance, Dovey helped Celia groom herself before dinner, joking slyly that perhaps Hal would return again. He did, and Dovey allowed Celia to abandon the clearing of dishes just so she could sit and have a drink with Hal in the backroom.

I drank with Hal in the backroom.

Hal.

The backroom.

The tinge of revulsion at this remembrance roiled her belly, and she shook her head in ineffectual attempts to cast the memory aside.

She was on the edge of the park now. A flock of sparrows flew overhead and the sun shone down from a brilliantly blue sky, but Celia felt cursed. Miserable, she leaned against a fence post and watched as a group of schoolgirls filed past upon the gravel path toward the Serpentine.

Though the students varied in size and age – some looked to be just Celia's age – they all wore the same dark blue muslin frock, overlaid with a crisp white apron. Upon their heads were identical bonnets secured there with narrow ribands tied in a bow just under the left ear. Small details like puffed sleeves and a frill of lace on the aprons distinguished them from being a group of maidservants out for an afternoon walk.

Celia had seen such groups of girls at other times, taking in the air and a bit of sunlight at the park, all lounging or frolicking together on the hills under the vigilant eyes of their dour chaperones.

What's it like to be a schoolgirl? Celia wondered longingly, not for the first time. *I'll never know, of course. A letter of recommendation might be needed to get into a school, as well as lots of money!*

She stood up and went down the gravel pathway, unwilling to gaze another moment on a bevy that would shun her if they only knew what she did. Walking for another hour on the city's streets, perhaps in circles, she stopped occasionally to stare at a building and think, but remained uninspired in spite of her desperation. Her throat ached with thirst as her worry urged her on. Drips of sweat ran down her back and between her breasts.

At a busy intersection, she paused, looking about her in all directions.

All afternoon and I've found nothing! Perhaps Honora would know what to do. If I tell her what the Bower is, she might believe me. I mayn't have to tell her everything.

But surely, I'll have to tell enough to draw her away from the kitchen where she's so happy to work…

Suddenly, her anxious mind was arrested as three girls in rough, almost colourless dresses walked toward her.

Many times before, she had seen a singular girl here, another there, dressed in this serviceably modest garb. Over their fronts was laid a coarse apron. Upon their heads they wore simple, close-fitting linen caps.

She had always wondered who these girls were.

Their clothing is not so fine that they likely think too highly of themselves. If they are from a school, perhaps Honora and I might gain a place there with the little bit of money we have and with the promise to do laundry or other tasks. Lord! Honora was trained as a governess. *Perhaps she could be a teacher there!*

Celia scanned the street to discern whence the girls came.

Another of them exited a large, brick building that had the words **LONDON LILY** painted in large, extravagant letters on its front. Tearing the linen cap from her head to shake her hair free, the girl skipped down the steps, a small burlap sack hanging empty in her other hand.

It's not a school. The truth suddenly occurred to Celia. *They* work *here and have just been let out for the day!*

One of these girls was drawing near and Celia knew she must say something or miss her chance should they all disappear. This was a slight girl with mousey hair peeking out in wisps from under her cap. Putting her usual reticence aside, Celia stood before her. When the girl dodged to go past, Celia darted to block her again.

A faint fear woke in the girl's eyes as she looked up at Celia who stood several inches taller than her.

"How'd you come to work there?" Celia asked, pointing at the brick building, wasting no time.

"Me cuzin took me to th'office to meet Mr. Tiller." The girl's eyes were wide, her voice solemn.

"Where's the office and what does Mr. Tiller look like?" Celia continued in a gentler tone.

"Y'alright, Polly?" asked another girl – the one who had removed her cap – as she sidled up to the two. A faint defiance and suspicion darkened her brow as she gazed steadily at Celia.

"I was just wondering how it is you came to work there," Celia explained.

"We've a right t'earn an honest livin'."

"There's no question of that," Celia responded, frustrated at the girl's defensiveness.

"Not all of us are fine ladies wit' money 'anded to us by our fadders and brudders." She looked Celia up and down, scorn twisting her mouth. "Some of us 'ave ta git our 'ands dirty to keep food in our bellies."

The gross irony of these words leeched out all of Celia's patience.

"Good lord!" she exclaimed, pushing past both girls. "I'll find the office myself, *thank you not at all.*"

The flow of girls exiting the building had been stemmed and only a few stragglers now came out of the door and down the steps, glancing curiously at Celia as she entered.

Once inside, Celia felt lost once again. It took a moment for her eyes to adjust to the dim entryway. A hallway stretched out on either side of her with many doors, most of them closed. It was a dusty, utilitarian place devoid of decorative touches and furnishings.

A man, whistled absentmindedly as he came out one of the doors and shut it behind him. He held a hat, looking as if he were about to put it on his head and go out into the street, but he stopped abruptly as he caught sight of Celia.

"Have you lost your way, ma'am?" he asked.

Celia's mouth felt drier than ever, but she licked her lips and spoke. "Can you tell me where Mr. Tiller is to be found?"

"Certainly." He tilted his head at her questioningly. "But mightn't *I* be able to help you?"

Taking a deep breath, Celia announced, "I would like to work here."

The man's mouth fell open, then twisted into a smile.

"*You?*" With a laugh, he gestured to her as if she didn't know where her body stood, then waved his hand at the building all around them.

"Work *here?*"

Standing to her full height, Celia nodded, her face burning. She felt ridiculous, like a fragile doll, standing there in the lovely dress, clutching a parasol.

The fellow continued to laugh as the door behind him opened and another man – a fellow with an outrageously large mustache – stood in the doorway.

"Someone to see me, Carlton?" the mustachioed man asked brusquely, eyeing the jovial fellow, then glancing at Celia.

"Yes, Mr. Tiller," Carlton replied, motioning toward Celia. "This lady here. Says she wants to *work* here!"

"In the future, Carlton, if someone asks to be directed to me, I expect you to comply promptly, and without including your implied opinions. Is that clear?"

Now somber, Carlton nodded. "Yes, sir."

"You may go now. I will see you on the morrow," Tiller continued, then turned to Celia. "I do apologize, miss. Please forgive my employee's uncouth behaviour."

"Sorry, miss," Carlton muttered as he stepped past Celia. She dipped her head though her cheeks still felt on fire.

"Please, come in," Tiller said in a warm voice as he pushed the door open fully. Though Celia could not see much of his mouth behind the whiskers, his eyes were smiling above them. As the door swung wide, it revealed a woman at a desk who had bounteous curly hair piled atop her head. She glanced up as Celia stood in the doorway.

"Please, come in and sit down, Miss…"

Celia hesitated.

Do you want out of the Bower? She asked herself. *Of course, I do!*

But her name stuck in her throat as she followed him into the room and sank gratefully, if for but a moment, into the proffered chair. The woman's curious glance at Celia had ended and she was soon engrossed again in examining a ledger on the desk.

"Here," Tiller said, putting a piece of paper and pencil before Celia. "Please write your name, age and the position for which you are applying. Oh, and next of kin. Would you care for some refreshment?"

"Some water would be very nice," she said, the thought of it suddenly making her thirst rage to new life.

"Of course," he said and walked over to a table where a pitcher and a tin cup were.

She took up the pencil and wrote – *Celia Woodlow, 17* – at the top of the paper in a clear, smooth hand.

'Position sought'? She clutched the pencil motionlessly. *What work do I hope to do here? What do those other girls do?*

Her mind scrambled forward.

And 'Next of kin'? I can't write Bill's name down here. Nan's gone. I don't even know Honora's surname. Reluctantly, she put the pencil down on the table just as Mr. Tiller returned to hand her a filled cup. Though she told herself to sip slowly, she drained the cup in seconds and silently longed for more, dabbing at her upper lip with her gloved hand. Mr. Tiller fetched the pitcher and refilled the cup without a word.

"Now, miss," he said staidly as he replenished her water for a third time, then sat down at his desk. "You say you want to work here."

At this, the woman's head shot up again. Celia refused to look at her.

"Yes," Celia affirmed, then drank the water.

"Do you know what it is that young ladies who work here do?"

It doesn't matter! Celia wanted to holler. *Anything would be better than what Dovey puts me up to.*

Feeling foolish that she had no response to this she shook her head and clutched at the cup, now empty again in her hand.

His demeanor shifted to one of quiet pride as he launched into a monologue that Celia supposed he had spoken many times.

"Within this large building," he lifted his hands to the walls around them, "is made the most exceptional soap in all of England – London Lily. Each cake is matchless in its cleansing capabilities – gentle enough to neaten the face of a newborn, yet powerful enough to tidy that of a coalminer."

He paused as if waiting for Celia to laugh. She only smiled faintly and he surged forward.

"The making of such a superior product requires the utmost precision. Some of our girls carefully measure the right quantities of the finest ingredients to be incorporated with the base. Other girls stand vigilantly and patiently stir each vat until it has achieved the proper consistency. Our cleverest girls are entrusted with the thermometers, that they might ensure the mixtures are at the precise temperature at every stage in order to achieve a successful batch of London Lily. Everything must be done correctly because the final product is transparent, you know!"

Here, he leaned slightly forward and winked.

"Oh," Celia murmured and nodded, though she had never held a bar of this soap in her hands.

"And, of course many hands are needed to sort and prepare the dried herbs and flowers that arrive in sacks at the backdoor. Others cut the paper and carefully wrap each cake once it is sufficiently cooled and hardened. I'm sure you have seen them – lavender striped ovals?"

Again Celia nodded, this time honestly as she had caught sight of them in the windows of shops where gentlewomen bought toiletries.

"Well, we are very proud of our girls, as most are diligent and do quite well." He said this solemnly. "However, it is *hard* work, and truly they are bone tired at the days' end."

He thinks me unable, or unwilling. Why'd I wear this dress? It ain't getting me the respect I thought it would.

"Mr. Tiller," Celia cleared her throat. "I'm sure I'm as strong as any of those girls I saw leave here just now. And I am not afraid of hard work."

Chewing his lip, Tiller looked thoughtful, but Celia wondered if she was being humoured.

He reached for the paper before her, then read aloud, "Celia Woodlow, 17 – ah, that's a fine hand you write."

Celia took a breath and nodded.

"And your kin are?"

"Dead. All of them."

Or they might as well be.

"Oh." His eyes lifted from the page. "For that, I am truly sorry."

His gentle, compassionate tone deepened Celia's guilt at having lied. The moment passed and he continued.

"And what sort of work are you presently doing?"

The question, though politely asked was like a slap across Celia's face. Her throat constricted and her pulse throbbed in her temples. Staring dumbly at the man, she saw his expression turn in a few seconds from one of good-humoured interest to one of understanding and then profound pity.

And the woman was looking up from her desk again.

Celia could not bear it. In one swift motion, she grabbed the parasol, bolted from the chair and was down the hall, hearing nothing behind her, seeing little in front of her. Out the front door she rushed, then down the steps to the pavement unaware of which direction she was going other than that it was away from the look in Mr. Tiller's eyes – away from the raised head of the woman who had probably always earned her living sitting at a desk, staring at virtuously white papers.

On she ran away from the brick building, and when she finally had to stop to gasp for air, she saw that in her hands she clutched not only her parasol, but also Mr. Tiller's tin cup.

SOMETHING IRREVERSIBLE, SHE HOPES

DAMMIT! DOVEY GLANCED at the clock on her mantlepiece.

Hours had passed since she gave Celia the gown. That part of the plan had gone off seamlessly as just moments later, she had watched the girl slip out the front door, dressed in her new finery. She knew Celia would stay out for hours.

But the other pawns Dovey had counted on had not yet materialized.

"Where is Rottem?" she asked aloud, as she stood at her window. *He always visits us on Tuesdays.*

She had watched from above as three men entered Titania's Bower in the preceding half hour, but Rottem had yet to darken its doorstep. Dovey was running out of time.

Perhaps I ought to wait another night – see if he comes tomorrow? No! It must be tonight.

Dovey knew that if she wanted to secure Honora's place at the Bower, she needed to do it promptly. Though Honora was shockingly ignorant, she wasn't stupid and once she realized where she was and what was expected of her, she would vanish – Dovey was sure of it.

The clever girls only feel bound to me once they are tainted. I can't let a pretty face like hers get away. Yes, it has to be tonight. But which man?

As she pondered this, one more fellow came down the street and stepped up to the door. Dovey noted that he glanced around furtively before putting his hand to the doorknob.

Hmm. Pilven might do.

He was a tall fellow, muscular build, but not so brutish looking as to arouse suspicion or fear in Honora at first sight.

This all must be done delicately, Dovey thought. *If he's too abrupt, she'll try to bolt. If he's not bold enough, the night will end unsuccessfully. Perhaps I'll need to give her a dram of my strongest drink. Well, if it's to be him, I'd better start now.*

With a final glance down the street which held no sign of Mr. Rottem, Dovey sighed resignedly and left her room to descend the stairs, her mind spinning to different angles she ought to take should the man balk at her offer.

He stood in the entryway, Molly having opened the door to him.

"Ah, Mr. Pilven!" Dovey said as welcomingly as she could, shooing the girl away.

"Yes?" The man bowed low, sweeping his arm out to the side histrionically. Inside now, he had transformed from his skittishness on the doorstep to a man of flirty condescension.

Clearly, he feels safe once he's on this side of the door, thinking no one on the outside world will find him out.

She took his hand in hers, noting how his eyes grew wide at her touch.

"I have something very special planned for you this evening."

Something between appreciation and confusion clouded his eyes as he looked down at their joined hands then strayed to Dovey's bosom.

Not with me*, you idiot!*

"A girl – a *new* girl!" She smiled knowingly, hoping he would catch the significance of the emphasized word. The use of the word 'virginal' might conjure up images of the two daughters Dovey knew him to have, and at this stage that was to be avoided at all costs. Titania's Bower was a place where gentlemen came to forget about the people who most relied upon them.

"Oh?" His face shifted into something Dovey could not discern.

Dammit. Where is Rottem? I'd know exactly what to expect from him. Well, just go on as if it's all been settled and he's the beneficiary.

"Yes, please go into the Mingling Room for some light refreshment. Afterwards, she will meet with you in a private room, and things can progress from there as you wish." Dovey tilted her head and smiled at him.

"A new girl? She is…that is, is she…?" His voice dropped off.

"Handsome? Oh, exceedingly!" Dovey was not pleased at the uncertain look on his face.

"No, not *handsome*," he interrupted. "I was going to ask if she is...*willing?*"

"What?" In spite of herself, Dovey recoiled and sharply replied, "Well of course she's *willing?* Where do you think you are, after all?"

This last bit was punctuated with a laugh which Dovey hoped would soften the words. Mr. Pilven's face informed her that it did not.

Don't you know what's being offered to you? Nearly any other man would jump at this chance?

Though she thought the words, something deeper in her knew they weren't true. Most men, knowing that a whore was unwilling, would shirk the tryst. In fact, the few that were aroused by a girl's reluctance and fear were the sort of men Dovey didn't want in her establishment – Rottem being an exception since he paid extremely well – as they were rough, rude and guided only by their own desires.

Seeing the unsure look on Pilven's face, Dovey knew she had lost her first chance with him but there was no turning back. Her second form of attack was dangerous, but she felt she must press on with it, so she clutched his arm and leaned toward him.

"I assure you, Mr. John Fordman of Maida Hill, that she is willing enough," she whispered in a firm but affable voice.

He stopped breathing at the sound of his real name and neighborhood.

"This evening, you will relish some intimate time with a very pretty girl – for that is why you came here, is it not? *And all will be well.*"

The man took a ragged breath as Dovey continued, "And tomorrow, should the chief cashier at Corrington and Boyce, ask you how you spent this evening, you can reply, 'Quietly at home, with my loving wife and two daughters' knowing that no one from Titania's Bower will gainsay you. That is, there will be no chance of contradiction, should you finish the task for which I have chosen you."

Here she paused, surveying his now ashen complexion.

Perhaps I've gone too far? But I needed to make my expectations clear.

Hoping to appeal to his ego, she let go of his arm, then smoothed the back of his jacket down past his rump, letting her hand rest there. Her voice flirty again, she purred, "I'm sure I chose the right man to *finish* the job. Didn't I?"

A bit of colour returning to his face, he swallowed, then nodded.

"Very good!" Slipping her arm through the crook of his elbow, she drew him steadily toward the Mingling Room. "And what will you have tonight? A slice of cake with your coffee, perhaps?"

So sure of her upper hand in the situation was she, that she hardly listened to his sputtering response. Her mind had moved on.

And now, to prepare Honora for what is next.

A BLUR OF FORMS

HONORA APPROACHED DOVEY'S bedroom door, mulling over their exchange in the kitchen that morning. She knew her comments on Doris's behaviour of the night before had likely seemed obtrusive – bordering on impertinence even.

Yet how could I stay silent? she reasoned. *If Dovey wants the Bower to be a place of finery, as Celia claims, then she ought to heed my advice. Having lived among the gentry all my life, I understand what polished society deems proper.*

In truth, Honora had enjoyed voicing her concern on the heels of Dovey's criticism of her appearance.

You didn't like the way I looked in the dress you chose for me? she had thought. *Well, I shall educate you in other matters…*

Dovey's response had been strange – her voice false and light as she said she would address Doris directly. Honora wasn't sure if she was being mocked.

Yet, I said my piece. Surely on further reflection, she will see it was right.

Emboldened by what felt like a victory, Honora was spurred to push the boundaries. As she now rapped upon Dovey's door, she readied herself to ask why she was required to wear anything other than her own perfectly respectable dress while serving cake.

The door opened and Dovey exclaimed, "So punctual, dearest! Delightful!"

Ushering Honora in, she waved her toward one of many wardrobes in the room. "Some of those frocks are certainly your size. Leaf through them and find your favorite. We'll see what we can do to make it fit properly."

A dress of my own choosing? Honora thought.

Pleased at the sight of so many options, she forgot to question Dovey.

She had always appreciated lovely garments, at times to her detriment. One day, when Lady Eliza was on a venture to London, fourteen-year-old Honora had crept into the room that held the late Lady Beeman's wardrobes. The outdated styles did not seem to stir Eliza's interest either for fashionable nor nostalgic purposes. So all forty seven of the gowns – Honora had tallied them up – seemed forgotten by all but Honora herself.

Eagerly, she pushed her arms elbow deep through yards of sarsenet, bombazine, and damask, thrilled by the varying textures, all mashed together, gleaming like jewels. Had she not taken so long admiring the kaleidoscope of colours and the fine details of lace and ribbons, she might have evaded capture.

But as she was about to strip to her shift, she had heard the familiar clearing of a throat behind her. She'd spun to see her father, his black-clad figure in the doorway. In an instant, he had crossed the space between them, creaking floorboards under the thick carpet, and laid hold of the bright blue evening gown in Honora's arms.

"This is not yours," he said somberly as he neatly returned it to the wardrobe.

"No one cares about them!" Honora insisted. "They've hung here for years, completely disregarded!"

His mouth hardened. "The wealthy often do not value what they have until you show interest in it. But then they will destroy you."

"Destroy me?" Honora had laughed quietly. "Father, you ought to blush at such exaggeration!"

"Do not make light of my warning, Honora," he had said, his face severe, and her laughter caught in her throat. "The destruction would not be physical, at least not directly. But they have power to thrust us out into the world with only our hats on our heads, bereft even of our reputations."

"Father! You have worked faithfully for Lord Beeman for nearly twenty years! Surely, he wouldn't…"

"*He* is not the only person of power in this household." He continued, sounding less angry but equally serious. "I will not always be here to protect and feed you, so you must learn the rules that the monied have set. This is possibly the most important of them: *You must never behave as if you have a right to something that is theirs.*"

With this, he lifted three more gowns from the chair where Honora had draped them and settled them back in their oblivion.

"You mustn't mention this to anyone, not even Polly, and don't ever let me find you pawing over what a jealous, wealthy girl might use against you. Now, go and study your mathematics so that you'll be a proper governess when the time comes."

Honora had stalked from the room flush-faced, muttering that she had damaged nothing. Within five minutes she was in the kitchen at Polly's elbow, separating egg whites from yolks for a meringue.

One minus a half equals another half, Honora had thought, still piqued. *There are your mathematics, Father.*

However, a week later when she had thought of all the ways Eliza had already undercut her, she had apologized to him. Never one for much demonstrative affection, he had patted her hand, stating, "I only want the best for you, my girl. I can't give much else, but advice I have in bushelfuls."

Now, as Honora stood before Dovey's three wardrobes, their doors open to reveal their many possibilities, she whispered in her mind, *As you see, Father, I'm getting my chance to wear finery after all.*

Of course, Mrs. Dovey wants me to look nice if I'm to serve her patrons. Maybe it is an especially fine group of people. Servants always wear what their employers want.

Lord! Where did she get all of these?

With a thrill of excitement, she stepped forward and began to touch the various garments stuffed inside. The third gown she examined was dark grey with clean, sharp lines and a starched collar, simple yet tasteful.

This could be a servant's gown, she thought, pulling it out.

"Oh no, dear!" Dovey exclaimed. "That is far too drab!"

A few moments more and Honora – now almost giddy – settled on a pink gown with frothy, cream-coloured lace at the neck and wrists. Once she had slipped it over her head, Dovey pulled it here, tucked it there, fastening it with straight pins, murmuring about how she had no time to take it in properly with needle and thread. It fit Honora quite well though it was lower in the front than she had anticipated. As she tried to tug the bodice into a more modest position, Dovey laughed and swatted her hands away.

"There's no shame in having a *bosom*, dear girl!" she laughed, then pushed Honora toward a chair before the looking-glass.

Polly mightn't agree with that, Honora thought as she saw the soft swells of her breasts above the neckline. Dovey began to comb her hair and twist it into a simple knot to pin at the nape of Honora's neck. Looking into the full-length mirror, Honora was quite pleased with her appearance.

Looking like this, I might turn that preacher's head right off his shoulders!

"Ah! You are pleased with your reflection!" Dovey said playfully, catching Honora's eye in the looking-glass. "I told you, you are quite lovely!"

In fact, Honora had never felt so pretty. At Stagsdown House, she had downplayed her attractive features at the urging of Polly who had told her on more than one occasion, "Lady 'Liza don't want to be outshone!"

Suddenly, the front doorbell sounded, visibly harrying Dovey. She hurried to the window and strained her neck, muttering under her breath, "Is that him, at last?"

Apparently dissatisfied with what she saw, she turned back to Honora and looked nearly surprised to see her sitting there.

"Still here, are you?" she asked, almost crossly. "Get down to the kitchen. They're arriving!"

Noting how quickly the amity in the room had evaporated, Honora hied herself to the kitchen where a large pile of dirty dishes and the cake awaited her.

Why, we're both in pink! She thought, delighted that her gown and the treat she'd carry appeared so congruous. It was a lovely creation, two tiers and delicately decorated, its icing blushing with the dash of beet juice she had added.

Wouldn't Polly be pleased, patting herself on the back for all she taught me?

A warm pride spread through her partially exposed bosom.

Yes, if I can work in this well-equipped kitchen, wear beautiful clothes at times and chat with Celia in the evening, I may be content here after all!

She knew better than to expect *happiness* as life at Stagsdown House had taught her that such an emotion was unlikely for someone born to her station, but *contentment* was something to be sought out and thankful for.

But then, Honora's contemplations were unsettled by the entrance of a stranger to the kitchen.

It was a girl, younger than herself with her thin dull hair pulled back severely in a tight knot. She came in through the back door, bobbed a hasty curtsey at Honora, then began to wash the dishes that were piled up next to the wash basin. She wore a grey dress, straight and plain, wrapped around with an apron. Honora felt almost regal by comparison.

"Good evening," Honora said, though she wanted to ask, 'Who are you and why are you here?'

The girl looked up shyly from the dishwater and nodded. "Evenin', Miss. I'll git these cleaned and shined up real quick like. Jes' you wait an' see."

Honora glanced at Sally, hoping for some explanation for the girl's presence and why she was doing one of Honora's chores. But Sally was picking through shreds of islinglass, and taking a long time choosing some of them to drop into the coffee pot[iii], Honora thought.

I suppose she needs the girl's help tonight as I'll be presenting the cake.

Suddenly Dovey appeared, once again boisterous and bright.

"Ah! Honora, how lovely!" She clapped her hands together looking at the cake from all angles. "Please, pick that up and follow me."

Dovey led her to the hall, then down another, through which Honora had never before ventured. They arrived at a door, smaller than the others they had passed. Opening it, Dovey stepped inside and beckoned Honora to follow.

There was a table, laid out with a white cloth and several sparkling plates and starched napkins folded into stiff triangles, along with several goblets and a decanter. This room had only one window, the bottom half of which was covered with a thick shade. Against the wall was a very large settee with numerous pillows, next to a small ewer table hung with a fresh hand towel. Three chairs were placed near it.

"Put the cake there," Dovey directed, waving at the table, then looked around the room with a sigh and a near-smile. "Oh! Before I go to lead them in…"

She moved toward the table and poured a purplish liquid from the decanter into one of the goblets.

"Try this," she said, surprising Honora by extending the drink to her. "It's new. I'm wondering if the guests will like it. Do you think it will complement the cake's flavor?"

Honora took the goblet and lifted it to her lips. The alcohol's miasma filled her nose, making her cough and she nearly declined the sample altogether.

"Don't be such a child!" Dovey laughed. "Taste it!"

Holding her breath, Honora tilted some of the drink into her mouth and swallowed hastily. It burned all the way down her throat to her stomach.

"Well?" Dovey asked with a treacly smile. "Do you think they'll like it?"

I don't know how anyone could like *that!* Honora thought, but the whiskey she had snuck from an abandoned glass at Stagsdown House had made her wonder the same thing. She simply nodded, murmuring, "They'll likely find it very nice."

She reached to put the goblet down, but Dovey said, harshly, "Oh no! That's costly and you're not to waste it, so finish it all. I didn't pour you much!"

Hoping that her acquiescence would hurry the woman out of the room, Honora forced down the remaining measure. Above the rim, she could see Dovey was smiling again.

"Good girl. See, I told you you'd like it!" The tall woman turned away and headed toward the door. "I'll return soon! Be ready to serve!"

As the door swung shut behind her, Honora's head suddenly felt as if it was tilting sideways. She was able to place the goblet back down, but her other hand grasped the side of the table as her legs slightly swayed beneath her. She had heard the expression, 'He doesn't hold his liquor well', and wondered if this was what was meant by it as the swaying grew more intense.

Dear god, that drink! Why didn't I refuse?

Gripping the chair rail on the wall, she led herself to the large settee and settled down upon it, fearful she might fall over if she remained standing.

Footsteps sounded in the hallway.

How can I serve cake if I can't stand upright? She wondered, her heart pounding rapidly.

The door opened, and Honora tried to rise, fearful that Dovey would chastise her for sitting, but the floor rocked under her feet. She fell back with a heavy thud then tipped over entirely on the cushioned surface.

Good lord! I'm drunk!

Dovey and a man entered, then stood, swimming on the far side of the room. Honora tried to focus her eyes but saw only the blurs of their forms.

Terrified and confused, Honora wanted to scream, 'Mrs. Dovey! Help me!' But no words exited her lips, only a moan that seemed to seep into the pillow upon which her open mouth rested.

Dovey turned to the man and said, "See? She won't even know."

The last thing Honora's eyes saw before heaviness overtook and closed them was Dovey reaching for the door handle.

Then, there were only sounds.

Dovey's voice said through the water that had filled the room – "Be sure you finish the job, Mr. Fordman" – followed by the door clacking shut and the man clearing his throat.

The weight of Honora's body seemed to fall deeper into the cushions.

Through her muddled mind floated a bit of a quiet conversation between a scullery maid and Polly that she had once overheard in the kitchen.

"They say the girl was ravished by Lord Ralley's footman," the maid had whispered, hugging herself tightly. At Honora's approach, Polly had turned, her ridged forehead a map of worry.

"Get thee gone, Honora," she'd said harshly.

Honora had left, annoyed at the unwarranted scolding, but curious as to what 'ravished' meant. Of course, she had never asked. Now the word hung in her mind as the clicking of Dovey's footsteps grew fainter down the hallway.

The man's grew louder as he came toward the settee.

Oh god — dear god!

And then a terrified Honora knew nothing but the smell of whiskey upon the man's breath and a hazy, urgent whispering that accompanied it.

THE POISONING OF INNARDS

I DON'T KNOW WHERE we'd have lived, anyway, Celia thought as she walked up the staircase toward her room. *If it had been a school, there'd be a bed and room for us. But if it was just a place to work . . .*

The sounds of the other girls, laughing and flirting with gentlemen downstairs drifted up to her. The pitying look in Mr. Tiller's eyes assaulted her memory once more and she shook her head to be rid of it. She had stayed out as long as she dared, walking off the nausea she felt at having accomplished nothing.

I must talk with Honora tonight, she determined, reluctantly. *Tell her the truth of it that we might plan together what to do. She'll be done in the kitchen soon, and I've the night off, so hopefully we can talk alone.*

She stepped quietly that her whereabouts would elude Dovey's ready notice. Now on the second floor, she tiptoed down the hall with a lit rush dip toward her bedroom door. Opening it, she went inside and heard a low moan from just feet away.

"Honora?" she whispered. "Molly?"

Another moan sounded and Celia turned, nearly dropping the light at what she saw.

Spread out on the larger bed was Honora, belly down, her arm and head hanging over the side as if she were about to slip off the edge.

"Honora? Honora!" Celia cried, setting the dip on the ewer table, then rushing to her.

Honora's mouth hung open, a strand of drool hanging from her lower lip. Her eyelids barely lifted, revealing unfocused pupils underneath before they snapped shut again.

"What is the matter?" Celia asked. "Are you ill?"

"I...I can't open...my eyes," Honora struggled to say, then began to weep.

She's been drugged. And Dovey got me out of the Bower because...because...

"It's alright," Celia stuttered as her own eyes welled up. "I'm...I'm here."

Climbing up onto the bed, Celia drew Honora's heavy head onto her chest, wiping Honora's tears and her own with the bed's counterpane.

"Dovey gave me...a drink," Honora murmured, her voice a little stronger and clearer now.

No, no, no, no!

"Shh..." With quaking hands, Celia stroked Honora's hair away from her face.

Celia's mind flitted back to Hal – the remembrance she was running from every time she rushed down the street, away from the Bower. But still, the memory was there, just beneath the surface until drawn forth in all of its sickening detail.

Dovey gave me *a drink that night.*

In the backroom.

With Hal.

Celia had felt so grown-up, flirting with this man whose doting gaze warmed her to her toes, holding a glass of what Dovey called sherry. Slowly, so slowly she had sipped at it, wanting the moment to last forever.

But a few minutes in, she felt the room begin to spin. Forcing herself to focus on Hal's eyes, so engaging as they spoke, she soon found she could no longer ignore the pitch and heave of the walls around her. She nearly excused herself from the room, but upon rising from her chair, she tipped over and Hal caught her in his arms. It seemed a chivalrous act and Celia tried to laugh, but then she saw that Dovey was gone and the door to the hallway was shut.

Suddenly, Hal had lowered her onto the settee and was pulling at her dress, his weak jaw set determinedly.

"No!" she had cried and slapped feebly at his hands as they found purchase past her clothing and upon her flesh. Staring through her tears up at the paneled ceiling, she had wondered how her admirer had been transformed into such a different creature. She looked to his glass upon the table and saw that it was nearly full.

116

He gazed no more upon her face, wholly distracted by what he was revealing with each tug of her bodice and skirt. When she screamed, his left hand clamped over her mouth as his right arm – so strong and quick – pinned her down upon the upholstered seat.

And then, he did something.

It hurt Celia with a pain, sharp and deep that she had never felt before, never imagined.

He's poisoning my innards! She had thought, utterly panicked. *He's killing me!*

It was over quickly, and he stood to adjust his clothing, leaving Celia laying there, raw and weeping. He took two quick steps to the table where he gulped down the amber liquid in his glass, then strode out of the door.

Celia had felt so absolutely changed that she wondered if she was dead already. But then she had heard the familiar sounds of the Bower just outside the door – a sharp bark of laughter, heavy footsteps down the hall. Several moments passed and she grew convinced of her lingering mortality. One thought kept ringing through her mind.

Dovey knew.

The very next evening, she had stuffed some day-old bread into a bag and run off into the dark.

As the first night set in, she fearfully curled up under a tree, smelling the scent of a roast mutton supper wafting through the air. After dozing off, she had been startled awake by a booted foot, nudging her cheek. Two members of the Night Watch had peered down at her, their faces lit by a handheld lantern.

"Move on, tarty," the one who had toed her said. The other had concern in his eyes, but said nothing as she had stood to wrap her shawl more tightly around her shoulders.

"Where can I go?" She had asked, sincerely thinking they would inform her of a place.

"Dunno," the first fellow had said. "Move on."

Over the next two days, she ate nothing and drank water from a rain gutter, watching smoke rise from chimneys and imagining the warming flames that produced it. She had thought of Bill incessantly. She never wanted to look into his eyes again, not after being poisoned by Hal.

On the third night, as she was leaning against a horse-tie, shivering and aching all over, a sot stumbled out of a public house nearby. He had staggered toward her, laughing, his arms outstretched.

"Ah, lookit what's waitin' 'ere fer me! Come 'ere, me li'l strumpet!" he had slurred.

Now knowing how a man could hurt a woman, Celia had run down the street and into an alley, nearly wetting herself with fear. As she hid behind a broken wooden box, praying for him to shuffle past, she knew, *It happens outside the Bower, as well.*

Yet, it was another worry that had extinguished her resolve entirely. As she sensed her weakened body mightn't ever leave the spot where she was hiding, she pictured Bill taking a short cut while carrying a message, just to happen upon her corpse there in the alley.

At this haunting image, she dug her nails into the gritty masonry and made the most difficult decision of her life.

Faint with hunger and fatigue, she stumbled back to the Bower before sunrise to knock on the door and rouse Dovey from her bed. With her eyes barely able to stay open, Celia promised the bawd that she'd never run away again. Dovey had made a great show of opening the door wide to allow her passage back into the Bower, declaring, "You'll do all the laundry you did before, as well as *all* the girls' monthly cloths just to keep my mercy fresh in your mind. But this is your only chance, so don't you dare ever run off again!"

Celia staggered inside and curled up on the dry soft carpet, thankful for the click of the door shutting and locking behind her.

"I won't," she had murmured before dropping off to sleep right there on the vestibule's floor.

But I should have! Celia thought now, holding Honora's head closer to her bosom. *How many times could I have warned her?*

"Honora, I'm sorry. So very, very sorry." The shaking of her body intensified and she began to sob. "I thought she might be p-planning it, b-but I thought we had m-more time. Had I known, I n-never would have..."

A breach in Celia's speech was filled with the far-off tinkling laughter of Doris in another room, another frame of mind.

"Celia, please..." Honora slowly lifted her arm to clumsily pat Celia's hand. "He didn't...ravish me."

"What?"

"He whispered...said he wouldn't hurt me...but said he had to make it...look as if he did. He called Dovey back...told her he'd done it...she told him to carry me up here."

Relief flooded Celia's body so that she felt it in her toes.

But wait…

"Honora, did Dovey lift your skirts and…look at you?"

"No, she was called away…just after he lay me here. Why?"

After Hal had left her on the settee, Dovey had stolen in to flip Celia's dress up. Pulling through the layers, she finally muttered to herself, "Ah, there's the proof. Good girl, Celia."

It was later, when Celia was cleaning herself that she had seen the blood on her skirt and undergarments.

Celia wiggled out from underneath the surprising weight of Honora's head and shoulders, saying, "She'll be here soon to look you over and make sure he's truly done it."

She stood and moved around the room, frantically opening every drawer, feeling under both beds.

"What are you doing?" Honora asked.

"Looking for something sharp."

"Oh no, Celia!" Honora tried to push herself up on the bed. "She's strong. You'll be hurt!"

"No, no! Nothing sharp to *harm* her! To *fool* her!"

Celia stood for a desperate moment thinking, then fell on the answer. Leaping onto the bed, she pulled the whole stack of clothes down to find Honora's linen apron. The wick trimmer was a hard lump in the pocket. Fishing it out, Celia held it in her hand and said, "I must take off your petticoat."

With a confused look and a faint nod, Honora struggled to help Celia with the removal of her underskirts. Flipping the petticoat inside out, Celia chose a spot and held it inches from her face.

This may work, but it will hurt.

That's what I deserve for not warning her. I owe this to Honora.

With the wick trimmer's stubby metal blades in her mouth, she braced herself and clipped the soft inside of her cheek. It stung exquisitely, but she snipped again until she tasted and felt blood in her mouth.

"What are you doing?" Honora's eyes were round in the candlelight.

Celia let blood and saliva pool in her mouth, then spat liberally onto the petticoat.

"She'll be looking for blood," she said, eyeing the splotch, the dark of it visible even in the dim room. Then she arranged the petticoat on the floor, careful to expose the bloody mark.

"When Dovey comes, she'll see that, and think he had his way with you. Now, let me help you out of your dress as if I'd washed you as she may look elsewhere."

With much difficulty, the two girls removed Honora's gown. Pouring water from the pitcher into the bowl, Celia wettened a rag and laid it over the side of the bowl. With her cheek still bleeding, she spat into the bowl and left it on the ewer stand. Just as she did so, the girls heard footsteps in the hallway.

Celia jumped onto the bed beside her friend, shoving the wick trimmer under her pillow.

"Cry!" she whispered. "She *must* believe it happened."

Putting her arms once again around Honora's now shaking shoulders, she began to croon as the door opened.

Molly entered, carrying a lit rush dip of her own and stared at the two girls on the bed.

Celia, her arms awkwardly wrapped around the crying mess of Honora, marveled at her friend's theatrics. Honora's quivering body lay strewn out on the bed beside her, her open mouth an ugly, rigid abyss, her leaking eyes squeezed shut.

"Hush now," Celia murmured. "Hush."

"What's got 'er goin'?" Molly asked.

Continuing to pat Honora's back, Celia whispered, "Mr. Pilven".

"Pilven?" Molly asked. "Well, 'e's not so bad. What's she cryin' for?"

"She didn't know what to expect."

This brought fresh wails from Honora.

"By the way she's 'ollerin', I thought surely Rottem got ahold of 'er." Molly's eyes fell upon the petticoat upon the floor, its smear offensive and telling.

"Hmph. I see the fine lady *is* one of us now."

Though Celia secretly rejoiced at Molly's words, she threw her a fierce look and waved her away.

Crossly, Molly stood, stuck her tongue out and headed toward the door.

"I'm only speakin' truth! What was she 'spectin'? It's only what we all do 'ere every day! And by the by, I'm done for the night and want to go to sleep, so when I come back from the ne'ssary room, I want 'er to be done wailin' and *you* to be gone from *my* bed, Celia."

"You can sleep in the little bed, Molly," Celia said, the inside of her cheek stinging with every word. "It's yours from now on."

Apparently surprised at this sudden munificence, Molly fell silent before exiting.

Honora ceased in her feigned sobbing as Molly's footsteps receded down the hallway.

"Good lord, that was some fine acting!" Celia whispered. "She's probably pleased to run off and tell Dovey about your bloodied petticoat."

"What would happen if Dovey *didn't* believe?" Honora asked.

"She'd likely shut you in a room with Rottem." Celia tasted blood on her tongue. "And there'd be no escaping him."

Honora took a deep breath before asking, "She makes you do that all the time, doesn't she? With men."

Celia's breath caught and the girls' eyes found each other. She barely nodded her head as she dropped her gaze again.

"Celia, we can't stay here."

"But where can we go? I was out all the afternoon, looking for a place. I found nothing. *Nothing.*"

"We'll think together on it," Honora whispered.

Hope stirred in Celia's heart.

"We'll have a few days," she said. "If Dovey believes you were tainted then she'll leave you alone for a while. Let you heal."

She helped to arrange the bedcovers over Honora before climbing into the bed herself. The sound of footsteps alerted them both.

They said not another word as Molly reentered the room, but Honora's hand reached over to Celia's, finding it under the blankets. Celia felt the heartening clutch of her friend's grasp until she finally fell asleep.

A FINE MORNING

"A LETTER, MR. BARCLAY," Martha said as she entered the breakfast room, extending to him a thin cream-coloured envelope. The other Durbins had all left just moments earlier, their dirty plates on the table a testament to their early morning appetites. Brushing the last crumbs of toast from his fingertips, Barclay took what Martha offered. Seeing the cramped, tight scrawl across the front of it, he knew at once from whom the letter came. His heart sank.

"Ugh," he said, settling deeper into his chair. "It appears Uncle Allard has decided to address me directly."

"On what matter?" Martha asked in the frank manner she used when the two of them were alone together.

Barclay laughed. "He seems determined to make me his curate."

Martha did not chuckle as he did, but stopped stacking the crockery to gaze pointedly at him and say, "I believe the Lord may be bringing this about."

All trace of Barclay's amusement vanished.

"But Martha, if I was to become a curate, I could no longer call-out in town, and you yourself suggested the practice in the first place."

"Yes well, perhaps that has been a good proving ground for you, but who else amongst God's Faithful might be given such a chance as this? Just as Isaiah said, 'Send me,' you can offer yourself and see what the Lord will do."

Suddenly, Barclay felt very alone. At times, Martha had been his one ally at Singer Hall in spiritual matters. Once, she had confided in him that she regarded herself as an instrument situated in his household, placed there by God's hand to bring about great good for His kingdom. This belief coloured most of the conversations she had with him. Though he had heartily agreed previously, he now found himself approving of her self-assured statements less often, sometimes balking at them outright. Withdrawing, he began to shutter his heart from her more and more as he aged. He suspected Martha mourned the loss of what they had shared in his younger years. He did as well, to a degree.

It seemed to him she had slowed in her clearing of the table.

Hoping I'll open the letter and share it with her, most likely, he thought.

"Well, I shall keep that all to mind," he said, standing and folding the envelope in half to tuck it into his pocket. "Thank you, Martha."

As he left the breakfast room, she murmured a reply and continued her tidying. Moments later, in the privacy of his bedroom, he tore through the paper to read:

My dear nephew —

I will speak plainly. It has been several months since you came down from University, and because of our previous conversations, I thought that by now you would be installed here as curate to aid me in the shepherding of Southby. I know your heart is for the Lord and the work He has for you. Believe me, there is plenty of it here and I find I must engage someone, if not you, to help me as I am not the hale, hearty fellow I once was.

Have your intentions altered? Please inform me presently as I'm beginning to feel like a spurned maiden whose flirtations have grown cloying to her lover. Regardless of the answer, I shall remain your fond, though aging —
Uncle Allard

In spite of the missive's troubling content, Barclay smiled at the analogy, envisioning the coarse, elderly face of his uncle coyly peering out from under a frilled bonnet, his eyelids fluttering coquettishly beneath his wildly hairy brow.

"Oh uncle," he sighed. "I would not break your heart in this, or any other matter, and yet…"

The memory of the many languorous bodies filling the pews at Southby's church accosted him, their faces dull with lack of inspiration.

I sense no life in the future he offers. How does one word such an answer? Particularly to a revered and favorite uncle?

Frustrated, Barclay laid the letter on his desk and headed out to the yard. He and Jasper had planned on going into town just after breakfast to call-out, and Barclay wanted to arrive in the stable before his brother.

Successful in this, it was moments later that he saw Jasper enter the yard. The boy's face lit up with a grin at the sight of Caleb hitched to the gig instead of the cart.

"I'm pleased to see you've come to your senses at last," Jasper said, climbing up to settle himself beside Barclay on the seat.

"My reasoning is, the gig will get us there faster, giving us more time to call-out," Barclay responded as he hawed the horse to start the journey. "We can stable it at a distance and walk to Crawton Green so as not to pose a distraction with such a fine vehicle."

Jasper said, "Perhaps you'll warm to the idea of taking the phaeton next week. I'm sure Clayton would allow it."

Barclay laughed. "Do not crow too loudly in your victory or I may reconsider. I don't want material objects to set us apart from those we try to reach."

"Yet *Providence* has set us so far apart from them already, in every way. You don't suppose that the moment they see our neat, clean clothes and hear our learned speech that they think of us as such different creatures from them?"

"Yes, yes, but things as grand as carriages only widen the rift."

"I suppose there is sense in what you are saying," Jasper conceded.

"At last! You admit I may be right about something!"

They exited the grounds of Singer Hall chuckling together, then merged onto the larger road.

"However, I *do* wonder at your use of the gig over the cart as never before. Could it be because we might be seen by a certain girl with a basket?"

Barclay tried not to squirm in the seat as he said, "Don't you recall, but a moment ago I said we would stable the gig *away* from Crawton Green which is the only place we've seen her thus far?"

"You needn't be ashamed of your desire to impress a young lady, Barclay."

"Brother, you know I go to London to minister."

"And yet, while you minister, there are women nearby who can be wooed. I give you leave to do both," Jasper said drily. "And I suppose the Lord Himself does as well."

How likely is it I will even see the girl with the basket again? Barclay considered.

"Two short conversations, do not a courtship make," he said aloud, tiring of his brother's sagacious penetration. "And you, why do *you* go with me so often to call-out? You rarely say a word to anyone whilst there. Are *you* looking for someone to woo?"

"You'd marry me off at fourteen, would you?" Jasper laughed out loud. "I go because when I'm home from school, I like the busyness of London. And it's dull as a graveyard at home when *you're* not there."

Barclay's chest warmed at the thought of his younger brother so valuing his companionship.

"And I want to do good for others, I suppose," Jasper added, pleasing Barclay further.

"Very good. With God's guidance, let's go and do good today."

"And meet with pretty young ladies," Jasper murmured under his breath.

"May God's will be done in that matter and all others," Barclay responded, smiling at his smirking brother.

AN INCREDIBLE BOON

AT CELIA'S URGING, Honora had not stirred from their bedroom on the morning after her presumed tainting.

"Dovey wouldn't think you'd be up and about today," Celia had insisted. "If you seem well enough, she'll think Pilven didn't do it to you."

Seeing the sense in this, Honora remained in the bedroom all the next day, accepting plates of food that Celia brought to her and emerging only to use the necessary room twice. But by the following morning, she couldn't bear the thought of staring at the same four walls for another day even as Celia encouraged her to do so, so she ventured out.

"Ah, 'ere y'are," Sally said when Honora appeared in the kitchen, but spoke not at all of Honora's absence on the previous day. Normally nervous, Sally seemed especially uneasy as Honora stepped past her toward the sink to begin washing the breakfast dishes. Any budding appreciation Honora had had for the cook soured into disgust.

This horrible woman knew exactly *what Dovey had planned for me all along and gave me not a word of warning!*

Honora readily excused Celia's reticence on the matter, but Sally was much older, supposedly wiser, and *she* offered no explanation as to why she had said nothing.

Evil could not make such headway in this world if the informed but spoke of it.

Yet, Honora's primary goal was to get Celia and herself out of the Bower and she knew that starting wars with other members of the household might interfere with that. Thus she stayed silent.

"Oh! Miss Honora," a chuckle escaped from Sally's throat. "I jes' recalled. A fella's brought you somethin'."

She inclined her head toward a wrapped parcel on the table. "Early this morning, 'e was rappin' on the window there, wavin' that 'round, smilin' like Father Christmas three months early." She chuckled again.

Though she didn't want to share in any joke with Sally, Honora's curiosity was piqued and she laid aside the dirty plate in her hand.

"Who was it?"

"An old fella. White 'air, 'ad most of 'is teeth. Dressed fine like a gent-man."

Gazing at the paper-wrapped package, Honora detected a faint scent of cinnamon and nutmeg. Across the top was written:

For Miss Honora:

You may hide this in September, and feast upon it come December.

Absolutely no peeking before then, though surprises await you!

Mr. S

Mr. Shiverly's brought me a fruit cake!

The absurdity of the gift was a welcome bit of levity in an otherwise horrific few days and Honora found herself smiling. Intending to show it to Celia at her first opportunity, she picked it up and was surprised at how heavy it was.

How thick is this plate? How dense the cake?

She carefully removed the paper, mindful of the heartbreak such a premature action would be to the man who had delivered it. Within, she found a dark, thick loaf. Its surface was studded with nuts and sultanas that must have cost a fortune, but the cake itself looked soggy and stodgy, and reeked of rum. The white plate it had been set upon was lovely – the porcelain rippled with swirls and flowers – decorative and refined.

From the other table where she stood kneading bread dough, Sally whispered, "That's a fine bit of china. Don't let Mrs. Dovey catch sight of it or she'll whisk it away for 'erself."

Honora bristled at the warning. *Is that the sort of thing you alert young women to? To keep their* plates *safe?*

Biting back her response, she focused on the cake again.

Shiverly didn't skimp on any portion of this gift, she thought, sparing a moment of near-appreciation for the elderly man. She imagined him younger, staying up all night with Gladys – the admired housekeeper of years past – mixing fruit into the thick batter together.

The thought turned acrid though as Honora pictured his doughy hands enveloping Gladys's in the bowl and what she may have been expected to submit to next.

This perception transformed the cake from an amusingly distasteful oddity to a sickly vile brick. Honora wanted every bit of it gone from the kitchen, even the scent of it. Lifting the plate, she carried it over to the food slops bucket.

"Yer goin' to chuck it out, ay?" Sally asked, a smile lightening her plain, haggard face. "I don't blame ya. Can't imagine eatin' anythin' that old fella put together! Blech!"

Ignoring Sally's attempts at solidarity, Honora tilted the plate over the bucket, watching the mass tumble onto a pile of potato peelings and onion tops.

The surprising glint of something in the cake's underside caught her eye. She reached after the loaf and dug her fingers into it to grab ahold of the object. A cry caught in her throat.

It was a gold coin.

Another flash elsewhere in the claggy mass arrested her gaze.

Sally was still kneading the bread a few feet away, so Honora reached, with what she hoped was unremarkable movement, into the bucket again with one hand and broke up the chunks of moist cake. In scattering the pieces over the rest of the swill, she was astounded to uncover nine more coins, all of equal size. They lay on top of the garbage, bits of cake sticking to them, like unwashed newborn infants.

With her heart pounding wildly within her chest, Honora muttered, "Ugh. This bucket reeks – stinking up the kitchen. I'll dump it out now."

She knew she was overexplaining herself and probably raising Sally's curiosity with every word, but couldn't keep her mouth from forming a single one of them. Still talking, she took the bucket toward the backdoor. "Give the place a chance to air out."

Once outside in the garden, she resisted the urge to glance around at any windows overlooking where she stood. She plucked each of the coins out of the muck, and gripped the gluey hoard in her fist.

With this, Celia and I might escape. Set ourselves up together.

The exultant realization was so completely true that it took her breath away. As a girl growing up surrounded by wealth, she had learned to temper her thoughts with the truth that none of it was intended for her. But with these ten coins in her hand, there was no need for a counter balance. There was only the question of when she and Celia would sneak away.

After slipping the coins into her apron pocket, she dumped the bucket into the midden. She retied her apron, lacing the long ties over the pocket to keep the coins still and silent. Still, she worried the moisture on them might soak through – a tell-tale mark of her incredible boon.

Soon, she was back inside the kitchen, willing a grin off her face and swishing a wet rag over the decorative plate. Feet away, Sally hummed a tuneless song as she continued to knead her bread dough.

Dovey shall have this plate with my blessing, Honora thought, drying it with care.

Unwilling to keep such news to herself any longer, Honora dried her hands and opened the laundry room door. Not finding Celia there, she went down the hall and up the staircase, two steps at a time. Going through their bedroom door, Honora was pleased to find Celia there, then disappointed to see Molly also, still under the covers of the single bed. The blonde appeared to be barely awake, but Honora would risk nothing.

Celia looked up from where she sat on the larger bed, darning a sock.

Repressing the smile she felt tugging at the corners of her mouth, Honora went to her drawer, desperate to exhibit some unremarkable behaviour before Molly. She retrieved a hairpin, then stood before the mirror and slowly pushed it into place in her hair. Catching Celia's eye, Honora gave her a meaningful look, full of all the lidded joy and excitement she felt.

We've done it! She tried to say. *We can be gone by tomorrow!*

Celia's brow creased inquiringly, but Honora faintly shook her head and suddenly wondered if the other girls could smell the spice-rich crumbs clinging to the money in her pocket. She slipped out of the room, hoping her friend would soon follow and paused at the door after clicking it shut behind her.

"What's between you two?" she heard Molly ask. "You want to share a bed and now she's throwin' you looks of longin'? You know that ain't natural, don't you?"

"Shut up, Molly," Celia snapped. "I'm sorry you know nothing of friendship."

I gave too much away. Honora worried. *We can't have Molly suspicious and watching us every moment.*

Down the hall she went, then the stairs, chiding herself. As her feet contacted the first floor, her heart skipped a beat.

Dovey stood before her, blocking her way.

"Ah, Honora!" said the bawd, staring down from her imposing height, with something a naïf might mistake as pity in her eyes. "I've wanted to speak with you and here we are alone together at last."

Feeling the immense weight of the coins in her apron pocket, Honora stuttered, "I…I have to get back to the kitchen. There's much to do there."

"Oh, who can think of cookery at a time like this?" She leaned toward Honora and whispered, "Listen, Molly told me what happened two nights past – that nasty business with Mr. Pilven."

Honora stood stock still, unbreathing.

Dovey reached out to take Honora's empty hand in her own. "It is such a shame how that turned out, your first time entertaining one of our gentlemen – well, someone I *supposed* was a gentleman! Believe me, dear girl, if I had known what sort of man he was, I would never have left you alone with him."

Dovey's voice, urging, *'See? She won't even know'* echoed through Honora's mind and the madam's touch became unbearable. Snatching her hand away, Honora knew the danger of glowering in shock and resentment at the woman, but she could not tame her features.

Clearly sensing the change and seeming to enjoy it, Dovey leaned in further to smile and whisper, "I promise you, the next time will be different."

The next time?

In unthinking rage, Honora swung at the leering face before her, the heel of her hand smashing into Dovey's mouth.

Stunned, Dovey reached up to her face and pulled her hand, now traced with blood, away. Her eyes were huge with disbelief and something else — something Honora would not stay to understand.

Instinct took over, and Honora fled out the front door, leaping down the stairs to the street below. She sprinted up the road — past startled pedestrians and amused drivers of carts — with nary a glance backward.

Just after bolting around the corner, her foot plunged into the very same pothole that Celia had saved her from but three days prior. Her ankle was wrenched terrifically and she fell to the ground clutching it as a sort of shock set in. Once the worst pangs had passed, she rose, as if in a dream — a painful, dizzying one — and began to lurch along, aware only that she needed to get further from the Bower.

BEFORE THE LOOKING-GLASS

DOVEY'S HAND SHOOK as she stood before the mirror, dabbing at her mouth with a handkerchief. More sickening than the bright red of fresh blood seeping from her gumline was the way her two top front teeth moved, like a child's loosened milk teeth.

Pulling her hand away, she grimaced into the looking-glass, turning her face this way and that.

God, no! I can't lose my teeth!

She was already dismayed at the pillowy bags now hanging under her eyes and the lines around her mouth which had started out fine and faint, but grew more numerous and deeper with every passing year.

That girl! That damned slut!

Usually, the hatred Dovey's girls felt toward her was displayed more subtly – sullen looks and words muttered under their breath – but she had experienced explosive rage on occasion. Years earlier, Dovey had informed a thick blonde called Harriet that she would have to henceforth satisfy herself solely with vegetables and chicken. At breakfast the following morning, Dovey had snatched a slice of bacon off the disobedient girl's plate. Harriet had reached up and scratched the madam's face. Prior to that, Dovey's shin had been kicked after she told a short girl called Clara to carry out a very full chamber pot. But nothing could compare to what had just occurred. Dovey was shocked that a sophisticate such as Honora – certainly the most refined girl she'd ever housed – could swing at her like that.

I'll punish her for this – put her in a room with Rottem every night for the next two weeks, without a drop of drink to dull any of it. And if my teeth do *fall out,*

133

I just might kill *her!*

But, she pondered, breathing slowly to calm herself, *when she first returns — they always do when they realize they have nowhere else to go! — I will pretend as if nothing happened as I can't let her — or any of the other girls — see that she's upset me so.*

And now, I must have my teeth looked at.

Taking a deep breath, she tossed the bloody handkerchief aside, smoothed her skirts and headed toward the hallway in search of someone who had no idea what had happened that morning.

She found her objective in the shape of Molly stumbling down the main staircase in her night clothes, sleepiness still dulling her face.

"Molly, dress yourself and go to Dr. Briggs," Dovey began imperiously. The words sounded strange in her ears. "Bring him back here as I've tripped and had a fall, and must be looked at."

Her mouth ached as she spewed the lie.

"Can't I go after breakfast? I'm 'ungry," Molly whined.

Dovey's tenuous hold on her temper broke and she lunged toward the girl.

"I am *injured*, you ungrateful little *bitch*! Go now or I will tear your hair out!"

Jumping back, Molly turned and hurried upstairs, leaving the bawd holding onto the stair rail, her chest heaving.

A WONDROUS OCCURRENCE

BARCLAY PLODDED ALONG, the sharp clip clop of the horses' hooves sounding on the cobblestones.

O Lord, today will I finally draw someone to You?

As they neared the stable where they would leave their gig, he looked hopefully but doubtfully at the masses milling alongside the street.

Alert beside him, Jasper suddenly pointed. "What's happening there?"

The river of pedestrians parted, making their way around someone. The object of their avoidance bobbed along, staggering and slow, yet steady. It took Barclay but a moment to recognize it as the girl with the basket.

He yanked the gig to a stop, nearly triggering a collision on the roadway, ignoring the angry cries of the drivers behind him. Jasper was off the seat immediately and beside the girl as Barclay jumped down himself. The horse pranced uneasily in place behind them.

Barclay touched the girl's elbow and she turned, flinching, but when her red-rimmed eyes fell on him, her strained face filled with hope. At such an expression upon seeing him, Barclay felt a surge of strength through his limbs. He stepped closer, his arms ready to steady her if she would allow it.

"You're hurt," he said, extending his hand.

Looking dazed, she placed her hand in his. At this, Barclay and Jasper moved to either side of her and helped her hobble toward the gig. Surmising it was the only way to get her out of the press of people,

Barclay asked, "May I lift you up?"

With a slight nod, she turned to face him, placing her hands on his shoulders.

"Oh…oh, no." Barclay stuttered and motioned with his hand. "You must turn. Put one hand on the dash here, and the other on the rail. And Jasper, hold Caleb. I don't want him startling."

The boy complied quickly.

Barclay blushed ferociously as he placed his hands on her waist. Never having lifted a girl before, he hoped he was up to the task. His face grew hotter as his palms pressed into the swell of her hips.

Trying to steady his voice, he said – "One, two, three!" – and lifted with all his strength. The girl was up and tumbled onto the space between the seat and the footrest, her bottom jutting into Barclay's face. The fire he felt spread from his cheeks down to his belly.

"Can you…can you climb into the seat from there?" he stammered, stepping back.

In but a moment, she had settled herself and the brothers were soon on either side of her, all three of them squeezed together to fill the gig seat to capacity.

"Where ought I to take you?" Barclay asked, very aware of her warm hip against his thigh.

Staring straight ahead, the girl replied, "Away."

I meant, to which place, Barclay thought, but urged the horse forward, merging back into the vehicular traffic. *I know no doctors in London. Perhaps Harding could look at her ankle. We could be to him within an hour. Once he has examined her, I could return her to her family in the phaeton which would be quicker than the gig.*

"May I take you to see my family's physician?"

The girl nodded faintly, murmuring, "Yes, away from here."

It seemed a strange answer, but as he found himself immersed in a wondrous occurrence altogether, Barclay slapped at the horse's hindquarters and they turned onto the busy thoroughfare.

"I must tell you that you won't be alarmed as we go, Singer Hall – our home – is a full hour's ride out from town. Is that alright?"

"Yes." She winced as the gig jolted over a rough spot in the road.

"Jasper, roll up that coat that she might wedge it under her leg. Elevate and keep the ankle swinging that it won't be jarred with every bump."

Jasper helped the girl as Barclay said, "I fear I never asked your

136

name. You may recall, I am Barclay Durbin. This is my youngest brother, Jasper. And *you* are…?"

"Honora," she said. "Honora Goodwin."

Jasper asked, "How did you hurt yourself, Miss Honora?"

"Oh, I…I stepped in a pothole."

"Have you lost your basket?" Barclay asked, realizing the item might be of great importance to her.

"I'm sorry?" She looked at him for the first time since getting into the gig, her eyes enormous.

"The basket you're always carrying – you haven't got it now," he explained. "Ought we go back and look for it?"

He readied himself to turn the gig around.

"Oh, no!" She reached toward his hands which held the reins. "Drive on."

The threesome fell to silence and Barclay began to regret his brash resolution to remove the girl from London though Jasper had not contested the plan.

Good heavens! Why does he trust me so implicitly? And certainly, Miss Honora was in no position to consent to leave town with two strangers, he thought, stealing a quick glance at her ashen face. He half-expected that upon his next return to Crawton Green there would be an armed rabble, ready to assault the young preacher who had reportedly kidnapped a young woman.

But as the gig emerged into true countryside, Honora remained still and quiet beside him, as if stupefied.

In for a penny, in for a pound, Barclay told himself, urging Caleb onward that they would arrive at Dr. Harding's as soon as possible.

AN URGENT NEED OF ICE

DR. BRIGGS wiggled Dovey's affected teeth with far more vigour than what she thought necessary.

"I didn't call you here to pull them!" she insisted, recoiling from his invasive finger and thumb.

"Of that, I am aware, Mrs. Dovey," he said, grabbing her chin and reaching back into her mouth. "But if I am to determine the extent of the damage, then I must have access to the teeth in question. You fell down the stairs, you say?"

There was more than a hint of disbelief in his tone. Dovey was accustomed to being spoken to this way by people considered *respectable* by one another.

You always find a smile when your ready palm is extended to me for payment, you greedy bastard, she thought, but said instead, "Yes, and hit my face upon the bannister."

"I see. Well, the roots have sustained serious damage. Only time will tell what that will result in. In the meantime, eat only soft foods to avoid jarring them further, and ice your mouth daily to harden your gums around the roots."

Ice? That would cost a fortune, especially at this time of year!

Morosely, she thanked him and paid the predetermined fee. He bowed his simpering head briefly as his hand closed over the banknote.

Yes, Dovey noted. *There is that pandering smile.*

And then he was gone, leaving Dovey alone with her endangered teeth and seething thoughts.

Where did Shiverly say he bought ice? Berkeley Square, was it? Surely Celia

139

knows where that is.

With a haste usually associated with doling out vengeance, she retrieved her money stocking from its hiding place. Peeling one note away from the others, she examined it, amazed once again that such a light piece of paper could represent so much toil, and promise so much gain.

I must save my teeth, her vanity chided her parsimony.

Grabbing a pewter bowl from a shelf above her, she opened her bedroom door.

"*Th*elia!" Dovey hollered out into the hallway, cringing as she heard a faint lisp as she formed the word.

She waited a moment, and heard no response. Out of her bedroom she went, stomping all the way down the hall. Throwing open their bedroom door, she found Celia and Molly lounging on their beds, both exceedingly startled at her abrupt entrance.

"You!" she said, shoving the bowl into Celia's hands. "Take thi*th* and go to Berkeley *Th*quare. Buy me enough i*th*e…"

Damn it, I am *lisping!*

"…enough i*th*e to fill the bowl and bring it back immediately."

A subtle look of wonder was exchanged between Celia and Molly, stoking the fire of Dovey's fury.

"Look at *ME* when I'm talking to you!" she roared, riveting Celia's eyes on her once again.

After taking a deep breath, she continued. "Thi*th* banknote will more than cover the co*th*t, and I want every penny not required to be returned to me. Do you under*th*tand?"

Clearly bewildered, Celia shook her head.

"You *th*tupid girl! You who are wont to roam all over – you know London better than anyone el*th*e here!"

She capitulated on trying to avoid her lisp.

"You are to go to Berkeley *Th*quare and get me a bowl of i*th*e. Now!"

The girl jumped up from the bed, ready to charge out of the door.

"No!" Dovey shouted, then pointed at the lavender silk gown hanging on a wall peg. "Wear *that* that you'll look re*th*pectable! And hurry back that it doe*th*n't melt or I'll beat you black and blue!"

Then, she dropped the banknote on the floor and stormed out.

AN EMPTY BOWL

GOOD GOD, WHAT brought that about? Celia wondered as she warily ran the tip of her tongue over the ravaged inside of her cheek. Though she was now several streets away, Dovey's red, raging face was fresh in her mind.

Berkley Square, Celia thought as she briskly crossed Whitcomb Street. *Berkley Square, where might that be?*

Though she wasn't sure where she had been commanded to go, Celia had readied herself quickly at the madam's behest. She was certain that the search for ice – though likely futile – would be less dreadful than staying near Dovey in her present state of fury.

Celia remembered Bill calling one roadway which branched off of Piccadilly "Berkley Street" and headed there, thinking that a good place to start searching for a square of the same name. Turning right onto it, she went past two very large houses and their grounds[iv] on her left. Hastening onward, she soon saw a large, ovular green before her.

A woman who looked to be a maid out on an errand was walking past.

Celia said to her, "Pardon me, but is this Berkley Square?"

"Yes, it is," the woman said curtly, hardly pausing in her paces to hear Celia's gratitude expressed.

Pleased at her good fortune, Celia continued forward and saw that the green was ringed with shops. Still uncertain on how to go about purchasing ice, she ducked into what looked like a tea house and asked the shopkeeper at the counter.

"Ice?" he asked, furrowing his brow, then waved her away.

Standing outside once again, she knew she could not return to the Bower so soon and without ice, so she asked at a second shop and then another. It was at the third that the proprietor said, "Oh, you'll be wanting to see Purvis just down the way there."

Locating Mr. Purvis was not difficult after that, but he laughed at her.

"Ice at this time of year – when last winter is as long ago as it can possibly be? Haha!"

Though she felt as foolish as a jester, Celia asked, "Where else might I get some?"

"Dunno! The last of mine puddled up my cellar floors in August." His face broke into a fresh grin as she turned to go and he called after her, "Don't worry! You'll get your ice in another month or two – at no cost! Haha!"

Now convinced that there was no ice to be had in all of London, Celia turned back toward the Bower with nothing but the pewter bowl and the banknote clutched in her sweaty hand. Such notes were an anomaly to her as the only money she'd held previously was of a round metallic nature.

It must be worth quite a lot, she supposed, scratching the paper's smooth, flat surface with her thumbnail.

Suddenly, it occurred to her that she could run away from the Bower at that very moment.

With this money and what I'd get from pawning the dish, I could stay off the street for a while anyway.

But the risk was too great and the outcome too hazy.

No. I can't be thought a thief. And how would I get word to Honora?

She was not far from the Bower now, the heavy bowl cumbersome in her hand.

Honora and I will get out somehow. She's promised it.

A WHIR

THE TREES OF an unfamiliar countryside passed Honora on either side as the sun rose higher in the sky. She felt as if she was drifting above her body until a sudden jolt of pain reminded her that she sat upon a gig seat between two street preachers. Glancing at her hand, she saw brown lines of fruitcake encrusted under her fingernails.

Did I dig through that cake just this morning? she thought incredulously, then began to recount the whir from which she had just emerged.

First, there was the cake of coins. But I could say nothing of it to Celia because Molly was there.

Then, Dovey was at the bottom of the stairs.

The memory of the bawd's sneering face looming just inches from her own turned her stomach.

And so I struck her and ran.

Honora recalled dashing over long stretches of pavement until – like the startling clutch of a vengeful corpse reaching up out of the ground – that pothole had swallowed her foot and twisted her ankle.

There she had sat, clutching at her leg as the masses of greater London streamed past, some gawking in surprise, others smirking in amusement, or annoyed that she blocked their path.

Nary a one made move to help me up.

Fearing that Dovey herself might appear at any moment, she had pushed herself to her feet and began to hobble lurchingly down the walkway, knowing not where she would go. When she had shambled on just a little further, suddenly *they* had been there – touching her elbow, then lifting her onto their gig.

As Honora thought through these events, Jasper chatted to her. She gave him minimal responses, alert now to her changing surroundings. Busy streets and encroaching buildings had given way to open dusty roadways bordered by hedges. Rolling hills, yellow now in mid-autumn stretched out before them, punctuated by church steeples near and far reaching up to the blue sky.

Where will we stop? Honora wondered, trying to quell a fresh wave of panic. *One thing at a time. I'm out of Dovey's clutches. I have an outrageous fortune in my pocket and these two young men seem to have no designs on me.*

By the time Barclay pulled the horse to a stop outside a house in a large village, Honora's queer sensation of floating outside herself had subsided.

Within a few moments, a Dr. Harding was up on the gig seat beside her as Barclay and his brother stood under a tree nearby. Honora supposed they stood at this respectful distance that they might not see her exposed calf during the examination.

"Have you pain here?" Harding asked, grasping and inverting her foot.

Honora's answer was a gasp and clutching of the gig's rail. The sharp pain pulled her fully out of her dream-like state.

"Hmm," the man said, then everted the joint. "And here?"

Honora gave a faint shake of the head though her ankle still pulsated from the previous motion.

"Push against my palm here with the ball of your foot," he said holding his hand against it.

As she complied, he ran his hand halfway up the back of her calf, squeezing and kneading the muscles, his brow furrowed in concentration.

"Hmm," he said again, then jumped down from the gig as Honora adjusted her skirt around her legs.

"All is well, excepting the lateral ligaments," he said, addressing Barclay who had stepped closer. "One or more of them is sprained and she ought not..."

"Please, sir," Honora said, annoyed that she was not the one being informed about her own ankle's status. "I am *here*."

"Ah, yes," he said, reverting his attention back to her. "You'll need to keep all weight off it for three days at least. Only then can you begin to..."

Honora interrupted, "Oh, but that is not possible, sir."

The man grinned knowingly. "Do not fret. You may not feel graceful whilst wielding a pair of crutches, but a healthy young lady such as yourself will master the use of them quickly. I'm certain the Durbins have a spare pair in one of the attics as each of the boys has needed them at some point with their many bashings and boutings in years past. Soon enough, you'll be well again, ready to spin and float at any ball you attend."

"I beg your pardon, sir, but it isn't a lack of grace that alarms me. Rather, to remain off of my feet is impossible."

"Your ankle begs to differ, Miss," he responded with a paternally patient smile.

Good lord! she thought. *What am I to do for three or four days with an injury such as this?*

As Barclay and Jasper climbed back up onto the gig, Harding asked, "Shall I add the charge for this to your family's account?"

Honora's breath caught. *Of course, there would be a cost! Why did I not think of that and decline?*

With wide eyes, she watched Barclay nod to the doctor, then turn to her.

"Such good news it is only the sinews, but the bones are sound enough," he said with a smile.

Honora nodded dumbly, her mind racing.

I ought to pay him now, myself, but how odd it would be if I pulled a gold coin from my apron pocket – and it sticky with cake! That would arouse suspicion on every front.

"Thank you, Harding," Barclay said as the man went to reenter his house. Looking back to Honora, he said, "You're pale. You'll be wanting a drink, and some dinner."

And how much will that *cost me?*

"Oh, no. I thank you. I really ought to be going."

Barclay's face fell as he nodded. "Yes, yes. Of course. Your family must be sick with worry. Jasper, when we get home, run in to ask Bess to pack up a picnic for us to eat on the way back to town while I tell Dervy to hitch up the phaeton."

"But there's not room for *all* of us in the phaeton," Jasper said, sulkily. "I'd have to ride alongside on horseback, and there's nothing to hear from the ten feet away as that would place me."

"I'm sorry for such disappointment, Jass, but my first object is to return Miss Honora to town as soon as possible."

As Jasper pouted, Honora reached into her pocket and slipped out one of the precious coins.

"Here," she said.

It pained her heart to lift it toward Barclay.

Oh, what good that could have done for Celia and myself!

"What is that?" he asked, smiling though he recoiled.

"The physician's fee."

"Oh, no!" Barclay shook his head vigorously. "You shan't pay a *farthing* for that, let alone a half guinea!"

"But…"

"'But' nothing! Put it away." He swiftly changed the subject. "Once we are back in town, to where shall I be delivering you, Miss Honora?"

The relief she felt at returning the money to her pocket fled.

"I…"

He could take me to an inn, but which one? Not one near the Bower as I might be seen by Dovey or one of the girls! And if I were to sleep at an inn, this ankle would keep me from going out to seek employment.

Seeing that Barclay was awaiting her reply, Honora could do nothing to keep tears from forming in her eyes. As they ran down her cheeks, she looked at her hands, empty in her lap.

This is precisely *the sort of behaviour that Eliza would accuse me of manufacturing to be pitied!*

"Is your ankle throbbing?" Barclay asked gently, producing a handkerchief from his pocket to hand to her.

"Yes," Honora nodded, dabbing her eyes, grateful for a different reason to explain her tears.

"Perhaps it will trouble you less once you are at home with your family."

Dammit! She felt the profane phrase burning on her tongue and longed to release it into the air around her.

"I have no home," she said, bluntly.

Barclay prodded, "Surely you have your people somewhere."

Celia's lovely, somber face as well as Polly's lumpy, florid one flashed into Honora's mind.

Yes, I suppose Celia is the closest to one of 'my people' as there is now, but she can be of no help. In fact, I need to help her. And as for Polly, what could she do if Barclay was to deliver me back at Stagsdown House? Hide me in the larder behind the apple bin until Eliza ventured off to Bath for the winter?

Might as well tell him at once.

With a sigh, Honora looked determinedly at Barclay, noting the enormous confusion on his face. Even in this flustered state, it showed kindness instead of irritation. She resignedly said, "I fear you must drop me at an inn – but not a *fine* one. Oh la! *You* being a gentleman probably only know of *fine* ones."

"Miss Honora," he said, solemnly. "As someone who *literally* loaded you onto a gig from the side of a street in town, I am presently responsible for your well-being. I understand you are feeling muddled – as I myself do – but we must determine to think clearly and get you back to your best place. Now, can you give me some indication as to where that might be?"

Good god, he thinks me an idiot!

Honora nodded and took a deep breath.

"I understand you perfectly, sir, and I do apologize. You see, this morning when you appeared, I had just turned my ankle after fleeing an attack by my employer."

"Attack?" Barclay and Jasper were visibly alarmed.

"Yes," Honora nodded. *Though she might argue that I attacked her.*

"What did he…?" Barclay started to ask, his lower jaw suddenly jutting out.

"Oh no, not *he. She.*"

"*She?*" the Durbins asked together, disbelievingly.

The brothers looked at her, then to one another before Jasper's face split into a grin and he laughed aloud.

"Two women fighting?" he asked, choking on his laughter.

Annoyed, Honora glanced at Barclay. She detected a twitching of the corner of his mouth, but when their eyes met, he grew serious again.

"Did you don her favorite apron without asking first?" Jasper chortled.

"Jasper!" Barclay said sharply. "Miss Honora's upset is no source of amusement."

"Of course," Jasper replied, biting his lips together as if to contain another peal of laughter. Then he took a deep breath and said, "I do apologize, Miss Honora."

"And surely there was no justifiable reason for this…attack," Barclay continued, "so we will not trouble you further by asking you to describe it. Please forgive our insensitivity."

A relief washed over Honora as she nodded numbly, sandwiched between the penitent siblings.

"Surely you can report her for her violence," said Barclay.

"Oh, no!" Honora declared. Her ardent response drew the eyes of both young men back to her and she offered reason for it. "Justices are notorious for siding with employers."

The disturbing reality that she had nowhere to lay her head that night settled over her again.

"And because I lived where I worked, I now have nowhere to go, but an inn."

"Very well," Barclay said, pleasantly. "You are in dire need of rest, sustenance and bonhomie, all of which can be provided abundantly at our home."

Jasper nodded, obviously pleased.

"Oh, but I couldn't!" Honora protested. "You have already rescued me and taken out credit for my doctor bill. Surely you must sense how mortifying all of this is for me to be taking and imposing all day long."

"Come, come," he chided. "I assure you, our mother and elder brother will have no qualms about it. We host guests regularly. Stay at Singer Hall a few days as you consider what you will do next. Mother is there, and Martha..."

Exhausted, Honora longed for the promised respite and offered no further objection. This silence was answered by Barclay hawing the horse onto the road and away from London.

HONORA HAS FLED

QUIETLY, CELIA ENTERED the Bower through the kitchen door and was surprised to see an unfamiliar girl hunched over the table. Though she wanted to put the pewter bowl on the table and creep upstairs, Celia knew she ought to return it directly to Dovey.

Though this girl looks meek, who knows if she might nick a bowl when our backs are turned.

The girl sniffled as she clumsily flipped a potato over to peel the skin off with a long knife.

"Don't bleed all over the damn 'tatoes!" Sally snapped.

Glancing at the girl's hands, Celia saw that her fingers had several nicks. Having peeled small, slippery potatoes herself, Celia didn't wonder where the little cuts had come from.

"Haven't you got a smaller knife for her, Sally?" Celia asked. "She's cutting her fingers to ribbons."

Instead of waiting for an answer, Celia looked into the cutlery drawer and withdrew a paring knife, placing it in front of the girl.

"That'll be wieldier," she murmured.

The girl said nothing as she lifted the proffered object, pausing for a moment to wipe her eyes on her sleeve.

"Are we eating soon, Sally?" Celia asked as she was unusually hungry.

"As you see," the cook replied, motioning toward the sliced bread and cheese she was arranging on a platter for the girls' dinner. "It's good I 'ad this 'un get started on supper before dinner's even served, as she's takin' years with them 'tatoes."

Celia could see the girl was making better progress with the smaller knife.

But who is this girl? And oughtn't Honora be peeling those, or baking one of her cakes?

"Where's Honora?" Celia asked Sally.

"Damned if I know!" the woman responded vehemently, tossing a dish cloth on the table. "'Aven't seen 'er since mornin'! Mrs. Dovey said she gone out to do the shoppin', but the basket's 'ere and there's no sign of 'er. Now I ain't got carrots to pair with them 'tatoes. Honora pro'lly run off – left me sloggin' along with this 'un!"

She waved her hand at the newest girl whose lower lip began to tremble. Two fat tears dropped out of her eyes.

"Damn it! Now yer *cryin'* on the 'tatoes!" Sally scolded. "No one wants yer tears fer supper!"

Ran off? Celia quickly calculated the time since Honora entered their bedroom and flashed her that meaningful look before Dovey barged in, demanding ice.

With the pewter bowl tucked under her arm, she headed toward her bedroom.

Molly was there, laying belly down on her bed, flipping through a copy of La Belle Assemblée.

"You look a fright, Celia. Your 'air is nearly wild. Did you get the ice?"

Ignoring the barb, Celia shook her head and asked, "When did you last see Honora?"

"Dunno. When she was makin' eyes at you this morning, I suppose. Why?"

"There's another girl in the kitchen and Honora's not been seen since mid-morning."

"Hmm. P'rhaps she was *taken* on 'er way to market, nabbed by gypsies and we'll never see 'er again." Molly shrugged, smirking. "Or maybe she run off."

She straightened suddenly at the sound of the dinner bell ringing downstairs. "Ah, dinner at last. I'm starvin'."

Did Honora run off? Celia asked herself.

Molly jumped up, brushing past Celia on her way to the door. "Aren't you comin'?"

Celia sank onto the bed, the pit in her stomach yawning into enormity. "I'm not hungry."

"Missin' your b'loved friend, more likely." Molly rolled her eyes, then said over her shoulder as she left the bedroom, "It's better this way. She'd've made a lousy 'arlot."

But what of me? I'm a lousy harlot, yet I'm stuck here all the same.

Celia imagined Honora hurrying down the street, away from the Bower and her heart burned with anger.

We said we'd run off together. I could've run off just now — even had a banknote in my hand! — but I came back for her sake.

Where'd she go? Back to that horrible Lady Eliza — not so horrible now!

Hugging her knees to her chest, she tried to keep her tears at bay, wondering how long it would be before Dovey appeared to slap her for not finding any ice.

SHE CANNOT BE MADE OUT

Singer Hall, later that same evening

SILENT AND NERVOUS, Barclay stood by the open dining room door awaiting Miss Honora's arrival that they might enter together. This would be the first time she beheld him without his hat, and the thought of her eyeing the entirety of his carroty head made him uneasy.

I'm not as red as Jasper, he thought, then began to chide himself for such vanity when he overheard his mother ask, "Well Clayton, what do you make of the girl?"

It was not Barclay's objective to eavesdrop on whomever was already in the dining room. However, at this question, he attuned his ears.

"What girl?" Clayton asked.

"Did you not know? Today, when they were calling-out, your brothers came across a girl who had just sprained her ankle along the street. Well, you know Barclay's tender heart!" Mamma chuckled fondly. "He bundled her up and brought her home to be tended to by Harding."

Overhearing his mother's good-natured retelling of the story pleased Barclay. He had felt foolish while introducing the two women earlier that day. Mrs. Durbin had been gracious of course, and Miss Honora had presented herself with the utmost propriety, but the situation was so peculiar that Barclay was anxious to hear what his mother had really thought of it.

"Mamma, you confound me!" Clayton cried.

"I scarcely believe it myself — and yet it grows stranger still as he has yet to return her, citing Harding's urgings that she remain off her feet for the rest of this week!"

"Surely, she would prefer to convalesce amongst her own people."

"And yet she remains!" Mrs. Durbin said with delighted exasperation as if there was nothing to be done about it. "She will be dining with us tonight."

"Who are her people? In which circle does her family move?"

"I've no idea. Truly Clayton, I cannot make her out! She is tidy in her person, and her manners are just what they ought to be. Her speech is refined though the cut and style of her clothing is nothing to speak of."

Barclay knew his mother's mentioning of Honora's clothing was not a criticism, merely an observation.

"Yet," she continued, "I cannot think what she was doing out in town without a chaperone!"

"Good lord — an urchin from the pavement directly to our dining table!" Clayton said, chuckling. "Barclay's biblical notions have run amok. What's next? A leper in the library? A foot-washing harlot in the salon?"

Mrs. Durbin's amusement evaporated instantaneously.

"Clayton!" she said sharply. "That is quite enough!"

It was not often that Barclay heard such a tone from his mother, but when he did, it was usually directed at Clayton.

"I'm only referring to what is described in the Good Book itself, Mamma," Clayton said.

"Your ribaldry is quite inappropriate."

"Forgive me!" Clayton cajoled.

Barclay could easily imagine Clayton grinning impishly, his hand snaking across the table to give their mother's wrist an affectionate little shake.

"Mr. Barclay?"

A voice at his elbow nearly made him jump out of his boots. There, just feet from him, stood Martha.

She thinks I was eavesdropping! he lamented, thoroughly chagrined. Simultaneously, the conversation within the dining room had ceased. *Ugh. They* all *think I was. Well, rightly so, I suppose…*

"I was awaiting Miss Honora so we could go into supper together," he pronounced loudly enough that he hoped his mother and Clayton would hear.

"Yes, well regarding your *guest*…" Martha began, her voice warbling unpleasantly on the last word. "She has asked me to beg your forgiveness as the pain in her ankle has dulled her appetite, and she wishes only to remain in her chamber where she can rest."

"Oh." Barclay felt his face fall, and Martha's close scrutiny of it.

Jasper came quickly striding down the hallway then.

"Miss Honora will not be joining us?" he asked, his eagerness for supper visually dampened.

"Well, it is understandable. She's had a trying day and is now in a strange place," Barclay said, trying to hide his own disappointment. Motioning Jasper toward the dining room, he followed him in, saying, "Martha, please take her some elderberry cordial and some of Bess's currant biscuits should her appetite return. Give her our best wishes for the evening."

"I shall, sir…" She bowed her head subserviently, but then surprised Barclay by stepping through the doorway after him, "…once the family is fed."

"Martha," Barclay said. "I should very much like you to do it now. There are no guests here and we Durbins can ladle our own soup."

The servant looked taken aback, glancing between the two brothers. Then, with tightly closed lips, she bobbed her head and turned away to honor Barclay's bidding.

He watched her walk down the hall at a quick clip, slightly rankled.

"Brothers!" Clayton bellowed dramatically from where he sat at the table. "Come tell me your tale for it seems you had an adventure today!"

The jesting tone stirred up a subtle defensiveness in Barclay.

"There is little to tell beyond what Mamma has shared with you already, I am sure," Barclay replied, eager to steer the conversation away from his capricious actions of that morning. He had difficulty understanding them himself and had no desire to lay them out in plain sight before his ever-goading brother.

"But *you*, Clayton," he said. "How was the shooting at Sparsvale? It must have been successful as it kept you from home until after dark."

Happily, Clayton launched into an account of his day's activities which lasted the length of supper. Barclay felt it a triumph when he left the table realizing that Honora had not been mentioned again.

That night, he retired early, tired from the wondrous occurrences of the day and marveling that just down the hall slept a young woman who had truly needed his help earlier.

Though it all was passing strange, he thought, climbing into bed. *I suppose it's fair to say that I did some good today.*

***

The next morning, when Barclay arrived in the breakfast room, he was pleased to see it was empty except for Miss Honora. She was seated at the table, her crutches leaning against the back of her chair. Her hair was pulled back into a smooth knot at the nape of her neck and her face had lost its dazed look of the day before.

"Good morning," he said, smiling warmly.

She nodded politely as he sat down across from her. "And to you, Mr. Barclay."

There were footsteps in the hall. Suddenly, to Barclay's dismay, Clayton stood before them, wearing a thick velvet robe – his copper-tinged hair sticking up in all directions.

"Ah!" he said, his eyes fastening on Honora. "So you *do* exist!"

The girl's faint smile stiffened.

"How ungracious you sound!" Barclay scolded his brother.

Honora stammered, "Yes sir, but if you would but direct me to an inn, then I…"

"Oh no! None of that! I simply meant that your rumoured appearance yesterday sounded as if it may have all been a joke," Clayton gibed. Then, bowing dramatically, he said, "By the by, I am Clayton Durbin. Very pleased to make your acquaintance, miss."

Without waiting for any reciprocation, he fell heavily into a chair and reached for the teapot.

Honora squirmed on her seat, looking as if she were trying to formulate an answer.

"Clayton, your careless teasing has perturbed our guest," Barclay said.

"Oh Barclay, I'm sure she knows I mean no harm." Clayton rejoined, lifting a piece of bacon to his lips with a laugh. "And today will bring even more guests to Singer Hall, so she will not be the only foreigner amongst us."

"Who are we expecting?" Barclay asked.

"Have you forgotten about Sir Richard Bradford and his cousins?" Clayton asked. "I told you he was coming out to shoot some birds, Barclay! It seems your head is now full of other things."

Here he looked pointedly at Honora who was very intent on spreading a spoonful of jam on her roll.

"I suppose Miss Emily Bradford will be with him?" Barclay asked, hoping to redirect his brother's focus.

"Of course!" Clayton said, ladling porridge into his bowl. "As well as Miss *Leticia*."

Here, he shot a look at Barclay.

Oh no. Today of all days!

"Very good," Barclay said, though he knew the words sounded unconvincing. "Miss Honora will have some young ladies to converse with as she convalesces as I'm sure we gentlemen would bore her immensely."

Honora smiled at this politely.

"Richard's keen on the shooting." Clayton said. "I hope you'll not forego going with us, Barclay. Three in the wood always makes a merrier group than two."

Keeping his eyes trained on the table cloth, Barclay mentally ticked off on his fingers.

This will be the Bradfords' first, second…third visit since Lady's Day. That is rather more often than anyone else's.

The proximity of Singer Hall to London allowed for a carriage to make the trip between the two places easily, that anyone staying in town could venture over to the Durbins' for a visitation and be back at their London lodgings by supper. In recent years, Barclay had noted a steady parade of Clayton's school fellows and their sisters or female relatives. As the practice continued, he supposed that Clayton was now searching for a bride. Or that a bride was searching for him.

Though Barclay's mother was assured of a place in her present home until death, Clayton's wife would replace her as the pre-eminent lady at Singer Hall. This could spell disaster for the amicable peace that prevailed there.

Therefore, it was with interest that Barclay watched as pretty girls, plain girls, quiet girls, brash girls, willowy girls, stout girls – in short, every type of girl imaginable – passed through the front doors at Singer Hall. Each had their stint in the parlor, delicately sipping tea from a fine bone china teacup. If that went well, they might progress to the dining table for a meal, where the proper use of their linen and forks might be noted by Martha and remarked on later to Barclay in private. Some were fortunate enough to be invited to stay a night or two, although Barclay had not detected that this implied a particular appreciation on Clayton's part for the present females. Often, it simply meant he wanted to extend his time with the male relatives who accompanied them.

When guests called at Singer Hall, Barclay was socially required to be present and available if he was at home. He was always nearby, ready to grant assistance whilst making his own silent observations, storing them away for his own amusement.

Most of the young women seemed to understand the nature of their inclusion in the visit to Singer Hall, primed no doubt by worldly-wise relatives, and informed of the honor and importance of such an opportunity. Though some girls struggled to keep their heads above the proverbial water, there were others who played their hands well, capturing Clayton's attention for varying amounts of time. Up until this point, however, all budding relationships had withered on the vine.

One especially awkward incident was when a Mr. Jameson had arrived with his sister in tow. A handsome carriage, the family crest emblazoned upon its door, rolled into the courtyard. Upon climbing out, the brother was greeted with a hearty handshake and a back slap from Clayton with the exclamation, "It's been far too long!"

Seconds later, *Miss* Jameson stepped out of the carriage. Clayton turned to face her, then burst out laughing, declaring, "Good god, Jameson! She looks *exactly* like you!"

Although Clayton followed the pronouncement with a proper bow and a gentle handshake, Barclay could see that the visit's purpose had been squashed from its onset. Any confidence the girl had had had clearly dissolved as she stood before Clayton, tugging at the bonnet that framed her crestfallen, fraternal face.

Though that was poorly done on Clayton's part, he was *right!* Barclay recalled. *Put a heavier brow on her and shear her hair off, and Miss Jameson would have been Mr. Jameson's twin. They were even the same height!*

Many girls would suddenly realize that Clayton was not interested in them and some of them would begin to cast their eye toward Barclay himself. The first time it happened, Barclay had shrunk away, absenting himself from the parlour, or from lingering at the dining table. But eventually he had warmed to it, sometimes engaging in exclusive, quiet conversation with a girl in the corner of the library or offering his arm as they ambled around the gardens together. After all, he knew he was not intended for a celibate life. But none of these girls had kept his interest for long. Generally, they either lacked the intelligence that his mind required or the depth of character for which his heart longed.

And so that grasping flirt, Emily, and her mysterious sister, Leticia, will come along with their cousin, Sir Richard Bradford.

Barclay suppressed a sigh at this thought, exasperated already, and buttered his bread.

At least it is clear that Emily's intentions are dead set on Clayton. She's hardly ever spoken to me. But Leticia…Emily joked about bringing her along next time to meet me. If she's anything like her sister, I won't be able to stomach her for long.

Still uneasy about the inevitable invasion, he smiled at Honora, noting that she had finally begun to eat some breakfast.

A QUESTION OF CONNEXION

MRS. DURBIN POPPED her head into the parlor where Honora sat reading.

"Come, dear. The Bradfords are pulling into the drive this very moment. You must not hide yourself away."

But that is precisely why I have settled here, Honora thought, as she dutifully rose from the settee and grasped the crutches' handles.

"Yes, ma'am."

When Honora reached the doorway, Mrs. Durbin placed her hand gently on Honora's back and murmured, "Don't be nervous."

Unsure how to respond, Honora smiled and said, "But I am so ungainly!"

"As anyone who has turned their ankle shall be," Mrs. Durbin rejoined as they began to make slow progress down the hallway.

Honora regarded Barclay's mother as a handsome gentlewoman of generous proportions.

When Barclay had introduced the two women the day before, Honora had appreciated how attentive and tender his mother's gaze was when she beheld and listened to her son.

And her eyes exude that fawning warmth even whilst looking at me.

The woman's face, though lax with the living of many years, was still pretty and Honora could easily envision her charming some blustery fellow long ago.

Approaching the foyer, they joined the Durbin boys who were finger-combing their hair and brushing off their coats. Through a window, Honora could see an enclosed carriage coming up the drive.

She stifled the sigh she felt forming in her chest.

How much petty vanity does that carriage presently hold?

Within five minutes, three young people alit from its confines in the courtyard as the Durbins stood by, ready to greet them. Honora felt a familiar and electrifying change in the air as she was suddenly very aware of herself and the others, what they all wore, how their hair was dressed, how they postured their bodies.

Immediately she saw which of the women – the shorter one – intended to sink her claws into Clayton. Emily – or 'Miss Bradford' as she was the eldest sister – moved to stand beside him and spoke so quietly that only he could discern her words. She surveyed the grounds with a shrewd eye when Clayton's attention was not on her, but when he turned to her, her face transformed to such rapturous levity that Honora had difficulty keeping her countenance as she witnessed it.

Near her was Sir Richard, who looked very pleased with himself in spite of the largish nose blighting his face. His eyes skipped quickly over Honora as if his quick perusal of her had told him everything he would ever want to know about her. Last of all, Honora's eyes fell on the taller girl, she who must be Miss Leticia – she whose name had clearly unsettled Barclay that morning at breakfast.

She's pleasant enough looking, Honora thought, noting the girl's hauteur was half that of her sister's.

Within moments, all necessary introductions had been made and the whole group was filing into the largest parlour. Honora learned that Sir Richard was from Shropshire and was Clayton's particular friend from their years together at Heath School for Boys.

Being the least noticed of all people in the room, Honora had the benefit of watching the others in their strutting, preening, and posturing as they found seats for themselves.

Leticia had greatly anticipated meeting Barclay, as evidenced by her eyes rarely leaving his face, though he was situated across the room from her. It was not long before she stood and made her way to stand near him, where she began to study a small ivory sculpture with marked delight.

"I've never seen anything of the like!" she exclaimed. "Where has this come from?"

"Hmm?" Barclay asked. He had been listening to the conversation between Clayton and Richard. "I believe it was brought from India to Singer Hall by my paternal grandfather, though I don't recall its precise story."

"What a shame! It is so intriguing!"

"Perhaps," Barclay responded noncommittally as he turned his attention back to the men who were enthusiastically discussing their previous shoot.

Poor Leticia, Honora thought though with a smile behind her masked front. *Oh, but it looks as if she is not yet finished!*

The determined girl had sat herself down, rather heavily next to Barclay on the settee.

"Have you been to town lately?" she asked, leaning toward him.

"Mm, yes," Barclay replied, looking a bit ill at ease. "Just yesterday, actually."

"What!" she swatted at him as playfully as Emily had previously batted at Clayton. "You were in London and you did not call on us? What were you doing that we were neglected?"

He was scraping the likes of me up off the pavement, Honora thought.

"I go regularly into town to call…that is, to proselytize."

"Prossa…prossel…?" Leticia furrowed her brow. "Enlighten me, do!"

Ah, that is not within the range of your vocabulary, Miss Leticia? Honora thought. *And would you ask for an explanation if he was shorter than you or married already?*

Oh Honora, be fair! She urged herself. *Perhaps she is not as you suppose.*

At the girl's apparent interest, Barclay brightened, sitting up straighter.

"I stand on a green where I declare the good news of God's love and plan to all who will listen."

"Oh!" Leticia exclaimed with delight. "How very good of you!"

This response surprised Honora, and seemed to hearten Barclay.

"And what do you tell them?"

He needed just this minor encouragement to launch heartily into a thorough description.

Leticia listened so fixedly, asking questions with an open and easy air that invited more discourse, that Honora began to second-guess her prejudgment of the young woman.

The pleasant conversation was suddenly brought to a halt by Sir Richard's loud declaration of, "Why are we yet here, shut inside this dreary parlour?"

Motioning to the window, he continued. "The sky is blue, the air crisp! A perfect day to trek out for a brace of pheasants – say you not, good fellows?"

He waggled his eyebrows at Clayton and Barclay.

"Oh!" Emily exclaimed, grabbing ahold of Clayton's arm. "I would that I were a man who could tromp out into the woods and play all day!"

"I've a second great coat you could don, if you'd like!" Clayton offered her jokingly.

"Hmph! You're so broad, I'd drown in it!" Emily replied, pouting as she slumped dramatically into the settee.

"It seems your cousin's plans must postpone further conversation until supper," Barclay said to Leticia. "I have enjoyed speaking with you, Miss Leticia."

He stood and her eyes lingered on him as if to hold him in the room.

"But Miss Honora is a good conversationalist," he said, waving his hand in Honora's direction.

When have I had opportunity to prove myself thus? Honora wondered, thinking of her shocked near silence during the ride to Singer Hall from London, and her absence from the supper table the night before. His implicit faith in her abilities amused her.

"And I am sure she will keep you in fine company in my absence."

Barclay turned his eyes to her, an appeal visible in their blue depths.

Honora nodded a faint acquiescence though she wondered what she could possibly say to this girl and her sister that would be of interest to them.

The gentlemen left, ribbing one another over who would return with the most birds and who was most likely to shoot off their toes. Unexpectedly, Mrs. Durbin rose and left at the same time as the men, begging the pardon of the girls she was leaving behind, but offering no explanation.

This troubled Honora. Though she had only known the woman for one day, her pleasant nature made her a preferred companion. But once the exodus had occurred and the doors swung shut with a definitive click, it was only Miss Bradford and Miss Leticia with whom Honora found herself.

The change in the air was immediate. The sisters began an abundant discussion on the lives and fashions of their many acquaintances, all loudly enough for Honora to hear clearly, though they did not direct any of its bounty toward her. Though pleased at the omission, Honora wondered, *Would they not have exhausted such topics having been shut up together in a carriage just this morning?*

And so, Honora's mind was free to ponder matters other than the ostrich feathers that Miss Claremont had dripped with at the Royal Opera House just the night before – *a bold choice* according to Miss Leticia.

My ankle is feeling a bit better already. She stretched her leg out and rotated her foot in every direction, noting that it smarted only slightly.

It was at this moment that she noticed the chatter had stopped and both of the sisters were looking at her foot which was still stuck out from the settee. The shoe exposed to their examination was neither fashionable nor new, hardly something to excite interest. And yet, it seemed to have served a reminder to them that they were not alone together in the Durbins' parlour.

"Miss Honora?" Leticia said. The haughtiness in her voice promptly convinced Honora that her momentary grace toward the woman had been ill-served.

Oh la, she thought. *Now it will begin.*

Through the parlour window, Honora saw the gentlemen as they struck out down the gravel drive toward the woods beyond. Sunlight glinted off the guns' long barrels as two dogs barked excitedly, dancing around the men's feet.

"Yes?" Honora said, looking steadily back at Leticia. Emily, who was seated across from her, also gave Honora her full attention, though silently.

"What exactly is your *connexion* with the Durbin family?" Leticia asked. Her voice had lost the girlish pitch it had while talking with Barclay, yet she gave a little laugh. "I confess, I did not quite understand when it was explained earlier."

Hmm. It seems the Bradford sisters had the same tutor in torture as Lady Eliza. Well, I shall cut to the chase and give her exactly what she wants immediately.

"There is no connexion other than their beneficence."

"What can you mean?"

"I mean that yesterday Barclay and Jasper came across me as I sat upon a London pavement, having just wrenched my ankle. They took me to their family physician who prescribed a week's rest and so I am here at Singer Hall, convalescing."

Leticia looked flummoxed. "What do you mean they 'came across you'? You had met them before at someone's home or a ball, and then they found you yesterday injured in Mayfair or Regent's Square?"

"Near Seven Dials, actually," Honora replied.

Oh, that hit its mark! she thought as the girls' upper lips collectively curled.

"And no, we had not met in some formal setting prior to it, though I had spoken with Barclay and Jasper before as they proselytized at Crawton Green."

This was met with a blank look.

'Proselytized', Miss Leticia. Remember that word that you were so pleased to have Barclay explain to you just ten minutes ago?

"Well, I had heard of his recent ordination..." Leticia said.

Ah! And you imagine you might as well be a clergyman's wife as not, Honora nearly snickered.

"...and then he met you by chance," Leticia was saying, "...and brought you here. But why would he bring you *here*? Where was your chaperone?"

Honora could not suppress a smile as she informed them, "I am my own chaperone."

Leticia drew back and exchanged a look of alarm with Emily.

"But who is your family that you could simply disappear into the countryside with a pair of unknown brothers for a week at a time?"

Looking Leticia straight in the eye, Honora stated, "As you would certainly learn upon further investigation, my family, when they were alive, were not people of consequence, either in name or fortune."

"Oh, I see," Leticia said, her eyebrows lifted in disapproving surprise. She looked at her sister and bit her lips together, then rose from her seat to stand by the window. "What a lovely day. Perfect weather for a walk around the grounds, isn't it, Emily? Miss Honora, would you like to join us for..."

Turning, her eyes caught on the crutches leaning against the settee where Honora sat.

"Oh, how silly I am. I forgot. Of course, we can't go walking today."

"By all means, do go. I hope to never curtail any pleasure that might be afforded you."

"But to leave you alone here in the parlour..." The sisters exchanged a look of *faux* regret.

"Truly, I am leaving the parlour myself presently." Honora hoisted herself up to steady her weight on the crutches. "Unlike many others, I do not dread singularity. Now, if you will please excuse me."

She dipped her head politely and started toward the door, trying not to smirk at the expressions of surprise and confusion on the sisters' faces. A plan was brewing in her mind, one that would likely further the girls' consternation.

You ladies may walk in the garden as you gossip about me. In the meantime, I will show you what I can do.

Out into the hallway she galumphed, wishing it was easier to make a graceful exit whilst juggling crutches and one's pride.

"Miss Goodwin?" she heard, then felt the door being shut behind her. Martha, the solemn, ever-present servant stood just two feet away, her eyes settling on Honora's ankle. "May I be of service to you?"

"Yes, please direct me to the kitchen."

"The kitchen?" The servant's eyes snapped back up to Honora's face.

Honora recalled that the only guests at Stagsdown House to ever make their way to the kitchen were either children in search of treats, or young men who were ravenous an hour before the next meal was scheduled.

"Yes, I would like to bake a cake, or some such confection," she said quietly, hoping the Bradfords would not overhear it.

"A *cake*, Miss? Bess may have one planned for this evening, but it's not likely in the oven yet, let alone out of it."

"No, Martha. I do not *seek* to eat some cake, but rather to *bake* one myself, if I might. The mess will be cleared away entirely by myself once I'm finished, even in spite of my injury." She motioned to her leg. "You can assure Bess of that. *And* the finished product will be worthy of the Durbin's table. Of that I am certain, as well."

Setting her jaw determinedly, Honora stood stock still as Martha regarded her. She could tell the woman was puzzled – and likely annoyed – by her.

But how could she not be? I am requesting access to one of the places regarded by the servants as sacred in their own lair. Where else but the kitchen can a servant linger for a moment, a cup of still warm tea in their hand, chattering for just a sentence more before setting out to answer the bidding, absurd or otherwise, of any member of the great family?

And she doesn't know what to make of me. I am not one of the gentry, yet I am regarded by the Durbins as a guest. Yes, there was definite reservation in her air toward me last night when she brought the cordial and biscuits.

"Baking is what I choose to do when I am pleased…or frustrated, as occasion dictates." Honora explained further, casting a telling glance at the parlor's shut door.

Martha eyed the door wonderingly, before a look of knowing dawned across her face.

Ah, yes. You, being a servant in a household with three young gentlemen, know what is at play with these visitors, don't you?

Honora didn't doubt the woman's perceptiveness. Servants relied on their ability to correctly read diverse situations, and accommodate or change them in whatever manner they supposed their employers would like.

The silent deliberation inside Martha's head seemed to end and she said, "Very good, Miss Goodwin. Right this way, please."

Delighted at her victory, Honora followed Martha as they began their slow but steady journey down the hallway toward the kitchen of Singer Hall.

THINGS LEFT BEHIND

SHE IS GONE.

Fuming, Celia thrust the tablecloth into the sudsy depths of the large wooden tub and swirled it with the posser. Her mind was still reeling with nothing but Honora's disappearance the day before.

Celia envisioned Honora quietly entering their room when she knew it would be empty, shutting the door behind her, crouching down beside the wall to pull her coins out from underneath the chair rail, and dropping them into her apron pocket.

Then she came back later, threw me that silly smile as if to say goodbye and snuck out the front door, never to return.

I oughtn't have shown her that hiding place.

A realization sent a shock down Celia's spine.

Did she take my *money as well? It was only a few coins, but they might have covered her coach fare back to that Stagsdown place.*

Dropping the posser with a splash, Celia hurried through the kitchen and down the hall to the staircase. Soon, she was within her bedroom where Molly lay on her bed, staring at a fashion plate page in one of her periodicals.

"Molly, Dovey wants you."

Molly sighed. "What for?"

"I dunno. She called your name when I was coming up just now. Must've thought I was you when she heard me on the stairs."

Tossing the 'La Belle Assemblée' aside, Molly sighed again and stood. The second she was out of the bedroom and the door was shut, Celia dropped to her knees by the chair rail. Her anger evaporated at what she saw. Not only were her own coins wedged under the thin slat, but so were the two gold pieces belonging to Honora. Her heart felt as if it skipped a beat.

If her money's still here, but she's gone...

Celia's stomach fluttered as she sat herself on the bed, thinking.

...then she did not leave on purpose.

Celia glanced at the shelf above the bed. Honora's stack of clothes was still there, and hanging beside them on a peg was the pelisse.

Molly's heavy tread clomped down the hallway and the door burst open. "Dovey didn't want me. Check your ears, Celia!"

She never meant to leave. She must have left for some errand, and someone stole her off the street.

"Did you hear me, Celia?" Molly stood akimbo before her.

Something or someone kept Honora from coming back.

"Piss off, Molly," Celia murmured, heading back out the door before Molly could see the tears forming in her eyes.

A BLATANT SUPERIORITY

FRESH FROM A BATH, Barclay stood before his wardrobe, its doors flung open wide. Normally, he thought very little about what he pulled out of its recesses, but today he was unsure what to wear. The Durbins would be hosting an early supper so that Sir Richard and his cousins could return to London before the evening had grown too late. This evening held a strange opportunity for Barclay as two young women would share his table, one of whom intrigued him. The other had initially held no enticement for him but the attentive interest she had shown in his calling-out had lit a flickering of possibility in his mind.

Though she hasn't the charm of Miss Honora, he mulled, *Miss Leticia might prove to be a good steady helpmeet. What does scripture say? "Whoso findeth a wife findeth a good thing"?*

He acknowledged the sense of this phrase but wondered why he felt a distinct heaviness of heart. Dressed now, he reached for a green, silken cravat. His hand froze.

No, not that one, he thought. *It is too fine. Miss Honora will still be wearing her only dress and it would not do to make her feel underdressed. The other ladies will undoubtedly do that already.*

He rolled his eyes, thinking of the absurdly stylized clothes some of Clayton's would-be inamoratas had worn at Singer Hall's supper table.

Purple turbans and fur-edged tippets – bah!

Selecting a plain, white cravat, he tied it deftly and exited his bedroom. Just as he came down the stairs, he saw Martha coming out of the dining room.

171

He drew close to her and asked in a low voice, "Martha, does Miss Honora appear nervous at all about tonight's supper?"

The servant tipped her head in confusion, and asked quietly, "Why would she?"

"It occurred to me a moment ago that the other ladies will be dressed in all their finery and…" He stopped as Martha's face had shifted to displeased realization.

"Oh!" she said. "You meant for her to join you all *here*? I supposed she would be eating with the servants in the kitchen later in the evening."

"What?" Barclay said, much louder than he meant to. Looking around the still empty hallway, he dropped his voice and began again, fervently. "No, Martha. Please find her wherever she is and inform her that supper is nearly served here in the dining room with the other guests."

Expecting an apology of some sort, he was surprised when the woman merely dipped into a silent curtsey and then hurried away.

Why would Martha presume such a thing? he wondered, embarrassed for Honora, and hopeful that it had not been stated to her outright that she would be excluded from the family's supper party.

However, he had little time to ponder the matter as Jasper — ever the eager eater — suddenly appeared. Barclay said nothing of the matter to his brother as they entered the dining room together.

Immediately, their attention was arrested by the sight of an elaborate patisserie on the sideboard. At nearly two feet high, scores of profiteroles had been stacked up on top of one another into a cone shape. Bright sprigs of herbs had been decoratively tucked here and there between the golden balls of dough.

"Bess has outdone herself today!" Barclay exclaimed. "But to what purpose?"

With a furtive glance at the empty doorway, Jasper said quietly, "Perhaps Miss Emily has secured Clayton at last and this is their wedding cake."

Barclay snorted. "What, married just this afternoon? And we not invited to the ceremony?"

The brothers stifled their chuckling as the others arrived — Clayton with Mrs. Durbin, then Richard and Emily with Leticia. One by one, they entered, noticed the towering confection, and commented on its elegant grandeur.

"Oh!" Emily cried. "A croquembouche – how lovely!"

Last was Honora who quietly thumped into the room on her crutches and, glancing quickly at the sideboard, remarked nothing. Relieved, Barclay noted that she appeared neither upset nor embarrassed, and wondered how Martha had conveyed to her that she was to be counted amongst the party there. He wanted to catch her eye and acknowledge her with an affirming nod, but she did not look his way.

"Shall we sit?" a voice asked beside him. Turning, he saw Leticia, her eyes riveted on him as she moved to the place at his right side.

"Yes, of course." He pulled out her chair that she might settle herself, then noted with some discomfort that Clayton was doing the same for Honora directly across the table from him.

I shall have to work very hard not to gaze at her throughout the meal.

Once everyone was seated and their plates heaped with food, Leticia said, "So please tell me, Mr. Barclay, why have you chosen such an unusual way to practice Christianity?"

"You mean by standing on a greensward in town and declaring God's love to all who pass?" Barclay was pleased that Leticia's interest in his devotion had not waned since the morning. "That method is most similar to what our Lord and His disciples did though they stood in the desert or at a lakeside."

"Yet many men make sermons but once a week, and are *paid* for it," Leticia said, smoothing her napkin in her lap.

The bite of roll in Barclay's mouth suddenly felt very dry.

"Yes," he conceded after swallowing it. "But I prefer to speak to people who perhaps have greater need to hear of God's pure religion."

"Pure religion?" Honora said from across the table. "I recall that being described as 'visiting the fatherless and widows in their affliction'."

"Why, yes," Barclay said, turning to look at her. She had been so quiet at breakfast, that her forwardness at a crowded dining room table surprised him. "That is in the book of James, I believe."

"That verse struck me even before I found that I myself had been orphaned."

This observation brought about a pause in the natter around the table, finally broken by Mrs. Durbin.

"And why is that, do you think, my dear?" she asked.

Honora smiled thoughtfully. "The hardships of being without an advocate in the world were spelled out plainly to me when I read *Mrs. Margery Two-Shoes'*."

"I read that," Leticia interjected, but was ignored.

Honora spoke on. "Knowing that scripture acknowledged orphans and widows, and exhorted the fortunate to care for the unfortunate gave me great comfort."

Yes! Barclay thought. *Very good!*

"And the benefit of that care," Honora continued, "is compounded when the advantaged prepare the disadvantaged to live the rest of their lives. Is that not why you aim to open a school for the impoverished, Mr. Barclay?"

Here, Barclay saw five surprised faces turn toward him. Jasper alone continued to eat.

"What is this, Barclay?" Mrs. Durbin asked. "A school?"

"Is this why you are hesitant to accept Uncle Allard's offer?" Clayton inquired, looking doubtful.

Mine is a good goal, Barclay reminded himself.

In a confident voice, he said, "I would like to enable the capable downcast to learn skills that they might support themselves."

"Hm. Where do you plan on housing these *protégées*?" Clayton asked, looking around as if searching for space there in the dining room.

"Well not here, of course, Clay, as this is *your* home," Barclay insisted. "You needn't worry! If founding a school is in my future, then God will provide the particulars."

Lifting his goblet as if in a toast, Clayton declared mock-solemnly, "Well then, to my brother, Barclay Durbin: Headmaster of the Foundling School!"

Richard tinked his glass to Clayton's and they chuckled together like school boys while Emily nearly cackled in forced glee.

"If God wills it, yes," Barclay said knowing that if no guests were present he wouldn't mind Clayton's teasing so very much.

As the amusement subsided. Martha reached past Clayton to retrieve an empty platter.

"What's Bess been up to?" he asked, his goblet-clutching hand motioning toward the croquembouche, sloshing claret onto the tablecloth.

"That's not Bess's doing," Martha replied rather stiffly.

"What?" Clayton laughed, a bit tipsy Barclay was sure now.

He and Sir Richard must have been tippling in the billiard room before supper. "Who's made that then?"

For a moment while she wiped at the tablecloth, Martha was silent, but Clayton's eyes were still upon her so she replied in a low voice, "'Twas Miss Honora."

Quiet fell over the whole table.

"Our half-crippled houseguest has made...*that?*" Once again, Clayton motioned, spilling more wine. "Oh Martha, you must be deeper in your cups than am I! I'll not be duped by silly tales!"

The maid said nothing and stepped away from the table, her arms full of serving ware.

Had Barclay not been so shocked by Martha's revelation, he would have chided his elder brother for such careless words. Instead, he turned to Honora and asked. "*You* made that?"

With her chin high and a subdued gleam in her eye, Honora nodded.

"You and what staff of bakers?" Leticia asked, an edge in her voice.

Delicately buttering a bit of bread, Honora shrugged and answered, "Bess showed me where the bowls and spoons were."

Standing and walking over to the sideboard, Barclay examined the object in question. Up close, he saw each round of dough was filled with a thick cream and had a delicate drizzle of golden caramel across its top. He felt the brush of Leticia's skirts against his hand as she was suddenly beside him, also leaning in to scrutinize the wonder.

"Astonishing!" he declared.

"Anyone with a stocked larder who can read a page of *Le Cuisinier Impérial* or *The Experienced English Housekeeper*[i] could do the same," Honora stated before forking a bit of roast into her mouth.

"And is that what you aspire to be?" asked Leticia. "A *housekeeper?*"

Barclay noted the ugliness of a smirk on her lips. His estimation of her was plummeting.

Tilting her head thoughtfully to the side, Honora swallowed and said, "If I was to have the good fortune of a gentleman's family offering me such a position, I would consider it very seriously."

Behind her napkin, Emily giggled, setting the peacock feather in her headdress aquiver.

"The *good fortune* to become a *housekeeper?*" Leticia rejoined looking around the room for agreement in her scorn. As their eyes met, Barclay made sure she did not find an ally in himself.

"Well, if that wondrous creation tastes half as good as it looks, I shall grow stout on it, indeed," Mrs. Durbin announced in the jolly raised voice she always used while attempting to cover over the verbal sins of another. "Now gentlemen, please tell us…who got the most birds?"

Clayton and Richard took the bait, springing together into a retelling of the afternoon's exploits, but Barclay's mind lingered elsewhere.

A scorning shamer is no helpmeet at all, he thought gloomily as he returned to his seat, regretting Leticia's ever-presence at his elbow. Glimpsing Honora, who was calmly dabbing the corners of her mouth with her napkin, he thought he saw the hint of a smile there.

Surely not all gentlemen's daughters are spoiled and catty like these Bradford sisters, and yet where are such ladies?

His heart felt heavy. Leticia was speaking to him again, but he only grunted in response. As Barclay began to push the food around on his plate, he silently dreaded how the rest of the evening would proceed, but by the time Martha began to clear the plates away, Leticia had ceased to chatter at him, apparently aware of the change in his mood.

After supper and a sampling of the croquembouche – which even Leticia begrudgingly described as "rather nice" – the Bradfords bid the Durbins adieu. Climbing into their carriage, they drove off into the darkening night. Barclay was pleased to see them go, and it seemed to him that Clayton – who had not once asked to speak with Miss Bradford privately – was, as well.

THE BLANDNESS OF AN EGG

EGGS FOR SUPPER!

Dovey scorned the soft yellowish mass on her plate. Forking a bit of it into her mouth, she tentatively chewed. Her belly hungered for the substance that a slice of roast beef would impart.

But if I am to save my teeth…

She swallowed and put another bite far into the back of her mouth.

Insolent, stupid girl!

Dovey repictured the startling swing of Honora's fist just before it collided with her jaw.

Why was she so angry? Her tainting? It's only the touching of flesh! I can't recall a time that men weren't touching me. Why, before my tenth year, I had learned to use it to my advantage.

The bawd's chin quivered with indignation.

I showed that girl a kindness -- kept her off the streets. It took Celia three days out there to come to her senses. She probably told Honora that I took her back. Well, not this time! I don't house wild animals!

Upon hearing the ring of the doorbell, she hollered into the hallway, "Molly, an*th*wer the door!"

Damn this lisp!

Dovey could not bear to face her clientele as she heard such a death rattle every time she opened her mouth. She looked out the window, noting how the sky was darkening earlier and earlier each evening. Below, she heard troddings of the newly arrived men downstairs.

Won't be long now before she comes back, pleading. She is a pretty girl…It's a damned shame to lose her. I suppose if she's timid and sorry, she might be tamed

177

into obedience. But I shall make her life hell!

She pushed the scorned egg around, then set the plate aside and poured herself a third glass of wine.

PONDERING IN THE GALLERY

WHEN SHE ARRIVED at the breakfast room the next morning, Honora was surprised to see that although the table was laden with food, no one else was there. She had left the crutches in her room as her ankle, though still tender, could support her weight now if she moved cautiously.

As she nibbled a cut apple, the solitude at the table kept her thoughts turned inward. Though the events at the previous night's supper had seemed like a triumph of sorts, it felt sorely won. The recollection of all the shocked faces at her mention of Barclay's future school made her cringe.

They didn't know? Why would he speak of it to me – a stranger just days ago – but to none of his family?

I shall have to apologize to him. But when? She set her buttered roll aside and gazed at the empty chair he had most recently occupied. *Well, although I may have trod recklessly in one direction, I'm pleased at my progress in another.*

Honora smirked at the memory of Miss Leticia's feeble contributions to the meal's conversation.

Maybe I have saved a good-hearted street preacher from an imprudent match.

But what is Mr. Barclay to me that it should please me so?

He is humble and kind – two attributes I thought fine gentlemen could not acquire before the age of fifty. And there is a pleasing glint in his eye when he smiles.

Oh dear, it seems my stay here ought to end soon.

Draining her tea cup, Honora stood from the table and hobbled out into the convolutions of the great house. She limped down the hall to the many-windowed gallery at its very end which was richly decorated. As she stepped into the long room, she gazed up at the paintings with which the northern wall was festooned. A row of portraits – likely of yesteryear's Durbins – stared back at her, many with a tinge of copper in their hair, some stodgy, some stern.

"You ought to thank me really," she quietly told one fellow who appeared tormented by his starched ruff, "as I made plain the true character of an unworthy conniver who wanted to weasel her way into your family. And as for me – another interloper in your eyes, most likely! – I shall be leaving here as soon as I am able."

A tall window behind her looked out upon a wide expanse of grass. A light rain fell onto the luminescent green blades.

"But I cannot go today. Surely none of you would wish me out in all that wet," she whispered, stepping toward the window, and settling herself upon a chair.

And what must Celia think of my absence? Certainly, Dovey did not relay the truth of what happened to her.

Hmm, I sense my desire to meddle improperly here growing and my concentration on what is truly important waning.

Yes, I must leave soon. I can take a coach to an inn on the outskirts of London and plot how to get a message to Celia. Certainly, Mr. Shiverly's coins will keep two intelligent girls alive until we can decide how we are to support ourselves in the long term.

Looking out, Honora admired the apple orchard to the east, its gnarled trees having lost most of their leaves. To the west, she noticed a rose bush that stood alone near a hillock. A few white blossoms lit its branches with a merry glow in the grayish gloom, but it seemed strange in its solitary placement.

It looks as out of place there as I feel here.

Perhaps tomorrow will be dry and I can strike out then. But good lord, what to do in the meantime?

A sudden movement in the yard caught her eye as Clayton emerged from the stables. Wrapped in his greatcoat, he strode quickly to the house on a path that ran the length of the gallery. She noted that his reddish hair was a shade lighter than Barclay's.

What a swaggering fellow this one is! Honora thought, recalling how he had badgered Barclay at supper the night before. Witnessing it, she had formulated several responses to him – all of them completely inappropriate to deliver to a fellow at his own supper party.

Just feet away from her now, he was startled at the sight of her face in the window. He smirked and she lifted her hand in apologetic salutation. Then he had passed and Honora heard the heavy front door shut followed by his footsteps in the foyer. They diminished as he made his way elsewhere.

Where is *everyone? Barclay? Jasper?*

The strangeness of her isolation became nearly oppressive before other footfalls, these much lighter, reached her ears. She lifted her forehead from the coolness of the glass pane.

Martha stood ten feet away.

Honora uprighted herself. Pulling her sleeve down over her knuckles, she began to rub the window where her face had rested, murmuring, "So sorry. Don't want to leave a smear."

"May I be of service to you?" the woman asked brusquely. Her manners were more direct and authoritative than those of the servants at Stagsdown House.

Eliza might have called her brazen, Honora thought. *And I might have agreed with her for once!*

As the woman stood stiffly nearby, Honora once again sensed that the servant's disapproval of her. It verged on wariness.

"I did not wrench my ankle by design," she thought to say.

Yet, I do understand she probably does not know what to make of me. Last night, when she insisted I go down and join the family and their guests for supper, she did not seem to actually believe that I ought to. And here she is asking if she can be of service to me though I suspect she'd rather chivvy me to go polish the silver.

But no, I shan't play games with servants. I'll be honest with her. Her response is her own concern.

"Actually, yes," Honora sighed, looking around the gallery restlessly. She did not ask where the younger Durbin brothers were, though she suspected the maid knew. Instead, she said, "I find myself in need of occupation."

"The parlor is full of books and solitary games."

"I thank you, however it is not entertainment I seek, but rather *useful* activity. I cannot please myself with such idleness."

Immediately, shame flooded Honora's heart.

"Forgive me. I mean no ingratitude to the Durbins and their generosity."

Martha reached to straighten the flowers in the vase just beyond Honora's left shoulder while stiffly asking, "Would you like to bake another mile-high treat?"

Honora wondered if she was being mocked.

"Thank you," she responded. "But I believe that half of yesterday's remains. It was silly of me to make such a large croquembouche as there were only eight of us at supper last night!"

She watched to see if her self-deprecation would soften Martha's demeanor – which it did not – then continued, "And I was hoping to do something of greater import."

At these words, Martha flinched as if suddenly prodded.

"I know just the thing! A family in the village has lost their little boy to a fit. The mother is out of her mind with suffering, yet there're other little ones to feed. Bess has sent over a huge pot of stew, but if you baked some fresh bread to fill up their bellies a bit more, that would make the heart of God smile, to be sure."

"Oh, yes!" Honora said, a weighty mix of concern and inspiration filling her. The maid's altered demeanor surprised and pleased her. "You say there are other children?"

"One boy and two girls."

"What are the girls' ages?"

"'Bout seven and nine, I'd suppose."

Immediately Honora thought of how alone and sad she felt when she lost her mother at the age of ten.

That's when Polly pulled me into the kitchen and taught me to bake my first tart – apples and custard.

A thought struck her.

"Martha, could you bring those girls here so I could make the bread *with* them? They'd probably like a stint out of their grieving household. Oh!" She stopped and bit her lip. "Good lord, that's a bit much to ask of Bess, isn't it? Two more strangers invading her kitchen?"

Honora saw Martha's eyes brighten as never before.

"Do not worry about that, Miss. Bess is the good sort. Hers is a big kitchen and I'm sure you can keep two little girls out of her way. I'll send for them straight away."

Instantaneously, Martha strode away and out one of the gallery's many doors.

Oh, dear. Have I just lost Bess's goodwill? Honora thought, the emptiness of the room once again pressing in on her. *I shall now go discover my fate.*

It took her several minutes to wamble her way through the house, her ankle smarting with the effort. As she entered the kitchen, Bess looked up from the pot she was scouring with a smile. "Morning, Miss!"

"Good morning, Bess."

"What'll you be making today? A marchpane castle?" The portly woman chortled at her own suggestion.

Honora obliged her with a simper, then answered, "I was thinking something a bit more nourishing and less grand. Some Brentford Rolls[vii], perhaps."

"Oh? I was 'bout to start a batch of white baps myself, but if yours are as beauteous as your cakes, then by all means, conjure 'em up! I'll get you what you'll be needing."

The cook wiped her hands on her apron and bustled right and left, plunging her strong arms into the cabinets to retrieve ingredients and implements which she placed on the table. Before she had finished, Martha suddenly appeared in the doorway. Behind her were two frightened looking, skinny girls, their hair pulled back in tight plaits, rivulets of rainwater running down their faces.

"What's this then, Martha?" Bess asked, her smile vanquished.

"Ned Bryer's girls, Bess. They who just lost their brother. Miss Honora's going to teach them how to bake a bit of something to cheer their mumma. Isn't that right, girls?"

The taller girl barely nodded, her wide eyes scanning the kitchen. The other stood petrified, clutching her sister's hand.

"Hmm, I see," Bess said, her eyes narrowed, her lips pursed.

Come now, Bess. You have a heart! Honora thought, willing the cook to welcome the children. When a moment passed and the woman had neither welcomed nor banished them, Honora took charge.

"Over here, girls. Warm yourselves by the oven for a moment, but we must stay out of Bess's way as she has much important work to do."

The youngsters tiptoed over to stand beside Honora who made a hasty introduction of herself. She learned, though it was all stated in low, tremulous voices that the girls were called Mary and Susan.

"Very good, my dears. Now the first thing we must do, is wash our hands thoroughly, so please step this way and we'll all give ours a good scrub."

ANSWERING UNCLE ALLARD

BARCLAY STARTED AS his bedroom door was flung wide open.

"Of course, here you are!" Clayton exclaimed, shaking his head at the sight of Barclay sitting beside the window. "Will you stare out at the drizzle with that Bible open in your lap all morning? If I didn't know any better, I'd think you were hiding. Emily and Leticia are gone, God be thanked! Next time Richard wants to come to shoot, I'll request he leave that squawking pair behind in their cages. By the by, whilst you are tucked away up here, there is a hobbled bird in the gallery looking very dull indeed – probably longing for some attention from a fellow who carted her here all the way from London."

Barclay threw his brother a sharp look.

Were my feelings evident last night even to an inebriate such as Clayton?

"Why do you dig at me this way?" Barclay knew he sounded like Jasper when he was very cross, but was too frustrated to amend his tone. "There can be no future in it."

"There *could* be if you took the damn curacy at Southby, you blockhead!"

Barclay felt amazed hope dawning over his face. "Is that so?"

"Well, it would be right in God's eyes," Clayton laughed, reaching to tweak his brother's ear. "How Uncle Allard's eyes see it…well, that would likely remain unknown until you ask him."

Marry Miss Honora? We hardly know one another. Would she have me? And how could I possibly be content making sermons amongst those slumbering masses?

"I must think on it longer" Barclay said, running his hands through his hair.

"Ugh, Barclay!" Clayton sighed in exasperation as he turned back to the door. "My uncle is likely to *demand* an answer very soon. Last he spoke of it, he said he could have you set up there within a fortnight. God knows why he's so intent on securing *you* for the placement – he may change his mind at any moment! And keep to mind that Miss Honora's ankle is healing every day. Soon there will be no reason for her to stay any longer."

"Clay!" Barclay called out as his brother was about to disappear. "What do you think Mamma would say of such an arrangement?"

"She'd be pleased to have you situated at Southby, and regarding marriage…" Clayton shrugged, a wry smile on his face. "Does it matter? *You're* the one who will be wedding and bedding whichever girl you end up with."

The door swung shut with a definitive click.

He speaks sense, though crassly. And truly, I've never known Mamma to scorn a person because of their lowly station in life.

But could I be content at Southby? With Miss Honora by my side, building a life with me, it would feel meaningful. Yet, it would certainly put an end to my going to Crawton Green.

An unwelcome thought that often pulled at his sleeve pushed itself to his mind's forefront.

When Martha recommended I go to preach to the downtrodden, I thought the plan providential, but what has it accomplished? Not a single sinner saved that I know of. Yes, the tracts are taken by grasping hands, but is that primarily because they make good fodder for the hob?

The only good I see from it is time spent with Jasper, a humbling of my own soul…and meeting Miss Honora.

A warmth spread through Barclay's chest.

Father, was meeting her the sole purpose of my trips to London all these months?

Something deep within him told him this was true and his heart began to pound.

Honora's in the gallery, is she?

Feeling suddenly heartened, he stowed his Bible upon its shelf and was about to set out to find her when his eyes fell suddenly on Uncle Allard's letter, pushed aside on his desk.

Nearly a week, and I have yet to answer him. Perhaps he has cast his wandering eye elsewhere already. That would serve me right for my negligence!

Scratching his head over how to answer him, Barclay sat down and took out his writing implements. After crumpling two dissatisfying drafts which he tossed into the fireplace, he finally determined to simply be forthright and wrote:

My esteemed uncle—

Please forgive my tardy response. My only excuse is in not knowing how to answer your thoughtful and generous offer. As you spoke plainly with me, I shall return the courtesy.

I am hesitant to become your curate, not for lack of appreciation of you or the benefits such an arrangement would afford me, but for two specific reasons.

The first is, my frustration with my classmates at Cambridge. Perhaps when you were at University, the halls there were not filled with dissolute, debauched creatures as they are now. I grieve to think on the men who are England's future celebrants of Christian charity and duty. Therefore, I am reluctant to align myself with this up-and-coming generation of clergy.

My second disinclination to donning a surplice at Southby is because God has made it clear to me that I am not intended for celibacy. Though you spoke in the past of me living with you in the rectory, I cannot presume the offer would be extended to a potentially much larger party, resulting in your resentment of myself, my future bride and our offspring.

By drawing these two issues to the fore, I hope to explain myself and give you an opportunity to address them. Again, uncle, I mean no ingratitude nor disrespect by my reluctance, as I am ever your

appreciative yet prudent nephew –
Barclay

Reading over what he had just written, Barclay was pleased as he lidded the inkwell. It was not a complete explanation as he made no mention of his dissatisfaction in Southby's congregation – but he had successfully delivered his criticism of clergymen away from Uncle Allard and his ilk by directing it at his own peers. Also, he did not blush at his pronouncement that he must marry at some point – the certainty of that conviction was too strong to be ignored.

With a prayer and a flourish of his pen, Barclay wrote the direction across an envelope and stuffed the letter inside before sealing it with a weighty blob of maroon wax. The splotch of colour on the paper's pale edge was still warm as he left his room. Once he was down the stairs and had put the letter on the credenza with the other outgoing correspondence, he went in search of Honora.

He pondered excuses for his morning absence that would be honest without sounding insipid, but when he stepped into the gallery she was not there. Though he then went from room to room looking for her, it was all in vain.

Surely, she is still at Singer Hall, he encouraged himself, looking out a window at the drear. *She might be in her room, but of course I cannot meet with her there.*

The kitchen!

With renewed vigor, he made his way to the room that would most obviously hold her.

Bess looked up from the pullet she was trussing, surprised and clearly a bit aggravated at his appearance in the doorway. Past her, Honora sat on a stool next to two young girls who looked vaguely familiar to Barclay. She was speaking quietly to them as they each folded and kneaded their own great blob of dough on the tabletop. Their smiling faces were dusted with flour.

"Good morning, Miss Honora. Girls." He ducked his head as he stepped over to them. "You are all very busy indeed! Might I ask what you are doing?"

"Miz Honora's teachin' us ta make Bentfud Rolls!" the older girl said as the smaller girl nodded shyly, their hands working inexpertly.

Barclay turned to look full on at Honora. "Is she?"

Her face was full of its usual good grace and humour.

"Yes, *Brentford* Rolls," she said with a smile. "They're going to take them home to their mother and father to be paired with the nourishing soup Bess sent over earlier."

Across the kitchen, Bess grunted and carried on with her fowl and twine.

"Well, I shall leave you to it," Barclay said, exceedingly pleased. With another glance at Honora's pretty face – flushed with the exertion of kneading – he retraced his steps out of the kitchen in search of the atlas in the library as he wanted to study the geography around Southby.

TO SEE THE SEA

THE MOMENT HONORA came into the breakfast room the next morning, she saw it, and her heart sank. She had sensed it the evening before at supper, but with the Durbin's gathered around the table energetically discussing the Bradfords' visit, it had not thrust itself forward. Now, as she entered the quiet room, there on Barclay's face, plain as a cloudless sunrise, was his obvious appreciation of her. It lifted his head, lit his eyes, and softened his mouth. He was up on his feet instantaneously to pull out her chair as she made her way toward the table. Clayton was there as well, silently reading a newspaper, his feet propped up on his end of the table.

Once Barclay had regained his own seat, his gaze remained riveted upon her face, as if any other thing or activity in the room was superfluous to her mere existence.

"Did you sleep well, I hope?" he asked, motioning for Martha to pour Honora some tea.

"Yes. I thank you," she responded quietly, nodding in appreciation at the servant as the steaming golden arc spilled into her teacup.

She had, of course, noted hints of his interest in her flittering across his honest face as they nattered on together at Crawton Green. There, it had been flattering, amusing, but as inconsequential as a passing breeze. Here however, in his own home, it had gale-force potential.

What further complicated things was that he had saved her, and from so much more than he could possibly know!

Honora tried to look anywhere but at him while the silver domes of covered platters shone in the morning light on the table between

191

them. She lifted the teacup to her lips and bit its rim, anxiously.

This is all so like Stagsdown House, she thought, peering around at the damask curtains on the windows and the ebonized Scafe clock ticking away quietly on the mantle. *And not only due to the costly furnishings.*

At Stagsdown House, on more than one occasion, Honora had had to deflect the attention of various young men. To describe their attention as *unwanted* would not be accurate, as Honora found any instance of being preferred gratifying. However, even as a little girl, she had learned that no attention paid to her by any of the gentry's boys could ever amount to anything.

When she was nine, Lord Flathom had brought his three sons, ages five, ten and twelve, to Stagsdown House for a week's time. The kindness Honora showed to the youngest boy earned her his undying devotion. Her willingness to build a fort in the lakeside mud – the progress of which little Lady Eliza had pettishly watched from the upper lawn – had gained her much esteem in the minds of the elder two.

On the Flathoms' final night, as they prepared to play at Pick Up Sticks before supper in the rose parlour, all the boys were arguing over who could claim Honora as a teammate. She overheard the adults chuckling as they observed the fracas.

"She's a favourite. That's for certain!"

"Yes, but that won't help her in the long run, will it?" Lord Beeman had said under his breath. "She's intended for a governess,"

"Ah, yes," Flotham had muttered regrettably. "Such girls don't stay in favour for long, do they?"

She had pretended not to have heard, but even then, Honora had understood. She was not of their class, and though the boys found her entertaining now, they would eventually view her as a lesser being, ultimately as someone to be disregarded.

And Barclay has no idea where I've spent the last few weeks, she thought, taking a tentative sip of the scalding tea and glimpsing him over the rim of the cup. He faintly smiled as their eyes met.

I could put an end to this bewitchment at this moment by divulging the facts of my last month! How his head would spin!

"What plans have you made for the day?" Clayton asked peering over his paper at Barclay before his eyes drifted knowingly over to Honora.

Good lord! Is he in on this as well?

At this moment, Jasper interrupted, stumbling into the breakfast room, his vibrant hair a comical mess. Yawning enormously, he gazed out the window, then absent-mindedly noted, "G'morning. Sea fog's rolling in."

Gratefully, Honora seized on this distraction.

"Does it often drift in this far from shore?" she asked as Jasper lowered himself into a chair.

"Quite often in autumn. Too often, really."

"Oh," she said, peering out at the gray mist. "Well, I think it lovely, so cooling and mysterious."

Barclay perked at her enthusiasm. "It's even more so when you're enveloped in its midst."

"*Amidst the mist?*" Honora joked, then thoughtfully said, "I have never seen the sea."

"What?" the younger brothers said together and looked at one another.

"Well, that must be rectified," Jasper said, grinning boyishly at Barclay.

"Yes, indeed." Barclay said, a smile spreading across his face. "*At once.*"

Clayton's face was again obscured as he dryly said, "Well, it seems you now have plans for the day."

The thought of journeying to the seaside thrilled Honora. Each summer, Lord Beeman and Lady Eliza would return from Weymouth to rave about the long stretch of warm golden sand and the row of large-wheeled bathing machines all lined up along the water's edge. This day, Honora knew would not afford the warmth nor a dip in the waters, but just to see the massive expanse would be something to remember for a lifetime.

But would it be wise to go? Seeing me with beads of sea mist clinging to my tresses might enamor Mr. Barclay further.

Honora nearly giggled at the absurd notion though she couldn't deny its possibility.

Pushing his empty plate away, Barclay left to ready the gig as Jasper swallowed his breakfast quickly.

Moments later, as Jasper and Honora made their way toward the front door, Mrs. Durbin was descending the stairs.

"Good morning!" she called cheerily. "Where are you off to?"

"The seaside!" Jasper replied.

"In this weather?" His mother asked, her wide eyes turning to the windows that flanked the house's entrance.

Jasper grasped the door handle. "Well yes, as at breakfast, Miss Honora divulged the shameful truth that she has never ever seen the sea."

"Ah, so you're not just spewing nonsense!" She smiled. "But wait! Miss Honora will need something warmer than that."

Earlier, Honora had considered this herself, but was willing to forego warmth in pursuit of the plan.

"Martha?" Mrs. Durbin alerted the servant who was standing by the door. "Please go fetch one of my warmer pelisses and a matching bonnet for Miss Honora as the sun may make an appearance later."

Honora could not help but notice a souring of Martha's face before she headed up the staircase to complete Mrs. Durbin's bidding.

Why are some servants displeased by a mistress' kind attentions to someone of a lower class? Does Martha consider me unworthy of warmth? She was pleased enough yesterday when I taught Mary and Susan to bake.

Ah! Perhaps because teaching the girls did not put me in such near proximity to a certain young man. She thinks I'm setting my cap for him.

Aloud, Honora thanked Mrs. Durbin for her thoughtful generosity.

"Say nothing of it," the woman replied as she continued toward the breakfast room. "Enjoy yourselves, remembering you're only young once!"

WEE BABY MOSES

BY THE TIME Honora and Jasper arrived at the yard, Dervy had rigged up a simple but sturdy ramp that would enable Honora to more easily board the gig. It could be collapsed and stowed in the gig itself, then easily reconstructed so that throughout their journey, she could disembark and reboard with little trouble.

When Barclay, Honora and Jasper were finally situated and departing the grounds of Singer Hall, much of the fog had burned off. A moderate breeze blew, making the ribbons framing Honora's face to dance about.

Barclay recognized the bonnet and pelisse that Honora wore as his mother's. Though it was finely made, and the colours complimented her complexion, he wondered what Honora would look like in something cut for her figure and of a style more appropriate for someone her age. Still, even encased in rather billowing, dowdy garments, her beguiling vivacity shone through.

Jasper began to talk excitedly, asking Honora many questions. Thus, Barclay learned about her, pleased that he never once appeared to be prying himself due to his inquisitive brother. She had grown up in a lord's household, having been born to his steward. First, she was bereft by the death of her mother, then more recently orphaned entirely by the passing of her father. They learned of her father's intention for Honora to become a governess that she would have a ready way to support herself throughout life, and thus the extensive education she had received alongside the lord's daughter.

"As interesting as that all is," Jasper said after nearly an hour, "it does not answer how you came to be in London, forever carrying a basket past the green we ourselves frequent."

"Oh, well," Honora looked flustered. "I...I simply decided I did not want to be the governess that they all had intended for me to be, so I left Stags – my childhood home and set out to find employment."

"And you found it buying produce for a place near Crawton Green?"

Barclay saw her blink and swallow, wondering if she had come to regret leaving her home.

"Yes. And you? I have been talking all this while," she said. "Tell me of yourselves."

"Us?" Jasper lifted his eyebrows. "There is not much to tell! Born to John Durbin of Singer Hall, to be educated at Heath School for Boys for far too many years. As you must know, because we are the two youngest brothers, we need to find our own ways in the world as a limited inheritance is all either of us can expect."

Barclay suppressed a smile at Jasper's succinct summary of their situations.

"And which direction have you determined to go, Jasper?" Honora asked archly, seemingly as entertained as Barclay felt. "Will you distinguish yourself in the military? Politically? Or in trade and commerce, perhaps?"

Apparently unaware of the amusement he was providing to his travel mates, Jasper replied, "That remains a source of mystery to me which I hope to soon resolve. Clayton is not mean and has promised to help me find a tolerable solution."

"Has Clayton rendered any assistance to *you*, Barclay?" Honora asked, turning to look at him.

Jasper answered as Barclay drew breath to respond. "Uncle Allard has, but Barclay wants none of it."

"Uncle Allard?" Honora's eyebrows rose coyly. "Did he seek to establish you as a miller by a stream? Or a haberdasher, perhaps?"

"In the church, actually."

"Oh? And you *declined*?" Her surprise was obvious. "The church was my first thought for you! I would think you'd like making sermons, seeing as you do so often on Crawton Green."

Perhaps I haven't declined, Miss Honora. You may hold the key to that!

"Well, I hesitate because the placement he's offered would put me in the midst of people whose souls I'm not concerned for – though I mourn for their characters." Realizing how judgmental this sounded, he added. "I want to help those for whom the benefit would be more apparent – the poor, the needy."

Again, Jasper butted in. "Barclay's always wanted to help people – even dead people."

"Jasper!" Barclay exclaimed, knowing what story was about to be told but disliking the way it was being introduced.

"Help *dead* people!" Honora cried, laughing aloud. "And what service can you render those who breath no longer? An extra pillow for their casket?"

"Dead babies, actually," Jasper said.

Barclay shook his head in embarrassment. "So macabre! In truth, Jasper, that story was not shared with you that you might frighten young ladies."

"I am not the least bit frightened, but *am* utterly intrigued." Honora leaned forward. "Do go on, Mr. Jasper."

It was with a mixture of pride and discomfort that Barclay listened to his younger brother retell – in mostly correct detail – an incident that had occurred nearly sixteen years earlier, when Barclay was seven and Jasper had not yet been born. As it was relayed to Honora, Barclay recalled it with acuity as it was one of the most formative moments of his life.

One day when he and Clayton were returning to Singer Hall after a fruitless morning of fishing at the pond, they came across a small bundle on the front doorstep. Thinking it nothing more than a pile of rags, Barclay had nearly stepped over it and into the house.

Why would a servant leave laundry here? He had wondered, glancing down at the loose cloths. His body froze. There was a tiny, still face amongst the folds of fabric.

Seeing it in the same instant, Clayton had gasped and drawn back.

It was an infant's face, the eyes closed and the lips retracted from the tiniest dark cavern of a mouth imaginable.

"Wha...what's he...?" Clayton had stuttered as he continued to examine the little person from a distance.

"He's like Wee Baby Moses," Barclay breathed softly, crouching over the stoop.

"But with no basket," responded Clayton, who stretched out his foot to nudge the baby's rigid hand, frozen into a little fist. Though the gesture was done gently, Barclay wanted to swat his brother's foot away.

Instead, he peered uneasily at the tiny bundle, noting the grayish skin, and how the closed eyelids were wrinkled a bit over the orbs underneath them. The lips, perfectly formed, were parted slightly, revealing a ridge of whey-coloured gums.

"He's dead," Clayton had declared solemnly.

"No! You think so?" Barclay asked, his stomach sinking. He studied the blanket over the chest. It didn't move. Neither did the tiny fist or lips.

So he is! Barclay had thought, marveling at the wholeness and fine detail of even dead creatures, his heart racing in his chest. "Where'd he come from?"

"Dunno." Clayton shrugged.

Had the brothers bothered to unwrap the tattered cloth, they would have seen that the infant was actually a girl, but the thought of touching it was repulsive.

"But why would someone just...*drop* him here?" Barclay's last three words quavered as the thought of abandonment struck him.

"Perhaps he was dead beforehand and his Mamma didn't have a coin to pay the digger. He's a piddly little thingy."

Yes, maybe he was dead beforehand, Barclay had considered. The thought was slightly comforting as he imagined himself on a doorstep, dead and therefore unable to see his mother's back as she walked away, leaving him behind. *But why drop him* here? *Why at* our *door?*

Ah! Perhaps because Mamma lives here. All the people in the villages know of her kindness.

Clayton's toe slowly edged forward toward the baby's bare cheek.

Prepared this time, Barclay would not allow it. Reaching out, he surprised even himself by lifting the bundled infant from the step, away from the looming foot, and stood.

Never before had his brother, two years his senior, looked at him with such awe and respect. He felt proud for an instant, knowing Clayton thought him brave, but then was hit by a shameful realization.

I cannot hold you close to me, Wee Moses, Barclay silently apologized to the nominal weight in his outstretched hands. *You have nothing, yet I cannot even give you that.*

There was one kindness he could give the baby, however.

"I'm taking him to Mamma," he had announced, his shaking arms stretched out before him.

Still stunned into silence, Clayton had opened the front door for his brother.

As if in a dream, Barclay walked through the entry and drifted down the passageway to the parlor where he knew his mother would be, most likely leaning over her writing desk.

Rushing ahead of him, Clayton opened that door, too, and Barclay entered. She was just where he had predicted.

Mrs. Durbin had looked up from the paper in front of her, a look of unperturbed inquiry on her face.

"What have you there, darling?" she asked as her eyes rested on the tiny burden Barclay bore.

"It was on the front doorstep," Clayton explained solemnly.

"What is it?" she asked, her eyebrows lifting in question, a small smile on her lips. But as Barclay drew closer, she gasped and sprung out of her chair, reaching to take the bundle.

"Whose…? Where…? Oh, little one…" Cradling it in the crook of her arm, she tenderly touched the little cheek. Beginning to weep, she had murmured, "It's gone already."

Barclay watched as his mother rocked the baby, clutched next to her bosom.

That is how one ought to hold a baby, he had thought as his mother's weeping suddenly swelled into sobs.

"Ought I not to have brought him to you?" he asked, tears welling in his own eyes. "Mamma?"

His mother had looked up, bewildered, as if remembering Barclay was there and stifled her cries.

"You did well, my dear." She reached out to touch Barclay's cheek.

He willed himself not to draw back though it was the same hand that had been stroking the dead baby's face.

"You did exactly what you ought." Her voice caught. "You found him on the doorstep, you say?"

"Yes, Mamma."

Barclay watched as his mother wiped her eyes, saying, "You two, go to Bess. Tell her you need some warm posset as you've had a horrible fright."

She smiled wanly through her tears at the boys, then hurried toward the door. "And should you see your father, tell him what has happened and that I've gone to find the…the poor mother. Oh, the poor, dear mother!"

Sobbing again, and with the tiny bundle cradled in her arms, she rushed out of the door and down the hallway.

Shaken at witnessing the ferocity of his mother's emotion and the lingering sensation of the dead infant in his arms, Barclay had stood quietly, resting his quivering hand upon the back of the settee.

Feet away, Clayton had solemnly studied the face of his brother for several moments.

"You picked him up," he uttered with such a voice that Barclay realized Clayton hadn't even *thought* of doing it himself. Here was his strong, brave, elder brother, openly marveling at his courage.

For years after, Clayton would occasionally mention to friends at school that Barclay had once carried a dead baby through the house and every time, Barclay's chest would swell as all eyes turned toward him curiously.

Relishing the sensation of having been heroic, he had determined that he would spend his life doing this again and again.

Now, here was Jasper, regaling a young woman with the tale, ending with, "So, though he was only seven years old, he carried – what did you call it? Wee Baby Moses? – into the house and down the hall to our mother. And *that* is the sort of brother I have!"

It seems I have impressed my brothers most thoroughly with what I accomplished as a child! Barclay lamented.

Honora looked thoughtful, no longer jovial, as she turned to face Barclay.

"Do you recall much from that day?"

"Every moment," Barclay responded truthfully.

She tilted her head to one side and Barclay perceived a softening in her eyes as she looked at him. "And why is that?"

It seemed a strange question, but Barclay was pleased to consider it for a moment before replying, "If I hadn't felt how light and seemingly inconsequential an entire human being can be when lifted, then I don't think I would now value God's goodness as thoroughly as I do. Nor would I be so concerned that all might experience it."

"Hmm," Honora said. Then quietly, "And what of the mother? Was she found?"

"No. In spite of an inquiry around several villages, she was not. Thus, Wee Baby Moses was laid in an oaken box with a fine, soft blanket. A deep hole was dug in our southern lawn to receive him. There is a rosebush there for his headstone."

Rounding a curve in the road, a thatch-roofed public house came into their view.

"Ah! And here we are now at the Black Swan!" Barclay said. "We always have our dinner here on journeys to the sea as the pigeon pie is especially tender and flavorful, though you may choose something else of course."

"Pigeon pie sounds delightful," Honora responded.

Thinking they would eat upon the gig-seat, he steered the carriage to a shady spot under a large oak. Pulling the horse to a stop, he took a few coins from his pocket and handed them to Jasper.

"Tell Barbara we'll be having a picnic out here today."

As his brother hopped down, leaving him alone with Miss Honora, Barclay couldn't help but turn to gaze at her though he had no words to say. It seemed – though he may have been imagining it – that the look she returned to him was softer and more lingering than before.

Does she think more highly of me now? What magic does the story of Wee Baby Moses possess that all who hear it regard me differently?

The familiar feeling that perhaps all of his courage had been spent in his seventh year during that one act gripped him. Another memory badgered him, one of shame.

When Barclay had first arrived at Heath at the age of ten, a boy – one year his elder named Biles – had fixated on him.

"Little Durbin", he had dubbed Barclay, which was not an unlikely appellation since Clayton also attended the school. But the way in which Biles pronounced it, with a sneer, made it seem an insult. He would wait for Barclay after dinner when Clayton and his friends were headed across campus to Latin class. When Barclay emerged from the refectory alone, Biles would stride up to him, tousle his hair roughly and ask, "Looks like you ate too many carrots again today, Little Durbin! When will you learn?" Then he would shove Barclay into the stone wall and run off laughing. So often did this occur that Barclay took to dashing out of the dining hall to avoid the encounters. The predation confused Barclay because he had seen Biles himself harassed by a group of older boys.

Why does he not want to be friends? he had wondered. *Then we could walk together and perhaps neither of us would be pestered.*

One day at dinner, the cook served pretty biscuits, dotted with chopped cherries and pecans. So taken was Barclay with them, that he tucked an extra one into his hand and left the hall distracted by his good fortune. Twelve steps out of the door, he saw Biles – his chin up and chest puffed out.

"What have you got there, Little Durbin?" he had asked, advancing on Barclay, herding him into a corner. "Does the little baby like his treats?"

Recalling his mother's frequent recitation that 'charity shall cover the multitude of sins', Barclay's heart had pounded as he extended the biscuit to the boy and said, "I've already had one, if you'd like this one. It's very nice, with cherries and such."

Biles's eyes had flickered, and Barclay had supposed himself victorious until Biles suddenly spat liberally upon the offering. Barclay watched disbelievingly as the viscous blob of saliva dripped in all directions, over the sides of the golden delicacy, onto his hand.

"Since you like baby biscuits so much, eat *this* one," Biles had said.

Aghast, Barclay had shaken his head.

Biles had grabbed him by the collar and shoved him up against the wall.

"I said, *eat it,*" he said, raising his free hand in a fist, ready to arc it down into Barclay's face. "Now."

Barclay gripped the dripping biscuit so tightly that it began to crumble. Looking around, he saw no one nearby to deliver him from his tormentor.

"*Now,*" Biles had breathed through gritted teeth.

Quaking with fear, Barclay lifted the biscuit to his lips and took a little bite of the dry part.

"The whole thing," Biles insisted, his mouth twisting with demented pleasure.

Barclay had gagged again and again as he choked down the remainder, and Biles didn't lower his fist until it was gone.

"There now. Wasn't that delightful?" he had asked.

Barclay had said nothing in response. The bigger boy finally let go of him and walked away laughing, leaving Barclay alone and nauseous.

A month later, Biles had developed a raging stomach ache in mathematics class for which he had to be physically carried out of the room. The pupils were told at breakfast the next morning that Biles had died during the night, a fact for which Barclay felt strangely guilty due to the relief it brought him.

Shamed at his utter cowardice, Barclay had never told Clayton of the incident. He had in fact, never told anyone, not even Martha.

Now here beside him under the boughs of an oak tree on a beautiful morning was a lovely young woman who seemed impressed by his one heroic act of childhood while knowing nothing of the Biles story. Staring at the reins in his hands, he wondered if she would ever find him out.

HONORA'S MULLINGS

THE BLACK SWAN was a homey-looking hovel near the bank of a stream. As Honora sat upon the gig seat, the scent of roasted meats and baking pastry filled the air and she breathed in deeply.

Her hunger was immense as she had hardly eaten anything at breakfast since Barclay's admiring observance had sapped her appetite. Now, though it was only a few hours later, Honora knew something within her had shifted. She valued the gentle and mature way Barclay corrected Jasper's careless exuberance. Then, with the telling of the dead foundling story, Honora felt her heart blossoming toward him.

Even at such an early age, he sought to help the less fortunate. He is a genuinely good man, very different in disposition than Father, but similar in character.

The more she thought on it, the more pleased she was with having outed the true personality of Miss Leticia.

Now, Jasper was within the tavern and Barclay was looking earnestly at her again. This time it didn't worry her as much.

Oh, but careful there! she told herself. *Though he is a second-born, he is still a gentleman and you are naught but a steward's daughter.*

Suddenly, a coach pulled up beside them. Three travel-weary people spilled out its opening door. It looked to be a family – a husband and wife with their prepubescent daughter. The females walked about under the trees, stretching their legs. The postilion climbed atop the coach and began to hand down various boxes and bags along with a trunk to the man, who placed them all at the base of a large oak.

Within moments, the coach was in motion again, veering back onto the thoroughfare, leaving the family behind.

"We'll be wanting some dinner then, as we wait for the hackney," the man said to the woman, then ventured toward the inn. Jasper held the door open for him as he himself was just exiting.

The girl, drawn now to examine the boxes and bags beside the tree, suddenly exclaimed, "Mamma, it's not here!"

"What's that, Jane?" asked the woman.

The girl roughly upended every object before her, then burst into tears exclaiming, "I'm telling you, my writing box is not here! I must have left it in the coach."

The commotion was such that Honora felt no shame in staring. Barclay, too, was engrossed for a moment until he sat upright, struck with an idea. Hopping down from the gig, he unhitched Caleb and said to Jasper, "Jass – ride after that coach that's just left and get the girl's writing box."

Turning back to the frantic girl, he asked, "What colour? Where was it left? On the seat or in the rear boot?"

With hope now glistening more brightly in her eyes than her tears, the girl answered, "Cherrywood. Likely under the rear seat."

Jasper was astride the bareback horse already, repeating the description quietly to himself, then hawing the horse into swift motion down the dusty road. The fluid movements were done with such ease, that Honora's wistful eyes steadily held sight of him and the horse as they rounded the bend and disappeared.

"You men are awash in freedoms that women can only dream of," she murmured.

"Hmm?" Barclay asked, turning to look at her.

"No woman would be allowed to do that," she responded, flicking her hand in the direction Jasper had gone after the carriage. "Even if she possessed the skill to hop on a horse and ride pell-mell after a coach – and he is but fourteen! In fact, no woman could even sit here prim and still to purchase and await a roasted joint of beef alone without raising suspicion or lewd thoughts."

The words, nearly whispered, she realized were nothing more than her own contemplation as Barclay studied her face.

And yet, my thoughts have value. If he merely wants to look upon me, admire my figure as it walks across a garden, then I am actually nothing to him.

She met his intent eyes as he said, "I am sorry society is unjust to your sex in this way."

Surprised at his perceptiveness, Honora said nothing.

At this moment, a woman then exited the Swan bearing a heavily laden tray and headed straight for the Durbin's gig.

"Ah, thank you, Barbara," Barclay said as she handed up to him three hefty portions of pigeon pie and three flagons of small beer.

"It's nothin', sir," the frowsy blonde answered, smiling warmly.

"Your pigeon pie could never be called 'nothing'!" Barclay responded as he offered a wooden plate of it to Honora. "I've dreamt of it in my absence."

"It's bin too long since ya come by. I's sayin' ta Robin jes' th'other day, 'It's been long since we seen the Coppery Gent'men'. Glad yer 'ere now! That li'l brothera yers 'as grown!"

Barbara chuckled, shading her eyes as she looked up at him, then turned her gaze to take in Honora. Saying nothing, the woman's eyes glowed mischievously and Honora saw her wink at Barclay before turning to make her way over the yard, back to the Swan's front door.

"No sense in letting it cool while we await Jasper's return," Barclay said, lifting a forkful of steaming tender crust and gravy to his lips. Honora did likewise.

Ah! she thought. *We are alone together at last!*

Swallowing, Honora put her fork aside and said, "Mr. Barclay, I owe you an apology."

Chewing a very full mouthful, Barclay was only able to open his eyes wide questioningly in response.

"When I mentioned your future plans to open a school, I did not suspect it to be news to your family. You spoke of it so readily to me upon our first acquaintance, I had supposed it to be common knowledge, but seeing how Mr. Clayton responded...well, I do apologize."

Vigorously shaking his head, Barclay was finally able to say, "Please do not worry yourself. Clayton is forever teasing me, so if it hadn't been over that subject, it would have been another."

"It *is* an admirable venture," Honora said, about to take a bite. "I hope that someday you will be able to help the less fortunate in the ways that you desire."

"It did not escape my notice that *you* were doing something of a similar nature just yesterday with Ned Bryer's girls," Barclay said thoughtfully. "What I hope to do in the future, *you* are doing already!"

"Hopefully Bess wasn't grossly offended at the invasion of her kitchen!" Honora forked a hot chunk of fowl into her mouth.

"Ah, Bess!" Barclay laughed. "She has a good heart, though she *is* possessive over her territory!"

Suddenly, Jasper was cantering back into the yard, a plume of dust billowing behind him and a small writing box clutched under his arm. This earned him a standing ovation from everyone under the oak trees as he slid from Caleb's back to the ground below.

"Thank the kind gentleman, Jane!" The mother exhorted, pushing the girl from behind. "He's done you such a service today!"

The girl came shyly forward to retrieve her recovered item. She murmured her thanks, and Jasper his demurring, their eyes never meeting in between.

Honora glanced at Barclay with a knowing smile, and murmured, "The young are so sweet in their awkward ways."

Putting his food aside, Barclay jumped down from the gig to take Caleb's reins, and Honora handed down a plate to Jasper.

"You sit a horse well, even with no saddle," she said.

Jasper shrugged, but Honora saw a faint blush across his cheeks as he began to quickly swallow his meal.

Once the plates had been emptied and returned to the Swan, the three recommenced their journey for the shoreline. After half an hour of light chatter and clopping along, the mist returned and thickened like porridge. Honora pulled the pelisse tighter around her shoulders.

Suddenly, she felt a change in the boys' alertness. They glanced at one another and were silent, speaking to each other only with their eyes as the gig passed through a stand of trees.

And there it was.

Honora gasped. The sea spread out before her, its gray immenseness stretching from right to left.

The ethereal mist rested lightly upon the water's surface, its tendrils reaching up onto the flat shoreline. A smooth expanse of beach stretched all the way from right to left, ruffled with multiple foamy waves which rushed onto the sand, then retreated just as quickly. The grayish blue bulk of fog floated above and beyond the reach of her eyes.

The enormous desolation of the sight struck Honora. A sense of loneliness and insecurity overwhelmed her.

What am I to do? My parents are dead. I've flouted the scheme that Lord Beeman made on my behalf. Polly knows nothing of my whereabouts. Celia knows only that I am gone from the Bower, but knows not why. The only kindness and consideration now shown to me is from the Durbins who are veritable strangers and who probably would cast me out the second they heard where I'd last been living!

The feeling could not be pushed aside and her eyes filled with tears. Dabbing the pelisse's sleeve against her eyelashes, she was mortified to realize both brothers were watching her.

Jasper turned away, clearly embarrassed as Barclay said, in a hushed tone, "I'm sorry we couldn't command the sun to shine brighter."

"Oh no, that is of no consequence, honestly," Honora replied, sniffing. "I...I miss my father."

It was true, though that was only a portion of her melancholy.

"Ah," Barclay said. "That we can understand, can't we, Jasper?"

The brothers bowed their heads as Honora continued to tidy her face, though the feeling lingered. Involuntarily, she shivered as if suddenly cold and was heartened to feel the boys lean in on either side as if to warm her.

"Please forgive me," she said, steadying her voice. "I am truly glad to have come here today."

"It's actually very nice on a sunny day, though it's far too cold to dip our feet in now," Barclay said somewhat apologetically. "That bit's not as mucky as it looks."

"It's lovely, just as I had expected," Honora said as Barclay began to turn the gig around.

As she adjusted the brim of the bonnet in the strengthening sun, she resolved to be cheerful all the way back to Singer Hall.

Their kindness has certainly earned them a return trip free of soppy sentimentality, she thought.

Within moments, Jasper had resumed regaling Honora with tales of his time at Heath School for Boys and she had rallied herself enough to laugh with sincerity.

THE SERPENTINE'S CENTER

CELIA'S EYES FLUTTERED open. She stared for a long moment at the ceiling as she realized anew that she was still in the Bower.

And Honora was still gone.

Today marks a full week, she thought though her eyes remained dry. Her tears had become fewer as the days had passed.

The room was brighter than when she normally rose to begin the laundry, but she did not bolt out of bed.

The linens will be washed, all in good time. And if they are not, what does it matter?

Slowly, she threw back the covers and stood, gripping the bed post as a faintness assailed her. Her already sparse appetite had all but disappeared in the previous few days. As she stood, awaiting the encroaching blackness to recede, she heard the tromping of hurried footsteps in the hall, followed by excited squeals.

The bedroom door flung open and a jubilant Molly burst in to declare, "Celia, we ain't got to work the whole day!"

"What?" Celia gripped the bedpost harder. "What can you mean?"

"I mean, the Princess Charlotte's died and Dovey's givin' us all day for mournin' and such!"

"Molly!" Dovey's voice boomed from downstairs, followed by the heavy but quick tread of her steps up the staircase.

A whole day off? Celia marveled. *Well, I shan't spend a moment of it here.* She began to dress herself.

Suddenly looming in the doorway with a wreath of black, silk flowers in her hand, Dovey scolded, "Thi*th* day i*th* meant to be *th*pent in *th*olemn contemplation."

With tears in her eyes, the bawd continued. "Fir*tht*, the royal baby, and now our very own prin*theth*."

Celia marveled, keeping her face impassive as she watched the woman dab at her nose with a handkerchief.

"Thi*th* day'*th* re*th*t will honor her…"

Ha! Honored by the likes of you! The princess would spit at you if she passed you on the street.

"…but we will re*th*ume bu*th*ine*th* tomorrow, a*th* many gentlemen will need comforting in thi*th* time of great lo*th*."

'Comfort'? Celia cringed as she folded her nightgown. *Is that what you've taken to calling what we do?*

"Now Molly, when you have dre*th*ed your*th*elf, I want your help hanging the mourning wreath*th* and the black draping*th*. Do not be long about it."

"Of course, Mrs. Dovey," Molly said with forced solemnity.

The girl's penitence contented Dovey who drifted down the hallway, but it evaporated instantaneously once the door was shut.

"Did you see 'er teeth?" Molly whispered, astounded.

Celia had hoped Molly would dress quickly and depart.

"They've gone gray as gravestones!"

"Hmm," Celia murmured, lifting the lavender gown over her head. As one who looked at Dovey as little as possible, she hadn't noticed.

"And she i*th* talkin' funny, a*th* well," Molly said in a perfect imitation of the procuress. "Surely you've 'eard that."

Celia nodded as she tied the sash and slipped on her shoes, thinking, *All of that from falling down the stairs?*

As she had done many times since the mysterious incident, Celia envisioned Dovey's toe catching on a step and her face colliding with the bannister. She smiled faintly as she smoothed her skirt over her petticoat. After tying her hair back, she headed out of the door, leaving Molly behind. Within half an hour, she was crunching along the gravel pathways of Hyde Park but the heaviness of her heart had returned in full force.

The remaining leaves on the trees, bright in their autumnal colour, drifted down from the high boughs on gentle breezes to rest on the ground below. The sky was a brilliant blue backdrop to a scattering of voluminous, high-flying white clouds which sailed by in lazy languor.

The beauty around Celia barely penetrated through the pall of her own personal grief. A few other amblers passed by, soberly contemplative, likely never guessing that the princess's death was the furthest thing from the mind of the somber, dark-haired girl they passed.

Nana is gone. Bill is as good as gone. And now Honora is gone.

Sunshine glinted on the Serpentine. As she stepped toward the dazzling vision, she saw a toy paper boat several yards from the shore, bobbing along. The sight of it instantly transported Celia back to the Grand Jubilee of 1814 when other miniaturized boats floating upon this very waterway had arrested her attention. On that first day of August, Nan had let her off laundering so that the Woodlow siblings could go to the park for the celebration.

"Come on! Let's get closer!" Bill had called back to her before disappearing into the crowd lining the Serpentine's banks.

I'm going to lose him! Celia had worried, pushing roughly into the horde. Though Bill knew the way around London better than she did, she felt responsible for the thirteen-year-old since she was a year his senior.

"Not so fast, Bill!" she had cried as he darted around the many tents set up upon the lawn.

There were dancing pigs in tutus, and tumblers who spun and whirled over the shorn grass in their bright blue and purple pantaloons. Bill's dark head dipped in and out of the throng, getting ever closer to the Serpentine.

Finally, he could go no further without swimming and Celia had caught up to him, plucking at his sleeve irritably. "Nan'll dunk my head in the tub if I return home without you."

Bill had grinned impishly, not penitent in the least.

"But we had to get to where we could watch the battle properly." He had pointed upriver. "Look at them, Celie!"

Many yards upstream, floated a fleet of miniature frigates. Each one bobbing about on the placid waters had three sailors aboard, waiting for a signal that would commence a reenactment of the Battle of the Nile.

"Well, I hope it starts soon," Celia had griped, "as I've got to piddle."

"Oh! Look!" Bill exclaimed. "There is Mr. Sadler!"

Following his pointing finger once again, Celia had shielded her eyes from the bright sun to see way up above them the dot of a red and yellow balloon drifting, its gondola-shaped basket hanging under it. She learned later, that the aeronaut had dropped little messages to the crowds below, tiny parachutes breaking their falls.

Seeing that Bill had no intention of helping her find somewhere to relieve herself, Celia had settled herself and tried to focus on the delicious smells wafting toward them from the many vendors' tents. Nan had packed them up some dinner but this didn't keep Celia from enjoying the rich scents of browned suckling pigs turning on spits over open fires, bits of their haunches sliced away. Offering oysters and whelks, some stalls had massive buckets besides them to collect the shucked shells. One tent just twenty feet from the riverbank had a large sign with red lettering. A man stumbled out from behind it as Celia read: **GIN - full drunk for 1 penny!**

In spite of her physical discomfort, she had felt a deep sense of contentment sitting there with her brother whose enthusiasm never ebbed for a moment. In good time, the mock battle had begun, startling Celia with the crack of guns firing from the miniaturized ships' quarterdecks. Soon, the *faux* French fleet sank into the Serpentine's depths to the triumphant sounds of music played by a merry band ashore. The masses around Celia had cheered so loudly, that her ears rang. She had never imagined such unified elation, but felt herself to be a part of it – she was proud to be English, thankful to be alive.

When finally the crowds had dissipated enough to make their way out, Celia had stood. Her legs were cramped from sitting so long that she nearly tumbled into the river, but Bill's hand had shot out to steady her. They had laughed together, though they knew their grandmother's patience at their absence was likely running out and that their remarkable day was quickly coming to an end.

Now, three years later, Celia looked at a spot alongside the Serpentine. *There. That may be right where I almost fell in.*

That seems so very long ago, she lamented, a fresh wave of grief overwhelming her. *And I am not the same girl that I was.*

Stepping to the edge, Celia stared down at the image of her face rippling across the water.

It looks as if I'm there, beneath the surface, she thought, noting the weariness in her eyes, the dangle of a single lock of hair, escaped from its knot.

What must it be like under the water?

She imagined the sensation of the river filling her mouth, her nostrils, her throat, her lungs.

A choking beyond all others. She shuddered. *And then – nothing.*

No more men. No more Dovey. No more wondering if Honora is alright.

But it would be horrible, horrible *for a moment before the endless nothing.*

How deep is *it?* She craned her neck to see out to its middle, but only the mirror-image of the perfect, autumnal sky met her intense gaze. She envisioned herself tossing her parasol aside onto the lawn, jumping into the water and thrusting herself toward that elusive center.

Looking around, she saw that no one stood nearby, ready to yank her dripping, sputtering person out of the watery depths and back into the nadir of her sorrow. The clamour inside her raged on, interrupted suddenly by the scurry of small feet across the embankment.

"It's here!" cried a happy little voice. "I've found it!"

Beside Celia had appeared a boy who looked to be about six years old. He wore a navy coloured skeleton suit, the many buttons across its front shining in the bright sunshine. Such was his joy that it could not be contained, and he shivered and trotted about in place, a frolicking caper that almost made Celia smile to see it.

"Thomas!" a far-off voice cried, at which the boy glanced over his shoulder.

"It's here!" he repeated with a wave of his arm, then crouched beside the water's edge.

The object of his intense interest, Celia soon surmised, was the white paper boat, which had evoked her memories and was drifting toward the shore. This was an especially large toy vessel with two sails. Impressively, it even had a little paper captain propped up against the mast, a hat upon his head.

The boat was slowly making its way toward the little boy's hands which were outstretched to pluck it up. But a sudden ripple across the surface of the water changed the boat's course just enough to keep it out of reach. Standing and brushing past Celia to stand on her other side, the child knelt again, ready to retrieve his prize. But the ship was now drifting back toward the Serpentine's center where Celia's dark thoughts had been focused only moments earlier.

"My boat!" the boy cried, looking up at Celia for the first time. His lower lip was pushed out in despair, but his eyes were full of hope as if he expected she would salvage the situation for him. Kneeling beside him, she grasped the end of the purple parasol and extended its curved handle out over the waters. Hooking the taller of the sails, she drew the toy toward them.

The boy clapped his hands together and squealed as only an excited child can. When it was near enough, he caught it up in his arms and gazed up at Celia with bright, sparkling eyes.

"You saved it!" he said, water dripping down the front of his little suit. "Thank you!"

"My pleasure," Celia replied, dipping her head.

"Mamma! Papa!" the boy shouted looking past Celia but pointing directly at her. "She saved it!"

"We saw, darling!" a woman's voice said, growing closer as it continued. "Perhaps you will never disparage a lady's parasol again, seeing what service it can render!"

Celia froze. She wanted no attention from any adult accompanying the boy.

"Miss?" the woman said, then more insistently at Celia's lack of response, "Miss?"

Turning slightly, Celia lifted her eyes. A rosy cheeked woman whose hair pins could not maintain hold of her frizzy chestnut hair stood feet away, her arm linked through that of a man.

"I thank you for your kindness to Thomas. We sat all the morning folding and refolding that monstrously large piece of paper to ensure seaworthiness. It would have been a shame to lose it to the depths of Hyde's Serpentine Sea."

"It was nothing," Celia murmured with a faint smile. Then her cheeks grew warm as she realized the man's eyes lingered on her face. His voice soon followed his intense gaze, and what he said startled Celia beyond anything.

"Miss Woodlow, is it?"

Not having the presence of mind to either affirm or deny the man's assertion, Celia looked at him fully for the first time. There was something familiar about him — the gray eyes, the grandiose mustache — and her heart thumped wildly.

Please don't be a rutter from the Bower!

Every time she was stuck with a man alone in a room, she hoped that he would begin to think on his family and suddenly depart.

She glanced again at the woman and child, the former smiling winsomely at her whilst the latter crouched, launching his craft anew on the waters, seeming to have already forgotten his near loss of it.

"Ah! So you are acquainted with my husband already?" the woman asked. "It seems he knows *all* of London!"

Wanting to turn and run, Celia couldn't gasp in breath for the effort.

"It seems she doesn't recall," the man said, extending his hand with a smile. "Barton Tiller...of London Lily Soap?"

Mr. Tiller!

As she diffidently reached out to shake his hand, the memory came flooding back – entering the large brick building, seating herself upon the wooden chair before his desk, stating her name, the look of sudden perception and pity toward her on his face. Then she had fled and run down the street only to find she had stolen his tin cup.

"My wife, Anna," he said, waving in the woman's direction.

Anna's hand shot out to envelop Celia's. Celia wondered if she could feel it quivering.

"Anna, certainly you remember Miss Woodlow. She came into the office just over a week ago."

"Oh!" Mrs. Tiller exclaimed as if having a revelation. "Of course! Yes, I remember now."

She grinned familiarly as her husband continued.

"I'm sorry that our interview was interrupted," he said. "We could complete it if you found the time to return. I must say, I noted the neatness of your handwriting on the paper you left behind and believe that you would make a fine labeler."

"Labeler?" Celia asked softly, feeling as if she might faint at any moment. Clutching the handle of the parasol, she rested her weight on its slender body, digging its point deeply into the ground.

"Yes. You see, because of the soap tax[viii], only wealthier families can afford our product, and they tend to prefer packaging of the most attractive sort. Therefore, each of our labels is beautifully handwritten. We are always looking for girls who can write a fair hand as they are not as plenteous as one might think." He laughed and motioned toward his wife. "Anna keeps the books and she is a sorceress at ciphering, but her hand appears as Sanskrit upon all the pages of the ledgers!"

"Barton!"

The woman swatted at him playfully, then clutched at the crook of his arm again as he insisted, "You know it's true, my love!"

"Perhaps, but you needn't shame me before another lady!"

Just wanting away, Celia nodded her head – at what, she wasn't sure

– and murmured, "Good day to you both."

"Might we then expect you sometime next week," Mr. Tiller asked.

"Uh…perhaps. I…I wish you both a fine day," Celia said, then turned and headed back to the greater lawn area, just beyond the trees. Once she had gained the distance, she glanced back to see the couple gazing at her retreating figure, both their heads cocked to the side contemplatively. Anna raised her gloved hand in adieu.

He was offering me work, Celia marveled, hurrying herself onward. *How could he, knowing what he does about me?*

She shuddered at the recollection of the sympathy in his eyes when he had asked her where she was presently employed.

I couldn't be looked at like that every day.

Heading back toward the Bower now, Celia stumbled on a stone on Park Lane. Recovering herself, she lifted the hem of her skirt to examine her right shoe. The sole at the toe box was flapping open.

There's not a chance Dovey will pay to have that mended.

Though Dovey dressed her doxies' figures well, footwear was regarded as an unnecessary expense.

"My girls don't need shoes to do their work!" Celia had once heard Dovey quip jollily to a group of gentlemen in the Mingling Room.

As she stood, recalling how they had all laughed, a cart rolled past. From the corner of her eye, Celia saw the ovals of two faces turn toward her.

Ugh, men! Well, no wonder they're gawking as I stand here, raising the hem of my skirt, she thought, dropping it back into place and willing the men to cease in their study of her person. Expertly, she adjusted her parasol to shield herself from their gaze as the cart continued past.

"Celia?" A familiar voice rose above the common clatter and hub-bub of city life around them.

Bill.

Celia's heart felt set to explode out of her chest, but she managed miraculously to propel herself forward as if completely unaware and disinterested in anything she might have just heard.

"Walter, stop the cart!" The voice was louder this second time, though further away now. "Celia? Is that you?"

Steady on. Do not glance. Do not flinch, Celia urged herself, taking more steps though she felt she might collapse. *He cannot ask me where I have been and what I have done.*

"'Ey, Bill, the lady ain't int'rested! Leave 'er be!" a rough voice

218

laughed, presumably that of Walter. The sound of his mockery faded into the background as the cart rolled on.

A moment more, and Celia was sure her brother had been swallowed up into the greater traffic of the city, pushed along by the ever-hastening vehicles behind it, but still she would not look back.

Tears stung in her eyes. *Ah, Bill! What I'd give to be back living with you and Nana! But she's dead and I'm ruined. You're far better off without me.*

On shaky legs, Celia finally arrived back at the Bower where she sank onto the front doorstep and sat a good long while, dabbing at her tears with her skirt.

A MOTHER'S APPROVAL, A MAID'S DISTASTE

WHEN BARCLAY ENTERED his mother's parlor to retrieve a pen knife, he did not anticipate the gravid conversation in which he would immediately be engaged.

"Barclay," Mrs. Durbin said, looking up from her writing desk. "I have noticed that Miss Honora's ankle is much improved, and it has been a full week now that she has been at Singer Hall. Has she mentioned returning to her people?"

The question jarred him.

Are you anxious for her removal? he nearly asked, but instead banked on his mother's compassionate heart. "As you may recall, when I asked to whom I would be returning her, she faffed about before admitting that she has no family."

"Yes, so tragic," Mrs. Durbin clicked her tongue and shook her head, then pulled Barclay down to sit in a chair very near her own. "But she lived *somewhere* before arriving here. Surely she's thinking of returning there now."

"Verily, Mamma," Barclay continued, "this I have not told you before: The woman she was working for had just attacked her. That is why she had run out into the street and injured her ankle."

"Attacked?" Mrs. Durbin pressed her hands to her chest. "Ugh, it breaks my heart how often girls like her are ill-used. I must confess that I for one am delighted with her!"

This wholly unprovoked accolade startled yet thrilled Barclay.

"She *is* a remarkable young woman," he conceded, holding back the extended praise that pushed on the base of his tongue.

"Truly, Barclay," his mother said, reaching for his hand. "I cannot but wonder if her presence here is *Providential* in nature."

Barclay was shocked into silence.

But Mrs. Durbin quickly extinguished his ecstasy as she went on to whisper, "I'm thinking that as my youngest boys are bound to be off and about in the future, Miss Honora might make a suitable companion for me. Oh! And her skills in the kitchen! That croquembouche she made – what sorcery!"

A companion for herself. Not a spouse for her son. Barclay forced a steady smile upon his face as she looked to him for his response.

"Were you not astonished by it, Barclay?"

"Hmm?"

"The dessert?"

"Oh yes, of course."

Suddenly, Barclay could feel his mother's eyes on him, studying him attentively.

Her voice dropped. "Barclay, I am compelled to ask you, what is the nature of your attachment to this girl?"

Am I so transparent?

"Mamma, I have done nothing unseemly, if that is your concern."

Mrs. Durbin bit back a chuckle. "No, my dear. That is not my worry. After all, it is not *Clayton* to whom I am speaking!"

The amusement passed and her eyes settled again on him, patiently.

Goodness, is she really requiring an answer of me?

In that instant, Martha came through the doorway, a letter in her hand.

"Mr. Barclay," she said extending it to him.

"Ah! Thank you, Martha!"

Barclay jumped up from the chair and took it. It seemed to him that his mother was about to say something, so he headed for the door, asking, "Martha, do you know where Jasper is? I promised I would review his Latin with him and this afternoon is as good a time as any."

Falling into step beside him as they exited the room, Martha responded, "I believe he's in the gallery."

"The gallery?" Barclay was surprised at this as he and Martha made their way down the hall. "Why ever is he *there*?"

"I believe Miss Honora asked him to tell her the tales of all your ancestors in their portraits."

Even when Martha was striding alongside him at a quick clip, Barclay could sense when she found something distasteful. There was something in her voice, and the way she held her mouth when she had finished speaking.

"And you disapprove of this pastime?" he asked teasingly, but immediately regretted it.

"It is not my place to either approve or disapprove," she responded.

Yes, this is very true, Barclay thought. *And I oughtn't give you leave to think otherwise.*

"Well, I shall go and break up their unbefitting behavior." He hoped his joking would end the conversation.

It did, conversationally. However, when they reached the gallery's door, Martha turned her eyes to him and Barclay read far more there than he wanted to.

Solemnly, he stared back at Martha's plain, aging face with a message of his own.

Yes, I know you see that Miss Honora means more to me than you think is proper. No, her presence here has not drawn me away from our Heavenly Father and His purposes for me.

Martha's gaze dropped and she bobbed a solemn curtsey before turning and heading back down the hall. Once she was gone, Barclay did not yet enter the room whence he could hear Jasper and Honora's voices emanating. Instead, he leaned against the wall and tore into the letter to read:

My dear boy –

Thank you for entrusting your bared heart to me. When you were a young aspirant, your enthusiasm for entering the ministry thrilled me, but now I see you have matured – as is proper for any bearer of the gospel! — and you have valid concerns that ought to be addressed.

As for the first matter: Yes, there have always existed within our ranks those who are not properly inspired for this vocation. Because of such, St. Paul urged Titus to "hold fast the faithful word as he hath been taught, that he may be able by sound doctrine both to exhort and to convince gainsayers." But nephew, as your devotion is true, I encourage you to come join the assembly of likeminded clergy — we do exist, I assure you! In fact, just this Thursday, I shall venture to the home of my long-time friend near Luton where six other reputable clergymen will be assembled. We meet together twice a year to boost one another's spirits and sharpen our minds. (There used to be ten of us, but alas! Death does have a temporal sting.) I will stop short of insisting it is your duty to bulk up these faithful troops, as I don't want to be regarded as dictatorial. But think on it, do!

Regarding your determination to be husband to a wife: I know well the fires that burn in most men's bosoms and am forever grateful for the twenty years of wedded harmony I shared with your dear Aunt Hetty — a joy I would willfully withhold from no one. Having visited my home many times over the years, you will recall how expansive it is — certainly large enough to comfortably house you, your future wife and any squalling fruits of your loins. As long as the little blessings can learn to stay out of my chamber and study, I think we would all get on quite merrily in this drafty edifice. Come! Visit Southby again with appraising eyes and tell me what conclusion you yourself draw.

I will stop there in my advisement to remain your perhaps tiresome but well meaning–
Uncle Allard

Cheered beyond what he had expected, Barclay tucked the letter away within his waistcoat, now determined that he ought to ask for Honora's hand, and soon.

However, he did not want to promise her his unending affection and companionship there in the gallery before his younger brother, so he stole away down the hallway toward his room where he could ponder how to befittingly word such a proposal.

ANOTHER CONFECTION, ANOTHER GRAN

"ONE CUP. TWO CUPS. Three cups," Honora said as Susan dumped flour into a bowl. "Always count aloud, girls, that you won't lose your way and mismeasure."

And it will help you learn your numbers, she added silently.

"Yes, ma'am," the Bryer girls said in unison. They had arrived moments earlier, running to stand beside Honora, clamoring with questions as to what they would bake that day. After a lively debate in which Mary extolled the virtues of strawberry tarts, and Susan angled to make a fresh plum cake, Honora informed them that the necessary ingredients for both treats were not in season. Their disappointment quickly turned to joy when she suggested instead that they create a dozen gooseberry jam tartlets. Now the table before them was littered with bowls, measuring cups and spoons.

"Please, may I see into the bowl?" Mary asked, bobbing a little curtsey at Honora's elbow.

Suppressing a smile at the solemn gesture, Honora hooked her hands under the girl's arms to lift her up at the high table. Just as her arms were beginning to shake with the effort, she heard Bess's voice at her side.

"Here y'are, Miss." She placed a stepping stool down beside them. "No need to harm yourself whilst making the wee ones happy."

Honora's heart swelled with appreciation toward the woman.

Aw Bess, you're not as flinty as you'd have us all believe!

"Girls, what do we say to Miss Bess for her kindness to us?"

"Thank you, Miss Bess," the Bryers chimed.

"Mm-hm," the cook half-grunted as she went back to the other side of the kitchen where a leg of lamb awaited her.

Once all the ingredients had been mixed, Honora dumped the ball of pastry onto the table, split it in two even portions and set one before each girl with a rolling pin. Honora was thankful that getting it thin enough for the tins would take a lot of time and concentration on the girls' part as it would give her time to think.

It had been four days since their trip to the seaside and her shameful outburst. That day had offered more than just a glimpse of the sea. Clearly portrayed before her had been Mr. Barclay's deep-seated desire to help the disadvantaged.

Such compassion can't be taught, she thought warmly.

In the meantime, another instinctual sentiment had become more and more obvious to her.

His appreciation of me has only increased. Deeply.

This was evident by the way his eyes constantly caressed her face as he listened to her every word. In conversing with him, she often consciously made reference to her 'steward father' and her 'intended career as a governess', anxious to remind him once again of her place in society, so undeniably beneath his own. Though he clearly heard her words, he never once shushed her as if she need be ashamed, nor puffed up before her as though pleased at his superiority.

No. He is always steady, always true. Valuing what he ought and disregarding what he should, never pleased by vanity. He is so completely unlike the dandies and devils who frequented Stagsdown House! Yes, he is an uncommonly good gentleman.

And he has intentions toward me.

"Are your arms flagging, Susan?" The girl's rolling had slowed considerably. "Hop down from the stool and I'll take over for a spell."

But what would his family think? Clayton knows already. I can see that in his smug glances. And it seems Jasper is there with him, though he is more tactful.

It's the mother who would likely quash it all.

When she and Eliza had their schooling, the governess had set them to read Mr. Richardson's *Pamela*. At its end, Eliza had stated, "I did not like the heroine, or the book really at all. Her grasping at greatness was not believable as she was successful and then accepted by the upper class. Such things do not occur."

Hearing these words, Honora knew their utterance had been meant for her as a warning at best or a threat at worst.

Yet, unlike Eliza, Mrs. Durbin is kind to me — seems to genuinely like *me even! Perhaps she, like Barclay, is not impressed by the pomp and vanity of polished society.*

Oh, but Honora, have you already forgotten? Under what roof did you recently spend four nights — two in ignorance, two in awakened horror?

Yes, if the Durbins were to learn of that, they'd turn me out in an instant, for certain.

Honora's heart pounded just at the thought of being discovered.

I didn't know where I was! I needed food to eat and a place to sleep. What creature — animal let alone human! — ought to be denied such things?

"Give the filling a stir, Mary," she said, her mouth dry. "Mix it well."

Who knows of my time at the Bower? Only the others who live there and that horrible celery root woman. She recalled the look of disgust on the grocer's face and doubled down on the idea forming in her mind.

No one need ever know. It wouldn't be difficult to avoid that part of London — or stay out of London altogether.

So if my time at Titania's Bower is the only impediment to my future with Barclay...

Oh, how I let my mind fly away!

As Honora stifled the chuckle forming in her chest, she felt a sense of pure, hopeful joy budding there as well.

Little Susan, looked up just then. Seeing the glint of happiness on Honora's face, she answered it with a smile of her own.

"Thank you for teachin' us to make tartlets, Miss Honora," she said. "They smell like somethin' my gran made once."

"What was that, Susan?" Honora asked, the smile slipping from her face.

"My gran made somethin' that smelt like this."

The childish observation pricked Honora's heart at the recollection of another, older girl saying similar words — a girl with dark hair and the saddest eyes Honora had ever seen. A girl still imprisoned in the Bower.

Dear Celia, forgive me. I haven't thought of you in days.

A MORE HONOURABLE GOAL

"MY GOODNESS, GIRLS!" Barclay exclaimed, staring in exaggerated awe at the many little tartlets upon the kitchen table. Their crusts were uneven and broken in places, but their colourful fillings were pretty and the rich scent of jam filled the air. "Are you expecting the Prince Regent himself?"

Susan and Mary giggled, though shyly.

"Oh, Mr. Barclay, how fortuitous of you to arrive at this moment," Honora said with a sigh. "We were just contemplating how to get all of these safely to the girls' house. Would you be willing to carry the platter there?"

"I would be honored," he replied, bowing to the children.

"You mustn't trip and tip it into the lane!" Mary warned, solemnly.

"I shall do my utmost to mind my feet," Barclay promised, and was surprised when the quip didn't earn him a smile from Honora's lips.

"And what will we make next time, Miss Honora?" Susan asked, her brown eyes large with anticipation.

"Oh." Honora's face fell. "Next time? I hadn't really…"

Barclay noted her furrowed brow. *Perhaps she's tired… or worried that Bess will mind yet another foray into her lair.*

He glanced at the cook who was stirring a large copper pot on the hob, looking as contented as could be.

"I shall have to consider that, Susan," Honora finally said. "In the meanwhile, *these* are ready for your mother to see. I'm certain she will be delighted with it as you girls did such a lovely job."

"Thank you, Miss," the girls said together.

"Well, shall we?" Barclay asked, lifting the platter and carrying it to the kitchen's outside door. He turned back, expecting one of the girls to follow in his wake, excited to get the door for him. Instead, he saw Honora tenderly embracing both girls in her arms, her eyes closed. Then Susan hurried to open the door for him while Mary said to Honora who still sat on a stool, "Thank you again, Miss."

I suppose this means she's not coming with us. Barclay masked his disappointment.

The Bryer's house lay on the nearside of the village, so delivery of the sisters and their bounty took little time.

"Did you girls empty every last jam jar to make all of these?" he joked, eliciting a giggle from each of them.

Upon arrival at the humble house, the girls' mother greeted Barclay with the pleasant but shy deference that most villagers showed to any member of the Durbin family, apologizing profusely for the state of her home. As gallantly as he could, he placed the tartlets on the room's one table and departed.

Alone at last, Barclay was plunged once again into anxious introspection.

Will I truly speak to her of it this evening? This very hour even? Will she say yes?

How could she not?

Though Barclay cringed at this pomposity, he knew it to be a valid question.

She is a poor girl who must work to keep herself fed. Could she possibly decline an offer of marriage from a gentleman though second-born, even if he has flaming hair?

Singer Hall appeared through the trees, the door into the kitchen plainly in sight. Barclay's stomach flipped over.

Is now the time, Father?

But Honora seemed so somber this afternoon. Perhaps the girls misbehaved today. Ought I to wait for a pleasanter time?

A robin twittered in the distance as the sky grew rosier on its western edge.

No. It is a lovely evening. Let it be now.

He took a deep breath and grasped the handle. The door opened with a squeak, revealing Honora wiping down the table with a damp cloth. She looked up, obviously surprised at his reappearance.

"Oh, I hurried, hoping to return in time to help you tidy up," Barclay said. "But you are done now. Miss Honora, will you walk with me on the lawn?"

At this, Bess stopped paring vegetables and looked back and forth between the two young people.

Bess, mind your turnips! Barclay thought. *But if Miss Honora and I are to be engaged, Bess will know of it soon enough.*

Honora nodded and said nothing as they headed outside.

Barclay bit his lips. So anxious was he, that they were down the front steps and well on the gravel path before he noticed the tightness in Honora's jaw, and the way she clutched her elbows with her hands.

"Is everything alright?" he asked.

Honora swallowed hard and replied simply, "No."

"What's troubling you?" he asked, his resolve to propose crumbling.

Silence prevailed. Skirting the kitchen garden, they stepped out into the tall grass. When they reached the top of the hillock overlooking the valley, and she still had given no answer, he turned to her and asked, "Are you not happy here?"

This revived her from her mulling. "Oh, no! I am quite content. Happy even, conversing with you and Jasper, baking with the girls – seeing the sea! But I…"

She fears my intentions toward her are not sincere, that I'm toying with her.

"I cannot stop thinking about someone," she finished the sentence softly.

Barclay's breath caught in his throat.

"Someone very dear to me," she continued.

She loves another.

Damn! He cursed silently, and was struck with contrition, then cursed again. *Damn! Of course! Why did I not consider this before? Of course, a woman of such beauty and wit – though poor – has caught the attention of other men!*

The two were silent for a long moment.

"Well," he was finally able to say, "If you have prayed and determined him to be a worthy man…"

"What?" Honora looked at him, her eyes wide. Then she laughed, her head tipping backward that the sound of it reached toward the sky. "It isn't a *man* of whom I speak, but a friend – a *female* friend!"

"Oh." Barclay laughed as well, though the sound of it was queer, devoid of breath.

Good lord, what a fright that was! he thought, the tightness in his throat subsiding.

"So, this friend of yours – is she ill??"

Seriousness settled back over Honora.

"No."

"Are the two of you at odds?" He tried again, still feeling the rush of relief.

"No."

"What then?"

"She is enslaved."

The quiet words hung in the air, jarring and mysterious, as visions of dark-skinned peoples, chained and beaten, jumbled through Barclay's mind.

"But Wilberforce and the Saints outlawed slavery *long* ago," he said after a long moment.

"Not *that* sort of enslavement," Honora murmured, turning away again. "Another sort – one that the people here mightn't dare speak of."

"'The people here'?"

"Your family, Mr. Barclay – your very good and proper family, and the people who consort with you. There are some things that you needn't bother yourselves with though they are very real indeed."

Barclay began to feel that this conversation could never swing around to the topic for which he had started it.

"Miss Honora, I want to understand…"

Honora took a deep breath as she finally turned to him, and said in her straightforward way, "My friend is a harlot."

Barclay flinched. The few times he had heard that word before, it had only been whispered – by a man, never a woman.

Does she even know what that means? he wondered. *Great God, don't make me be the one to explain it!*

He recalled the girl on the barrel in the alley, her spilling bosom and lascivious gaze.

How can Honora be acquainted with someone like her*? And well enough to call her 'friend'?*

Taking a deep breath, Barclay asked, "What do you mean she is a *slave* and a…a har…?"

"I *mean*, she doesn't *want* to be a harlot…"

Barclay cringed at hearing the word again.

"…but she is confined in a brothel."

Ugh, another vile word.

He nearly said, *I assume she is not chained to the wall.* But thinking better of it, he simply said, "She is 'confined', you say? Why does she not leave?"

Barclay watched as Honora's face fell from concern to frustration, knowing it was at *his* words.

"Where would she go? What would she do? She has only a few coins to her name. They would be spent by the end of one very frugal week."

"Of course," Barclay murmured, thinking of the filthy, rag-wrapped children he had seen lurking in London's alleys nearly every time he went there. He always wondered where they slept at night – how often their mouths tasted food. These were the people he longed to elevate, to help.

But to resort to the selling of one's body? Surely God provides another way to those who ask Him.

Of this he was certain, but his mind veered elsewhere.

Honora has befriended a prostitute! An influx of emotions flooded his heart as he tried to make sense of it all.

Christ did not draw away from the woman who washed His feet with her tears. And the woman at the well, she who had five husbands – she might as well have been a doxy. Yes, He did not spurn sinful woman. And Honora hasn't either.

That is commendable, though what are the risks?

Honora jolted him out of his mental convolutions, saying, "I must leave here and help her."

"What? Why would leaving here allow you to do so?"

"I can do nothing for her whilst in this idyllic place." She spread her hands out to indicate all of the Durbin estate. "My ankle is well enough now. I must return to London to help Celia."

"Celia is the name of…your friend?"

Honora only nodded and began to walk forward again, the stalks of long grass clinging to her skirt as she passed them.

She can't leave! Barclay moved after her, scrambling in his head. *But what could be a more honorable goal than to help deliver someone from light to darkness? She says the girl wants out of her life of sin.*

Yet, God's Faithful might decry it as dancing on a line of intimacy with darkness.

But aren't those then like the Pharisees who scorned our Lord for His mingling with sinners? Yes! That is so and they are to be disregarded.

Yet, are we not to respect those in authority over us?

But what is God more desirous of than a lost sinner being found, a prodigal returning home?

Thus convinced, Barclay placed his hand on Honora's shoulder, stopping her. Looking startled at his touch, she pulled back slightly.

He stated with resolved determination, "I will help you."

Shock filled Honora's face, and was soon replaced with the spreading warmth of happy disbelief.

"Oh, I…that is, I hadn't expected that you…oh!" The worry lines on her forehead smoothed, and the apples of her cheeks lifted into a smile – a smile full of wonder and appreciation. And it was all because of something *he* had said.

Reaching forward to grasp his hands, her eyes glowing, she murmured, "Thank you."

He asked softly, "How are we to save Celia?"

With her eyes shining, Honora replied, "I confess, each plan I've concocted seems impossible, but with *your* help…ah, there is hope now!"

She laughed a little unaffected laugh. "Very well then, let us think…Celia is a great walker, always making her way to Hyde Park when she is able – often on Fridays."

A prostitute in Hyde Park! So they don't always stay in the alleyways of Covent Garden? Barclay marveled, thinking of all the times he had meandered through the park apparently unaware of who was walking past.

"And tomorrow, as you know, is Friday, so if we were to go to London, perhaps…"

Honora continued her scheming as Barclay watched her face, savoring the sensation of her hand in his.

This was how he had hoped their walk on the lawn would end – their hands clasped together, her eyes peering deeply into his with a fervency that stopped his breath. Certainly, there was a vital, missing element – a marital engagement – but all the emotions he'd longed for were present, abundantly so.

And our joint rescuing of her friend will surely bind us together. The wedding will come. I'm sure of it.

***

That evening, as Barclay was exiting the necessary room, something occurred to him.

On our way to town tomorrow, we'll be going right past the road to Southby. If Honora could but see the rectory – it is an impressive house!

But Uncle Allard…

Though Barclay treasured his aging relative, he cringed at what the eccentric man might say or do in Honora's presence.

Oh! Did he not write that he would be traveling to Luton today? Certainly, he will not have returned by tomorrow.

"Barclay?"

Jasper was suddenly behind him.

"Will Miss Honora be going with us to town tomorrow?" he asked, looking worried. "Will we be returning her to her home?"

Barclay cringed slightly. He hadn't even considered how to keep Jasper uninvolved on the morrow.

"No, but Jass…"

"What is it?"

Exhaling largely, Barclay said, "Well, you see, I was hoping that she *alone* would accompany me tomorrow."

Instead of the petulant response he expected, Barclay watched in wonder as a smile spread slowly across his brother's face.

"I see," Jasper said, nodding. "Was that because you had a *particular question* that you wanted to ask her for which privacy would be best?"

Although Jasper's assumption was incorrect, Barclay immediately saw that it could be put to good use.

I am not being deceptive exactly, Barclay reasoned with his conscience, *as I do intend to ask for Honora's hand very soon. It nearly happened today and could happen tomorrow.*

Jasper was still grinning wolfishly as Barclay smiled sheepishly back, neither affirming nor denying Jasper's question.

Yes, my silence is not a lie; it is strategic honesty.

"Very well, big brother," Jasper said, patting Barclay roughly on the back. "I shall honor your request. I know when I'm not wanted!"

A sudden thought struck Barclay.

"Uh, Jass, please say nothing of this to anyone," he said as lightly as he could. "I want to broach the topic with the others in my own good time."

"Don't worry yourself," Jasper said more quietly. "I'm sure she'll say yes. How could she not? I guess this means you'll be telling my uncle you want the curacy at Southby after all, ay?"

Yet again, Barclay was astonished at the boy's perspicacity.

"You needn't answer that, brother." With a final pat on the shoulder, Jasper walked away, saying over his shoulder, "I doubt you'll get a bit of sleep tonight, but good night anyway."

ASSESSING THE RECTORY

"HERE YOU ARE," Barclay said, handing Honora a small linen-wrapped bundle as they sat beside each other on the gig seat. It was mid-morning while they hurried toward London – making good time as far as Honora could determine.

"Why, thank you," she said, curious. Putting it on her lap, she flipped aside the napkin's corners, and found two golden rolls inside.

"I thought you might be hungry since you missed breakfast."

"How thoughtful you are!" Honora said, marveling that both had been carefully cut down the middle and generously spread with butter and black currant jam, just like she had prepared for herself nearly every morning since arriving at Singer Hall. She laughed. "Truthfully, I've been hungry since dawn, but avoided the breakfast room out of fear I might say something to give away our plans for the day!"

Immediately, she regretted the implication that the two of them were doing something wrong. Nothing could be further from the truth, but Honora knew Barclay had a very particular moral conscience.

She smoothed over her blunder with a moan of appreciation as she bit into one of the rolls.

"Yes," he answered. "I had to bite my tongue once or twice myself. But somehow, we escaped the grounds with our scheme undiscovered."

Perhaps he is not as missish about all this as I had supposed, she thought, taking another bite. Her approval of him blossomed anew. She was still surprised he had offered to help her in this venture.

But will we meet with success?

Her nerves rose up again and at her third mouthful, she could eat no more. Enfolding the remnants back in the napkin, she placed the bundle aside, thinking, *Maybe Celia will be hungry and want that when we whisk her away. Ugh! What will we say to the Durbins when we arrive back at Singer Hall with her in tow?*

She tried to keep her toes from tapping on the floorboard as her mind raced. There were many particulars about their plan that they had not precalculated.

And yet, all is well so far. Jasper is not with us. How did Barclay manage that?

She stole a glance at him, admiring the determined yet cheerful set of his mouth and jaw in profile as he held the reins and scanned the road ahead. His eyes flitted over to hers.

"Miss Honora," he said. "I hope you don't mind, but in a mile or so, we'll be veering off course for just a moment. I should very much like to show you something."

"Oh, of course," Honora replied.

Soon, they took a turn in the road and the gig crested a hillock. Below them and to the right was a village in the near distance, its many buildings brightly reflecting the morning light.

"Southby," Barclay said, then took a deep breath.

Within minutes they stopped before a large, stone house, very near the church.

"This is the rectory. My father's brother lives here with only the Wilfreys – a married couple who serve him." Barclay made no move to climb down from the gig.

"I wanted to show it to you as it is prettily situated. My brothers and I spent many happy times here as boys, climbing the trees and splashing through the stream you see flowing just there." He pointed past the house to a bubbling brook. "Uncle Allard has been a second father of sorts to us since Papa passed."

Barclay has felt the sting of loss, Honora thought.

"He must be a wonderful person. And his home is beautiful," she said, gazing upon the house's heavy gray walls looming up before them. Then, to lighten the moment, she went on, "Rather large for someone who lives practically alone."

"Yes," he smiled, nodding enthusiastically. "It is *quite* spacious."

Suddenly, in the window closest to them, the mob-capped head of a woman appeared, her face full of joy and surprise.

"Ah! Mrs. Wilfrey," Barclay said, lifting his hand to acknowledge her.

The woman began to beckon excitedly, pointing toward the house's front door.

"I think she intends for us to come in. Oh, dear," Barclay said, but looked pleased.

Honora hid her dismay, knowing the less time she and Barclay were at the park, the less likely they would catch sight of Celia.

But certainly, I cannot complain to him.

She bit her lips and hoped for the best. Seeming to sense her concern, Barclay assured her, "This will take but a moment. I believe my uncle is in Luton today, and his housekeeper will only want to say hello."

Now he was off the seat, securing Caleb, then beside her, offering her a hand. Though her ankle was nearly healed, disembarking still caused a bit of pain. Her hand felt small in his as she alit from the carriage, and he seemed slow in letting go of it even once she was safely on the ground.

They stepped into a tidy courtyard. The walkway to the front door was lined with several jardinieres which overflowed with heather plants. Though it was late in the season, there were still some blooming white and purple stalks. Honora knelt down to breathe in their fresh, earthy scent when the door of the house was flung open.

"Nephew!" a jolly voice bellowed.

"Uncle Allard?" Barclay halted in his tracks.

Honora stood and beheld a fellow on the doorstep with his arms extended. He was stooped in stature and thick about the middle. Two unruly eyebrows fought for space on his forehead, but the smile below them was of the most congenial sort imaginable.

"Oh ho ho!" he said at sight of Honora herself and waggled his head.

What a strange fellow is this! Honora thought, swallowing her amusement.

She stepped forward to stand beside Barclay who seemed frozen on the doorstep, a look of embarrassment on his face.

Thrusting his hand out at Honora, the elderly man formally stated, "Allard Durbin, Rector of Southby."

"Honora Goodwin," she responded, shaking his hand heartily. It was gnarled but steady in her grasp.

"Very good. And you, my dear boy." Allard reached to embrace Barclay though the effort clearly pained him.

"Uncle," Barclay sounded concerned as his arms enveloped the man. "You are not well?"

Allard waved his hand dismissively.

"Just a touch of the rheumatism, dear boy. Nothing to wonder at in a man of my age." He pantomimed dragging Barclay through the door saying, "Do come in!"

Honora followed them into the foyer, touched and amused by the affectionately playful display.

"Sorry, Miss Goodwin. You'll have to bear the sight of my balding pate as I didn't know you were coming," Allard said, running his fingers through his sparse hair. "I'm exempt from the license[ix] you know, so I could have powdered and donned my wig!"

"Your shoulders are cleaner this way," she said, caught up in the jollity, recalling the fine white dusting that had often billowed off of Lord Beeman's head to settle on his great coat.

"Ah, yes! No snow is falling on these fields today," he said, brushing dramatically at one shoulder, then laughed. He ushered the young people down the hall toward a sitting room, hollering, "Mrs. Wilfrey, tea please!"

"The water's heating, sir!" a voice called from elsewhere.

"Oh no, Uncle," Barclay spoke. "I regret that we cannot stay, as we – that is, we are expected in town shortly."

"Oh?" The delight fell from the man's face as he looked back and forth between the two young people. But then it was replaced by a look of knowing.

"Ahh, I see!" he said, gazing hard at Barclay for a long, odd moment. "You've brought those *appraising eyes* of yours at my invitation, as well as an additional pair – the second much lovelier than the first!"

Is Uncle Allard a bit barmy? Honora wondered, looking away for fear of laughing as Barclay squirmed.

"Very well then, let's get right to it," the elderly fellow said, rubbing his knotty hands together, then clearing his throat. "Here we stand in the foyer of Southby's rectory, built in 1742, home to no fewer than four consecutive clergymen and their families. Please note the fine oaken lintels above the windows and doorways, which you will see throughout the house. Now, if you will follow me this way…"

He motioned them down the hall, past the sitting room that he had previously been urging them to enter.

"You will note that from every window on this north side of the house is a view of the lovely, green churchyard."

Next, he ushered them into the kitchen where a startled Mrs. Wilfrey stood at a table, arranging little cakes on a serving plate.

"I've nearly got it ready, sir," she said, her hands hovering.

"Of course," Allard said. "I'm just showing them that the kitchen is fitted with all the modern comforts."

The discomfiture on the woman's face made Honora think that this was not a normal practice when guests arrived. She saw the housekeeper and Barclay exchange bemused smiles, but there was little time to join in as Allard was now bustling them through to the dining room.

A small chandelier hung low over a large table, and a burled elmwood sideboard stood by, laden with crockery.

"Plenty of room for supper parties, as you see," he said. "Though I eat most of my meals in the kitchen with Mr. and Mrs. Wilfrey."

The poor dear likely has few visitors, Honora thought, looking at the man with new eyes, and she regretted the sense of hurry she felt for her own time there to be done. *Perhaps he is eager to show his fine home because he wants to impress anyone who stops in.*

Merrily onward, he hied them, his aging body pitching side to side in his ungainly gait.

"There is still the second parlor and the breakfast room to see. Oh! I did not point out the larder. We will have to circle back to see it, as it is especially nice. Come on, then!"

Honora caught Barclay's eye and smiled conspiratorially though she could not read his thoughts as he gazed earnestly back at her. They hurried on to follow after the elderly man as he was disappearing through a doorway.

Each room was described with enthusiasm until they stood at the base of the staircase. It looked as if Allard was determined to lead them to the upper story.

"Uncle," Barclay said. "I don't think a perusal of the bedrooms is in order."

"No?" the man looked surprised. "But there are so many of them — and there are not one, but *two* necessary rooms — both nicely situated! Surely Miss Goodwin wants to see them!"

He beamed proudly, his hand on the bannister, his foot on the bottom step.

Barclay turned to Honora, his eyes pleading.

"Sir," she said, fixing her eyes on the eager gentleman, and praying she wouldn't giggle. "I am sure the upstairs is as beautifully kept as is the downstairs. But I am eager to sample the cakes Mrs. Wilfrey has laid out for us."

"Ah, yes — she is a wonderful baker!" The man's fervor veered again as he headed back down the hallway whence they had come. "Very well, let's sit in the parlor for a quick *tête-à-tête* before you must rush off to your next engagement. Oh — *Engagement!* Ha ha!"

He laughed, then turned to look at Barclay who blushed brightly.

Honora felt suddenly quite shy.

Of course, his uncle thinks we are an intended couple! What else is he to suppose when his nephew arrives at his home for a visit, bringing with him only a young woman?

Upon glimpsing Barclay's face, Allard cleared his throat and murmured something that might have been an apology under his breath, as he continued back to the parlor. When they arrived there, Honora saw that Mrs. Wilfrey had brought in a tea set with a steaming pot and filled plates.

A somewhat awkward ingestion followed, Honora deducing that the others were just as uneasy after Uncle Allard's *faux-pas* as she herself felt. The elderly man looked like a scolded dog, sitting on his chair, his shoulders even more hunched than before as he nibbled halfheartedly at a little cake. After a few sips of tea and a cursory sampling of Mrs. Wilfrey's offerings, Barclay rose from the settee and declared that he and Honora must be going. Determined to end the otherwise delightful time happily, Honora said as she stepped toward the doorway, "It was a pleasure to meet you, Rev. Durbin. Thank you for your unparalleled hospitality."

He brightened a bit, rose creakily from his chair and shook her hand, saying, "Yes my dear, I am very pleased to have met you. If my rheumatism had not flared up so voraciously yesterday, I should have missed your visit as I'd be in Luton at this very moment. I was sorry to miss the journey, but your visit has blunted the sharpness of that disappointment."

He turned to Barclay and opened his arms wide. "Thank you for stopping on your way into town, nephew."

Barclay embraced the old fellow. "I hope to return and see you again soon."

"Do! Do!"

Mrs. Wilfrey drifted in, a towel-wrapped object in her hand.

"Sir, I've a warming stone here should you like to sit down with it." She situated the bundle on the settee and Allard immediately tottered over to it.

"Thank you, Mrs. Wilfrey. Barclay and Miss Goodwin, please forgive an old man for not seeing you out properly. I fear running all over the house just now has finished me for the morning."

The two voiced assurances on their way out the door, also bidding the housekeeper adieu.

Once they were atop the gig again and headed toward London, Honora said, "What a pleasant creature he is."

"The finest of men," Barclay agreed, then added solemnly, "His physical state has certainly deteriorated since I last saw him."

"Well, Mrs. Wilfrey appears to be an attentive caretaker," Honora offered.

"Hmm. Yes, he has her to help him at home, though I wonder how he can possibly continue to fulfill his church duties."

It seemed that Barclay was lost in thought as he directed Caleb back onto the road. This suited Honora as her own mind had settled again on the difficult task they had set before themselves that may or may not be awaiting them at Hyde Park.

A STROLL WITH MOLLY

CELIA CREPT DOWN the hallway toward the vestibule. She had already finished laundering many sheets that morning and had hung them to dry. She half-expected Dovey to appear, telling her that since she had had the whole day off yesterday, she would not be allowed out today.

But it is Friday, and I shall have my Friday walk, she resolved.

Though the prior day's encounters with the Tillers and Bill had shaken her, she could not bear to closet herself away in the Bower.

As she turned the corner, she nearly ran into Dovey who was moving a potted lily plant to the marble topped table.

Damn.

"You got them sheet*th* done?" the procuress asked, looking the girl up and down, her eyes critically assessing.

Celia nodded. She had noticed that Dovey often slipped into unrefined speech when no gentlemen were around to despise her for it.

"Well, if yer goin' out, take Molly with you."

As Celia absorbed this distasteful dictate, Dovey added, as though it was an afterthought, "*Thinth*e that Honora-girl wa*th* nabbed, I don't want any of my girl*th* goin' out alone."

'*My girls*'. Celia bristled, but said nothing as she turned to ascend the stairs. When she found Molly in their bedroom and told her of Dovey's commandment, the petty blonde looked out the window at the encroaching drear and said slyly, "Dunno if I wanna go."

She knows she's doing me a favor if she does. Celia studied the calculating look on Molly's face.

Making a gamble of her own, Celia shrugged and headed for the door, saying lightly, "Suit yourself."

"Oh fine, I'll go!" Molly said, glancing quickly in the mirror and patting at her hair before rushing down the stairs after Celia. "But if it rains, and flattens my curls – yer not gonna be walkin' this fast all the way there, are ya?"

Then they were out of the door with Celia two steps ahead at every turn until Hyde Park's tree tops came into view, a green ruffle against a gray sky backdrop.

"Slow down!" Molly insisted for the fifth time, and Celia finally did.

Bill won't be here in the park, she thought, taking a more leisurely pace toward the Serpentine. *And I can keep my eyes open for the Tillers.*

There weren't many other people there, perhaps kept at bay by the threat of rain.

"There's no one here now," Molly muttered, twirling her parasol above her head.

Celia sighed, gazing down into the Serpentine's shallows

"I thought there'd at least be *a few* gentlemen strollin' about."

Will you never stop speaking of gentlemen? Celia didn't bother to ask.

"Oh!" Molly's cried. "'Ere comes *one* fella!"

The man indicated was headed toward them. Celia noted the brown curls that peeked out from underneath his top hat, tickling at his collar. Unwittingly, she imagined him with his hat off – she'd seen so many men unhatted. They'd enter the Bower bedecked in all their finery, then hang their hats in the vestibule, revealing the uncouth deformation of their hair. Once she was alone with them, they took off their coats, exposing yellowish stains in the armpits of their shirts. Then they doffed their trousers, baring shapeless linen undergarments. Celia shook her head to halt the furtherance of the thought.

Men are stupid, greedy pigs. Why does Molly insist on flirting with such beasts?

The man was passing by them now, clearly aware of the interest he had elicited in Molly. He winked, at which Molly giggled, declaring loudly enough for him to hear, "Oh, 'e's a lovely one!"

"None of them truly like you," Celia said, equally as loudly.

"What?" Molly said half-listening, glancing again and again at the fellow. He was lingering by the edge of the Serpentine, gazing out across it, but intermittently, he looked back at Molly.

"Gentlemen. None of them care a fig about you. They only care about the way you make them feel and the moment you stop making them feel that way, they forget you're even breathing until they're hungry again. You're like the potted roast they want for supper."

"What're you talkin' about?" Molly asked, wrinkling her brow, then grabbed Celia's hand. "Oh! He's comin' over!"

Celia glanced and saw that the man was in fact moving toward them. She didn't have the stomach for whatever it was that he and Molly would say to one another, so she shook off Molly's hand off and stalked away.

"Celia!" Molly cried. "We're s'pposed to stay together!"

"I won't tell if you won't." Celia threw back, noting that Molly didn't even seem to hear her answer as the man was beside her already.

Good god, Celia thought as she settled her bottom onto a large rock. *Just look at her!*

Molly was giggling ferociously, swaying her parasol over her shoulder as the man reached out to touch one of her blonde curls. Celia focused on the glassy stretch of the Serpentine before her. Little pebbles littered the ground beside her and her fingers itched to pick them up and toss them into the water, though she knew ladies didn't do such things.

Dammit all. She sighed and leaned over to lift a smooth small stone from the damp earth beside her.

How can I forget what I've done with her *tagging along beside me? Everyone can see what she is. And me alongside her.*

Celia nearly stood to leave, but two notions stopped her.

If I return to the Bower without Molly, Dovey'll never let me out again. And, *dim-witted Molly mightn't be able to make it back without me to guide her through the streets.*

Though she despised Molly, Celia couldn't let her get lost in London. She didn't want that for anyone. Convinced that Honora had been abducted whilst out alone, Celia considered that pretty Molly might be regarded as an even greater prize. Thus, she sat and waited, wondering when the ridiculous rendezvous would end.

The low clouds which had been drifting in from the west settled over the park, and unleashed a faint drizzle.

Suddenly, Molly skipped over to where Celia had been tossing pebbles into the water.

"'E says 'e'll see me at the Bower!" she declared triumphantly.

"And why is that a good thing?" Celia asked, standing and brushing off her skirt.

"Oh, Celia! You can't be as thick as you pretend. If 'e comes to see me, maybe 'e'll fall in love with me and take me away."

"That will never happen."

They began to walk down the path.

"And why not? If *Lyla* dunnit, why can't I?"

"You don't know what Lyla did."

"I do! As do you! She run off with Mr. Shaw!"

"She very well may have *run off* with him three months past, but even if Lyla still *is* with Shaw, she's likely holed up in a dark, little hovel somewhere above a bakery or haberdashery where he visits her twice a week. He certainly didn't take her back to his family estate where she could put on fancy dresses, sip from a pink teacup and meet callers in the drawing room. If that's what you're dreaming of, you're even stupider than you look."

When no sharp retort came back at her, Celia glanced at Molly. The girl's face had melted into a portrait of misery. Celia watched in surprise as Molly stopped on the pathway and burst into tears, her hands now covering her face, her shoulders quivering.

"Why're you so mean?" Molly asked. "I never 'eard you talk so much as today, and now I never wanna 'ear you talk again."

Ah, look at her now. I only spoke truth, Celia thought, staring hard at the astonishing sight. *But maybe that's too stark a tale.*

"I'm sorry, Molly," Celia said, surprising even herself at the tender sound of it.

Molly sniffed, wiping her eyes with her fingers.

Reaching up, Celia squeezed the girl's quaking shoulder. "I just don't want you to set your heart on fairy stories. You'll only be disappointed!"

Molly dabbed at her eyes and asked, "What else 'ave I got?"

Celia stood a moment, digesting these words as the mizzle around them grew into something more like rain.

Nothing, she knew she couldn't say. *You've got nothing but fairy stories, Molly.*

So she said not a word, but took her fellow prostitute, now docile as a lamb, by the wet hand and led her out of the park, then through London's streets back to Titania's Bower.

THROUGH THE SPYGLASS

BARCLAY EXTENDED THE umbrella to shield Honora.

She hardly seemed to notice that it had just begun to rain as she darted ahead down the gravel path, clutching his spyglass in her hand. The sparse crowd in the park had thinned even more as the clouds rolled in. He watched the swish of her skirt as she veered off the path to climb a small grassy knoll.

"Up here," she called back to him. "We can survey the breadth of the park."

Barclay followed though he lacked her enthusiasm. His heart was committed to helping Honora and her friend in this noble venture, but just as they were stabling the gig, his mind had begun to waver at their plan.

What will Mamma and Clayton say when I arrive home with another *young woman? That will be the second one in so many weeks! And will it be clear to them with one glance what she is? God Almighty, help me in this!*

Honora stood upon the summit of the hillock, pressing the spyglass's eye cup to her right eye, her left eye scrunched shut, her mouth tight in a little knot.

In spite of his worry, Barclay smiled at the sight of her determined face as she scanned the landscape below them like a sailor in a crow's nest.

"Do you see her?" he asked, still gazing at her face. They had already thoroughly searched the western end of the park to no avail.

Even to himself, Barclay didn't want to acknowledge the faint hope within him that this sector would yield similar results.

"Not yet, but she must be here." She bit her lip, still peering hard through the cylinder. "It's Friday, after all — oh! *There she is!*"

She shoved the spyglass into his hand, pointing wildly toward the Serpentine.

"Right there, sitting on a rock by the water!"

Placing the spyglass to his own eye, Barclay looked in the general direction Honora indicated. It took a moment of dizzying searching through the lens to locate a woman in a simple cream coloured dress — *a proper length and coverage,* he thought — seated alongside the Serpentine.

"Oh, no!" she cried, her eyes still riveted on the spot below. "Someone is with her!"

She grabbed the spyglass back out of his grasp. "Is that…is that *Molly!*"

Another young woman, this one with blonde, ringleted hair, was traipsing up to the girl in cream, her movement conveying how pleased she was about something.

"Celia and Molly don't get on at all!" Honora continued. "Why would they walk in the park together?"

"Well, shall we?" he asked, extending his arm to Honora again.

"What? Go down to them?" she asked, incredulously. "If Molly was to see me talking to Celia, she'd run back to Dovey and tell her everything."

Dovey? Molly? Who are these women? He nearly asked, but Honora had turned to him, a look of inspiration in her eyes.

"I know! You can go down yourself and engage Molly — she's mad about young gentlemen. If you walk a ways away with her, I could then wave Celia over somewhere out of sight and speak with her."

Barclay squirmed.

"Who is this 'Molly'?" he asked, dubiously.

"That girl right there with Celia," Honora answered, waving again down the hill.

"Yes, but *who is* she?"

"She also lives at the Bower, but she doesn't seem to want out."

Barclay recoiled. Honora's attention was down the hill again.

She knows two *prostitutes?*

"Are they quarreling?" Honora asked seemingly of herself, prompting Barclay to look again.

It did appear that sharp words were being exchanged between the girls as they started down the walkway together. But then, the blonde's head tilted forward, obvious sadness settling over her. Celia looked at her, and appeared to deflate, then put her hand on Molly's shoulder.

In but a moment, Celia gently reached for Molly's hand and began to lead her down the path, away from the Serpentine.

"Oh, no! They're leaving!" Honora exclaimed.

He tried to ignore the relief he felt.

"Well, let's get back home," he said as they watched the two girls disappear around a bend in the path.

Once again, he offered his arm to Honora who had finally turned away from the place they had last seen Celia. This time she took it, swelling Barclay's heart as the warmth of her arm seeped through his coat.

In silence, they made their way through the park back to where they had stabled Caleb and the gig.

I shan't ask her in the next hour. Tonight at dusk, we'll walk on the lawn and I'll do it then.

Barclay felt pleased at the conviction that he would in fact be bold enough to do so.

The skies now let loose a true shower, and though they walked under an umbrella's protective span, he thought of offering her his coat, envisioning himself peeling the garment off his own frame to drape it around her narrower one.

Would the scent of her linger in the fabric's folds after she returned it to me?

These were pleasant meditations. However, one little memory niggled at the back of his mind.

How was it she expected me to approach a prostitute and engage her in conversation?

Pushing this thought away, he concentrated on the sensation of her slender arm pressed against his side as they walked on together. After but a moment, he realized she was walking more slowly than usual and her head was down.

Of course, he thought, slowing his pace. *She is disappointed. We are going home without Celia in tow.*

"Do not be troubled, Miss Honora," he said. "We will hone our plan and try again another day."

I shall have to cheer her on the ride home. I want all thoughts of prostitutes banished when I ask her to be my wife.

WHOSO FINDETH

HONORA'S STOMACH RUMBLED as they pulled up alongside the stable and Dervy emerged from its door.

How can I hunger when I've just seen Celia headed back to the Bower?

Barclay had chattered happily the entire way back from London. Although Honora, understood his kind intentions, she felt heavy with disappointment as the gig seat bumped incessantly beneath her.

It was very good of him to try and help me – unbelievably so! Even when he learned what Celia is, he did not balk.

This continuous thought kept her smiling faintly each time he turned to her to share some cheery little nothing on the road back to Singer Hall.

Gingerly, she climbed down from the gig, resting much of her weight on his shoulder as her ankle was prone to smarting. Once on the ground, she turned toward the house.

"Will you walk on the lawn with me for a moment?" he asked, surprising her.

But we've just spent nearly an hour together in the gig. She snuck a look at him and saw a definite change in his demeanor. Where he had been smiling and joking a moment before, he now looked solemn, both of his hands clutching at the brim of his hat.

What's this about? Honora wondered.

His eyes were soft, and she allowed hers to gaze warmly back, then wondered at the prudence of such a response.

"Of course," she said in a more business-like manner. "I'd like to stretch my legs."

They headed out toward the hillock, the stately hall well in sight behind them. The rain had ceased, and now a few billowing gray clouds sailed overhead as the sun sank closer to the horizon. The skyline was just starting to pinken.

"Thank you for the kindness you showed me – and Celia – today," Honora said. "It's such a shame that Molly was there to ruin it all."

"Don't fret over it," he responded. "Sometimes what seems like a failure to us is just a part of the Lord's greater plan."

Honora remained silent as they walked on, his words unsettling her. *This is one thing about him that I cannot reconcile – his constant talk of the Almighty's 'plan'. Certainly, Celia returning to the Bower to be ravished by men for another week isn't part of some divine design.*

"Miss Honora, can we...can we stop a moment here?"
Yet he seems to be reasonable in all other matters.

They stood on the top of the hillock now. Nearby was the rose bush which Honora had deduced marked Wee Baby Moses's grave. A few white blooms on its starkening branches fluttered in the breeze, shining brightly in the waning sunlight. The vantage point allowed for a view of a great distance of rolling, green hills dotted with church steeples and stands of trees.

"Regarding the Lord's plan," Barclay began again. "I believe I have perceived it correctly as it pertains to me – pertains to *us*."

The intimacy of such a statement startled Honora as she forced herself to continue looking out over the valley.

*Is he about to...*she wondered, her stomach fluttering. *Is he going to...?*

"Miss Honora, we have known one another for only a brief time, but – "

Here, he gently reached for her hand. She let him take it and turned to face him, feeling that the vigorous beating of her heart might burst her eardrums.

"But, my admiration for you in this short period has grown to immensity. Your hard work and thoughtfulness as you teach those girls in the kitchen. Your disinterest in vain and worldly things – psh! To see you alongside Emily and Leticia! Your merit excels far beyond theirs without you even having to try! And with these virtues is paired your delightfully playful manner which never fails to lighten and brighten a room – or a lawn!"

He laughed nervously, motioning to the grassy expanse around them.

"And of course, in addition to all of this is your intelligence, wit and undeniable beauty. Miss Honora, forgive me if this seems premature, but I for one am convinced of the prudence of it…"

How am I to answer him?

Honora ceased to breathe as she noted how pink was Barclay's face, how his chin quivered in the pause.

"Miss Honora, might I have the honor of gaining your hand in marriage?"

The query hung in the cool, darkening air between them.

Good god!

"Oh!" Honora gasped as a dizziness overtook her. "I did not…that is, I…oh, forgive me. This is all such a shock. I must sit down."

Pulling her hand away from him, she dropped to the ground with an ungraceful thud, feeling the world whirl around her.

Looking up, she saw him, half-way into a crouch, his face concerned and embarrassed. She felt the earth's dampness begin to seep through the layers of her skirts.

What a strange day this has become!

"Mr. Barclay, please forgive me," she said. "Will you not sit for a moment as I compose myself?"

He dutifully lowered himself beside her and waited, his face fully blushing.

I cannot accept him, Honora thought, fixed in place by consternation. *His family would never accept me as one of their own.*

Through the heady silence came the call of a chaffinch in the distance.

And yet, his offer is possibly my best chance at happiness – my best chance at survival! I've been here just over a week – every hour borrowed from inevitability – and I have no clear idea of my future otherwise!

He is a good man.

She stole a glance at him. It saddened her to see his shoulders hunched forward – how his face had lost its determined grit.

Poor fellow. This is certainly not turning out as he intended!

"Mr. Barclay," she began, attempting to soften his chagrin though she was still unsure how to answer him. "I am certainly flattered by your offer, and truth be told I am very tempted to agree to it, yet my intelligence that you referred to a moment ago makes me wonder at doing so."

"Having prayed in earnest about it, I myself have no doubts," he said, though his tone lacked the fervency of moments earlier. "Our every interaction – from our first moments together on Crawton Green, to finding you injured on the pavement, to your time here at Singer Hall – has been steeped in Providence. I know you would make an excellent wife, and if you would allow me to prove it to you, I would make a…a good husband."

He stared down at his hands as if she had rejected him already.

"I…I believe you would," Honora said. "It's just…"

She paused, unsure how to summarize all she was thinking.

"Is it my hair?" he asked quietly.

"Pardon me?" she asked, confounded.

"Is your hesitance to accept me because of the colour of my hair?" His shoulders and chin rose in forced dignity as if he was bracing himself.

"Your hair?" Honora asked seriously, then couldn't contain a giggle as his head slightly nodded. Her amusement grew and the giggle swelled into a laugh that threw back her head with its escape.

"Sorry," she said in the lull of it, drying her eyes, "But are you asking me if I might reject the best offer of marriage I'm ever likely to receive all because of your cheerfully orangish hair?"

He brightened somewhat at her levity, his head lifting as a sheepish smile tugged at the corners of his mouth.

"But you said a moment ago that I am 'intelligent'. And truly," she continued, reaching for a tuft of hair just under his earlobe, "I think it's quite lovely."

At her touch, he turned to face her fully, hope revived in his eyes. A frisson of affection twanged Honora's heart and she let go of the lock reluctantly.

Great God! What am I to do?

"Barclay," she said, consciously dropping the formal 'Mr.'. "My hesitance lies neither in your endearing hair colour, nor in your impeccable character, but in our stations within society. *You* are a gentleman and *I* am nothing close to a gentleman's daughter."

"I have thought this through," he interrupted, reenergized. "I am a gentleman's *second* son, so a grand marriage is not expected of me. And you! You outshine all the daughters of gentlemen I have ever known! With your manner of speaking and genteel comportment, if you would but don a silken gown and dress your hair, no one would wonder at your heritage, but take it for granted that you are high born."

Honora's bosom warmed at his sentiments so prettily stated.

"I thank you. I do. However, your mother, your whole family, would know who I *truly* am," she said measuredly.

"My mother lives a quiet life here at Singer Hall, disgusted by gossip. Have I never told you that she herself was a saddler's daughter?" Barclay asked.

At another time, the charm of this revelation would have danced within Honora's heart, but she was hardly listening as an ugly truth had crept forward in her mind.

No, the Durbins would not *know who I truly am.* A cold finger traced down her spine. *And neither would Barclay.*

Just yesterday I determined to never tell a living soul about the Bower, but could I truly hope to build a life with someone with whom I'm unwilling to share the truth of myself?

Something vast shifted inside her as she turned to study the man who was pleading his case.

Unaware of the change, Barclay continued, his face alight with brightening hope, "Father fell in love with her when he stopped into her family's saddlery one day – smitten the moment he saw her sitting in the corner, sorting through a box of rivets. He wooed her, married her and they were enormously happy together! Honora, my family would be happy if they knew *I* was happy. Clayton cares nothing for social conventions, and Jasper – he already prizes you above all women! And truly, all Mamma wants is for me to be situated at Southby as Uncle Allard's curate. That's why I wanted to show you his house today. He's said we could live there with him."

Good gracious! A house to live in – that big, beautiful house? How can I decline this offer? I must, yet I must not!

If I am to truly consider becoming this man's wife, *I need to tell him the truth. If he cannot accept my past, then it would be best to know now.*

Her heart rebelled at her mind's logic.

More time! I need more time before I reveal all to him.

No. It would be best to be done with it.

"Barclay," she said, feeling a tremor in her voice. "I must tell you more of my history."

"Very well," he said. "I shall be pleased to hear it."

And he settled in to do so.

A SIGHT OF DISCONNEXION

ONCE AGAIN, BARCLAY'S plans had not been realized. This time, he had got the words out, but his proposal was yet unanswered. However, as he sat beside Honora on the lawn overlooking the valley, he felt a sense of contentment. He felt he had played his part well, and she had not *refused* him. Rather she was voicing her sensible concerns.

Proving herself once again to be wise and circumspect. As a husband, I would naturally want my wife to exhibit these traits.

He admired a faint furrow in her brow and prepared to hear more of her history, as she was set on telling it.

"After Lord Beeman died," she began, "Lady Eliza became the tyrant that she was born to be. Suddenly, she was the only one who had any say over my life – or so she thought. This, combined with her notion that possible suitors who came to Stagsdown House often seemed to prefer me over her resulted in a *very* unhappy household."

"I can imagine so," Barclay said, bristling at the idea himself.

She hurried on. "One night, she invited me to join her and her guests at supper. Once there, she announced that she had found a place for me as governess to four children and that I would be leaving Stagsdown House in a week's time. Sir Roderick and his sister, and a few others were with us that evening. She favored him above all other young men, and I knew she wanted him to hear that not only was I destined for the lowly position of governess, but that it would be off in Yorkshire, more than a hundred miles away from his own estate in

Sussex. Now, I had little reason to believe that Sir Roderick would care about my location as *he* had never shown me especial attention – Eliza was ridiculously jealous! – but she had relayed all her plans for me at the table with a particular lilt in her voice. I had grown up hearing that lilt many times and knew exactly what it meant – the placement she'd found for me was horrendous and she was beyond pleased to relegate me there.

"Not wanting to mar the supper party, I merely thanked her for looking into the matter on my behalf, but made no indication that I was accepting the position. Meanwhile, I knew that a plan I had been devising for weeks must now come into play. Back in my room, I had a satchel packed with all the things I needed to leave Stagsdown House, including the little bit of money I'd found amongst my father's things at his passing – all my inheritance in the world. I supposed it would support me until I could find work. On my nightstand beside my bed were a number of recent newspaper clippings of employment opportunities. I would leave early the next morning with all of this and go and make my own way in the world."

"How exceedingly brave of you," Barclay said, then thought. *Had she not fled, she would likely be in Yorkshire now, not here with me.*

Honora laughed.

"The timing of my escape was especially delicious because Sir Roderick was leaving that morning also and it may have seemed to Eliza that I had run off with him. Of course, his many companions would have vouched that nothing of the sort had occurred but how I wish I could have seen her face if that thought occurred to her!

"I arrived in London before noon and began to seek out the various addresses I had read in the newspapers. After much walking and knocking on doors, I learned that the first two positions had been filled."

Here she paused, inordinately long.

"And then…" he encouraged.

"Barclay," she said, a quaver in her voice. "I have been honest with you, honest about my parents, about my life at Stagsdown House. But there are things I was not ready to speak to you about. But now…"

She smiled faintly and took a deep breath. "Now, I want to make it prodigiously clear why I went where I did next. It was something like a coffee house off of St Martins Lane. Truly discouraged, I urged myself to smile and exude confidence as surely that would help me to be hired. I would not – *could not* – return to Stagsdown House. I *needed* a job and a place to sleep. Well, I found what I needed there – became gainfully employed in their kitchen."

"The Lord provided for you in your time of need." Barclay said. *And working there ensured you could walk past Crawton Green at just the right time and meet me.*

Honora seemed to grow flustered, then continued. "It was a very nice establishment, finely furnished and serving good fare. I was pleased at the success of my plan."

She paused again.

"I lived and worked there for but five days when I learned that the coffee house was actually something quite different than what I had been led to believe."

"Yes!" Barclay said. "When we found you near Seven Dials, you had just been attacked by your employer!"

She seemed not to have heard him as she looked out over the hills. "You see, it was there that I met Celia, and discovered what she did under threat of physical injury."

"Celia frequented the coffee house?"

Honora would not look at him.

"Celia lived there…as did I."

Barclay ceased to breathe. *A prostitute lived where Honora worked?*

"So you see," she continued slowly, "If I have not made myself clear: I am determined to get Celia out of Titania's Bower because I saw what she endures, having lived amongst the harlots there."

Even seated, Barclay felt light-headed.

Honora lived at a…

She herself was a…

In his befuddlement, a vision appeared in his mind.

The girl in the alley near Covent Garden, she who had leaned forward that her loosened bodice would cease to hold its secrets – she sat on her barrel again, but this time above the pale fullness of her revealed bosom, luridly painted and smirking, was Honora's face.

No! This is Honora! He reminded himself, blinking hard. *I have seen her goodness when she works with the children — heard such sense each time she opens her mouth to speak!*

He studied her lips for a moment, thinking of the kisses they must have dealt out. Then, he closed his eyes to keep them from traveling down her body as he wondered how else she had been touched and how the length and breadth of her had responded.

The silence endured for a moment longer before he finally forced out the words, "Your determination to save your friend is to be commended."

His voice strained as he went on. "As for living there — at this…place — it seems you felt you had no alternative."

"I did not *feel* it to be so. I *knew* it."

She was staring steadily at him now.

"Yes, well," he began haltingly, then paused as his mind staggered ahead.

If we confess our sins, he is faithful and just to forgive us our sins, and to cleanse us from all unrighteousness.

All unrighteousness. Yes, it is written as all *unrighteousness.*

Thus fortified, he stammered on, "G-god forgives us for our sins if we but ask. By Him Who is merciful…all will be forgiven"

"All will be forgiven?" she asked.

"Yes," he insisted, looking at her steadily, hoping to convince her as well as himself. "If we but confess our sins."

Her eyes grew wider.

"You believe that I *sinned* in this matter?"

She doesn't think she deserves such mercy.

His mouth opened and closed like a fish, though he said nothing.

A curtain seemed to fall somewhere behind her eyes and she exhaled a lengthy breath. Suddenly, she was on her feet.

"Miss Honora?" he asked, leaping up himself. She wouldn't look at him.

"Ah, there you two are!"

Barclay, in a state of mortified wonder at her sudden transformation, glanced over his shoulder.

Jasper was advancing on them, taking long steps over the grass.

"I saw that Caleb was back in his pen and came looking for you!" he said, jovially. "Supper's ready."

Barclay said nothing, but looked from his brother's youthful face, now losing its good humour, to Honora as she stood, still as a marble statue. Through a ringing in his ears, he heard Jasper ask with an uncomfortable little laugh, "Is everything alright?"

Honora replied in a foreign voice, "I'm afraid I've been put off my supper tonight, Jasper."

"Oh!" His face fell. "Well, perhaps Bess could make you a poached egg and a bit of toast if you are unwell."

"No, though I thank you," Honora said, hurrying toward the house now and saying over her shoulder, "Please excuse me for the evening, as I will keep to my quarters."

"Alright then," Jasper said, his voice full of polite confusion as he and Barclay began to follow after her. "I'm sorry you're not well."

Barclay studied how her shoulders were hunched slightly forward, her head down. He would not have recognized her if he saw her walking across a street in this state.

What did I say that so upset her? He wondered, recalling how her eyes had dimmed and her mouth – laughing about his hair just moments earlier – had hardened into a thin line.

'Forgiveness'…that's what it was.

"Is she truly feeling poorly?" Jasper asked, then, "Barclay?"

"So she says."

"She didn't…" Jasper started to ask, his voice full of gentle astonishment. "She didn't *refuse* you, did she?"

"She…I…" All other words caught in Barclay's throat.

Yes, let him think that. I cannot begin to explain the truth of it.

He clamped his mouth shut and stared hard at his brother.

"Simply unbelievable," Jasper finally breathed and said nothing more as the two brothers started up the steps into the house, but his hand rested firmly on Barclay's shoulder.

A PLAN TO FLEE

FORGIVENESS? HE THINKS I need forgiveness *for getting trapped in a bawdy house?*

Honora held her anger in check as she ascended the staircase to her room.

And what exactly does he suppose me to be guilty of? Drinking that diabolical drink Dovey forced upon me? Stupidity, perhaps? No…ignorance. But how is one guilty when acting out of total ignorance?

As her hand grasped the doorknob to her bedroom, realization hit her.

He must think I was a harlot!

But I never said such a thing…

Still, what else would he think as I lived among them? Truth be told, I would have been one had Pilven not been so reluctant.

The memory of the man leaning in to whisper into her ear filled her eyes with tears. His quavering hand had pushed her hair back as his breath was hot upon her cheek.

"I won't touch you," he had said as she had lain upon the settee completely immobile. "But you must behave as if I had or Mrs. Dovey will tell my wife I've been here, and I *can't* have that!"

His quiet voice had grown almost frantic as he continued, "And that Dovey, she'll just send another fellow in to do it to you, so you might as well act like I done it!"

The remembrance of the terror raging inside her whilst her limbs had lain weightily, uselessly, churned her stomach.

But even if he had *touched me, I still wouldn't need to ask for forgiveness.*

The thought was like a slap in the face. She sat down heavily on the bed, brushing her hand over her leaking eyes.

Celia's been touched that way many times, but she doesn't need forgiveness either. She needs a way to make it stop!

I cannot stay here and flirt with a man who will not understand a most basic truth. I'll leave tomorrow. And when I am able, I will *get Celia out of the Bower.*

With a sickened, heavy heart, Honora curled up on her bed and wept.

A STORE OF COURAGE

BARCLAY STARED AT the bowl of soup before him, stirring it absentmindedly, noting again the emptiness of the chair that Honora usually occupied.

"I am sorry that Miss Honora is not feeling well, Barclay," Mrs. Durbin's voice broke through his miserable musing. "Did you have dinner in town? Perhaps something did not agree with her there."

"She seemed well enough until we arrived back here." Barclay said, laying down his spoon. "Truth be told, I'm not feeling well myself. Please excuse me."

He rose to leave and felt the appraising eyes of Jasper, his mother and even Martha on him.

Ask me no questions, any of you! He silently begged as he made his way out of the dining room.

He heard Clayton mutter, "I hope I'm not to catch what's ailing you both as I'm leaving early tomorrow for town."

Within minutes, Barclay was slumped in the window box of his room, remembering how it had felt as if the lawn was opening beneath him when Honora confided in him.

She said she was tricked? But how can one mistake a brothel for a coffee house? he wondered. But then it occurred to him, that when he had seen Celia through the spyglass, she had appeared to him as any other young woman at Hyde Park.

I suppose if a prostitute can be camouflaged, a brothel can be as well.

But could Honora really have been a...a doxy? he asked himself. *Father, is this not the woman You have promised me?*

He thought back on all that had seemed to confirm this notion.

Yes, she must be my Intended.

He envisioned her beautiful face, lit by her playful sagacity, then the dousing of her esprit at a few words from his mouth.

'...you believe I sinned in this *matter?' she asked, and I did not answer.*

His head ached at the memory — how she had stonily turned away just moments after caressing a tuft of his hair.

Am I wrong, Father? Was it not sin?

There is forgiveness for such things.

How many women in scripture were 'delivered from the power of darkness, translated into the kingdom'? The woman at the well...Mary Magdalene...the woman with the spikenard. Yes, they were redeemed and now are revered amongst all Christendom.

And how many men committed the same act and yet are called the pillars of our faith?

Reflexively, he reached for the Bible on his armoire, but he did not open it. He knew well what it said.

David had countless concubines. Jacob bedded his wives' handmaidens. Worst of all, Lot offered up his daughters to the townsmen!

The persistent and urgent demands of his own flesh, solitarily appeased, roared to the forefront of his mind. The few bites of soup he had swallowed at supper roiled within his belly.

God, why are we such a rotten people?

His eyes filled with tears. He wiped at them with one hand while the other still rested on the book's worn, leather cover.

When King David called Bathsheba to him, she was not able to refuse. She must have wanted out of his palace — just as Celia wants out of this Titania's Bower — but who can refuse a king?

Celia wants out! She's being held there against her will, enslaved, as Honora said.

An inkling stirred in his mind.

I could help her. Just as Joshua's spies spared Rahab whilst Jericho tumbled down, I might save Celia from this Titania's Bower.

Father, is this why I met Honora? Not to find a wife, but to free another girl from a hell in London?

All I've ever wanted is to help those in need. Well, here is someone who is desperate for my intervention. Yes, even if Honora will never speak to me again, saving Celia is my Christian duty.

His eyes were dry now as the inspiration hardened into resolve. Still, he was frightened and prayed that God would loosen within him a store of courage, yet unknown.

BEGIN AGAIN, AGAIN

EARLY THE NEXT morning, Honora crept down the large staircase, preparing to leave Singer Hall forever.

Surely no one will be in the blue salon at this hour, she thought, hardly able to make out the handrail in the faint morning light. She carried very little with her since she had arrived at the estate with nothing more than the clothes she wore and a pocketful of gold coins.

To her relief, the salon's door did not creak at its opening, and no Durbin lurked within the room's confines. Going to the last place she had seen a newspaper, she found it again – the light was much brighter here due to the eastern facing windows – and leafed through it for the advertisement section. Expecting to hear the ever-present Martha hastening down the hall at any moment, Honora folded a few pages into a manageable square and tucked them into her bodice.

I can pore over that in the coach.

The idea rang hollowly in her mind due to the disastrous results of her previous attempt at doing so. Now, armed to head back to London, she snuck down the hallway and out Singer Hall's front door. The brisk air was colder than she had expected and she missed Mrs. Durbin's pelisse. Skirting around the side of the house, she picked her way past the kitchen garden to a hedge which ran parallel to the lane. She found a narrow opening in it and pushed her way through.

Emerging on the other side, she began to walk toward the stage coach stop she had noted on her few trips back and forth to town with the Durbins.

Had I kept silent, I might be engaged now. In a simpler world, I could be lying awake fretting over what would be served at our wedding breakfast.

Unwittingly, Honora drew forth the memory of Mrs. Durbin, her eyes alight with interest, her voice soft with a gentle answer – and that of Jasper, his mouth twisted into a cagey grin – and her heart ached.

Now they will remember me as the rudest guest in Singer Hall's history, departing at the crack of dawn without a word.

But what else was to be done? Though they may never know it, I've spared them.

Then there was the image of Barclay, his earnest, kind face peering intently at her, his vibrant hair haloing his face in the light of the setting sun the evening before.

'All will be forgiven', he said.

Honora's eyes pricked with tears, but she urged herself to center on the anger she felt rather than the disappointment.

Forgiveness! I might as well beg pardon for having been born a steward's daughter, or for having large feet!

She pinched her pocket and felt the hard lump of coins – her only hope now.

A wide, stone pillar came into view down the way at the crossroads, and soon she had situated herself on a stump there. The pillar supported her back as her ankle protested at the exercise it had just endured.

Such frailty! she chided her body. *There's likely a bit more walking that will be required of you today.*

As she leaned forward to massage the flagging member, she heard coming up behind her the wheels of a vehicle on the road. It sped past, headed toward London. At once, Honora recognized the Durbin's gig, and the back of the fellow driving it.

Barclay! Has he come to chase me down? Good thing the pillar hid me. Does he think me able to travel so quickly?

The absurd thought of herself running madly away from Singer Hall made her smile, but it faded immediately.

What does he want from me? To insist further how desperately in need of forgiveness I am?

A sudden burning behind her eyes warned Honora that she must veer away from thinking about such things if she didn't want to be a weeping mess once the coach rolled into view.

Now there was the hard scrabble upon the road of a horse approaching behind her. A rider, his bright carroty hair peeking out from underneath his hat, cantered past, taking the same route as the gig.

Jasper! Why would they not travel together?

She sat a good twenty minutes pondering.

Surely those boys didn't think I could have got that far away in this amount of time. Perhaps they weren't chasing me after all. And the coach — did I miss it? Does it not run on Saturdays?

As she sat morosely contemplating her situation, there appeared down the road coming toward her, two girls swinging their joined hands happily between them.

Susan and Mary. Oh, I did invite them back to the kitchen today, didn't I?

The girls hailed her and began to run, happily tripping on their own feet. "Miss Honora! Miss Honora! 'Ave ya come to meet us?"

Almost simultaneously, the mail coach rumbled into view, its maroon and black body shining in the sun. Honora knew that if she waved at the driver, the scarlet wheels would stop, and she could disappear behind its door and reach London in a few hours' time.

Good god, to disappoint these girls right before their eyes? How could I bear it?

"Mumma loved the tartlets! And we've told 'er 'bout the toad-in-a-'ole biscuits[x] we're makin' t'day!"

With as sunny an answer as she could assemble, Honora rose from the stump, took both Byerlys by the hand and headed back to Singer Hall, knowing that today, for the sake of two excited little girls, she would not yet flee to London to begin again, again.

LIKE MOSES UNTO PHARAOH

THE WORDS ABOVE the door were painted in a stately font: **Titania's Bower**.

Barclay stood for a moment, examining the building's respectable-looking front, breathing in a rich, enticing aroma.

It does look – even smells – like a coffee house.

His heart pounded in his ears. All the way into town, he had considered what he would do and say upon entering this devil's lair.

'I have come to deliver the girl called Celia from this den of wickedness. Do not hinder this scheme or the wrath of God will be upon you.'

And then he would wait for Celia to pack her bag which he would carry for her as she walked beside him back to the stables. He would then retrieve the gig and drive them back to Singer Hall.

This was the first fantasy that had run through his mind as he hawed Caleb toward London. As the unrealistic nature of it quickly became apparent, many other versions wound themselves out, but they all ended in the same manner – Celia seated alongside him in the gig, her face jubilant with realized liberation.

Now, as he stood outside the Bower, he knew that he could not stride in and demand Celia's release as Moses had commanded the letting go of his people from Egypt. Though he had never faced one before, he was certain that no bawd would relinquish one of her girls any more easily than a fox would release a hen from its jaws.

And what if a strongman opens the door? The image of Biles, clad in his Heath School uniform and forcing dripping biscuits upon him, flickered into his mind.

I would do my best to fight him, if it came to that.

Then there was the additional problem that Celia had never met him, and was not acquainted with his character.

How to get her to come away with me, a stranger? he wondered, his stomach churning.

Lurking under all of this was a fear, even more personal.

The young women inside this place are schooled in enticing men. What if I am tempted beyond what I can bear?

The alarming thought made him reconsider the entire scheme. As he stood, contemplating his own shameful lack of self-restraint, a verse of scripture burst into his mind like a brick thrown through a window.

'The Spirit of the Lord God is upon me...he hath sent me to bind up the brokenhearted, to proclaim liberty to the captives, and the opening of the prison to them that are bound.'

Yes, he thought, staring hard at the Bower's front door. *There is a girl inside there who wants out. And I may be the instrument God uses to liberate her.*

The street preacher took a deep breath.

Lord, preserve and guide me!

With this desperate prayer on his lips, he was about to step toward the door when it suddenly opened.

"Good morning!" a tall, finely dressed woman called to him pleasantly.

Barclay froze.

"It i*th* rather early," she said with an affable smile and a wave of her hand. "But we are ready for you. Plea*the* come in."

A PREACHER IN THE BOWER

JUST A MOMENT earlier, Dovey had been upstairs gazing broodingly out her bedroom window when a strange young man stepped into view on the street below. She watched as he stood there for an inordinate amount of time peering intently at the Bower.

Will you come in or not, sir? she thought, but then made the decision for him by quickly descending the stairs to open the front door and invite him in.

At this, he marched up the stairs and through the door with an air of determination that surprised Dovey.

Perhaps he knows what he wants after all, she thought. But once inside, he looked around the vestibule – examining it from ceiling to floor – as if he'd never entered a building before.

She stood between him and the exit expectantly, yet patient. When his visual perusal of the entryway ended, he suddenly announced, "I've come for Miss Celia – the thin, dark-haired girl."

"Oh? And how are you acquainted with my dear *Th*elia?" Dovey asked.

"I...I saw her at Hyde Park."

Dovey could not have been more astounded though she masked it well. *Celia's been playing the coquette whilst out on her walks? That fine silk gown has done its work!*

"Very well, *th*ir. Right thi*th* way, if you plea*th*e."

She led him down the hallway where she encountered an inquisitive Molly to whom she whispered a hurried directive. As Molly rushed off to fetch Celia, Dovey opened the door to the backroom and waved the man inside. Again, blocking the doorway, the procuress spoke.

"*Th*elia, a*th* I'm *th*ertain you could tell, i*th* one of my mo*th*t beloved girl*th*. Therefore, the time a gentleman *th*pends with her i*th*, well..."

Dovey laughed her tinkling laugh at that moment in this practiced speech.

"Time with her i*th* more co*th*tly than time with *th*ome of the other*th*."

The fellow looked as if he'd been hit upside the head, his eyes gibbous with astonishment.

Did you think you'd be getting it for free, you imbecile?

"But you, *th*ir." Dovey scanned him up and down approvingly, taking in the quality of his coat, the unscuffed leather of his boots. "Clearly a gentleman of *your* caliber will have no trouble affording *one* guinea."

Here she extended her hand to him, palm up, smiling unctuously all the while.

After standing dumbstruck for a moment, he muttered something that sounded like, "Yes, well Hosea paid for Gomer". Then he patted at his pockets as if he wasn't sure where he would find the requested payment.

But soon, Dovey's fingers were closing over a warm, metallic coin.

"Very good, *th*ir," she purred. "Mi*th* *Th*elia will be with you in but a moment."

A STRANGE RUTTER

CELIA WAS DOZING on her bed when Molly burst through the door.

"Celia, there's a gentleman 'ere to see ya!" she sang out.

Celia's eyes fluttered open, and she noted the brightness of the sunlight coming through the window.

"What? Now?" she asked, propping up on her elbow. "It's not even dinnertime yet."

"Not all appetites run on the same clock. Dovey says yer to ready yerself and come down at once."

Molly settled herself on the edge of her bed while Celia stared at the wall uneasily.

"Come on, then!" Molly urged, then giggled. "'E's a bit of a strange rutter."

"What do you mean?" Celia sat bolt upright in bed, her eyes narrowing. A vision of Rottem flashed into her mind, his matted curly hair, the look of malevolent boredom in his eyes. The dreaded cull had never shown any interest in Celia herself, stating once as he stared at her chest, "You haven't got a set of baps to bat about. I need a bit of flesh to wrestle with."

Therefore, she had never suffered the rough treatment he doled out to the plumper girls, but she knew he wasn't the only brute in London.

"Oh, you'll see!" Molly replied in an irritating sing-song voice. "'E asked for you in partic'lar. Dovey knew it 'ad to be you, when 'e said 'e saw a skinny dark-haired girl walkin' in the park —said no one else'll do!"

What? Alarmed, Celia thought back to their jaunt through the park the day before. Molly, of course, had flirted with the fellow by the Serpentine, but Celia had kept her head down when anyone passed, just as she always did.

"Come on, then!" Molly urged again. "She's gonna be angry for certain if you don't get down there quick like!"

Celia climbed out of the bed. Her head felt fuzzy and light, as if she had gulped down a large tumbler full of wine.

"Leave me," she said in a voice that seemed to come from outside of herself.

With a final giggle, Molly exited the bedroom.

Once alone, Celia went to the mirror and stared for a long moment into its depths. Her face was gaunt and there were bluish circles under her huge eyes. There was no colour in her cheeks and her dry, cracked lips were pale as if coated with frost.

This is the girl he saw and followed? she marveled.

The thought that she now had nothing to herself assaulted her. Her body, she had conceded long ago, but now even her walks in the park were no longer her own. Within the walls of the Bower, she could not be herself, but out on the gravel paths under the leafy overhang of the trees and at the edges of the various waterways, she had been free to act as she wanted, think as she wanted, if only for a little while. But all of that had just been ripped from her tenuous grasp. Now every time she went out, she'd be glancing over her shoulder for anyone who might be following her, watching her with overt regard, ready to follow her back to the Bower.

I'll let this bastard see me as I truly am — maybe that will ward him off for good.

Slipping out of her nightgown, she stepped into her laundering dress, pleased for once at its thinning, faded material. She neither combed her hair or washed her face.

Soon she was descending the staircase to stand before Dovey. Molly, snickering again, stood behind the bawd.

"Drumming up bi*th*ni*th* in the park, were you? Good, clever girl!" Dovey said quietly, a glint in her eye, then looked the drab dress up and down. "An odd choi*the* for a morning tumble. But he already paid – a whole guinea! – *th*o no harm there. Follow me."

Celia was dragged down the hall to the backroom where Dovey announced flirtatiously, "*Th*ir, here i*th* the girl who caught your eye."

The man who turned to face her was young, only a few years older than herself. Standing awkwardly by the fire grate, his hat was still on his head and his empty hands hung at his sides, working nervously. But his mien was most surprising of all. Surrounded by a shock of coppery hair, his face looked nearly angelic in its wide-eyed earnestness.

Celia could determine much about how a dalliance would progress within the first three seconds of seeing the cull. Looking at the anxious fellow before her, she took a deep breath, then exhaled.

He followed me back here from the park last evening? He does not look so bold as to attempt that. I may be able to talk him out of what he came here for, Celia realized. She had done such a thing before with a nervous would-be patron.

"Celia?" he asked staring, then pointed at her. "You...*you* are called Celia?"

Dovey pushed her forward.

"Ye*th*, and what i*th* she to call you, *th*ir?"

The man looked around, uneasily and replied nothing.

"*Mr. Park*, perhaps?" Dovey asked, filling the awkward silence. "Will that do?"

He stared at the women dumbly.

Good lord! Did he really come here, expecting to be caught up in the throes? Celia marveled, her relief growing as she seated herself upon a chair. *Just look at him – a fish out of water. Surely, he wouldn't know what to do if a girl stood naked before him.*

"Well, I will leave you to it," Dovey murmured, finally moving towards the door. "Will you want any refreshment – coffee? cake? – to round out your time here, Mr. Park?"

The man shook his head faintly, still staring at Celia.

Dovey did not entirely disguise a chuckle as she exited and shut the door behind her.

THE CRUSHING OF JASPER

PUSHING MOLLY RATHER roughly out of the way, Dovey squatted beside the closed salon door and pressed her ear to the thinnest of its panels. Molly knelt right up against her.

What can he possibly think to accomplish in there with a living, breathing girl? Dovey wondered, snickering. She pressed her ear harder against the door. There was the susurration of quiet voices on the other side.

And now we will learn if he is pleased with his purchase. She held her breath, unsuccessfully straining to make out the couple's words. Suddenly, their *sotto voci* ceased.

Perhaps he's making a go at it after all, Dovey thought, wanting to pat the fellow on the back. She had just settled in to overhear the familiar sounds of rhythmic thumping when there was a knock upon the Bower's front door.

Yet another at this early hour? she marveled.

But she was intent on hearing whatever she could of the strange occurrence taking place within the salon, so she bumped Molly, waving her toward the vestibule.

Molly skulked down the hallway and disappeared around the corner.

A few more seconds of virtual silence beyond the door, and an ache in her compressed ear, convinced Dovey to stand. As she sighed in frustration, a squeal from the Bower's front arrested her attention.

Who's at the door, then? she wondered and headed there. Stopping at the hall's end, she had a perfect view of the scene unfolding itself in the vestibule.

Upon the doorstep was a much younger version of the strange fellow who had just been ushered into the salon with Celia. With a brighter shade of hair, he was shorter and thinner. His face was all eyes and nose as he gazed out from under the brim of his slightly too-large hat. Though he was awkward, he had all the markings of a fine gentleman in the making.

He gaped at Molly who leaned against the doorframe languorously.

Dovey loved to see her artful girls play well at their game, so she silently hung back to watch.

The boy's mouth, fringed with the beginnings of a moustache, worked stupidly. It was a long moment before he uttered in a newly broken, genteel voice, "Please, ma'am, I'm looking for...for my brother. I believe I saw him enter this building a few moments ago."

Mr. Park's brother? Of course!

"Aye sir, 'e's come in 'ere, asking for Celia." Molly said in a most affected manner, her sleeve slipping off her shoulder. "'E's in the back with her at present. Did ya want a li'l of what 'e's 'avin' fer yerself?"

She looked him up and down suggestively.

Ah Molly, that's my girl! Dovey thought proudly.

"It seems that with fine gent'men, you cain't ever start too early," Molly added.

The boy's face turned different colours.

Don't take it too far, Molly-Girl. Be sure of your mark.

At that moment, there was a creak in the floor at the top of the staircase. Doris appeared, dressed in only her thin nightgown, her pert curves silhouetted by the sunlight coming in through a window in the hallway above.

"Who's this then?" she asked. Her loose, wavy hair fell about her shoulders and Dovey thought she almost looked pretty as she drifted down the stairs to pose seductively in the doorway alongside Molly.

"Comin' in for a bit, sir?" she asked.

Yes Doris, my love! Dovey approved. *One such as him might be frighted off by a beauty like Molly, but your plain girlishness might be just what he's after.*

288

The boy, dumb in confoundment, looked from one prostitute to the other several times before beginning to shake his head.

"No," he murmured, quietly, his hand reaching toward his mouth. "No."

Then, his shoulders lurched forward and his jaw dropped open, his chest heaving below it.

"Good god!" Molly cried, all amusement and coquetry fled. "Don't puke 'ere!"

The boy was able to tame his sudden retching and turned to flee down the stairs to the street.

However, the mere display proved too much for the delicacy of Doris's stomach which upended itself. Dovey watched in horror as the girl bent over and vomited onto the floor, splattering Molly's feet.

"Ew!" Molly screeched, delicately lifting the hem of her dress to examine her ankles as she stepped to the window, away from the mess. "Ewwww!"

Doris sank to the floor completely and whimpered in shame as Molly began to wipe her feet with the long curtains.

"Molly!" Dovey said sharply, stepping out of the shadows. "Don't you dare!"

The blonde looked up, clearly startled to see the bawd standing so close by.

Dovey's delight had soured along with Doris's belly. "And why would you *th*care a young gentleman away like that? If I *th*ee you read a cull wrong like that again, I'll box*th* your ear*th*."

Sticking her lip out defiantly, Molly stalked away.

"And Dori*th*, get that floor cleaned up immediately," Dovey hissed.

From the floor, the girl moaned. "But I…I…"

"*Th*till your belly and grab your mop, you *th*tupid girl."

But Doris only crawled away, not even bothering to duck when Dovey's hand swung in to smack the back of her head.

As Doris began to stumble up the stairs, Dovey went to retrieve the implements to clean the floor herself. She hadn't pressed the issue with Doris for fear of sparking another wave of vomit and she wanted the doorway clean before Mr. Park stepped back through it. Suddenly the guinea she had earlier tucked into her bodice didn't feel as weighty.

IN THE BACKROOM WITH BARCLAY

LOOKING MOONSTRUCK, the fellow stood by the fire grate, still staring at Celia.

"Have you had a fine morning, sir?" Celia asked. When left alone with men who did not seem urgently intent on a dalliance, Celia had learned to ask them questions. She hoped to remind them of their other lives – their real lives – which she knew were full of people who relied upon them and who probably didn't know they were then at the Bower. On occasion this ploy had stopped the visit from progressing its usual way even though the fee had already been placed into Dovey's outstretched hand. This kept the bawd happy and Celia happier.

Ignoring her query, the man took a deep breath and said quietly, "Celia."

Have you not yet understood that that is who I am?

"Yes?"

"I've come because of…because of Honora," he stuttered.

Celia's heart jumped within her.

"She said it broke her heart to leave you behind, but she had to flee when she did."

Tears filled Celia's eyes. Standing from her chair, she moved closer to the man, then pulled him down to sit next to her on the settee. He looked alarmed at the sudden proximity.

Celia whispered, "Where is she?"

"At Singer Hall, my home. I've come to take you there."

Celia choked back a cry and bit her lips.

She looked hard at the fellow before her, his solemn eyes peering out intently from underneath his thatch of vibrant hair. Her heart whispered to her, *Here is a good man. Honora wouldn't have sent someone untrustworthy.*

She thought of all the men that she couldn't trust. The vast number was uncountable. Then, she recalled the men she could rely on.

Father — what I remember of him. Bill. Yes, such men do exist. Possibly Mr. Tiller.

"Let's go now," he said, his voice far too loud, and stood as if their departure was imminent.

"Shh!" Celia urged, pressing her finger to her lips and pulling him back down onto the settee beside her. "I cannot simply walk out with you at this moment."

He looked perplexed. "But it's just up Mile End Road, past Romford. We'll be there within an hour if we leave now."

Honora did not send a bad man, but she may have sent a fool.

"Dovey would beat us both if she knew what we meant to do. We'll have to go later today. But for now, I must pretend as if all is normal. When the gentlemen start arriving tonight, I'll sneak out and meet you…at the corner of Hyde Park where the Road from Uxbridge meets Park Lane."

His eyes looked doubtful.

"Will that do?" she asked, willing him to agree.

It must — don't leave me here!

"Yes," he said, nodding as if trying to convince himself. "Yes. Hyde Park. Where Uxbridge meets Park. I will meet you there this evening."

Celia contained the sigh of relief that welled up in her.

"You ought to go now," she said. "Dovey will get suspicious if you don't come out soon as we've had enough time to finish you off."

He flinched as Celia reached forward to remove his hat and muss his hair.

"What are you…?" he stuttered, pulling away.

"You look as if nothing's happened." She pulled him back toward her to loosen his cravat and undo the top two buttons of his shirt. Celia noted his horror at the familiar ministrations, but she was so happy, she felt no shame.

Once she was done with him, she turned her busy hands on herself, pinching her cheeks to pinken them and tucking a bit of her skirt so that it was caught on her petticoat.

Folding her hands over her chest, she whispered "Thank you, Mr. Park, from my very heart."

"Oh, don't ever call me that. I am Barclay Durbin." He squashed his hat back on his head and took a breath as if steeling himself for his exit. "I will wait for you at the park."

Speaking more loudly than necessary, he said, "Thank you, Miss Celia." Then he cringed again, perhaps realizing what he seemed to be thanking her for.

"Of course, sir," she said at an equal volume.

Nodding silently at each other, he rose first and headed toward the door.

Then, he was gone.

Honora is well! And thinking of me!

It was with great difficulty that Celia smothered the smile that tugged at her lips, ironing her face into its usual denial of emotion.

This time, great good had actually come of being alone with a man.

SPARING MOST DETAILS

DOVEY STOOD IN the entryway, arranging and rearranging a vaseful of silk flowers, determined to be present when the anomalous Mr. Park finally emerged from the backroom with Celia.

Likely with a similar motivation, Molly had returned. Her feet and ankles now clean, she was wafting the sickly air of the vestibule out the front door.

"*Th*ay nothing of the man'*th* brother to him," Dovey warned the girl fiercely. "The boy'*th* up*th*et i*th* between the two of them and Mr. Park will learn of it later or he won't. It'*th* none of *our* con*th*ern."

When Mr. Park finally did make his reentrance, looking perhaps even more awkward than he had before, he came down the hall alone.

Of course, Celia wouldn't do the proper thing and see him out, Dovey thought, irritated as she adjusted a large pink peony for the tenth time. *That girl has no business sense!*

In her much-rehearsed gracious voice, she said, "We do thank you for your cu*th*tom, Mr. Park. I hope you found Celia a*th* plea*th*ant a*th* you had anti*th*ipated. Plea*th*e remember her in the future."

The man hardly paused in his passage to the door, just nodding slightly before rushing out. Once Molly had shut it behind him, she and Dovey hurried to the backroom, tittering all the way.

They found Celia, her skirts askew, sitting on the settee.

"Did he keep his hat on the whole time?" Molly asked excitedly.

Dovey giggled, as she had wondered the same thing.

"What happened?" Molly insisted as Celia wasn't answering, looking lost in thought. "Celia!"

"Oh," she said as Molly jabbed her in the ribs. She shook her head. "He...he couldn't..."

Here, she extended her index finger and waggled it.

Dovey and Molly burst out laughing.

"Well that'*th* not *th*urpri*th*ing!" Dovey said, wiping her eyes. Through the years, she had seen that some impotent men never returned, ashamed to show their faces. Yet others came back the very next day, bent on proving themselves, usually asking for a different girl that they could blame some factor other than their own physique. "He may be back for another try."

"Oh," Celia said, the spell she'd been under suddenly broken. She shook her head. "I don't think he'll return."

"Why? Did you not try your be*th*t to plea*th*e him?" Dovey asked cuttingly, shifting back into her usual state of avarice.

"I did what I could, Mrs. Dovey," Celia said, a faint glow in her eyes. A smile seemed to be teasing at the corners of her mouth.

He was much more palatable than most of the crusty old hoppers who frequent us. Well, if I'd known all it took was a youthful chap to perk her up, I'd have lured one in long ago!

Hmm, but most likely of all, she's happy because she thinks she's done working for the day. Can't let her get too comfortable with that notion.

"Well, the fun i*th* over. A*th* alway*th*, I want all your daytime dutie*th* taken care of before you need to do your work thi*th* evening."

That did the trick! Dovey thought as Celia's face resumed its usual sullenness and Molly shuffled out of the room. With a great sense of contentment she hadn't felt since Honora's fist had struck her face, Dovey turned to go, Mr. Park's coin slipping within her bodice.

Ah, yes! I shall drop this into the sack in my drawer with the rest of my money and exchange it for paper soon.

On the heels of this pleasant thought was the unsettling recollection that she would have to face the bankers with her newly-acquired lisp.

296

A GROSS MISAPPREHENSION

"LIKE THIS, MA'AM?" Susan asked, tipping the mortar so that Honora could see into its hollow.

Honora chuckled to herself as she examined the consistency of the girl's pounded almonds. *Will I ever grow accustomed to being called 'ma'am'?*

"Very well done, Susan. Nice and fine. Now mix it in with the Lisbon sugar."

The girl beamed, her missing front tooth a dark window in her joyful smile, as she poured the paste into a bowl.

Honora pretended not to see Mary sneak a dried cherry from the pile on the table into her mouth.

Just over the girl's shoulder, a dark mass streaked past the window, startling Honora from her good humour. Stepping forward, she pressed her forehead against the glass pane, and caught a glimpse of a horse just inside the paddock. Its sides were heaving as its slim rider slipped off to the ground.

Jasper has returned. She waited a moment to see the gig drive in behind him, but it did not appear. *But where is Barclay?*

After his hasty dismount, the boy stumbled back from the horse's flank, and planted his hands on his knees as if to stabilize himself. Immediately, Honora could see this was not mere recovery from a raucous gallop.

Good god, what is the matter?

The boy righted himself and reeled right and left as the groom emerged from the stable to take the horse's reins. Dervy looked as alarmed at the sight of the boy as Honora felt, and put out an arm to steady him.

Is he drunk? No, not Jasper...

And where is Barclay? Surely, he would want to be here when his brother is in such a state.

The boy shook off the groom's hand and reeled toward the front of the house.

"Girls," Honora said in as level a voice as she could. "Keep stirring until it's entirely smooth. I shall return in but a moment."

Then she was through the swinging kitchen door, headed toward the foyer. Within seconds, she heard the front door open and the quick, heavy slap of boots running upon the parqueted floor. Peeking around the corner and down the long hall, she watched Jasper pass through the door into his mother's favorite room. She nearly called out to him, but the preponderant silence of the lofty entryway around her stilled her tongue as she rushed forward.

He had left the door flung wide. Honora glanced around as the sound of his voice spilled out into the hallway. No one was there to see her creep closer and lean against the wall.

"Jasper! Have you gone wild?" Mrs. Durbin gasped. "Come sit beside me. Martha, please fetch him some wine."

A sob escaped the boy's throat. Honora ducked behind the corner just in time as she heard Martha rush out of the door and down the hall.

What has happened? Honora marveled. *Is Barclay hurt?*

Her stomach churned at the thought.

"Now Jasper," the soothing sounds of Mrs. Durbin's voice drifted out of the doorway. "What's got you all in a lather."

"Mamma, you must brace yourself to hear it." Here, his voice broke with another guttural sob.

Good lord! Honora drew closer to the doorway.

"This morning, Barclay was not at breakfast," the boy began. "I saw him riding out of the stables. I knew he was troubled so I went after him toward London, hoping he would confide in me on the way there. But he hurried so, I could not catch him."

"Jasper, please tell me, is Barclay injured or in danger?" his mother asked.

Yes! Get to the crux of the matter!

A scornful laugh erupted from Jasper.

"Oh, I think his *body* is perfectly sound, indeed! It is his *soul* that we ought to be concerned for!"

"Jasper!" Mrs. Durbin was alarmed. "Why would you answer me in this way?"

"Because, Mamma, I followed him to a…once in town, I saw him enter a…"

"Where, Jasper?" There was a note of dread in her voice. "*Where* did Barclay go?"

The boy inhaled with a slow but shaky breath. "He went to Titania's Bower."

Honora's blood turned to ice water.

He went to get Celia!

"It's a…a bawdy house," Jasper whispered the last words.

"No!" his mother gasped.

Silently, Honora lurched forward, gripping the doorjamb, gazing in horror at the two Durbins upon the settee.

"And I'll never speak to him again, Mamma. I swear it! I'll never look upon his face…"

"No, Jasper!" Honora stumbled into the room, her hands pressed to her chest. "Barclay's done nothing wrong!"

Mother and son looked up at her round-eyed as if sighting one risen from the dead.

"Honora!" Jasper stood. "You ought to know what he truly is. You were right in rejecting him! At first, I thought you treacherously ungrateful after all he'd done for you, but I see now!"

Understanding began to dawn in Honora's mind.

He knew of Barclay's proposal?

"That the rejection of a good woman would hurt him deeply, yes, that is understandable," the boy went on. "But to then – less than a day later! – throw himself in the way of – of *harlots*?"

Here he burst into fresh tears, not the leaking sort which quietly run down the faces of overcome ladies, but the noisy, messy sort of heartbroken little boys.

Honora reached for the boy's shoulders. "Jasper, please calm yourself. Nothing good can come of this state you are in."

"Nothing good can come of anything! Not now, not ever!"

"It is not what you think!" Honora urged. "Please, do not think ill of him!"

"But if you could but see these...*girls* who were there! With no discretion – no modesty! – they met me at the door, nearly pulling me inside. And the things they said! – I won't taint your ears."

Honora's heart beat wildly.

I must tell him – and his mother – here and now.

"Listen to me and your pride in your brother will be restored in full force – *greater* force, truly."

Honora could not keep her eyes from flitting in Mrs. Durbin's direction as she quavered over how to begin. The woman's eyes were huge, her face inscrutable.

Oh Mrs. Durbin, what will you think of me in the next moment?

Honora sank down upon the settee, pulled Jasper down beside her and took a deep breath.

"Jasper, you must believe me when I say he went there to accomplish good. You see, I told him of a girl who is trapped inside that place – the Bower as it were."

"Trapped?"

"Yes. Celia. Her name is Celia."

"*Celia*! That is who the horrible blonde girl said Barclay had asked for."

Oh, good lord, poor Jasper met Molly!

"How did you know of this girl?" Jasper asked, his eyes grieved and pleading.

Sitting up as straight as her faint head would allow, Honora replied, "Jasper, just as you did not know where you were when you knocked upon the Bower's door, neither did I when I first arrived there. And suddenly, I found myself employed at what I thought was a coffee house."

She felt the sealing of her fate as the words lifted off her tongue. The clock on the mantle ticked loudly as her heart pounded in her ears. She had expected Jasper or his mother to cry out at her last sentence, but both just sat, panting through their open mouths. With the faint hope that they might listen to an explanation, Honora continued with tears coursing down her face.

"So you see, because of my ignorance, I too lived at this…brothel."

There was a sudden exclamation, though not from either of the Durbins.

"Out!" Martha rushed in through the doorway and over to the settee, wine sloshing out of a bottle in her hand.

"You!" She jabbed a finger at Honora, her face contorted with fury. "OUT!"

"Martha!" Mrs. Durbin said sharply but the servant was too enraged to heed her.

"You have been a canker here from the day you arrived, tainting this godly household!" Martha shrieked. "Limping along as if injured – toying with Mr. Barclay's heart! '*Honora*'? Ha! No one was ever so poorly named! You must go! *Go now!*"

"Martha!" Mrs. Durbin snapped again and stood to snatch the splashing bottle of wine from the frenzied maid's hand. "Stop your hateful speech this instant!"

Martha blanched as if slapped, then looked at her employer and the great purple splotches now dampening the settee and rug.

"Martha, leave us now," Mrs. Durbin said starchily. "We will not be requiring your services for the rest of the day."

"I beg your pardon, ma'am," the servant said, then left the room looking dazed.

"Miss Honora, I am terribly sorry," Mrs. Durbin said, her eyes on the door. "I will address her further, when this uproar has subsided."

Which cannot happen until I am gone from here, Honora thought.

"Mrs. Durbin," she said. "You have been so terribly kind to me, and I cannot tell you how I appreciate it, but I must go now, leave you and your family…"

"Oh no! Of course, we don't want you to leave in this state. Please, promise me you won't disappear before Barclay returns and we can sort all of this out."

Her eyes still stinging with tears, Honora nodded and quietly said, "I shall remain until Barclay returns."

I must see him – thank him before I go.

"Please excuse me now," she murmured.

"Of course, dear."

With a final glance at Jasper's indecipherable face, Honora left the salon and went to her room. The window there allowed a full view of the approach to Singer Hall, and she posted herself beside it to watch for Barclay.

A note of joy sang in her heart in spite of what had just occurred.

Will Celia be with him? she wondered. *He went to help her even after I spurned him! Oh, Barclay, you very good and proper soul!*

Celia still knows nothing of Mr. Shiverly's coins. How pleased she will be!

She continued to ponder what their next steps would be as she sat, staring out the window.

An hour passed.

And then another.

There was no sign of Barclay or Celia beside him on the gig seat. Honora had just begun to worry earnestly when there was a knock at her door. As she rose to her feet, Honora realized how stiff her back and legs felt from sitting so long.

Upon opening the door, she saw Bess with a tray, looking completely out of place in the hallway, the evening shadows lengthening behind her.

"Mrs. Durbin asked me to bring this up to ya, Miss," she said, then bobbed a curtsey as the tray changed hands. "I made a nice supper, but it seems no one's feelin' up to eatin' it in the dinin' room as everyone's keepin' to their rooms t'night. I hope nothin's goin' 'round."

She stepped back cautiously, her eyes fixed on Honora's face as if she was wondering at the temperature of the girl's forehead.

Honora nearly said she was sure whatever ailed those in the house was not catching, but thought better of it, pleased actually that there was an excuse for such unusual behavior. She was sure that Bess would be informed eventually as to what had transpired at Singer Hall that afternoon, but she herself would say nothing of it. Looking down at the food, she murmured her thanks.

Bess began again. "Susan and Mary were pleased to carry home the Toad-in-a-Holes to their dear mam."

"Oh!" Honora exclaimed. "I'm so sorry, Bess! I forgot all about them!"

"'S'alright, Miss. I told 'em you'd taken ill. I dropped the batter onto the paper for 'em and they were pleased to push the cherries into the middles. Them biscuits looked quite nice comin' outta the oven, I must say." She smiled warmly then turned to go. "Nice little girls, them. Now you rest and eat all that you can. Must keep your strength up."

The cook departed and Honora retreated to her window, tray in hand. She settled herself back into her chair and picked at bits of roast chicken, watching again for Barclay's return as the sun slipped over the horizon.

AN ABSENCE OF CLOTHS

PRETEND THAT ALL is as it always is, Celia reminded herself as she realized she was walking lightly and almost humming a tune.

Now she was alone in the laundry room, where she needn't be so careful at allowing her joy to show through. There she could think and rejoice.

I mustn't catch Dovey's eye. Just as Honora left her things behind, so will I.

She lifted a drenched sheet from the vat, sloshing the front of her dress with tepid water.

But the money, she thought. *I must take all of that. I can give Honora back her two coins.*

I'll be free!

A thought crept in, dampening her joy.

I'll be free, but at Singer Hall, I'll be even further away from Bill.

After fitting the wet sheet into the rollers of the wringer, she turned the crank, watched as the water squeezed out, then put it aside.

She retrieved a kettle from the hob before it began to sing and poured its contents into the vat, readying herself to launder the repulsive bucketful of Molly's menstrual cloths. She was tempted to disregard them, knowing she wouldn't be at the Bower long enough to suffer the wrath of not having washed them.

No, all need be as it always is and I must keep myself busy until evening, she reminded herself as she upended the bucket over the washing tub.

Ugh. Celia held her breath as the gory cloths swirled around in the water.

Doris's ought to be here as well, but it seems I'll never have to clean hers again.
As she poured more water into the vat, this niggled at her.

When was the last time Doris's cloths filled this tub?
A terrifying little whisper answered that question.

She's always regular as the sunrise...but now she's a week or more past due.
The posser grew still in Celia's hands. With her heart thumping loudly, she released it into the water and turned toward the door. Clutching the monthlies' bucket with especial strength, Celia scaled the staircase, then timidly knocked on one of the bedroom doors.

"Come in." Celia heard, so she pushed it open. Inside, Doris was standing by her little mirror, smoothing her hair into place. She turned with a smile and her eyes fell on the familiar bucket dangling from Celia's hand. They lingered there a moment as the smile faded. Her eyes grew large and frightened, then rose to meet Celia's. The lock of hair she had been twisting fell from her hands which reached to clutch at her belly. She stepped toward her bed and sat down upon it heavily as her eyes filled with tears.

There was a thick silence in the room as Celia shut the door and placed the empty bucket upon the floor. Moving to the bed, she sat down beside Doris, and laid her arm over her shoulders.

After several moments, Doris asked in a small voice, "Celia, what am I going to do?"

Celia only tightened her embrace and asked herself, *And me, what am I to do?*

Tonight is my one chance to leave the Bower, she thought. *But I'd be leaving Doris behind.*

Perhaps I needn't meet Mr. Barclay tonight. Where did he say his home was — up Mile End Road?

But surely I couldn't just appear on Singer Hall's doorstep some other day — he may be very cross if I don't meet him tonight. He was probably doing a favor for Honora by coming here.

How long will he wait tonight, I wonder? I promised to be there!
Her mind circled around again.

Yet, how could I leave Doris? How would I feel, alone, knowing a baby was growing inside me? And then, the only other person who knows disappears?

But I might be *her any day now — even* now *perhaps!* Her hand reluctantly strayed to touch her own belly. *I must get out of the Bower!*

After a lengthy spell of silence, Celia heard the supper bell ring.

"We'd better go down," Doris said in a small voice, rising from the bed and wiping her eyes. "Dovey'll wonder why if we don't."

Knowing she had a decision to make and that her choice might require nourishment for strength, Celia stood and followed Doris down to the dining room, her hand on the girl's shoulder.

A QUIET HOMECOMING

THE SUN WAS RISING when an exhausted Barclay steered the gig onto his home grounds. Everything was still and quiet. Dervy did not appear, tousle-headed and yawning, so Barclay unhitched the gig and led the horse into the stable himself, anxious to feed and water the poor animal.

This was the homecoming he'd hoped for upon returning with Celia, one of quiet solitude, that no questions would be immediately asked and no opinions could be formed. Though he had prayed all the way to London the previous morning, no proper explanation for him coming home with yet another unknown young woman beside him had presented itself.

But it was all for naught as here I am, returning alone – a failure.

He had waited at the corner of Uxbridge and Park, certain that Celia would come as she had seemed so sincerely happy at the prospect of leaving the Bower. But an hour passed, then several more, and as the streets darkened and thinned of their daytime crowds, finally holding only the occasional group of marauding men carousing the streets, his certainty wavered. The one thing that kept him posted there was the thought that Celia might finally arrive only to find him departed. He couldn't be the source of such cruel disappointment. By the time even the straggling men, weaving unsteadily and singing drunken ditties, had disappeared, Barclay finally set Caleb in motion toward Singer Hall.

Now as Barclay was leading Caleb into his pen, he heard the crunch of pebbles on the stone floor behind him.

"Barclay."

Whirling around, he made out the shape of a woman in the light of dawn streaming in through the open doors.

Honora.

He wished to sink into the stable floor, disappearing from her sight.

Ought I to tell her what I've attempted? Would she even believe me?

She stepped forward and he could see her expression was open, rapt.

Emboldened, he hung the halter on its hook, strode over to where she stood and stated simply, "I went to get Celia."

There was no shifting of her countenance as she replied softly, "Yes, I know."

"You *know*?" His hand halted in removing his hat. "How can you *know*?"

Honora inched toward him, surprising him with the intimacy of such proximity.

Opening her mouth, she said in clearly measured words, "Jasper told me."

Jasper?

He clutched at the stall's railing as a wave of horror crashed over him.

"What did he...? How can he...?"

Reaching for him, Honora grasped his shoulder, offering support more necessary than she likely knew.

"He thought we had quarreled yesterday and he pitied you. Not wanting you to be alone, he followed and saw you enter the Bower, then returned here, ferociously upset." Her voice dropped off. "So I told him why you had gone there. I told him all of it."

"All of it?"

"Yes. Your mother heard it as well." A faint smile soured on her lips. "As well as Martha."

"Why did you tell them so much? You didn't owe them that."

"No." Through the lightening gloom, her eyes found his. "But I owed it to *you*."

Barclay swallowed hard.

"I couldn't have Jasper think ill of you, especially knowing that it was *my* words that sent you to the Bower."

She sacrificed her repute to salvage mine.

He could see now how tired she was. Her eyes were ringed with dark circles and her head sagged on her shoulders.

She must have been up all night, waiting for me.

This thought fanned a faint hope within him.

"Honora, please forgive me. I see now how trapped girls are blameless. I am aggrieved to my heart knowing that I – "

"Shh," she said, reaching for his hand with both of hers. "Barclay, it is not your fault such horrors were unfathomable to you. You have lived in a good world of good people who treat each other well. It is wonderful that some can have such an existence."

The cold tips of his fingers rested in her soft, warm palm.

"Please believe me," he said, "that I have wanted little else but to help others since finding a dead infant on my doorstep – but whom have I ever helped? I mean *truly* helped? I meant to finally accomplish that yesterday, but as you see, Celia is not with me."

His voice caught and she shushed him again.

"You are the bravest, kindest man I've ever known, Mr. Barclay. And with the wisdom you now have, your beneficence will fill the earth with goodness."

Suddenly, there was a gruff throat clearing and hasty footsteps on the staircase from the groom's quarters above the stable. Honora dropped Barclay's hand as Dervy stepped into view.

"Sorry, sir," the groom said, stifling a yawn. "I was up watchin' and listenin' for ya last night, but I musta' dozed off. I'll mix up a nice bit of mash for Caleb if ya want to go inside yerself."

"Thank you, Dervy," Barclay replied.

Though his hand ached to reach again for Honora's as they left the stable to walk silently toward the house, he did not allow it to.

TURNIPS IN A GARDEN

THE SKY WAS LIGHTENING as Dovey stood at her bedroom window, sucking nervously on her teeth when a small, wiry figure hurried up the front steps of the Bower.

Ah, here he is.

Though the previous day had offered much amusement in the form of the strange Mr. Park, the foreboding truth of Dovey's dental predicament lingered on.

She had left the front door unlocked and soon footsteps could be heard clunking up the staircase.

Damn you, Briggs, she thought. He was not being quiet as she had urged when these plans were laid. *Now any of the girls might awaken and wonder who is here.*

Before he could knock on her bedroom door, rousing the prostitutes further, Dovey opened it, admitting the doctor and his dreaded leather bag. The one lit beeswax candle in the room illuminated his jubilant face.

"Good morning, my dear," he said, jovially.

She would have slapped the spectacles off of his face if she didn't believe him to be the only possible saviour of her pride.

"Not much light in here. But do not fear," he said, grinning with pride. "I could pull a tooth whilst blindfolded."

Dovey's stomach fluttered.

You are positively delighted in the midst of my suffering, aren't you, you vile little man?

"Shall we begin?" He set his satchel on her bed. Opening it, he pulled a small, lidded tin cup from its depths, which he shook with a slosh and a rattle. "These were freshly drawn this morning and I assure you they are perfectly matched."

Removing the lid, he extended the cup toward the candle that Dovey might peer into its recess. There, in a shallow pool of what smelled and looked like milk were two human incisors, their long, tapered roots naked and gleaming.

Dovey did not ask whence he had acquired the pair, but imagined some young, indigent woman, now huddled in an alley, pressing a cloth to her bleeding mouth with one hand while she clutched a golden guinea with the other. Some of the girls she had brought into the Bower off the street had been nearly as desperate for a bit of coinage.

Shame. Such a girl could no longer work for me, her smile marred. The truth sharpened the dagger in Dovey's heart. *And who will continue to attend the brothel of a toothless hag such as myself? This* must *work!*

Her hero was now sorting through the tools in his bag, muttering to himself about each one's efficacy. Finally, he selected a pair of pliers and motioned toward the bed.

"Please, my dear, situate yourself here with your mouth turned this way. Once I've drawn your teeth, I'll put *these* in their place. Because the roots are fresh, they will adhere to your gums as would turnips in a garden."

Then why have you not charged me anything? Dovey wondered. *You only want to experiment on me — see if teeth can be swapped mouth to mouth. Isn't that right?*

It was clear to her, however, that her own teeth were dead. Grayish-yellow, they now wiggled with her every word, every bite of food.

He'd have to pull them soon anyway. And without these others to replace them, I'd be left with a broken window for a face.

Desperation, a sensation she had not felt for many years, positioned her uneasily on the bed's coverlet as she readied herself for the brutality sure to follow.

With a sudden solemnness, Dr. Briggs doffed his coat. Tossing it aside, he then wrapped his spindly arm around her, clamping his left

314

hand onto her forehead. She recoiled at the smell of stale perspiration on his shirt. The little finger of his right hand, tickled at her chin, easing her mouth open into a rigid rictus.

"Yes, yes. There we are," he purred, as if to a fretful animal as he fitted the pliers' jaws around her front right tooth. "I shall be done in no time."

Dovey clutched her quivering hands together over her chest. With a nauseating crunch and the sensation of something much longer than a mere tooth root being pulled from her mouth, the grayer of the teeth was suddenly out and plinking into the cup's lid.

She exhaled, hoping the doctor did not hear the shakiness of it.

"There. You see?" he asked, his arm still encircling her, his smiling face mere inches away from her face. "We managed that quite well, did we not?"

"Get on with it," she said crossly, trying not to gag on the trickle of blood that ran down her tongue.

With similar finesse, he gripped the left tooth with the pliers and began to tug. Dovey squirmed, trying not to whimper.

"Hmm." His brow wrinkled. "It seems this one will not be unseated so easily."

The tooth's reluctance was an affront to the doctor who began now to twist and pull more vigourously, rendering Dovey a yelping, flailing mess. With crackling that reverberated through Dovey's skull, the incisor was finally dislodged, though it was multiple broken pieces that Briggs fished out of the hole in her gum, each removal sending Dovey into fresh spasms of torment.

At its conclusion, Dovey lay back upon the bed, faint with agony, knowing the man had not yet finished.

"There!" Briggs said with satisfaction. "Now to replace them."

With the same pliers, he grasped one of the new teeth in the tin cup, and examined it closely by the candle's light.

"I believe this was the left incisor," he muttered, squinting at it as its milky wash dripped onto Dovey's coverlet. Then he looked down at her body, draped across the bed. "Ah yes, being supine may allow for easier placement."

With nary a word more, he leaned his chest across her own, pinning her forehead down with his left hand while his right positioned the pliers and began to wriggle the tooth into the recently gaping hole. The *removal* of Dovey's teeth had been painful, but Briggs's new occupation was exquisitely torturous and she lost all control of herself. Screaming, she writhed with such force that the small man was thrown off the bed, sending the tooth in his grasp skidding across the floor.

Out in the hallway, hurried footsteps of more than one person, padded to a stop just outside the door. Dovey rolled onto her side, staring at the doorknob, yet it did not turn. No one even knocked.

Sprawled on the carpet, Dr. Briggs indignantly declared, "My dear lady, if you will not cooperate, I *cannot* help you."

Though she was a strong woman, both in spirit and body, Dovey knew her limitations. Those two teeth, freshly yanked from some healthy mouth just an hour or so before, would never find their way to being implanted in her own.

"Doctor," she said, her voice weak. "There mu*th*t be another way."

What could only be described as irritated disappointment spread across the man's face.

"I went to great lengths to acquire those incisors," he responded, testily. "Of course, a set of dentures could be made, but they would not be as *natural* of a cure."

"Then denture*th* it *th*all be," she said, abhorring how sloppily her lips flopped over her pillaged mouth. Tears leaked out of her eyes. "I will pay hand*th*omely for them."

With a tetchy sigh, the doctor climbed up off the floor. "Very well, but I shall have to take measurements."

Retrieving a set of calipers from his bag, he set about peeling back Dovey's lips to thrust the tool around her gory gums, holding the candle so close that her nose felt it may burst into flame. When he had finished, he scribbled down his findings with a pencil, shoved all of his belongings into the bag and headed for the door. "I shall inform you when they are ready. Do not be startled at the exorbitance of their cost."

There was a frantic scurrying in the hallway as he swung the door open. Once he had shut it, the madam lay upon her bed for more than an hour, aching all over and weeping, wondering why not even one of her girls came to inquire as to her well-being.

REVELATIONS ABOUND

HER HEAD ACHING with grief and fatigue, Honora ascended the stairs to the front door of Singer Hall with Barclay at her side for what she supposed would be the last time. Once inside, she was startled to see Mrs. Durbin standing in the foyer, as if awaiting them.

"Son!" the woman stepped forward, her arms outstretched to receive Barclay. "I've been worried to death about you all night!"

She did look exhausted, Honora realized, her hair amuss, her face drooping.

Honora saw how Barclay relaxed into his mother's arms, his weary head large against her small, rounded shoulder.

The woman's face was placid as it suddenly turned – her embrace not ceasing – and said, "Good morning, Miss Honora."

"And to you, ma'am," Honora replied, wanting to skirt the familial reunion and dart up the staircase to the solitude of her room. Now that she had said what she needed to to Barclay, she was hoping to sleep for a few hours before beginning her trek back to the unknown in London. Yet, Mrs. Durbin had been nothing but kind to her – even after her shocking disclosure of the day before – and she knew she ought to express her gratitude before evaporating into the countryside.

"Mrs. Durbin, I thank you for the generous hospitality you have shown me," she began, then looked down the hall. "I had hoped to thank Mr. Clayton as well. Will you please tell him on my behalf?"

"Oh, are you leaving us this morning?"

Was that not your intention once Barclay was home safely? Honora thought, tilting her head instead of giving an answer. She expected to see Martha – smug in her victory – drifting silently by toward the breakfast room. But it was Jasper who appeared, his hair vivid in the early morning light. Silently, he stepped forward to embrace Barclay. The brothers held each other for a moment. As Jasper stepped back, his eyes settled on Honora's face, sadness weighing down his gaze.

"What a shame you are set on leaving," Mrs. Durbin continued. "You have been a delightful guest, teaching the children and bewitching us all with your delicious baked goods."

The woman's gracious response and Jasper's presence loosened Honora's tongue further.

"I am sorry for the…for the disquiet that my presence here has…"

"Oh no, dear girl. None of that. Come, come," Mrs. Durbin frowned, waving her hand. "It seems you are determined to leave us, but will you not breakfast with us first?"

Honora had learned all too well that sight of determination – politely masked – on the face of a member of the upper class. Although she knew she would not be able to choke down more than two bites of food and she wanted nothing more than to stretch out on her bed, she nodded and followed the Durbins to the set table in the breakfast room. Once the three young people were seated, Mrs. Durbin shut the doors to the rest of the house saying, "I have requested that we be left alone for our meal as I want to broach a topic with you. All of you."

She peered directly at Honora and sat, reaching for the tea pot.

Honora's back stiffened.

Will she shame me now, thinking it gracious due to the privacy?

As Mrs. Durbin passed around the teacups she had just filled, Honora knew that she could excuse herself and slip out of the door. But the sight of Barclay, directly across the table, staring at her – looking as if he hadn't heard a word his mother said – kept her seated.

This is the last I'll see of him, the best man I now know.

His expression was neither glum nor sullen, but solemnly attentive as if he was memorizing the curve of her cheek and the length of her lashes. Over every feature, his eyes traced, as she in turn became lost in doing the same to him.

Jasper's voice interrupted her heartfelt exercise.

"Miss Honora, I'm sorry that I thought ill of you, even for a moment, and I'm sorry that…" He broke off, his lip and voice quavering, then lifted his teacup abruptly as if to drink, but didn't, his eyes brimming with tears.

"Oh Jasper, say nothing of it. It was all a confusing mess with the best of intentions on every side," she replied, then continued primarily for Mrs. Durbin's benefit. "I told your brother about a girl in dire need, and he, with his sympathetic and courageous heart, went to help her."

"Yes," Mrs. Durbin said. "He's always found purpose in aiding those in distress. I imagine you heard the family lore of Wee Baby Moses, Miss Honora?"

Honora nodded.

The woman motioned that everyone ought to lift the lids off the platters and fill their plates, though no one moved. "It is a favorite tale amongst my boys, so I knew that either Jasper or Clayton would likely have told it to you. Barclay, my dear, why did you bring the baby to *me* straight away all those years ago?"

Roused from his determined perusal of Honora's face, Barclay pondered his mother's question before answering, "It was silly as I knew he had passed already, but I suppose I thought you the one most likely to help him…and to help me in that moment."

Honora noted how thoughtful Mrs. Durbin looked at this. "That heartens me greatly, son."

A silence fell over the group and Barclay resumed his peering at Honora.

"And did you ever wonder why I rushed out of the door, anxious to find the poor child's mother?"

Barclay merely grunted, and Jasper who had now apparently found his stomach empty in spite of the emotion that ringed the table, was lifting a slice of ham onto his plate, along with a wedge of toasted bread.

"It was because," Mrs. Durbin continued, "although I didn't know who she was, I *did* know the terror, grief and horror that she faced as she was likely an unwed mother who could not care for her child in its life or its death."

Neither Barclay nor Jasper seemed to be listening, but a strange notion stirred in Honora's mind at the words. She remained silent, aghast at her own assumptions.

Surely, she misspoke, or I have misinterpreted her.

With a little huff of frustration, Mrs. Durbin said, "Barclay, stop mooning over Miss Honora, and Jasper, stop crunching that toast. Listen as I tell you that upon marriage to your father, *I was with child.*"

The orange heads snapped to the right in unison, their faces awash with astonishment. Honora felt her own face burn as she knew not where to look.

"Yes, boys." The woman nodded, sitting straight up in her chair and gazing steadily at them both. "Clayton's beginnings were mired in shame and secrecy. Fortunately for me, your father loved me in spite of our quiet disgrace and carried on with our engagement and marriage. But for three days – three *horrible*, tear-drenched days before I told him of my trouble – I carried a child out of wedlock, loving it in spite of the ruin it signified for my life, wondering what would become of both of us. God knows what my parents would have done had they known."

Mrs. Durbin? Honora marveled, thinking of the refined manners and gentle demeanor of the aging woman just three feet away. *This woman, mother to the preacher Barclay Durbin, did what Celia and Molly do with men all the time? Well, of course it wasn't for money and yet, she did that outside of a marital bed?*

It seemed impossible. If anyone but the woman herself had suggested it, Honora would have shushed them severely.

Barclay finally found his voice. "But how…"

"The circumstances are not your concern," his mother interrupted rather sharply. "I tell you any of this simply to say that a person's character is not proven by the circumstances they find themselves in, but rather how they respond based on the resources and knowledge afforded them. Consequently, that may look different for everyone. What is done is done, and we oughtn't let it ruin us if we can help it."

Spooning a bit of sugar into her tea, she gave it a delicate tinkling stir with the thin silver spoon and went on.

"As for what I have just revealed to you, I trust you will all guard it wisely. I did not share it out of a sense of obligation, but only because it seemed beneficial for the situation we all now find ourselves in. I

320

have never informed Clayton of this matter as I've not thought it prudent to do so, and," here she scoffed slightly, "I suspect that he with his cavalier humour might revel in it. As for society at large, we needn't tell the world all of our stories. Just as swine will trample pearls, so will they tread carelessly or intentionally upon tender truths."

Honora could barely lift her eyes from the table as Mrs. Durbin addressed her.

"Miss Honora, I am terribly sorry for how Martha treated you yesterday. It lacked grace, compassion and propriety entirely. I spoke to her this morning as she brought in our breakfast, then dismissed her."

Dismissed her?

The alarm on Honora's face prompted an unfamiliar giggle out of Mrs. Durbin. "I dismissed her from the breakfast room, dear, not from service at Singer Hall altogether! I wanted to speak privately with the three of you as Martha need not know my history any more than she ought to have known yours.

"As for your *future*, dear girl, you need not flee here in such haste. I have greatly appreciated your teaching of the young village girls in the kitchen – as I believe it may help them in their time to avoid some of the difficulties that young women are wont to face – and would hate for it to cease. I lack the skill and energy to carry on what you do there and Bess lacks the time. But of course, your life is your own and if you have better plans for it then I heartily encourage you to pursue them."

She held her plate out to Barclay.

"And now, my dear, if you will fork that littlest slice of bacon and a roll onto my plate, I think I've found my appetite."

At this, Mrs. Durbin began to eat her breakfast in earnest, leaving the three young people astonished in the wake of her speech. Finally, after several disbelieving glances and unsteady clearings of throats, they themselves proceeded to have their breakfast.

She says I can stay here. Honora thought, slowly chewing a bite of egg. *Says she wants me to continue my work with the girls. But would she still feel that way if she knew that Barclay had already proposed marriage and how close I came to accepting him?*

Across the table, Barclay must have been of the same mind, because he blurted out, "Mamma, I thank you for entrusting your story to us, and now that we are being quite frank, I must tell you that I am in love with Miss Honora and want to accept the curacy at Southby to provide a home for her if she will have me."

For the second time that morning, Honora was jolted by the revelation of bald truth, and she crouched internally, waiting for what the next minute might bring.

Mrs. Durbin looked nonplussed for the first time that morning.

"I had suspected that that was the direction things were moving for the two of you," she said, pushing her now empty plate away. "And if I disapproved, I would not have invited Miss Honora to stay here longer. My one concern is that the two of you know so little of one another. Yes, much has happened in the last fortnight, and you admire what you've seen in each other thus far, but youthful infatuations have been proven many times over to lack staying power. More time before a permanent union would be my advice."

At this declaration's conclusion, Mrs. Durbin stood and bid them all a good morning. In spite of what Honora now knew about her, the same sense of awe she had always felt in the woman's presence settled over her as she watched her leave the room.

With her gone, the three young people looked at one another.

"Had you any idea of that, Barclay?" Jasper asked in hushed tones.

"I'd have been less surprised if she had told me she herself was Queen Charlotte."

"As would I," Jasper replied. "I feel strange now."

"She is still our mother," Barclay said, wiping his chin with his napkin. "Still the same woman who has cuddled us, helped us, reprimanded us through all these years."

"Yes, of course." Jasper nodded, then baffled asked, "What else do you suppose we don't know about her...or about Father?"

Suddenly, Honora felt that she was trespassing on a private moment between brothers.

But they see me sitting here and are continuing the conversation.

Lifting his eyebrows, Barclay said, "I suppose if there was something that we *ought* to know, then she would tell us, and if she doesn't deem it beneficial, we'll never know."

"So we shall have to content ourselves with trusting in her wisdom," Jasper said.

"Indeed." Barclay drew in a deep breath and turned to Honora.

"Are you still intent on leaving Singer Hall?" he asked simply, his eyes full of hope.

Am I? she asked herself. *Is knowing that my past does not hinder Mrs. Durbin from looking upon me, from sitting at table alongside me, enough to allow me to continue on in this household?*

Truly, I have no where better to go, and I can continue to teach Susan and Mary. There's that benefit.

But what of Celia? And how is it that Barclay was not able to bring her out from underneath Dovey's thumb?

She realized she had not even asked him what had happened in the day before, but felt her fatigue might overwhelm her at any moment. Locking eyes with Barclay, she said, "I will consider staying longer, but now I must sleep."

He nodded, his own eyelids drooping heavily.

Rising from the table, Honora left the room and wearily ascended the staircase to fall into bed.

THE SLEEPY LITTLE FOOTMAN

AFTER LYING AWAKE most of the night, Celia had finally settled into the deep sleep of utter exhaustion. Just after dawn, she was jerked back to consciousness by a yelp from down the hallway.

"What's that?" Molly asked, propping herself up on her elbow, worry filling her voice.

Startled out of all drowsiness, Celia replied, "Doesn't sound like Doris, and it's far too early for any rutter to be here anyway."

Another cry of what was clearly pain, resounded through the walls, and both girls threw back their covers to stand. Opening the door a few inches, they pressed their faces into the space and heard the faint click of other doors opening all up and down the hall.

"I think it's comin' from Dovey's room," Molly said, then stepped through the doorway and tiptoed toward the procuress's door. Celia could discern two other nightgowned figures there already, crouching in the near-dark, straining to hear. Their patience was rewarded as the strange sounds suddenly swelled into agonized screeches.

The cacophony ceased and there were several seconds of silence before the bawd's door suddenly swung open, sending the three eavesdroppers running in all directions like spooked specters. A small, wiry man with a large bag emerged, nearly slamming the door behind him. As he strode past her, Celia recognized him as the doctor Dovey called to tend to any of her girls' teeth. He said nothing as he hurried past the doxies and down the stairs. In a moment, there was the sound of the Bower's front door opening and shutting.

Molly scurried back to Celia. Closing the bedroom door behind her, she leaned on it as if out of breath.

"What's happened?" Celia asked.

"Dr. Briggs done pulled summa Dovey's teeth – prob'ly them front two!" Molly whispered excitedly, then clamped her hand over her mouth to laugh quietly into it.

Celia smiled, imagining Dovey wriggling anxiously under the doctor's humbling tools, then glaring miserably into the mirror at the new emptiness in her mouth.

"She's goin' to look a fright now!" Molly said, biting her lip. "She's asked 'im to make her a 'set of denchers'. What're those?"

"False teeth, I suppose," Celia answered.

"I'm gonna go tell Doris and Nancy."

Celia watched as the beautiful blonde giggled, then headed out to inform others of Dovey's misfortune.

What would Dovey think if she saw that even her favorite girl hates her so?

But Celia's mind did not linger there. She began to dress hastily, thinking, *Certainly, Dovey won't stir from her room this morning. And perhaps, just maybe, Mr. Barclay is still at Uxbridge and Park. If I got there in time, I might explain to him – thank him but tell him why I cannot go with him.*

Within minutes, she was dressed and hurrying down the street in the early morning light.

***

Standing stock-still, Celia glanced at any man who ventured near her. She had been at the chosen corner of Hyde Park for an hour at least and had yet to see a single flash of coppery hair beneath a top hat. Only delivery men and a few maids on errands bustled past, as it seemed there were no members of polite society out and about in this early hour.

Don't be stupid, she scolded herself. *Of course, he's not here. Hasn't been for hours.*

She studied a horse tie on the side of the road.

Is this where he stood? How long did he wait for me?

326

She envisioned Mr. Barclay shifting his weight from one foot to the other, peering up and down the street for her appearance, growing impatient as the sky darkened.

The knot in her stomach tightened.

He won't be back. Ever.

Celia resigned herself, and started back toward the Bower, though altering her route, almost hoping to get lost in the convoluted streets of London. Once the sun was well overhead, she found herself on Piccadilly with Green Park to her right when a great carriage jostled past. Two little footmen who looked to be about seven years old, dressed all in purple and black, sat on the board at the back. Their tricorn hatted heads bobbed about as both seemed fast asleep. Surprised that anyone could slumber while being jarred so violently, Celia watched them, relieved to feel slightly amused by something. However, her appreciation changed to horror when one of the young boys fell off his perch and tumbled into the road. So quickly was the carriage traveling, that none of its occupants heard his startled yip. The other child remained in place and asleep, the purple blot of his livery fading in the distance.

Fortunately, a man walking by ducked into the street to draw the squalling boy out of it. But that was where his interest ended, as he deposited the boy on the side of the road and continued on his own way.

Hurrying to the child, Celia crouched down, using her parasol to shield him from the rest of indifferent humanity. His mouth was shut now, but his eyes were so wide that his face could hardly contain them.

"Are you hurt?" she asked.

He proved he wasn't, jumping to his feet and knocking the lofty span of parasol aside to run in the direction that the carriage had disappeared. At a few yards, he stopped to gawp around him at the tall buildings which now formed a callous corridor around him.

In seconds, Celia was beside him again.

"They left me," he said, panic barely contained in his voice. "I don't know the way home!"

"Where do you live?"

"My lady's house, at Grosvenor," he said, acknowledging Celia for the first time. Then, with a note of hope, "Do you know it?"

It broke her heart to shake her head and see his eyes fill with tears. "What am I to do?"

Looking at his clean, little face, she could not bear the thought of him transforming into one of the pitiable gamins who lurked in London's alleyways.

"I will help you find your way," Celia said. "What is near your home? Tell me of the churches, of the markets."

Gulping down his terror, the boy thought for a moment.

"There is a large green just across from my lady's house, not a park as are Hyde or St. James, but big enough to run across." Then as an afterthought, he added, "And it is round."

With his index finger, he drew a large oval in the air.

Could he mean Berkley Square?

"I may know it!" Celia encouraged, noting the glint of hope her words sparked in the boy's eyes. "Come, this way."

She stepped forward and was startled as his warm little hand suddenly grasped at hers. She extended her fingers that he might adjust his hold. Thus, they set out, hand in hand, looking for the ovular green.

They crossed Piccadilly and turned left onto Berkley Street, their pace quickening until a large rounded green came into view.

Expectantly, Celia asked, "Do you see your lady's house?"

The boy shook his head. "Coachman calls this Berkley."

This is not it? Well, he could be from anywhere! Celia thought, disheartened.

"The green is bigger at Grosvenor," he added. "With more trees, and square paths in the middle."

"Oh! I think that is not far from here!" Celia was sure she knew where he meant now, it being a place of very fine residences.

They started north, and within minutes, the boy cried out happily, "That's the tree we pelt with apple cores! And here, Coachman always stops to shout at the baker. This way!"

Now, he was leading *her* through the busy streets, pulling her along hastily. Another rounded green, this one with trees and a square path soon appeared before them.

"There it is!" he cried, dragging her toward the servants' entrance of a palatial house. At their approach, the door flung open from inside. The other little, purple-clad footman burst out, yelling, "Fred!"

"Bill!" Celia's companion hollered back.

Her heart surged at the sound of her own brother's name. She smiled as she watched the joyful reunification, seeing at once that the boys were actually twins, identical in every way, from the blonde hair on their heads down to their sharp little chins.

"What happened?" Bill asked. "I woke up at the mews and you were gone!"

Tom said, "I fell off into the road."

The embracing boys began to giggle, then dissolved into fits of laughter.

A matronly servant appeared in the doorway.

"See, Billy! I told you 'e'd make 'is way back! No need to blub! Coachman don't need to go out searchin' after all."

"This lady brought me home," Fred said, turning to Celia, his eyes shining brightly up at her.

"Aw, what a dear thing she is!" the servant said. "Will ya come in for a moment's refreshment, miss?"

Unable to meet the woman's eye, Celia shook her head and muttered something about getting on her way.

"Oh, but we do thank ya for bringin' our Freddie back to us. My lady woulda been outta 'er mind with worry once we told 'er 'e was missin'. Now boys come inside, and Freddie, don'tcha ever fall asleep on the back of that carriage again! Neither of ya!" She shook her finger which set them to giggling once again.

Celia turned and began to retrace her steps but was suddenly grabbed about the waist by one of the boys. Looking down to see him grinning from ear to ear, she wondered which of the twins was clinching her.

"Billy!" the woman scolded. "Don't jostle 'er so! She ain't used to rough treatment!"

"Thank you for bringing my brother back to me!" the twin said, then let go as abruptly as he had seized her to dart back into the house.

The servant threw her hands up, then chuckled, looking pointedly at Celia. "What's to be done with boys! We thank ya again, dear lady."

Then the door was shut.

Celia could still feel the fierceness of little Billy's determined grip around her person. Those same little arms had also clasped his brother, Freddie, recently lost but returned to him – returned by her.

If it wasn't for me, little Freddie would likely still be down on Piccadilly, running about in a mad panic, she thought. *Or sitting on the pavement bawling his eyes out.*

The thought lifted her chin and shoulders, and she stopped to look again at the door through which the happy boys had disappeared. She imagined the delight that was certainly still spuming just beyond it, and yearned to be a part of it, if only at its edges.

Why did I not go in when asked?

Because I am a doxy, and oughtn't darken their doorstep.

Yet, I am the one who just rejoined two brothers.

Yes. Though I am a harlot, I did some good today – returning a lost boy to his brother, Billy.

With an unfamiliar warmth in her chest, Celia headed back to the Bower, her head held a bit higher than usual.

AN UNCLE'S APPROVAL

FINALLY AWAKE, BARCLAY pushed the covers aside and rose from bed. His grumbling stomach told him it was long past dinnertime so he headed downstairs. As he passed the credenza in the hallway, he saw an envelope there with his name on it. Leaning against the wall, he tore into it and read:

My dear nephew —

I fear I may have embarrassed you during your visit here. Please forgive an old man for his foolery.

She is a bright May morning. Secure her hand as quickly as you can and you shall both be installed here at the rectory by Christmas.

Affectionately—

Uncle Allard

Oh uncle, I wish it were as simple as that.

Barclay sighed and stuffed the letter into his pocket, noting suddenly that his head was aching. He went toward the kitchen in search of some biscuits to eat while he began plotting his next attempt at liberating Celia.

DELIVERANCE

I SHOULD HAVE gone to meet him, Celia thought as she measured lye into the vat. *But what of Doris?*

This was the circuit upon which her thoughts had run every moment of each of the six days since Barclay's departure.

Yes, what of Doris? She wasn't at breakfast this morning. Is she alright?

After starting another kettle of water to heat on the hob, Celia went in search of her.

The girl was lying on her bed, her face ashen and beaded with sweat.

"Doris! What's happened?" Celia asked alarmed, shutting the door behind her. As far as she knew, Doris had told no one else of her pregnancy.

"I think I passed it," the girl said, her hands resting over her belly. Though her face was furrowed with pain and fatigue, she smiled. "I woke this mornin' with a nasty bellyache and by dinner, the bleedin' was enormous. I went to the necessary room and, well…"

"How did this happen?" Celia lowered herself onto the bed, resting her hand on Doris's knee. *Did she hurt herself to make it so?*

"Just lucky, I s'ppose. I didn't throw myself down the stairs or anythin', if that's what you're wonderin' – though I thought about it. That's what Molly did last year when it 'appened to 'er." Her head dipped in obvious shame. "Celia, I was so worrit I'd have a little baby girl. And then she'd grow up to be just like me, doin' what I'm doin'. I couldn't bear that."

Celia shook her head, trying to disperse the images such words conjured.

"So then I found myself 'opin' it'd be a boy, but that ain't much better, is it? 'E'd either be one of them poor little scamps runnin' the streets to pick pockets, or..."

In the pause that followed, Celia's own mind selected multiple misfortunes that could befall a boy, but Doris continued, "Or it might be Rottem's child and 'e' could turn out just like 'is pappy."

The two girls looked steadily into each others' eyes, silent yet loquacious in their understanding.

Celia took a shaky breath. "Good lord! Doris, we've got to get out of here."

"What – out of the Bower?"

"Yes!"

Doris sat upright. "But where would we go? There's no place for girls like us. Not *now* anyway."

"That's not true. We could clean! You're quick at floors, and you could learn to tend to other things, as could I along with laundering. I have a little bit of money, enough to rent a room for us to share. Then when we earn more, we could..."

"No, Celia." Doris shook her head, her eyes large and solemn. "We'd starve. Or what if the people who 'ired us found out what we done while livin' 'ere? There's no forgivin' you and me! They'd throw us out on our ears. Don't talk of it!"

"I *will* talk of it," Celia said, fiercely. "Doris, it's going to happen again."

She touched the girl's belly.

"It won't," Doris responded, pushing Celia's hand aside. "I'll be more careful from now on."

"More *careful?*" Celia asked, incredulously. "How?"

Doris thought, glancing apprehensively at Celia. "I'll tell the rutters they must put on a *baudruche* before they come near me."

Celia shook her head. "They *hate* wearing those. They'll refuse!"

"And..." Doris went on "...and when I'm in the throes, I won't pretend I like it so much."

"That won't change *anything!*" Celia insisted. "It's just a matter of time before you have to hope for an awful bellyache again. Any time one of them beasts poisons our innards, it might happen. *We must leave.*"

"No, Celia. I'm not goin' anywhere and you oughtn't either!" Doris said this slowly, deliberately. "Dovey'd beat us and starve us if she knew we were even thinkin' 'bout it."

Celia felt Doris's eyes studying her and a new anxiety stirred in her heart as she thought back on all she had just said.

Why'd I tell her I have money? What if she tells Dovey?

"I suppose you're right, Doris," she lied, sighing. "We oughtn't think about such things. Afterall, I tried it once before and I nearly died."

Doris appeared relieved and lay back down on the bed. "Yes. We've a much better chance of bein' carried off like Lyla was than makin' it on our own. And who knows what 'appened to Honora?" Her face changed again. "Do *you* know what 'appened to Honora, Celia?"

"No." Celia said guardedly. "I can only hope she's alright. She left all her clothes and things behind, so she couldn't've planned it."

With the air of a disappointed mother, Doris sighed and said, "Yes, well Honora may be *worse* off than us now, poor girl."

Celia nodded though she quietly seethed.

I could be with her now if I hadn't stayed for you, Doris!

The memory of the little footman's hand in hers and his joy at reunification with his brother filled Celia's mind.

He wanted my help and all worked out well for him.

She regarded Doris's pale, homely face haloed by the tangle of her hair upon the pillow. The girl looked at ease, content almost, here in a bed in the Bower.

Something ticked within Celia's heart.

I will never again betray myself for the sake of someone else's fear or stupidity, Celia thought.

In that moment, she decided she would leave the Bower, and she would do so immediately.

"Very good," Doris affirmed. "Let's speak of it no more. Ugh, la! I'm so very tired."

"Rest well," Celia murmured, taking a moment to push a few wispy hairs back from the doxy's damp forehead. She wondered if it might be the last bit of tenderness the girl was ever shown by anyone.

Doris smiled and Celia stood to go. In the hallway, she crept quietly past Dovey's bedroom door on the way back to her own room.

Since the drawing of her teeth, Dovey had relegated her hosting duties to Molly. This challenge had proven to be too much for the fatuous girl and Celia had noticed a lapse in the Bower's business. She herself had not even gone to the Mingling Room to meet with gentlemen the previous two nights, pleading to Molly a headache, an excuse that was readily accepted.

Once back in her own room, Celia smoothed the lavender silk dress out upon the bed – its matching parasol and the gloves beside it – so that it would be the first thing anyone entering the room would see. She couldn't let Dovey accuse her of theft should the procuress track her down. Even her own parasol – the cheap one she had bought herself – she left propped up in the corner. Most of her temporary escapes from the hell of the Bower happened while she clutched that flimsy item in her hand, and she never wanted to hold it again.

She wore the dress in which she had arrived at the Bower. It had served as her chore and laundering dress for the last six months. She noted how worn in places it was, its sleeves thin and tattered from the constant plunge into warm water and the abrasion of scrubbing.

But it is mine and no one can say otherwise.

Now her heart began to pound as what she was about to do signified that she was undeniably running away. She held her breath and listened for a moment to the silence of the Bower around her. Satisfied, she crouched down under the chair rail and beheld the coins wedged there. Honora's two gold pieces were the easiest to remove, ironically, as Celia felt uneasy about taking them with her.

They are not mine. Yet she is certainly not coming back for them and their being stuck here is a perfect waste.

Dislodging the others required some leverage from the handle of the bone comb on the ewer table. Finally holding all the coins in her palm, she dropped them into her pocket and slipped her feet into her shoes.

Steady, she told herself as she exited the bedroom door. *If Dovey does hear me going past and questions me, I can say, 'I came upstairs to use the necessary room but now I must go hang the sheets I washed out to dry.'*

But the bawd's door remained closed as Celia passed.

On through the kitchen she went, where Sally and the newest girl were busy with the peeling of vegetables and kneading of dough.

Good. If they were idle, they'd likely take closer note of me.

Taking deep, slow breaths, she went past them and disappeared into the laundry room where the pile of damp sheets she had earlier abandoned awaited her. Lifting the top two, she draped them over her arm and headed toward the back garden to hang them.

Once I get them all up on the line, I'll sneak out back of the garden, down the alleyway, she thought. But as she passed again through the kitchen, she saw that Sally was no longer there.

It's now. Celia thought, her heart pounding in her ears. *With Sally gone, I must go now.*

But as she put her hand on the backdoor's knob, something made her pause.

It was the newest girl, standing by the butcher block. Though she wasn't crying today, she still looked miserably apprehensive as she picked another potato off the huge pile before her and began to peel it.

Maybe she doesn't know. She's not stuck here yet.

No! I won't betray myself again. Sally might return at any moment.

But, a word of warning and a little help might save her. Surely, I must give her that.

Ducking back into the laundry room, Celia dropped the sheets to the floor and grabbed one of Honora's coins out of her pocket. Back in the kitchen, she stalked over to the startled girl, and said in a fierce whisper, "Go home to your family and never return."

"Miss?" the girl stammered.

"Once Dovey's claws are in you, you'll wish you were dead because of the things she'll make you do."

Shock coloured the girl's face as the potato and paring knife slipped from her hands onto the table.

"Here." Celia shoved the coin into the girl's hand and closed her fingers over it. "This will feed your family until you find a job elsewhere. Go now!"

Not waiting to see if the girl would heed her, Celia nearly ran out the backdoor into the sunshine of the afternoon.

It's changed a bit, Celia thought, hugging her shawl about her shoulders as she looked around the street. Six months earlier – before getting trapped in the Bower – she and Bill had found this place together. Now, she stopped under the familiar overhanging window, its belly jutting out over the pavement below. Her heart was racing faster than it had earlier that afternoon when she went back to see Mr. and Mrs. Tiller.

And that turned out alright, she encouraged herself, thinking happily that she would return the next morning to their building where she would spend the day cutting paper for labels and writing *London Lily* upon them.

Go on. It's getting darker. Get it over with. Learn what you must learn.

"Bill!" she called out, looking up at the bow window. It remained shut, so a bit louder, she called again, "Bill!"

A head popped out to survey her on the street below.

"'Oo's that?" the man asked.

"Is Bill about?" Celia asked. "Bill Woodlow?"

"'Oo wants ta know, pretty lady?" He laughed roughly. "Even if 'e's not 'ere, *I* am!"

Pushing down her frustration, she forged ahead. "I'm his sister, Celia."

"Ah, yer 'is sista, are – Oi, watch it!" The man's head was pushed aside by a hand as another face thrust out of the window – one of pale skin, framed with dark, shaggy hair.

Bill.

The brother and sister stared at each other. Celia felt her heart was about to burst out of her mouth as her eyes searched his.

Anger? Hate? Joy?

She couldn't read what was there, and he said nothing so his voice rendered no clues.

"A 'appy return, I see!" the chatty man said, glancing back and forth amusedly between the siblings.

"Shut up, Sam," Bill said drily, his eyes never wavering from Celia's face.

"Come walk with me," Celia heard herself boldly say.

Bill bit his lip for a moment, then pulled his head back out of sight.

Unsure if he was on his way down or dismissing her, Celia determined to stand right where she was and call out to him again if necessary. But within a moment's time, he was stepping out of the door and up to her, staring down from his newly acquired height, a look of alarm on his face as the gap closed.

"God, Celie. You're skinny as a skeleton!" He lifted his hand as if to touch her cheekbone.

She nearly closed her eyes, longing for the faint warmth his clumsy fingers might impart.

But he let his hand drop and again, they gazed upon each other silently. Finally, she spoke.

"You've grown."

"Where've you been, Celia?" His chin jutted aside, tense.

Ah, anger. That's better than hate, I suppose.

"Somewhere I didn't want to be."

"Is that so?" His eyes flew wide with mock surprise. "Because it seems that where you didn't want to be was *here*!"

He threw his arm up toward the window. "Remember when we came here *together* months ago to let that single stinking room up there – to live in it *together* whilst you worked a job, and I worked another! Then you disappeared and I had to take in *bloody Sam* to help pay for and keep the place!"

" 'Ay! I'm a lovely roommate!" Sam protested from above, his head still hanging out of the window. "I pay on time an' even swept the floor a time er two!"

"Please walk with me," Celia said quietly, her eyes imploring.

Bill stuffed his hands deep into his pockets and began to pace ahead of her down the pavement.

"Come on, then," he said over his shoulder.

At least he's talking to me, she told herself as she hurried after him.

"Was that you in a purply dress on Park Lane one week past?" he asked, striding forward as if he had somewhere to go.

He did *see me.* She nearly tripped trying to keep up with him. "Yes."

He guffawed. "Seems you wanted to be where you were then, ignoring me, turning your back and spinning your parasol. Thought I'd seen a ghost in broad daylight – some grand lady dressed in finery with the face of my own vanished sister. I called out to you!"

Celia strode silently beside him. She had determined to tell him the truth, that she'd never have to fear him discovering it somehow on his own, but she suspected he needed to rage at her awhile.

"Last you told me, you'd got a job laundering at some fine coffee house. You came back home every night the first couple of weeks, bringing tasty little bits and pieces from their kitchen, telling me all about how nice and clean it was there. And then one night, you must have decided you liked it there better than here, because you didn't come back." He paused and cleared his throat. "I stayed up, worrying, waiting with a pot of soup on the hob. Already lost my ma and Nana, and suddenly my sister doesn't come home!"

His voice broke as his strides grew longer, his feet hitting the ground with wasted force.

Celia yearned to grasp his arm, to turn him toward her, but instead struggled to match her pace to his and said nothing.

"'She would have told me if she wasn't coming home tonight,' I told myself. 'Something horrible must have happened!' So I ran the streets looking for you, but hadn't the faintest idea where you might be! I hated myself for not asking you where this coffee house was or what it was called."

He finally stopped, his back rigid, biting his lips and staring at the ground.

"It is called Titania's Bower off St Martins Lane," Celia said quietly but clearly.

"Well that helps me considerably now," he said, sourly. There were tears in his eyes.

Seeing them, Celia knew, *He loves me still.*

She was tempted to say nothing to him of her plight – to let him think she had just run away for a while, happy to be free but had now returned, bored with her adventure. She supposed she could apologize for her selfishness and perhaps he would begrudgingly forgive her, allowing her back into his life.

No, she decided. *He would never truly trust me again if he believed that. And I need him to know I would have never left him willingly. I must tell him all of it.*

She reached up to grab his shoulder and said quietly, "Bill, you must listen whilst I have the courage to tell you this. Though I did not know it at first, Titania's Bower is a bawdy house."

Celia watched as the fire in Bill's eyes dimmed from injured sullenness to confused dread.

"A what?" he asked.

"Yes, you heard me. And while I was there, I was forced into doing things I *never* wanted to do."

Out of his pockets now, Bill's hands were balled up into fists and his shoulder quivered under Celia's grip.

"What man touched you?" he asked through gritted teeth.

Her heart swelled at the sensation of his muscles tensing at the thought of her being harmed. The proof of his fury did more to heal her spirit than the passage of ten thousand days ever could and she smiled.

"Don't be a fool, Bill. There's nothing to be done about it." After a deep breath, she added, "Last week, I pretended I didn't hear you because I couldn't bear to have you look at me."

"You looked such a fine lady, I thought a gentleman had fallen in love with you and offered you marriage, but said you must cut off with me."

Celia shook her head. "I nearly drowned myself in the Serpentine that day."

His eyes widened.

"Aw, Celie," Bill breathed, putting his arms around her. She melted into his warmth and enfolded his frame in her own arms, inhaling the nearly forgotten scent of his young, familiar body. They stood for a long moment, silent and still, holding each other.

Celia's thoughts tumbled over one another, and she finally let them spill out of her mouth, that they would haunt the solitude of her mind no longer.

"I hated myself for what happened to me." Her voice was muffled by his shirt. "I got another job today, nothing like the first. I made sure of that. But if you're done with me – if you want to keep things the way they are, you living with Sam and all – I'll find another place. But tell me now."

"Of course, I want to be together again, Celie," he answered, holding her tighter. "It's all I've wanted since you left."

A sense of peace and joy that Celia had not felt since her grandmother passed laid hold of her heart. The sky continued to darken and neither sibling loosened their hold on the other.

STUPID, STUPID GIRL

DOVEY AWOKE to a pounding on her bedroom door. There was a stinging ache in her gum and the metallic tang of blood on her tongue.

"What?" she hollered, wondering who would dare to awaken her and in this manner.

The locked doorknob jiggled and a voice bellowed, "I must 'ave at least *one* girl come 'elp me!"

It was Sally, louder and more truculent than she had ever been before.

I'll slap you later, you brazen hag.

"What are you talking about?" Dovey shouted, the words from her ravaged mouth ill-formed.

"That stupid girl run off this mornin'. First the cake girl did it," Sally railed, "and now this un ain't 'ere neither."

Dovey rolled on to her side, to stare at the door malevolently.

That new little slut is gone?

Sally continued, "I cain't make *every* bite of food for these girls and gent'men all on me own!"

"Oh, *Th*ally!" Dovey hollered. Pushing a hand to her mouth to lessen the flopping of her lips over the huge gap, she continued, "Choo*th*e any girl to work with, ju*th*t keep me out of it!"

Sally hmphed and began to walk away.

Dovey called after her, "And bring me *th*um porridge!"

She had hoped to remain barely seen and certainly unheard until Dr. Briggs had returned to fit her with her dentures.

But that could be a week or more, she conceded reluctantly knowing that a brothel could not be run without a present and attentive bawd.

And the money must continue to flow in as that selfish bastard wants half the cost up front, sight unseen.

In fact, he was returning that morning to collect the funds. Dovey had protested at the amount and the payment arrangement, particularly since she had not seen a single example of his work. But she knew that she'd pay anything to vanquish the shame of her lost teeth and he'd promised she'd never lisp again with the dentures he provided.

With a leaden gut, she rose from the mattress and pulled on her red, silk dressing gown. She smoothed her hair as she settled herself by the windows to await the doctor and watch the street below.

Ugh, dentures... she thought with a disdainful shiver.

In the early years of the Bower, when she had whored herself out to keep the place financially sound, there was one client who always removed his false teeth before their dalliances. She could not hear the word 'dentures' without envisioning his gleaming set coated in viscous, bubbly saliva, grinning from atop her ewer table as he pawed clumsily at her.

And there will sit mine each night as I sleep, she thought, glancing at the same bit of furniture next to her bed. Tears burned her eyes.

A faint tap on the door startled Dovey from her contemplation. In four strides, she crossed the room to open the door.

There stood Doris, holding out a bowl of porridge, her eyes on the floor.

"Good mornin', Mrs. Dovey," she said softly, dipping into a little curtsey.

The madam said nothing as she took the bowl, noting that no steam rose from its filled hollow. Peering at the colourless contents, she saw it was congealed and claggy. Furious, she pushed the whole mess back at the girl, who looked up in fear, then surprise.

"Oh, Mrs. Dovey!" Doris gasped. "What is the matter?"

At the sight of concern on an apparently caring face, Dovey's fury dissolved into self-pity. Leaning forward, she began to weep into her hands.

I can't let her see me this way!

But the tears would not stop flowing.

"Poor Mrs. Dovey," Doris said, coming into the room and shutting the door behind her. Placing the bowl on the floor, she took Dovey by the elbow and led her to the bed. They sat down together and Doris rubbed the bawd's back, crooning, "Now, now. Don't cry."

The heartening warmth of the girl's hand stirred a memory deep inside Dovey.

Mamma, she thought, recalling a hand occasionally straying to touch her back or shoulder when her father, always censorious, was haranguing her about the plainness of her face and form.

"I know it seems a bit much," Doris murmured. "But we'll get through this."

I must get ahold of myself.

With a blunt nod, Dovey wiped her eyes and stood, moving out of the range of Doris's hand.

But the girl clearly did not want to let go of the moment. She rose also and reached out to pat Dovey's shoulder, saying, "She may come back."

Ha ha! Yes, let her think that I am crying over Sally's loss of that kitchen girl, not my teeth.

"Doe*th*n't matter," Dovey muttered, saying as few words as possible.

"Oh, but I know how you care for all us girls, and Celia was a favori –"

"*Th*elia?" Dovey said sharply. "What are you talking about, Dori*th*?"

"Oh, uh – Celia." The girl stammered. "She run off. Ain't that why you're –"

"What! When?" Dovey demanded, edging closer to the girl.

"Last night," Doris whispered. "No one saw her after dinner yesterday."

Dammit! Dovey thought. *How can I pay Briggs when two of my girls have just run off?*

Fuming, she turned to glower at Doris. "You'd be*th*t not be getting any idea*th* your*th*elf."

"Oh no, ma'am!" Doris shook her head emphatically. "She asked me if I wanted to go with her – said she had some money saved up for it – but I told her…"

"*You knew?*" Dovey's voice rose to a screeching height and her hand shot out to slap Doris across the face.

"I…I thought she…she was talkin' nonsense!" Doris cried, stepping toward the door, clutching her reddened cheek. "'Ad I known she really meant to run off, I'da told you outright! I swear it!"

Surely, she's telling the truth. Doris knows she needs to keep me happy – needs to stay faithful to me. Who else does she have?

The thought calmed her slightly. Taking a deep breath, Dovey stalked over to stand by the mirror, gripping the wardrobe below it with both hands to steady herself.

And truly, who else does Celia have? She'll be back.

But money…

Dovey knew that if one had enough of it, they needed neither friends nor family.

"You *thay* T*h*elia had money?" she asked.

"I never saw it. Maybe she was telling tales," Doris said hopefully.

Hmm. Yes, Celia will be back, that stupid, stupid girl. She came back the first time.

Looking up, Dovey's face reflected back to herself in the looking-glass. She turned her head side to side, her lips slightly parted as she studied herself.

The swelling's gone down a bit. Briggs said it must be gone entirely before the dentures will fit nicely.

Over her shoulder in the mirror, she could see Doris watching her as she examined herself and bristled at the intrusion.

"Go," she said with a wave of her hand. She needed to count out the money for Briggs. "And when the doctor get*th* here, *th*end him up."

After Doris quietly left the bedroom, Dovey locked the door behind her and went to the middle wardrobe. Crouching down to open its bottom drawer, she reached behind several pairs of shoes stowed there and grabbed the money stocking from the back corner. As she lifted it, a cascade of paper scraps fluttered down to the floor.

Her heart plummeted as she stared in horror at little shreds surrounding her feet. There was an egg-sized hole in the sock's heel, out of which dropped more paper bits.

"No!" she cried aloud and plunged her hand into its depths. The inside now held a mess of shredded tatters and rodent droppings. Only one thin roll of notes appeared to be undamaged.

"NO!" she screamed again, flinging handfuls of the filth to the ground.

There was a pounding at the door.

"Mrs. Dovey?" Molly called. "What is it?"

"Go away!" Dovey hollered, clutching the single wad to her chest and dropping the scrap filled sack to the floor. "Leave me alone!"

Crying real tears for the third time that morning, Dovey stumbled toward her bed and flung herself onto its silken coverlet.

AN EVENTUAL RELIEF

STARING OUT ONE of the gallery's windows at the rain falling steadily upon the lawn, Barclay found himself praying the same few words again and again.

Father, what can I do? What can I do?

It had been a strange week – full of joy at the knowledge that Honora had chosen to remain at Singer Hall for the time being, but tinged by the haunting onus Barclay felt that he must do something to free Celia.

Jasper had come to Barclay's room one night before bed to ask, "How can we get that girl out of that horrible place?"

Looking into his brother's earnest eyes, Barclay had been too ashamed to admit that he was bereft of ideas. Instead, he replied, "I am praying for guidance."

"Well, include me in your plans – I want to help," Jasper said, pricking Barclay's heart with his fervent goodwill.

Barclay and Honora had discussed the situation at length several times, but all of their talk had come to naught.

"She seemed so sincerely happy that I was there to help her," Barclay said in their first conversation about it. "Why did she not meet me at the park that evening?"

"Something – more likely some*one* – kept her away," Honora said. "I *know* she wants out – more than anything."

Each time they spoke of it, Barclay felt he was more of a failure.

Once he asked, "Could we not send her a letter and…"

The look in Honora's eyes stilled his tongue. Though she did not say it, Barclay knew it was his stupidest suggestion yet.

Why didn't I insist she come away right then? he asked himself, remembering how Celia had sat next to him on the settee as they whispered to one another. *I should have known we couldn't gamble with the future – should have seized the moment.*

Good Lord, what's to be done?

"Mr. Barclay?" a quiet voice said behind him.

Turning, he saw Martha standing feet away.

The servant's haranguing of Honora days earlier had been described to him in extensive detail by Jasper. Infuriated, Barclay hadn't spoken to Martha for days afterward, but his hypocrisy in the matter found him out.

Did I not also blame Honora at first, though gently?

This conviction, paired with a report from Honora that Martha had privately apologized to her, lessened his ire, and soon he was trying to make amends with the woman.

Now as she stood before him, he pushed his own gloominess aside and said with forced brightness, "Yes, Martha?"

"A letter for you, sir," she said, holding it out to him and bobbing a curtsey.

"Thank you."

Their eyes met as he reached for it and he gave her a look of warm regard before glancing down at the envelope to read:

Mister Barkly Derbun
Singer Hall
Up Mile End Road from London
Past Romford

He smirked, intrigued and amused at the odd direction and the alternative way of spelling his name.

Martha had already drifted away and was nearly out of the gallery by the time he was opening the envelope.

He slid a single sheet of paper out of the narrow paper pocket. On it was written:

Mr. Barkly—

I want to thank you for your kindness. I could not keep my promise to you those weeks ago and for that I am very sorry.

The bemused smile on Barclay's lips disappeared and he read on eagerly.

But I got out all the same. If she's still there, please tell Honora I'm back home with my brother, working a new, good job and I like it very much. Also, please tell her that Mrs. D. lost her two front teeth which pleased me beyond anything.

You are brave and kind, one of the good men. Thank you for the good you do.

There was no signature. There didn't need to be. Before he had even finished his first read through, Barclay was off his chair and out of the library, heading to the kitchen.

Silently, he entered, making his way past Bess and the suet she was dicing to where Honora stood at a table teaching three girls and one boy. With a look in his eye that even a fool could see was admiration, he posted himself three feet away and watched as she explained to the children, "Now that we have piped out the batter in uniform measure, we must tap the pan upon the table to draw out any bubbles."

At a break in the tutelage, Barclay strode forward, holding the letter out before her as the children cacophonously declared who would do best at tapping the pan.

Raising her eyebrows questioningly at him, Honora leaned in to read what he held out to her. Almost immediately, she pressed her hands to her chest and her mouth transformed from an O of surprise to a hard-pressed line as a tear ran down her cheek.

With his free hand, Barclay reached to dab at the corners of her eyes which were devouring the letter for a second time. Smiling up at him, her face full of joy and hope, she whispered, "She got out."

Taking a shaky breath, Barclay bit his lip and nodded.

And then, with the unpretentious whim that compelled Honora in nearly everything she did, she pushed herself up onto her toes, placed her dough flecked hands on Barclay's shoulders and kissed his cheek with a tender warmth that few of his society would consider proper, but most would gaze upon with envy.

A RECTOR'S EPILOGUE

The Rectory at Southby
May 29, 1818

PLEASED, ALLARD RESTED his aching back against the bundled warming stone that Mrs. Wilfrey had just brought into the parlor. His feet were up and his spectacles were not yet hurting him behind the ears, so he happily settled in to read a few pages of the Bard's *As You Like It*.

Allard did not know if Barclay would approve of him reading something with such ribald passages so he had concealed the small volume inside a similarly sized, but emptied cover of Laurence Stern's sermons. However, anyone studying the ruse up close would not be fooled, so he chose to read from it only when he believed his nephew to be sufficiently busy elsewhere.

Allard smiled contentedly. Barclay and Honora had taken up residence with him just after the new year, having wed on the first of January.

Immediately after, Barclay had assumed the role of ministering to the Southby congregation. Each Sunday morning, Allard sat proudly on a hard, wooden pew, listening to his nephew espouse the virtues of kindness and forbearance in impassioned tones. Though the congregants seemed more alert to his nephew's interpretation and conveyance of scripture, there burned no jealousy in Allard's heart. He knew that his own waning enthusiasm had likely lulled his listeners previously.

And Honora – what a fine young woman she is!

Allard was certain he had grown more rotund in the past five months as his niece-in-law invited the village children over twice a week to bake all manner of goods – often things he'd never heard of, but thoroughly enjoyed.

Each Friday, the young couple borrowed his ancient gig to ride into town to stroll through Hyde Park. Allard wondered at their determination to do so as they continued the practice even when a drizzle would have deterred anyone else. But he would not begrudge them their pleasures, no matter how puzzling. Allard supposed that's where they were at that moment as he adjusted the book resting on his bulging belly.

Soon engrossed in Ganymede's banter with Aliena, he was startled as the parlor door suddenly opened. Fumbling wildly with his book of subterfuge, he smothered it tightly in his arms as Barclay and Honora entered the room.

"Hello there," he said. "I didn't hear the gig in the yard – didn't know you'd returned from town."

He knew he sounded guilty in his rambling, but neither of them looked suspicious at his words. In fact, they both appeared uneasy.

"We didn't go today," Barclay said. "Honora was unwell this morning."

"I am sorry to hear that," Allard replied, noting his nephew looked pale himself.

"Uncle," Barclay said as the couple simultaneously sat down on the settee directly across from him. "We have something of great import to tell you."

"What is it, dear children?" he asked, concerned.

"Earlier this year, you gained two new housemates, but…"

Are they not happy here? Allard's stomach lurched. *Perhaps they have determined to return to Singer Hall.*

Barclay pulled at his cravat. "…now it seems that by next Christmas you will have gained a third."

They are not leaving!

Relieved, Allard felt his face split into a merry grin. "Does Jasper want to come join us?"

Barclay seemed to blanch a shade lighter, and stammered, "N-no. You don't seem to understand."

Here, Honora reached a steady hand over to rest on Barclay's knee as she spoke. "No, uncle, though I do hope this third person will have hair as cheerfully red as Jasper's."

Her other hand, moved to rest on her belly.

Allard's heart leapt within him.

"Oh!" he cried, getting up as quickly as a portly, rheumatic gentleman might. The book slipped from his lap and landed on the floor in two telling parts, but no one paid it any mind. Reaching with his knobby hands, he cupped Barclay's face and kissed him sloppily on the forehead. He spared Honora this jubilant indignity, but patted her head with awkward affection as tears spilled from his eyes.

"Oh!" he said again, as he began to prance awkwardly around the room. "My dear children, now my joy is truly made complete!"

And as Honora and Barclay laughed together at such a merry display, so was theirs.

Other Books by A.E. Walnofer

A Girl Called Foote

Young Jonathan Clyde causes mischief for everyone at Whitehall, the stately home of his privileged ancestors. As he matures, however, he comes to despise the vanity and conceit surrounding him.

Misfortune requires Lydia Smythe, an exceptionally clever farmer's daughter, to seek employment at Whitehall. As a parlor maid, she feels stifled and harried by those over her. Still, she refuses to relinquish her independent mind and spirit.

From the moment Jonathan catches Lydia reading the books she is supposed to be dusting, he is intrigued by this unusual servant. Thus begins a clandestine relationship that is simultaneously amusing, confusing and enlightening. Just as it is evolving into something neither of them expected, an unforeseen truth comes to light, and the two wonder if their unconventional bond will be forever lost.

Set in England in the mid-eighteen hundreds, *A Girl Called Foote* is the coming-of-age story of two similarly impressive people leading very different lives.

With Face Aflame

Born with a red mark emblazoned across her face, seventeen-year-old Madge is lonely as she spends her days serving guests and cleaning rooms in the inn her father keeps.

One day, she meets an unusual minstrel in the marketplace. Moved by the beauty of his song and the odd shape of his body, she realizes she has made her first friend. But he must go on to the next town, leaving her behind. Soon after, while she herself is singing in the woods, she is startled by a chance meeting with a stranger there. Though the encounter leaves her horribly embarrassed, it proves she need not remain unnoticed and alone forever.

However, this new hope is shattered when she overhears a few quiet words that weren't intended for her ears. Heartbroken and confused, she flees her home to join the minstrel and his companion, a crass juggler. As they travel earning their daily bread, Madge secretly seeks to rid herself of the mark upon her cheek, convinced that nothing else can heal her heart.

Set in England in 1681, *With Face Aflame* is the tale of a girl who risks everything in hopes of becoming the person she desperately wants to be.

Notes to and Resources for Readers

If you at all enjoyed this book, please take five minutes to review it on Amazon. Indie authors like myself have difficulty marketing and every positive review improves the effectiveness of our efforts. If you're feeling especially generous, please post the same review on Goodreads, Bookbub and any other site that promotes my books. Thank you!

If you would like to receive updates on novels I write in the future, please let me know at aewalnofer@gmail.com. Check my website, www.aewalnofer.com for more information.

How does an author write a believable story about two women trapped in a brothel that neither sacrifices the dignity of her fictional characters, nor depresses her readers? This book is my attempt to do so, and to acknowledge the horrific reality of sexual slavery that countless people have been subjected to throughout the centuries. Sadly, stories of entrapment like Honora's and Celia's are not simply a dark reality from the past. According to the National Human Trafficking Organization's website: "Human trafficking still exists and is a form of modern-day slavery. This crime occurs when a trafficker uses force, fraud or coercion to control another person for the purpose of engaging in commercial sex acts or soliciting labor or services against his/her will." If you are suffering such things or encounter someone that seems to be, please call the National Human Trafficking Hotline at 1-888-373-7888 (TTY: 711) for help and resources.

You may wonder if Honora ever spelled out to Barclay exactly what she did and did not experience while in Titania's Bower. I purposely did not clarify this as I didn't want to effectively take a stance on there being a "right" way to deal with such situations. Hopefully the portrayal of their mutual affection and respect for one another makes their resolution of the matter credible.

It is unclear to me if the Battle of the Nile at the Grand Jubilee in Hyde Park was performed during the day or in the dark of night. Various contemporary depictions of it portray its occurrence at both times.

My limited research on the history of baby carriages indicated that during the early 1800's perambulators (prams) were pulled behind nannies rather than pushed in front of them.

Of course, there would be many more servants at Singer Hall to properly maintain a large estate, but I didn't want to clutter the story with all the Bobs and Betsies whose only purpose was to rake some leaves or polish the bannisters.

Please forgive me for any incredible details, remembering that this is a work of fiction, not a history book. Similarly, it is not a geography book. However, I'm hopeful any Londoners will keep in mind that while plotting out Celia's walking ventures, I referred continually to Richard Horwood's *PLAN of the Cities of LONDON and WESTMINSTER, the Borough of SOUTHWARK, and PARTS adjoining Shewing every HOUSE* which was produced between 1792 and 1799. Therefore, streets and places she frequented might no longer exist.

Acknowledgements

Thank you, Jenny Q of Historical Editorial for designing Out of the Bower's stunning book cover. I LOVE it!

To Mr. Richard Horwood, the indefatigable cartographer of the 18th century – Thank you so much for diligently plotting out and recording each building of London in the 1790's. Historians and anglophiles everywhere are in awe of your remarkable work and are deeply indebted to you though you are no longer around to know it.

Thank you to my beta readers, Rev. Rebecca Holland and Anna Bottoms, for your time, energy and helpful suggestions after reading Out of the Bower's first draft.

Special thanks to Allie Cresswell for her wonderful feedback and for combing through the minutiae to ensure the little bits and pieces of this story are sufficiently British. I hope I kept them that way in the final draft.

A bucket of heartfelt gratitude needs to be poured onto the doorstep of the novelist Lona Manning whose friendship has nurtured and sustained me through many a dry writing spell. You continuously inspire me, educate me and make me laugh. Astonishingly, we've never met in person – a travesty that *must* be remedied!

Finally, a thousand thanks to my beloved husband whose encouragement and indulgence makes writing novels a possibility for me. (And thank you for suggesting soap as Mr. Tiller's product as that was the perfect solution to my problem.) I love you immeasurably, Jeff.

Endnotes

[i] *La Belle Assemblée* or *Bell's Court and Fashionable Magazine* was one of the first women's magazines, published initially in 1806.

[ii] In Elizabeth Moxon's *English Housewifry*, 1764, the recipe for Sagoo Custards is # 259.

[iii] The recipe for coffee in the 1808 edition of Mrs. Maria Rundell's *A New System of Domestic Cookery* includes islinglass chips and fine Lisbon sugar.

[iv] Devonshire House and Lansdowne House

[v] This tale by John Newbery, published in 1765 is also known as *The History of Little Goody Two-Shoes*.

[vi] André Viard's 1806 cookbook and Elizabeth Raffald's 1769 cookbook

[vii] In the 1807 edition of Mrs. Maria Rundell's *A New System of Domestic Cookery* there is a recipe for Brentford Rolls.

[viii] From 1712 to 1835, there was a tax on soap in England.

[ix] Clergymen whose yearly income was under £100 were not required to buy an annual wig powder license.

[x] In Fredric Nutt's *The Complete Confectioner,* 1807, the recipe for Toad-in-a-Hole biscuits is #11.

Made in the USA
Las Vegas, NV
12 December 2023

82591817R00217